"You got something against cowboys?"

The deep, sexy voice coming from the front steps sent a jolt through Stacie. She dropped the picture to the table, turned in her seat and met an unblinking blue-eyed gaze.

It was him.

She had to admit Josh looked even better up close. He wore a chambray shirt that made his eyes look strikingly blue and a pair of jeans that hugged his long legs. There was no hat, just lots of thick dark hair brushing his collar.

The glint in his eyes told her he knew she'd put herself in a hole and was desperately searching for a way to shovel out.

"Of course I like cowboys," she said. "Cowboys make the world go round."

Josh's smile widened to a grin.

She'd been caught off guard. Startled. Distracted. By his eyes...and his timing.

Why, oh why, hadn't she kept her mouth shut?

MONTANA
★ COUNTRY LEGACY ★

HOW TO RESIST A RANCHER

⚒

Cindy Kirk

Teresa Southwick

Previously published as *Claiming the Rancher's Heart*
and *The Rancher Who Took Her In*

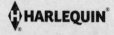

ISBN-13: 978-1-335-18992-9

Montana Country Legacy:
How to Resist a Rancher
Copyright © 2020 by Harlequin Books S.A.

Claiming the Rancher's Heart
First published in 2009. This edition published in 2020.
Copyright © 2009 by Cynthia Rutledge

The Rancher Who Took Her In
First published in 2014. This edition published in 2020.
Copyright © 2014 by Teresa Southwick

Recycling programs
for this product may
not exist in your area.

This edition published by arrangement with Harlequin Books S.A.

For questions and comments about the quality of this book, please contact us at CustomerService@Harlequin.com.

Harlequin Enterprises ULC
22 Adelaide St. West, 40th Floor
Toronto, Ontario M5H 4E3, Canada
www.Harlequin.com

Printed in U.S.A.

CONTENTS

Claiming the Rancher's Heart   7
by Cindy Kirk

The Rancher Who Took Her In   189
by Teresa Southwick

From the time she was a little girl, **Cindy Kirk** thought everyone made up different endings to books, movies and television shows. Instead of counting sheep at night, she made up stories. She's now had over forty novels published. She enjoys writing emotionally satisfying stories with a little faith and humor tossed in. She encourages readers to connect with her on Facebook and Twitter, @cindykirkauthor, and via her website, cindykirk.com.

Books by Cindy Kirk

Harlequin Special Edition

Rx for Love

The M.D.'s Unexpected Family
Ready, Set, I Do!
The Husband List
One Night with the Doctor
A Jackson Hole Homecoming
The Doctor and Mrs. Right
His Valentine Bride
The Doctor's Not-So-Little Secret
Jackson Hole Valentine

Montana Mavericks: What Happened at the Wedding?

Betting on the Maverick

The Fortunes of Texas: Cowboy Country

Fortune's Little Heartbreaker

The Fortunes of Texas: Welcome to Horseback Hollow

A Sweetheart for Jude Fortune

Visit the Author Profile page at Harlequin.com for more titles.

CLAIMING THE RANCHER'S HEART

Cindy Kirk

This book is dedicated with a thankful heart to my fabulous critique partners Louise Foster, Renee Halverson and Ruth Kaufman.

Chapter 1

"There's a whole herd of 'em." Stacie Summers stopped in the middle of the sidewalk and stared. Since arriving in Sweet River, Montana, two weeks ago she'd seen an occasional cowboy. But never so many. And never clustered together. "What's the occasion?"

Anna Anderssen, Stacie's friend and Sweet River native, came to a halt beside her. "What day is it?"

"Wednesday," Stacie answered.

"June second," Lauren Van Meveren replied. The doctoral student had seemed lost in thought since the three roommates had left Sharon's Food Mart. But now, standing beside Stacie in the bright sunlight, she couldn't have been more focused.

Though Lauren would normally be the first to say that staring was rude, she watched the cowboys pile out of the Coffee Pot Café with undisguised interest.

"Wednesday, June second," Anna repeated. Her blue

eyes narrowed in thought as she pulled a key fob from her pocket and unlocked the Jeep parked at the curb.

Stacie shifted the heavy sack of groceries to her other arm, opened the back and dropped the bag inside.

"Bingo," Anna announced with a decisive nod.

"They were playing bingo?" It seemed odd to Stacie that a group of men would gather on a Wednesday morning to play a game. But she'd quickly discovered that Sweet River was its own world.

"No, silly." Anna giggled. "The Cattleman's Association meets the first Wednesday of the month."

While that made more sense than bingo, Stacie wondered what issues such an organization would address. Ann Arbor, Michigan, where she'd grown up, was hardly a cattleman's paradise. And in the ten years she'd resided in Denver, not a single cowboy had crossed her path.

When Lauren had proposed moving to Anna's hometown to research male-female compatibility for her dissertation, Stacie had tagged along. The search for her perfect job—her bliss, as she liked to call it—wasn't going well, and a change of scenery seemed a good idea.

For some reason, she'd thought Sweet River would be like Aspen, one of her favorite towns. She'd expected cute, trendy shops and a plethora of doctors, lawyers and businessmen who enjoyed the great outdoors.

Boy, had she been wrong.

"I've never seen so many guys in boots and hats."

They were big men with broad shoulders, weathered skin and hair that had never seen a stylist's touch. Confident men who worked hard and lived life on their own terms. Men who would expect a wife to give up her dreams for a life on a ranch.

Though the air outside was warm, Stacie shivered.

Lauren's eyes took on a distant, almost dreamy look. "Do you know the first cowboys came from Mexico? They were known as *vaqueros,* the Spanish word for cowboys."

Stacie shot a pleading look in Anna's direction. They needed to stop Lauren before she got rolling. If not, they'd be forced to endure a lecture on the history of the modern cowboy all the way home.

"Get in, Lauren." Anna gestured to the Jeep. "We don't want the Rocky Road to melt."

Though Anna had injected a nice bit of urgency in her voice, Lauren's gaze remained riveted on the men, dressed in jeans and T-shirts and boots, talking and laughing in deep, manly voices.

One guy captured Stacie's attention. With his jeans, cowboy hat and sun-bronzed skin, he looked like all the others. Yet her gaze had been immediately drawn to him. It must have been because he was talking to Anna's brother, Seth. There could be no other explanation. A testosterone-rich male had never made it onto her radar before. She liked her men more artsy, preferring the starving-poet look over a bulky linebacker any day.

"You know, Stace—" Lauren tapped a finger against her lips "—something tells me there just may be a cowboy in your future."

Lauren's research involved identifying compatible couples, and Stacie was Lauren's first guinea pig—or as she liked to refer to it, research subject.

A knot formed in the pit of Stacie's stomach at the thought of being paired with a ropin', ridin' manly man. She sent a quick prayer heavenward. *Dear God, please. Anyone but a cowboy.*

A few weeks later, Stacie dropped into the high-backed wicker chair on Anna's porch, braced for battle.

When Lauren had arrived home after an afternoon run, Stacie had told her they needed to talk. She'd stewed in silence about the prospect of Lauren's proposed match for her long enough.

While she knew it was important for Lauren's research that she at least meet this guy, it seemed wrong to waste his time. And hers.

Stacie was still formulating the "I'm not interested in a cowboy" speech for Lauren when a cool breeze from the Crazy Mountains ruffled the picture in her hand. She lifted her face, reveling in the feel of mountain air against her cheek. Even after four weeks in Big Sky country, Stacie still found herself awed by the beauty that surrounded her.

She glanced out over the large front yard. Everywhere she looked the land was lush and green. And the flowers… June had barely started and the bluebells, beargrass and Indian paintbrush were already in riotous bloom.

The screen door clattered shut, and Lauren crossed the porch, claiming the chair opposite Stacie. "What's up?"

Stacie pulled her gaze from the breathtaking scenery to focus on Lauren.

"Your computer hiccupped. It's the only explanation." Stacie lifted the picture. "Does he look like my type?"

"If you're talking about Josh Collins, he's a nice guy." Anna stepped onto the wraparound porch of the large two-story house and let the door fall shut behind her. "I've known him since grade school. He and my brother, Seth, are best friends."

Stacie stared in dismay at the teetering tray of drinks Anna was attempting to balance. Lauren, who was closest, jumped up and took the tray with the pitcher of lemonade and three crystal glasses from the perky blonde.

"You're going to fall and break your neck wearing those shoes."

"Ask me if I care." Anna's gaze dropped to the lime-green, pointy-toed stilettos. "These are so me."

"They are cute," Lauren conceded. Her head cocked to one side. "I wonder if they'd fit me. You and I wear the same size—"

"Hel-lo." Stacie lifted a hand and waved it wildly. "Remember me? The one facing a date with Mr. Wrong? Any minute?"

"Calm down." Lauren poured a glass of lemonade, handed it to Stacie and sat down with a gracefulness Stacie envied. "I don't make mistakes. If you recall, I gave you a summary of the results. Unless you lied on your survey or he lied on his, you and Josh Collins are very much compatible."

She wanted to believe her friend. After all, her first match with Sweet River attorney Alexander Darst had been pleasant. Unfortunately there'd been no spark.

Stacie lifted the picture of the rugged rancher and studied it again. Even if he hadn't been on a horse, even if she hadn't seen him talking with Seth after the Cattleman's Association meeting, his hat and boots confirmed her theory about a computer malfunction.

A match between a city girl and a rancher made no sense. Everyone knew city and country were like oil and water. They just didn't mix.

Sadly, for all her jokes about the process, she was disappointed. She'd hoped to find a summer companion, a Renaissance man who shared her love of cooking and the arts.

"He's a cowboy, Lauren." Stacie's voice rose despite her efforts to control it. *"A cowboy."*

"You got something against cowboys?"

The deep sexy voice coming from the front steps sent a jolt through Stacie. She dropped the picture to the table, turned in her seat and met an unblinking blue-eyed gaze.

It was *him*.

She had to admit he looked even better up close. He wore a chambray shirt that made his eyes look strikingly blue and a pair of jeans that hugged his long legs. There was no hat, just lots of thick, dark hair brushing his collar.

He continued to lazily appraise her. The glint in his eye told her he knew she'd put herself in a hole and was desperately searching for a way to shovel out.

Trouble was, she couldn't count on Lauren, who appeared to be fighting a laugh. Anna—well, Anna just stared expectantly at her, offering no assistance at all.

"Of course I like cowboys," Stacie said, feeling an urgent need to fill the silence that seemed to go on for hours but lasted only a few seconds. "Cowboys make the world go round."

His smile widened to a grin, and Lauren laughed aloud. Stacie shot her a censuring look. Granted, her response might not have been the best, but it could have been worse. She'd been caught off guard. Startled. Distracted. By his eyes…and his timing.

Why, oh, why, hadn't she kept her mouth shut?

"Well, I can't say I recall ever hearing that saying before," he said smoothly, "but it's definitely true."

Okay, so he was also gracious, a quality sadly lacking in most men she'd dated, and one she greatly admired. It was too bad he was not only a cowboy, but also so big. He had to be at least six-foot-two, with broad shoulders and a muscular build. Rugged. Manly. A dreamboat to many, but not *her* type at all.

Still, when those laughing blue eyes once again settled on her, she shivered. There was keen intelligence in their liquid depths, and he exuded a self-confidence that she found appealing. This cowboy was nobody's fool.

Stacie opened her mouth to ask if he wanted a beer—he didn't look like a lemonade guy—but Anna spoke first.

"It's good to see you." Anna crossed the porch, her heels clacking loudly. When she reached Josh, she wrapped her arms around him. "Thank you for filling out the survey."

Josh smiled and gave her hair a tug. "Anything for you, Anna Banana."

Stacie exchanged a glance with Lauren.

"Anna Banana?" Lauren's lips twitched. "You never told us you had a nickname."

"Seth gave it to me when I was small," Anna explained before shifting her attention back to Josh. She wagged a finger at him. "You were supposed to forget that name."

"I have a good memory."

Stacie could see the twinkle in his eyes.

"I have a good memory, as well," Anna teased. "I remember Seth telling me that you and he preferred the traditional dating route. Yet, you both filled out Lauren's survey. Why?"

There was a warm, comfortable feel to the interaction between the two. Stacie found herself wondering if Josh and Anna had ever dated. A stab of something she couldn't quite identify rose up at the thought. It was almost as if she were…jealous? But that would be crazy. She wasn't interested in Josh Collins, cowboy extraordinaire.

"Seth probably did it because he knew you'd kill him

if he didn't," Josh explained. "I completed the survey because Seth asked and I owed him a favor." He shoved his hands into his pockets and rocked back on his heels. "I never expected to get matched."

He's no more excited about this date than I am, Stacie thought, pushing back her chair and rising, finding the thought more comforting than disturbing.

"I'll try to make the evening as painless as possible." Stacie covered the short distance separating them and held out her hand. "I'm Stacie Summers, your date."

"I figured as much." He pulled a hand from his pocket and his fingers covered hers in a warm, firm grip. "Josh Collins."

To Stacie's surprise, a tingle traveled up her arm. She slipped her hand from his, puzzled by the reaction. The cute attorney's hand had brushed against hers several times during their date, and she hadn't felt a single sizzle.

"Would you care to join us?" Anna asked. "We have fresh-squeezed lemonade. And I could bring out the sugar cookies Stacie made this morning."

His easy smile didn't waver, but something told Stacie he'd rather break a bronc than drink lemonade and eat cookies with three women.

Though several minutes earlier she'd been determined to do whatever it took to cut this date short, she found herself coming to his rescue. "Sorry, Anna. Josh agreed to a date with one woman, not three."

Lauren rose and stepped forward. "Well, before my roommate steals you away, let me introduce myself. I'm Lauren Van Meveren, the author of the survey you took. I also want to extend my thanks to you for participating."

"Pleased to meet you, Lauren." Josh shook her hand. "Those were some mighty interesting questions."

Stacie exchanged a glance with Anna. Obviously Josh didn't realize he was in danger of opening the floodgates. If there was one thing Lauren was passionate about, it was her research.

"I'm working on my doctoral dissertation." Lauren's face lit up, the way it always did when anyone expressed interest in her research. "The survey is a tool to gather data that will either support or disprove my research hypothesis."

"Seth mentioned you were working on your Ph.D.," Josh said. "But when I asked what your research question was, he couldn't tell me."

Stacie stifled a groan. The floodgates were now officially open.

Lauren straightened. "You're familiar with the dissertation process?"

"Somewhat," he admitted. "My mother is working on her Ph.D. in nursing. I remember what she went through to get her topic approved."

"Then you do understand." Lauren gestured to the wicker chair next to hers. "Have a seat. I'll tell you about my hypothesis."

"I suggest we all sit down," Anna said with a smile. "This may take a while," she added in a low tone only loud enough for Stacie to hear.

Stacie slipped back into the chair she'd vacated moments before. Josh snagged the seat beside her, his attention focused on Lauren. Even if Stacie wanted to save him, it was too late now.

Lauren's lips tipped up in a satisfied smile. "I was ecstatic when my subject was approved."

"And what are you studying?" Josh prompted.

Shoot me now, Stacie thought to herself. *Just put a gun to my head and shoot me.*

"Having relevant, personally tailored information about values and characteristics central to interpersonal relationships increases the chance of successful establishment and maintenance of said relationships," Lauren said without taking a breath. "It's a concept already embraced by many of the online dating services. But my study focuses more on what goes into forming a friendship rather than just a love match."

"Very interesting," Josh said, sounding surprisingly sincere. "What made you decide to do the research here?"

"Anna suggested I consider it—"

"I told her about all the single men." Anna poured a glass of lemonade and handed it to Josh. "And that I had a house where she could stay rent free. I decided to come along since there was nothing keeping me in Denver."

Josh shifted his attention to Anna. "Seth mentioned you lost your job."

"My employer was supposed to sell me her boutique." Anna took the last seat at the table. "Instead, she sold it to someone else."

Josh shook his head, sympathy in his eyes. "That sucks."

"Tell me about it," Anna said with a sigh.

The handsome cowboy seemed to be getting along so well with her roommates that Stacie wondered if anyone would notice if she got up and left. When her gaze returned to the table, she found Josh staring.

"It's been great catching up." He drained his glass of lemonade. "But Stacie and I should get going."

He stood, and Stacie automatically rose to her feet.

She adored her roommates, but going with her match seemed a better option than staying and talking research with Lauren or rehashing job disappointments with Anna.

Josh followed her to the steps. Though he'd already given her a quick once-over when he'd first arrived, she caught him casting surreptitious glances her way.

If the look in his eye was any indication, her khaki capris and pink cotton shirt met with his approval. Stacie felt the tension in her shoulders begin to ease. Anna had said he was a nice guy, and his interactions with her roommates had shown that to be true.

There was certainly no need to be stressed. But when she started chattering about the weather, Stacie realized her nerves were on high alert.

But if Josh found the topic dull, he didn't show it. In fact, he seemed more than willing to talk about the lack of rain the area had been experiencing. He'd just started telling her about a particularly bad forest fire near Big Timber a couple years earlier, when they reached his black 4x4.

He reached around her to open the door. When she stepped forward, he offered her a hand up into the vehicle.

"Thank you, Josh."

"My pleasure." He coupled the words with an easy smile.

Her heart skipped a beat. She didn't know why she was so charmed. Maybe it was because Mr. Sweet River attorney had gotten an F in the manners department. He hadn't opened a single door for her or even asked what movie she wanted to see. Instead they'd watched an action flick *he'd* chosen.

Josh, on the other hand, not only opened the door

without being asked, but he waited until she was settled inside the truck before shutting the door and rounding the front of the vehicle.

She watched him through the window, admiring his sure, purposeful stride. The cowboy exhibited a confidence that many women would find appealing. But as he slid into the driver's seat, her attention was drawn to the rifle hanging in the window behind her head. Her earlier reservations flooded back.

But how would she tell this nice guy that he wasn't her type?

"I can't get used to how flat the streets are," she said, buying herself some time. "When Anna talked about her hometown, I pictured a town high in the mountains, not one in a valley."

"It can be disappointing when things aren't what we expect," he said in an even tone.

"Not always." Stacie's gaze met his. "The unexpected can often be a pleasant surprise."

They drove in silence for several seconds.

"Did you know I'm psychic?"

She shifted in the seat to face him. "You are?"

"My powers," he continued, "are sending me a strong message."

"What's the message?" Stacie didn't know much about paranormal stuff, but she was curious. "What are your powers telling you?"

"You really want to know?" Josh's blue eyes looked almost black in the shadows of the truck's cab.

"Absolutely," Stacie said.

He stared unblinking. "They're telling me you don't want to be doing this."

Stacie stilled, and for a moment she forgot how to breathe. She adjusted her seat belt, not wanting to be rude and agree, but hating to lie. "What makes you say that?"

"For starters, what you said about cowboys." His smile took any censure from the words. "That, coupled with the look in your eye when you first saw me."

Though he gave no indication she'd hurt his feelings, she knew she had, and her heart twisted at the realization. "You seem very nice," she said softly. "It's just that I've always been attracted to a different kind of man."

His dark brows pulled together, and she could see the puzzlement in his eyes. "There's more than one kind?"

"You know," she stumbled over her words as she tried to explain. "Guys who like to shop and go to the theater. A metrosexual kind of guy."

"You like feminine men?"

She laughed at the shock he tried so hard to hide. "Not feminine...just more sensitive."

"And cowboys aren't sensitive?"

"No, they aren't," Stacie said immediately, then paused. "Are they?"

"Not really." Josh lifted a shoulder. "Not the ones I know, anyway."

"That's what I thought," Stacie said with a sigh, wondering why she felt disappointed when the answer was just what she'd expected.

"So what you're saying is this match stands no chance of success," Josh said.

Stacie hesitated. To be fair, she should give him a shot. But wouldn't that only postpone the inevitable? Still, there was something about this cowboy...

Cowboy. The word hit her like a splash of cold water.

"No chance," Stacie said firmly.

Josh's gaze searched her face, and she could feel her cheeks heat beneath the probing glance.

"I appreciate the honesty," he said at last, his face showing no emotion. "For a second I thought you might disagree. Crazy, huh?"

For a second she *had* been tempted to argue...until she'd come to her senses. Josh might be gentlemanly and have the bluest eyes she'd ever seen, but she could tell that they were too different.

"That doesn't mean we can't be friends," Stacie said. "Of course, you probably have plenty of friends."

"None as pretty as you," he said. He cleared his throat and slowed the truck to a crawl as they entered the business district. "If you're hungry we can grab a bite. Or I can show you the sites and give you some Sweet River history."

Stacie pondered the options. She wasn't in the mood to return to the house or to eat. Though Anna had given both her and Lauren a tour when they'd first moved to Sweet River, she didn't remember much of the town's history.

"Or I can take you home," he added.

"Not home." She immediately dismissed that option. Since they'd cleared the air, there was no reason they couldn't enjoy the evening. "How about you do the tour-guide thing? Then, if we feel like it, we can eat."

"Tour guide it is."

They cruised slowly through the small business district with the windows down. She learned that the corner restaurant had once been a bank and that the food mart had been resurrected by a woman who'd moved back to Sweet River after her husband died. He gave an interesting and informative travelogue, interspersed with touches of humor and stories from the past.

"...and then Pastor Barbee told Anna he didn't care

if she dressed it like a baby—she couldn't bring a lamb to church."

Laughter bubbled up inside Stacie and spilled from her lips.

"I can't believe Anna had a lamb for a pet." She couldn't keep a touch of envy from her voice. "My parents wouldn't even let me have a dog."

He looked at her in surprise. "You like dogs?"

"Love 'em."

"Me, too." He chuckled. "I better... I've got seven."

Stacie raised a brow. "Seven?"

"Yep."

She marveled that he could look so serious when telling such a tall tale.

"Wow, we have so much in common." Stacie deliberately widened her eyes. "You have seven dogs. I have seven pink ostriches."

Josh cast her a startled glance. "I'm serious."

"Yeah, right."

"Okay, one dog and six pups," he clarified. "Bert, my blue heeler, had puppies eight weeks ago."

He seemed sincere, but something still wasn't making sense. "Did you say *Bert* had puppies?"

"Her given name is Birdie." The look on his face told her what he thought of *that* name. "My mother chose it because Bert loves to chase anything with wings."

Stacie laughed. "I bet they're cute. The puppies, I mean."

"Want to see them?"

She straightened in her seat. "Could I?"

"If you don't mind a road trip," he said in a casual tone. "My ranch is forty miles from here."

He was letting her know that if she agreed, they'd be spending the rest of the day together. And he was giving her an out. But Stacie didn't hesitate. She adored puppies. And she was enjoying this time with Josh.

"It's a beautiful day," Stacie said, not even glancing at the sky. "Perfect for a drive."

"Don't give me that," he said, a smile returning to his face. "I've got your number. You don't care about the drive. Or the weather. This is all about the dogs."

"Nuh-uh." Stacie tried to keep a straight face but couldn't keep from laughing.

He did have her number. And she hoped this *was* all about the dogs. Because if it wasn't, she was in big trouble.

Chapter 2

Josh pulled up in front of his weathered ranch house and wondered when he'd lost his mind. Was it when he'd first seen the dark-haired beauty sitting on the porch and felt that stirring of attraction? Or when he'd started talking about the weather and she'd listened with rapt attention? Or maybe when her eyes had lit up like Christmas tree lights when he'd mentioned the puppies?

Whatever the reason, bringing her to the ranch had been a mistake.

He cast a sideways glance and found her staring wide-eyed, taking it all in. When her gaze lingered on the peeling paint, he fought the urge to explain that he had brushes and rollers and cans of exterior latex in the barn ready to go once he got the rest of the cattle moved. But he kept his mouth shut.

It didn't matter what she thought of his home; it was his and he was proud of it. Situated on the edge of the

Gallatin National Forest and nestled at the base of the Crazy Mountains, the land had been in his family for five generations. When he'd first brought Kristin here as a bride the house had been newly painted and remodeled. Still, she'd found fault.

"It's so—" Stacie began, then stopped.

Shabby. Old. Isolated. His mind automatically filled in the words his wife—ex-wife, he corrected himself—had hurled at him whenever they'd argued.

"Awesome." Stacie gazed over the meadow east of the house, already blue with forget-me-nots. "Like your own little piece of paradise."

Surprised, Josh exhaled the breath he didn't realize he'd been holding.

"Oh-h." Stacie squealed and leaned forward, resting her hands on the dash, her gaze focused on the short-haired dog, with hair so black it almost looked blue, streaking toward the truck. "Is that Bert?"

Josh smiled and pulled to a stop in front of the house. "That's her."

"I can't wait to pet her."

Out of the corner of his eye, Josh saw her reach for the door handle. Before she could push it open, he grabbed her arm. "Let me get the door."

"That's okay." Stacie tugged at his firm grasp. "I'll let you off being gentlemanly this once."

"No." Josh tightened his fingers around her arm. When her gaze dropped to the hand encircling her arm, he released his grip, knowing he had some quick explaining to do. "Bert can be territorial. You're a stranger. I'm not sure how she'll react to you."

He didn't want to scare Stacie, but last week the UPS man had stopped by and Bert had bared her teeth.

"Oh." A startled look crossed Stacie's face and she

sank back in the seat. "Of course. I don't know why that never occurred to me."

"She'll probably be fine," he said a trifle gruffly, disturbed by the protective feelings rising in him. "I just don't want to take any chances."

A look of gratitude filled her eyes but he pretended not to notice. He pushed open the door and stepped from the truck. He didn't need her thanks. He'd do this for any woman, including old Miss Parsons, who'd rapped his knuckles with a ruler in third grade. Yep, he'd do this for any female, not just for a pretty one that made him feel like a schoolboy again.

Josh shifted his attention to the predominantly black-and-gray-colored dog that stood at his feet, her white-tipped tail wagging wildly.

"Good girl." He reached down and scratched Bert's head. She'd been a birthday gift from his mother, six months before Kristin moved out. She'd never liked the dog. But then, by the time she left, Kristin hadn't liked much of anything; not the ranch, the house or him.

"Can I get out now?"

Josh grinned at the impatient voice coming from the truck's cab. Shoving aside thoughts of the past, he hurried to her door, Bert at his heels.

He paused and dropped his gaze to the dog. "Sit."

Bert did as instructed, her intelligent, amber-colored eyes riveted to him, ears up, on full alert.

"Miss Summers is a friend, Bert," Josh warned as he opened the passenger door. "Be good."

Despite the warning, the hair on Bert's neck and back rose as the brunette exited the vehicle. Josh moved between her and the dog.

"Nice doggie." Stacie's voice was low and calm as

she slipped around him. She took a step forward and held out her hand. "Hello, Bert. I'm Stacie."

Casting a look at Josh, Bert took a couple steps forward and cautiously sniffed Stacie's outstretched hand. Then, to Josh's surprise, Bert began to lick her fingers.

"Thank you, Birdie. I like you, too." Stacie's smile widened as the dog continued to lick her. "I can't wait to see your babies. I bet they're pretty, like their mama."

Bert's tail swished from side to side and Josh stared in amazement. For a woman who'd grown up without pets, Stacie certainly had a way with animals.

"Australian cattle dogs—that's another name for blue heelers—are known for being smart and loyal. They're great with livestock." Josh paused. "Still, not many would call them pretty—"

"She's *very* pretty." Stacie bent over and clasped her hands over the dog's ears, shooting Josh a warning look.

"My apologies." Josh covered his smile with a hand. "Would you like to see the six smaller versions in the barn?"

"Are you crazy?" Stacie straightened and grabbed his hand. "Let's go."

Her hand felt small in his, but there was firmness in the grasp that bespoke an inner strength. When he'd discovered that he'd been matched with Anna's friend from Denver, he'd wondered if Anna had monkeyed with the results.

He realized now that he and Stacie had more in common than he'd first thought. And he found himself liking this city girl. Of course that didn't mean she was a good match.

He'd been with a city girl once. Fell in love with her. Married her. But he was smarter now. This time he'd keep his heart to himself.

* * *

"I feel guilty." Josh stabbed the last piece of apple dumpling with his fork. "You spent the whole evening in the kitchen."

Stacie took a sip of coffee and smiled at the exaggeration. She hadn't spent the *entire* evening in the kitchen. They'd played with the puppies for the longest time. After that Josh had shown her all Bert's tricks, including catching a Frisbee in midair. By then, they were both hungry and she'd offered to make dinner.

"I told you," Stacie said, relishing the taste of the rich Columbian brew against her tongue. "Cooking is a hobby of mine. I love making something out of nothing."

Josh lowered his fork to rest on his now-empty plate. "You've impressed me. That noodle thing with the sausage and peppers tasted like something I'd get in a restaurant."

"And we didn't even have to go out." Stacie glanced around the modern country kitchen. After seeing the outside of the house, she'd been a bit apprehensive about the inside. But when Josh had ushered her through the front door and given her a tour, she'd been pleasantly surprised.

While the exterior needed some attention, the interior was up-to-date and exceptionally clean. When she'd complimented Josh on his tidiness, he sheepishly admitted that he had a housekeeper who came during the week to cook and clean.

"I'd have taken you out," Josh said, his gaze meeting hers. "I hope you know that."

"I do," Stacie said. "But this was more fun."

"I agree." Josh smiled and the fine lines that fanned out from the corners of his eyes crinkled appealingly.

He pushed back his chair. "How 'bout we take our coffee into the family room?"

Stacie rose. Her gaze lingered on the dishes in the sink before returning to the ones still on the table.

"Don't even think about it." He placed his hand in the small of her back and nudged her toward the doorway. "I'll clean up later."

Moments later, Stacie was sitting on a burgundy leather sofa listening to Josh finish his story about the fire that had threatened 180,000 acres several years earlier.

"I was fortunate," Josh said. "The damage to my property was minimal. It could have been so much worse."

Stacie studied the rugged cowboy who sat on the sofa a mere foot away from her. "You love it, don't you?"

He tilted his head. "Love what?"

"The land. Your life here," Stacie said. "I see it in your eyes. Hear it in your voice. This is your passion."

"From the time I was small, all I've wanted to do was be a rancher." His expression turned serious. "This land is part of me, and it will be part of my legacy."

"What about your parents?" Stacie asked, realizing that up to this point they hadn't discussed family at all. "Are they around?"

"They live in Sweet River," Josh said. "My dad runs the bank. My mother is the director of nursing at the hospital."

Bank? Hospital? "I thought you'd grown up on a ranch?"

"I did," he said in a matter-of-fact tone. "But my father was never into it. As soon as I returned home from college, he turned the place over to me."

"Sounds like the passion for the land skipped a generation," Stacie said in a light tone.

Josh lifted a shoulder in a shrug. "It's a great life, but definitely not for everyone."

Stacie wished *her* family had the same attitude. Why couldn't they understand that what worked for them didn't work for her? That's why she'd gone away to college and stayed in Denver after graduation rather than returning to Michigan. She wanted to find *her* passion, *her* purpose, not lead a life she hadn't chosen.

A coyote howled in the distance, the eerie sound drifting in on the breeze through the screened patio door. Stacie shivered. "It's so quiet out here...so isolated. Do you ever get lonely?"

"I have friends." The smile that had hovered on the edge of his lips most of the evening disappeared and his shoulders stiffened. "I see my parents at least weekly."

"But you live by yourself." Stacie wasn't sure why she was pressing the issue, but the answer somehow seemed important. "Almost an hour from civilization."

"Sometimes I get lonely," he said. "But when I have a family of my own, it'll be different."

"The solitude would drive me bonkers." Stacie took a sip of coffee. "I need people. The more the merrier."

"It's important to know what you want and what you don't." Josh's expression gave nothing away. "I need to find a woman who could be happy with this kind of life."

"Cross me off that list," Stacie said, keeping her tone light.

Josh's gaze never left her face. "I've never been much for lists."

Regardless of his obvious reluctance to hurt her feelings, she knew he'd made his decision, just like she'd made hers. No matter what the computer thought, she and Josh weren't meant to ride together into the sunset.

She took another sip of coffee and gazed out the screen door, feeling a little sad at the thought. Which made absolutely no sense at all. "The good thing is we haven't completed our first date and we already know it's not going to work."

"What's so good about that?"

Didn't he understand that she was doing her best to see the glass as half-full? "We don't have to waste time—"

"Are you saying tonight was a waste?"

She exhaled an exasperated breath. "No, but—"

"I don't think it was a waste at all," he said. "I can't remember the last time I've had this much fun or ate such a delicious meal."

He smiled and her pulse skipped a beat. Yikes. She'd never thought a cowboy could be so sexy.

Stacie placed her cup on the coffee table. "I should be getting home."

"Not yet." Josh reached forward and gently touched her face, letting his finger glide along her jaw.

He's going to kiss me. He's going to kiss me. He's going to kiss me.

The words ran through her head like a mantra. She told herself to pull away. To put some distance between them. To just say no. He was Anna's friend, after all, and he was looking for someone special. But instead of moving back, she leaned into his caress, her body quivering with anticipation.

He moved closer. Then closer still. So close she could see the flecks of gold in his eyes and feel his breath upon her cheek. She was already anticipating the taste of his lips when he abruptly sat back, his hand dropping to his side. "This is a bad idea."

Her heart dropped like a lead balloon and she felt like a child whose favorite toy had been snatched from her grasp.

For several heartbeats they simply looked at each other.

"You're right." Her pulse, which had stalled, began to thump like a bass drum. "It's late. I should get home."

When she stood he didn't try to stop her. By the time she reached the front door, her heart had settled into a regular rhythm. She paused on the porch and took a deep breath of crisp mountain air, hoping it would clear her tangled thoughts. Darkness had fallen, but thanks to a brilliant moon and a sky filled with stars, she could see clearly.

Out of the corner of her eye, she saw Bert racing across the yard toward her. Her spirits lifted and she stopped at the base of the porch steps to give the dog a goodbye hug. Bert reciprocated with a wet kiss to her cheek. She laughed and gave the animal another quick squeeze.

When she straightened, she found Josh staring.

"What can I say?" she said. "Animals love me."

"Of course they do," she thought she heard him mutter under his breath.

Though the truck in the drive was less than twenty feet away, the walk seemed to take forever. She quickly discovered that heeled sandals and a gravel drive weren't a good combination. Not to mention that every time she took a step, Bert pushed against her, forcing her closer to Josh.

When they got to the pickup, Josh reached past her to open the passenger door. Stacie inhaled the spicy scent of his aftershave and a yearning to play "kiss the cowboy" returned.

But instead of giving into temptation, she stepped back, putting a more comfortable distance between them.

She was congratulating herself on her good sense when sharp teeth sank into the back of her heel. She yelped and leapt forward, crashing against Josh's broad chest.

His arms closed protectively around her and a look of concern blanketed his face. "What's wrong?"

Stacie turned in his embrace to cast the dog a reproachful look. "Birdie bit the back of my foot."

The animal cocked her head and swished her tail slowly. Her dark lips curved upward until it almost looked as if she were smiling.

"Nipping heels is one of the ways she herds cattle," Josh said in an apologetic tone. "It's her nature."

"I don't like that part of her nature." Stacie wagged a finger at Bert. "Don't do that again."

The dog stared for a moment and then lifted a paw and proceeded to lick it.

"She's sorry," Josh said, a little smile tugging at the corners of his lips.

"Yeah, right." If Stacie didn't know better she'd believe the animal had wanted her in Josh's arms and had done what she could to make that happen.

"Nothing will ever hurt you," Josh said, his eyes dark and intense. "Not on my watch."

"Are you saying the cowboy will protect me against the big, bad dog?" she asked in a teasing tone.

"Most definitely." His gaze drifted to her lips.

Though she knew she was playing with fire, Stacie slipped her arms around his neck, raking her fingers through his thick, wavy hair. "What I want to know is, who's going to protect me against *you?*"

She wasn't sure he heard the question. Because the words had barely left her lips when his mouth closed over hers.

Chapter 3

"You kissed her?" Seth Anderssen let out a hoot of laughter that echoed throughout the Coffee Pot Café.

Josh scowled and wrapped his fingers around the small cup, wishing he'd kept his big mouth shut. After all, Seth's sister, Anna, was Stacie's friend. If Seth mentioned to her he'd been blabbing about the date, it might get back to Stacie. And she might get the mistaken impression that he was interested. Which he wasn't. Not in the least.

"Did she come back into the house?" Seth asked in an all-too-innocent tone. "So you two could get even better acquainted?"

Josh met his friend's blue eyes. "Are you asking if I slept with her?"

Though no one was seated nearby, Josh had automatically lowered his voice. When his marriage crumbled he'd provided more than his share of grist for the town's gossip mill, and he wasn't eager to repeat the experience.

Seth's gaze remained steady. "Did you?"

"Of course not." Josh responded immediately, making sure his tone left no room for doubt. "We just met. Besides, she's not my type. And I am *not* hers, either. She told me so."

A smile quirked the corners of Seth's lips. "Tell that to someone who'll believe it."

"She's Anna's friend." Josh ground out the words, irritated at the teasing, yet not sure why. Seth had always liked to rattle his cage. Why should now be any different?

"She's also very pretty," Seth pointed out.

"She's a city girl," Josh continued. "A hothouse flower not suited to this climate."

Just like Kristin, he thought.

"Sometimes those hybrid varieties can surprise you—"

"Then *you* go out with her—" Josh stopped himself, finding the thought of Stacie dating Seth strangely disturbing.

"I'm not her perfect match." Seth took a sip of coffee. "You are."

The words hung in the air for a long moment.

"I don't believe that bull," Josh said finally. "Look at Kristin and me. Everyone said we were a perfect match. Didn't even make it three years."

Though he now realized they were better off apart, the failure of his marriage still rankled. When he'd said his vows, he'd meant every word. He'd been willing to do whatever it took to make it work. But he'd learned the hard way that for a marriage to succeed, both parties had to share that commitment.

"That's because you and the wicked witch weren't matched by a computer."

"Get real. You don't believe in that stuff any more than I do."

"I filled out the questionnaires, didn't I?"

"Only 'cause you knew Anna would have your hide if you didn't."

"Speaking of which…" Seth's gaze settled on the doorway. "We got us some company."

Even before Josh turned around he knew who he'd find standing there. The click-clack of heels had been his first clue. The light scent of jasmine mingling with the smell of café cooking grease was the giveaway.

"Stacie… Anna…what a surprise." Josh pushed back his chair to stand, but Anna waved him down.

"Stay put," Anna said. "We're not staying. I saw Seth's truck parked out front and had a quick question for him."

Seth leaned back in his chair and lifted the coffee cup to his lips. "What can I do for you, baby sister?"

"I need more men." Anna cast a sideways glance at Stacie. "I mean, *we* need more men."

"I'm sorry Josh wasn't man enough for you." Seth's gaze focused on Stacie and his tone oozed sympathy.

Josh shot him a dark glance, warning him to back off.

The merest hint of a twinkle in Seth's eyes was his only response.

"I never said that." Stacie's cheeks turned a becoming shade of pink as her eyes sought his.

"Seth is a joker," Josh said, offering her a reassuring smile. He hated seeing her distressed. Her worried frown brought out his protective instincts and he wanted nothing more than to take her in his arms…

Whoa…where had that come from? He reined in

the emotion and told himself he was merely reacting to her appearance.

After all, she looked as pretty as the bluebells that filled his pasture. Instead of wearing jeans like most women in Sweet River, she had on a pair of shorts the color of the summer sky and a sleeveless, loose-fitting white shirt with something blue underneath.

Though the shorts came down midthigh and the shirt wasn't at all revealing, Josh remembered the feel of that body against his. In fact, he could still taste the sweetness of her lips and feel the softness of her hair against his cheek...

"I'm game," Seth's voice broke into his thoughts. "How 'bout you, Josh?"

Josh refocused to find the three staring expectantly at him. He quickly considered his options. He could admit that his mind had been traveling down a dead-end road or he could just go along. After all, Seth had already agreed. "Okay by me."

"Great." Anna smiled. "We'll see you at eight."

With their business concluded, the two women turned and headed for the door, admiring looks following in their wake.

"Should be interesting," Seth said.

"What?"

Seth grinned. "I knew you weren't listening."

It wasn't the smile that worried Josh; it was the gleam in Seth's eye. A sinking feeling filled the pit of Josh's stomach. "Tell me."

"Anna wants me to round up some more guys for the survey," Seth said. "Most ranchers from the area will be at the dance tonight. I promised I'd ask around."

A rush of relief flowed through Josh. For a second,

he'd let his imagination soar. "So all we have to do is recruit?"

"That's all *I* have to do," Seth said. "You have a different assignment."

Josh stilled. Why did he have the uneasy feeling the other shoe was about to drop? "Which is?"

"You're escorting Stacie to the dance." Seth motioned to the waitress for more coffee. "When the guys see how good your match turned out, Anna figures they'll want one of their own."

"This doesn't feel right." Stacie stared in the mirror and frowned. Dressed in blue jeans and a long-sleeved shirt with pearl snaps, she looked more like an extra in a Hollywood Western than a stylish twenty-first-century woman.

"I knew it." Anna's gaze dropped to Stacie's feet, to the Tony Lamas they'd picked up in town. "I thought you should have gone up a half size—"

"They fit fine." Stacie hastened to reassure her. If boots were indeed de rigueur for country dances, she'd found her fashion statement. The pink crunch goats had been the prettiest the Montana Western store had to offer.

"O-kay." Anna tilted her head, confusion clouding her blue eyes. "If it's not the boots, what doesn't fit?"

All the misgivings that had been plaguing Stacie since she first heard Anna's plan surged forth. "Me. Josh. This going-to-the-dance-together bit. I don't want to do it."

Anna's eyes widened as though this was the first she'd heard of Stacie's misgivings. Which didn't make sense, considering they'd been having this discussion off and on since Anna dropped the bombshell in the café. Frankly she'd been stunned when Josh agreed to the plan. When he'd taken her home after their first—and only—date, it had been clear to both of them that a romance wasn't going to work.

"I thought you liked him." Anna sounded hurt. As if Stacie was dissing her friend.

"I told you before… Josh is a wonderful guy." Stacie dropped on the bed and heaved a heavy sigh. "But he's not the man for me. And this—" she fingered the collar of her cowgirl shirt "—this isn't me."

For a moment Anna didn't say anything. Then she sashayed across the room, the rhinestones in her jean skirt glittering in the light. Once she reached the bed, she plopped down next to Stacie. "I'm not saying you have to stay in Sweet River and marry the guy. Just go to the dance with him. Have some fun."

"Going as his date just seems so…" Stacie struggled to find the words that would convey her feelings without insulting her friend.

Anna met her gaze. "Deceitful?"

Stacie nodded, relieved that Anna finally understood. "We *were* matched, but we aren't a couple."

"I believe," Anna pressed a finger to her lips, a contemplative look on her face, "you're thinking too hard."

Stacie blinked, stunned. It was the type of dismissive response she usually got from her family…as if she were too stupid to understand. She expected it from them, not from her roommate.

She lifted her chin, but when she met Anna's gaze, there was no condescension in the liquid blue depths.

"Why do you think most of the guys filled out the survey?" Anna asked when she remained silent.

"Because your brother made 'em."

"Good answer." Anna smiled. "Why else?"

"Because they're lonely and looking for their soul mates."

"Perhaps," Anna conceded. "Why else?"

Stacie shifted under Anna's expectant stare.

"Marriage or even a long-term relationship isn't really what Lauren's study is about," Anna explained.

"It's not?" Stacie couldn't keep the surprise from her voice. Though Lauren's dissertation topic wasn't fixed in her mind, she'd been sure the bottom line was matchmaking.

"You and Josh have a lot in common, right?"

Stacie thought for a moment. "I like to cook. He likes to eat."

Anna's lips twitched. "What else?"

"We both love animals," Stacie added, warming to the topic. "And he's easy to talk to."

"You enjoyed his company," Anna said matter-of-factly. "He enjoyed yours."

Stacie nodded. She couldn't deny it. In fact, when Josh had driven her home that night, he'd taken the long way, giving them more time to talk. He hadn't been uncomfortable, despite what happened. And though he hadn't kissed her again, the look in his eyes had told her he wanted to…

"Some guys *are* looking for a wife." Anna stood and moved to the mirror, pulling her long blond hair up in a ponytail before letting it drop back down. "But a lot of them would be satisfied with simply meeting someone who enjoys their company. Someone to go out with and have a good time. Someone to be their friend and take the edge off their loneliness."

Stacie took a moment to digest Anna's words. She thought back to her evening with Josh. She'd had fun and knew he had, too. Maybe that *was* enough.

"Okay. I'll do it," Stacie said reluctantly, hoping she wasn't making a mistake. "I'll do it. But I refuse to wear a hat. And square dancing is absolutely out."

Chapter 4

"All jump up and never come down, swing your pretty girl round and round."

Stacie twirled, the pink boots sliding on the sawdust-covered dance floor. Her breath came in short puffs and her heart danced a happy rhythm in her chest.

The large wooden structure that housed the Sweet River Civic Center was filled to capacity. The dance floor, brought in specifically for the occasion, took up a good third of the building. The rest was filled with tables decorated with red-and-white-checkered table-cloths. Baskets of peanuts doubled as a centerpiece.

Food supplied by ladies in the community sat on tables against a far wall, next to kegs of beer.

Though many of the younger men and women had left the floor when the square-dance caller took the stage, Stacie and Josh had stayed. She adjusted Josh's cowboy hat more firmly on her head during the promenade, a smile lifting the corners of her lips.

She'd been determined to remain hat free. But when Josh teasingly plopped his Stetson on her head, declaring her the prettiest cowgirl he'd ever seen, it seemed right to leave it there. And when the square dance had started and he asked her to give it a try, she hadn't had the heart to say no.

Surprisingly Stacie found herself enjoying the experience. But she hadn't realized how exhausting this style of dancing could be. The two-step and country swing moves had been challenging, but this—she allemanded left for what seemed like forever—set her heart pounding and turned her breathing ragged.

When the set ended and the caller started up again Stacie shook her head at Josh's questioning look. They'd barely relinquished their spot when an older couple took their place. Though it was almost midnight, the party showed no sign of slowing down.

Stacie wove her way through the tables, hopping aside just in time to avoid being plowed over by a drunken cowboy with a ten-gallon hat.

Josh slipped an arm around her shoulders, sheltering her with his body. He shot the man a quelling glance. "Watch where you're going, Danker. You almost ran into the lady."

Danker—all 285 pounds of him—stopped and turned. Stacie had never liked bulky linebacker types. Their size made her uneasy. But not this guy. With his chocolate-brown eyes and thick curly hair, he wasn't a grizzly but a teddy bear.

A huge, *drunk* teddy bear. His glassy eyes fought to focus.

"I did what? Oh." His gaze shifted from Josh to Stacie and a big grin split his face. "Is this her? Your new honey?"

"This is Stacie Summers," Josh said, then proceeded to introduce her to Wes Danker.

She learned that Wes raised sheep and that his ranch was twenty miles from Josh's spread. But when Josh mentioned Wes had recently returned to Sweet River after a stint in a Wall Street brokerage firm, Stacie couldn't hide her surprise.

"I need another drink," the man bellowed, punctuating his words with a belch.

Josh's gaze narrowed. "Tell me you're staying in town tonight and sleeping this off."

Wes's expression brightened as his gaze returned to Stacie. "I could sleep with you. If'n you'd let me."

Josh's blue eyes turned to slivers of silver in the light. "Ain't gonna happen."

Wes let loose a hearty laugh. "I was just kiddin'. I know she's yours." His expression sobered. "I wish I had a woman."

"That's why you need to fill out the survey," a familiar voice responded. Seth pushed through the crowd to stand beside Wes. "I told you, buddy. You want a woman. You fill out a survey."

"Probably won't get matched anyway." Wes grabbed two full plastic cups out of the hands of a man passing by. He took a big gulp out of one and then the other.

The cowboy whose beers he'd stolen just laughed and continued through the crowd.

"You won't know if you don't try." Seth's gaze settled on Stacie and Josh. "Look at Collins. Who'd a thought he'd get matched?"

"Hey." Josh gave Seth a shove. "Watch it."

"I want one as pretty as her," Wes said, as if placing an order for a side of fries, his gaze lingering on Stacie.

Was it only her imagination or did Josh's arm tighten around her shoulders?

Seth slapped the big man on the back. "You stop over at Anna's house tomorrow, fill out that survey and she'll do her best."

"'Kay." Wes finished off the beer in his right hand and crushed the plastic cup between his massive fingers. "I gotta take a leak."

As he stumbled off, Stacie swallowed the laughter bubbling in her throat. "I cannot imagine him on Wall Street."

A smile lifted the corners of Josh's lips. "He was good at what he did. Made bucket loads of money."

"Sounds as if he's going to do the survey." Stacie slanted an admiring glance at Seth. "Anyone ever tell you that you are one fantastic recruiter?"

Seth winked. "I'm not done yet." His eyes settled on a group of cowboys at a nearby table. "Five more and I make my quota."

Without a backward glance, he was gone.

"I hope Wes finds someone." Josh's expression turned thoughtful. "Though he's not at his best tonight, he's a good guy. Moving back to take over the ranch when his dad got sick was hard on him. I know he's lonely."

Stacie's heart went out to the gentle giant. In the past couple weeks she'd discovered what Anna had told her and Lauren was true: there simply weren't enough females to go around. Tonight, guys outnumbered women three to one.

"Seth is certainly doing his part to help make some matches," Stacie murmured as Josh led her to a table far from the dance floor. "Above and beyond the call of duty."

"He loves his sister." Josh pulled out a folding chair for Stacie. Once she sat down, he dropped into the chair next to her.

She thought Josh was clearly the handsomest man in the room. She inhaled deeply and her heart fluttered. He smelled good, too. The spicy scent of his cologne set her pulse racing.

"He's happy to have her back in Sweet River," Josh added.

"My parents and siblings would be happy if I were back in Ann Arbor, too," Stacie said with a wry smile. "It's hard to run my life from a distance."

Josh pulled a basket that sat in the middle of the table closer and grabbed a couple of peanuts. He handed one to Stacie. "I don't think you mentioned your family at all the other evening."

"Be glad," Stacie intoned in a ghoulish whisper. "Be very, very glad."

Josh didn't laugh or change the subject as she expected. Instead, with his gaze firmly fixed on her, he cracked the shell in his hand. "I take it you don't get along."

"I wouldn't say that." Stacie fought to keep her tone light. She never wanted to be one of those people who whined about their life or their awful childhood. It could be so much worse. After all, high aspirations for your child could hardly be considered abuse. "They're all very successful. I'm the token low achiever."

Josh's gaze searched hers. "Believing your family doesn't respect and value the person you've become has to hurt."

"Their opinion doesn't bother me." A lump rose in

her throat at his sympathetic tone, but she shoved it back down. "Most of the time, anyway."

Looking for an excuse to avoid his perceptive gaze, Stacie grabbed more peanuts. She shelled one and popped it into her mouth. By the time she met his gaze, her emotions were firmly under control. "Fact is, they're probably right."

His eyes never left hers. "You don't believe that."

Stacie hesitated, not wanting to lie, yet seeing no reason to bare her soul, either. "Sometimes I do. Other times, I tell myself it's just that I don't define success the same way they do."

"That's the way it was for me in college." Josh's eyes took on a faraway look. "Most of the guys I knew were all about making money. All I wanted to do was come back here and be a rancher."

"That's what I want, too." She paused and then laughed at the startled look on his face, realizing what she'd said. "No. No. I didn't—and don't—want to be a rancher. I simply want to be happy doing my life's work. But unlike you, I haven't found the avenue to my bliss."

Surprisingly, Josh didn't laugh. Instead, his expression grew even more serious. "If you could do anything, what would you do?"

He appeared sincerely interested and his tone invited confidences. Unfortunately over the years she'd learned the dangers of sharing her dreams. She'd discovered most men would happily run her life if she let them. Still, Josh didn't seem the kind to tell her what to do.

As if sensing her turmoil, Josh smiled encouragingly. "C'mon, tell me. I can keep a secret."

Maybe she'd gotten overheated on the dance floor and it had addled her brain. Maybe it was the knowledge that Josh was a man who understood money wasn't everything. Or maybe the beers she'd enjoyed this evening had loosened her tongue.

"I'd own a catering company and create fun dishes." She'd given up talking about her dream when it looked like it would never be a reality. "There's nothing I love more than parties and cooking and being creative. To be able to do that every day...it would be incredible."

A longing so intense it took her breath away rose up inside her. She thought she'd buried that dream, but intense emotion told her embers still smoldered.

"Based on the dinner you made the other night, I can see you being very successful." His supportive words and the sincerity in his tone warmed her heart. "Though I imagine you'd have to live in a large city to have enough clients to make a go of it."

"I did a business plan several years ago." Stacie flushed, embarrassed by the admission, yet not sure why. While she'd majored in business only because her father had insisted, she had to admit that some of what she'd learned occasionally came in handy. "The results surprised me."

Josh raised a brow. "What did you discover?"

"That it wouldn't have to be in New York or Los Angeles," Stacie said. "Or even in a city the size of Denver. A town with a population as little as two hundred thousand would work."

A look Stacie couldn't identify crossed Josh's face. It was gone quickly and his warm blue eyes refocused on her. "In this part of the world, you'd have to add the populations of Billings, Missoula and Great Falls together to get over two hundred thousand."

"Wow," Stacie said. "I guess I didn't realize those towns were so small. It—"

"Stacie, you've got to come with me." Lauren stood

beside the table, looking very much the part of the local scene in her tight-fitting Wranglers and cowboy hat.

Lauren's mission tonight was to mingle and to be on the dance floor as much as possible. She'd encouraged Anna and Stacie to do the same, saying it would be good advertising.

But if Lauren had come to drag her back on the dance floor, it wasn't going to happen. Stacie's feet ached and she was enjoying her conversation with Josh too much to cut it short. "I'm kinda busy at the moment."

"I'm afraid it can't wait. Or rather, your brother won't wait." Lauren's gaze shifted from Stacie to Josh, then back to Stacie again. "He insists on speaking with you *now.*"

Stacie dug her fingers into Josh's shirtsleeve. Paul called periodically, usually leaving a message about some job opportunity he thought she should pursue. But Saturday night was family time in his household. He'd never interrupt his time with his wife and children to call his sister. And why call Lauren and not her? Unless it was bad news and he knew she'd need her friend's support…

Dear God, had something happened to one of her parents? Her relationship with them might be tense at times, but she loved them dearly. She jumped to her feet. "Did he tell you what happened?"

She sensed rather than saw Josh move to stand beside her and then felt his arm slide around her waist, holding her steady.

"Paul isn't on the phone," Lauren explained. "He's here in Sweet River. Flew into Billings and drove straight over. He's waiting by the entrance for you."

The puzzle pieces that had begun to lock into place suddenly didn't fit. "Why would he come all this way to give me bad news?"

The confusion on Lauren's face was quickly replaced with understanding. "I'm not sure why he's here, but it's definitely not for that. I asked him how the family was, he said fine."

Stacie exhaled the breath she'd been holding and closed her eyes. Thank you, God.

"Why do you suppose he's here?" Josh asked.

"No idea." Stacie straightened her shoulders and shifted her gaze to Lauren. "Take me to him."

Josh stepped forward. "I'll come with you."

"No." The word came out more sharply than she'd intended. Stacie immediately softened the response with a smile. "Thank you, but no."

The last thing she wanted was to subject Josh to Paul's imperious manner or for her brother to get the wrong idea about her relationship with Josh.

"Are you sure?" Doubt filled his eyes and a frown worried his brow.

"Positive." Stacie removed his hat from her head and held it out to him. "Thanks for the loaner."

Josh took the hat, but didn't immediately put it on his head. "I don't understand why he'd show up here."

It was a question she'd like answered, as well. "No clue," Stacie said. "But I'm going to find out."

Chapter 5

Josh watched Stacie and Lauren disappear from sight, adrenaline spurting through his veins.

Though she hadn't said anything about Paul, the fact that she wasn't close to any of her family meant she wasn't close to this guy, either. And even though this wasn't a date in the traditional sense, Stacie had come with him. That meant he was responsible for her safety.

His mind made up, Josh pushed through the crowd, responding to friends without slowing his pace. He reached the front entrance, expecting to see Stacie and her brother, but instead found Pastor Barbee and his wife standing by the door.

The midsixties couple had been on the dance floor since the square dancing started, so Josh hadn't had a chance to say hello much less introduce Stacie. He could only hope they knew who she was.

"Have you seen Stacie Summers?" Josh kept his tone

casual and offhand. "She's Anna's friend. The one I was dancing with earlier."

"The pretty dark-haired girl." Mrs. Barbee nodded approvingly. "With the pink boots."

"That's the one." Josh cast a quick glance around, but once again came up empty. "You saw her?"

"She went outside." The pastor gestured toward the door with one hand.

"She was with a man," Mrs. Barbee added, a look of sympathy on her lined face. "Nice looking, but not as handsome as you."

Josh wasn't quite sure how to respond to that statement so he let it lie.

"Appreciate the information." Josh opened the door and stepped into the cool night air. He paused on the sidewalk and scanned the familiar street. At the far end of the block, he spotted her.

She and her brother stood next to a late-model Lincoln Town Car. Though her arms were crossed and her spine as stiff as a soldier's, she didn't appear in any distress. Now that he knew she was okay, good manners dictated he should go inside and give her some privacy. But he had an uneasy feeling about the situation and he'd learned to trust his instincts. So he leaned back against the building, keeping his eyes fixed on the pair.

He planned to stay out of it, truly he did. But when she raised her voice and the man in the dark suit grabbed her arm, Josh was down the street and at her side in a heartbeat.

"Get your hands off her," he growled. Brother or not, no man was going to raise a hand to Stacie. Not if Josh had anything to say about it.

The man whirled, releasing his hold on her arm, his lips thinning with displeasure.

Even if Josh hadn't known this was Stacie's brother, the resemblance between the two would have given it away. Although Paul was a good head taller than his sister and his hair a shade lighter, their almond-shaped eyes and patrician noses proclaimed them family.

"I don't know how it is where you come from," Josh said, "but around here we don't manhandle a woman."

Paul's gaze narrowed and Stacie took a step away, the action bringing her closer to Josh. It seemed natural for him to slip an arm around her shoulder, but she shrugged off the support, making it clear this was *her* battle.

A mocking little smile lifted her brother's lips. He shifted his gaze to Stacie. "Tell me you're not walking away from the opportunity of a lifetime for a two-bit cowboy."

"He's not why I said no," Stacie said in a calm voice. "Josh is an acquaintance, not a boyfriend."

Josh bristled. Acquaintance? He was *acquainted* with the librarian in town, but he'd never held her in his arms. Or felt her lips against his.

"Then this stubborn refusal of yours makes no sense." Paul's gaze remained fixed on Stacie. "Why would you turn down such a terrific offer?"

"That's what I've been trying to tell you," Stacie said. "But you just keep cutting me off."

Josh hid a smile. He'd only known Stacie a short time, but even he knew she was no pushover.

Paul crossed his arms. "I'm listening now."

Though his body language didn't indicate a willingness to consider any position other than his own, his tone was somewhat conciliatory. It must have been enough, because the tension left Stacie's shoulders and a glimmer of hope filled her eyes.

"I've never wanted to work in corporate America," she said in a soft voice. "It's just not me."

"You have a degree in business." Paul's entire attention was on his sister. "This position will allow you to not only use your education, but also be close to us."

Stacie opened her mouth but Paul continued without taking a breath.

"You don't even have to interview," Paul said. "The CEO is a friend and he's willing to hire you based on my recommendation."

"Paul—" Stacie raised a hand, but her brother was on a roll and seemed determined to finish.

"Best of all—since you're unemployed, you can start next week." He patted he suit coat pocket. "I have two return tickets. You can be back home tomorrow."

Stacie...leaving? An icy chill gripped Josh's heart.

"I'm not moving back to Ann Arbor." Stacie's chin lifted in a stubborn tilt. "Not tomorrow. Not in a week, a month or a year."

To Josh's surprise, Paul didn't immediately reply. Instead, his gaze searched Stacie's face for a long moment.

"I don't understand you," he said, his voice heavy with disappointment. "You have friends back home who miss you. Family that misses you. And now a great job handed to you on a silver platter. Why won't you at least consider coming back?"

Despite his heavy-handed methods, the man came across as sincere and made some good points. But when Josh glanced at Stacie, she didn't appear swayed.

"How many times do I have to tell you? I don't want to be stuck behind a desk." Her eyes flashed and Josh swore he saw steam coming from her nose. She reminded Josh of a bull ready to charge. "I only majored in business because Daddy insisted."

"Dad wants you to have a good life. A secure future." Paul's tone made it clear he agreed. "He loves you, Stacie. We all do. And we're worried about you."

Stacie raised a brow.

"Okay, *I'm* the one who's worried." Paul's voice broke. He took a moment to regain his composure before casting a sideways glance at Josh. "Send the cowboy back to the ranch. This is family business."

Though listening to their intimate conversation certainly wasn't his idea of fun, Josh kept his feet planted. He'd leave, but only if Stacie asked.

"He stays," Stacie said firmly.

Paul closed his eyes and blew out a hard breath.

"Mom and Dad have always wanted what's best for you," Paul repeated, once again sounding surprisingly sincere. "We all want that."

Stacie took a step forward and rested a hand on Paul's arm. "The problem is what you think is best for me is not what *I* want."

Anger flared in Paul's eyes. "What is it you want to do, little sister? Spend your life walking other people's dogs? Making lattes in a coffee shop? Or maybe you want to marry a cowboy and live in the middle of nowhere?"

Stacie's hand jerked back and her cheeks pinked as if she'd been slapped. But if her brother thought that harsh words and bullying tactics were the answer, all Paul had to do was look in her eyes to see that he'd lost any ground he might have gained.

"I don't care what you think of my choices, Paul." Her voice was icy cold, a stark contrast to her brother's heated passion. "Just because I have different goals, other things I want out of life…"

Paul's lips pressed together and he appeared to be fighting for control. "You and Amber Turlington, always searching for your damned bliss."

The words sounded like a curse. Still, Stacie couldn't help but smile at the familiar name. She and Amber had been best friends all through school. "Amber and I used to joke that we were twins separated at birth."

"She was never happy in Ann Arbor, either," Paul said, a surprising bitterness in his tone. "She always wanted something more. And look where it got her."

"Where it got her?" Stacie's voice rose. She couldn't believe his arrogance. "The school where she's teaching in Los Angeles may not be nationally acclaimed, and she may not be making the big bucks, but every day she makes a difference in the lives of her students."

"You haven't heard." It was a statement, not a question. The bleak look in Paul's eyes sent a shiver of unease up Stacie's spine.

"Heard what?" She knew Amber and Paul kept in touch. A long time ago Paul had desperately wanted to marry her friend. Though he'd moved on and married another woman, Stacie knew Amber still held a special spot in his heart.

A tiny muscle in Paul's jaw jumped. "I thought Karen and you would have talked by now."

Karen was one of Stacie's sisters. She'd left a handful of messages the past week, but Stacie hadn't gotten around to calling her back. "Karen and I haven't connected. Did she hear from Amber?"

"Amber is dead." The muscle in Paul's jaw began twitching. "Some punk shot her in the school parking lot."

His words seemed to come from far away. Stacie turned hot and then cold. A vision of Amber—auburn hair, bright green eyes and an ever-present smile—flashed before her. How could her friend be dead? She'd been the most alive person Stacie knew.

"It's not true." Stacie shook her head, trying to dispel

the picture of Amber lying in her own blood. "You're making it up. You want me to move back. To give up my dreams. Just like you wanted Amber to give up her dream for you. But she didn't and I won't—"

"Shh. It's okay." Josh moved to her side and this time when he placed a steadying arm around her shoulders, she didn't resist.

"The funeral was Thursday," Paul said, sounding incredibly weary.

Stacie swallowed a sob. It seemed easier to focus on her anger, rather than the pain tearing her heart in two.

"Why didn't you tell me?" Her voice sounded shrill even to her own ears. "I'd have come. She was my friend. My best friend."

"Karen and I both left messages asking you to call us back," Paul said simply. "I couldn't leave that news on voice mail."

Regret mixed with shame washed over Stacie. She leaned against Josh, drawing strength from his support. She'd been wrong to blame Paul. It was her fault for not calling back. She'd put off dialing his number for one reason: every time she talked to him or Karen, she hung up feeling like a big failure. Now Amber's parents probably thought she didn't care enough to come back for the funeral. "I can't imagine how hard this is on her family."

"I know exactly how they're feeling," Paul said. "That's why I'm here. I love you, Stacie. I want to make sure what happened to Amber doesn't happen to you."

Midmorning sun streamed through the lace curtains of the kitchen window and the heavenly aroma of freshly brewed coffee filled the air. Stacie stared down at her steaming cup of French roast, still unsettled by last night's events.

She lifted her gaze to find Lauren and Anna staring, waiting for her to finish the story. "I convinced Josh that my brother could see me safely home. Paul and I spent a couple of hours talking…crying…talking some more. He slept for three or four hours then headed back to Billings to catch his flight."

Though she and Paul disagreed on most issues, they'd both loved Amber. Stacie felt tears sting the back of her lids, but she blinked them back. She'd never liked crying in public. Even if in this case the "public" were her close friends.

Anna, sponge in hand, interrupted her counter cleaning to eye Stacie with a thoughtful look. "I'm still confused. Your brother wanted you to move home because a high school friend of yours died. I don't get it."

"I do." Lauren took a dainty bite of her egg sandwich. "Amber was looking for her bliss and she died. Stacie is doing the same and Paul is worried something may happen to her."

"That doesn't make any sense." Anna took a swipe at the kitchen counter. "Stacie's in Montana, not big, bad L.A."

"Her brother lost someone he loved." Lauren tapped a finger on the tabletop. "When Stacie didn't return his calls, he panicked, thinking something may have happened to her, too."

"I think he knows better now," Stacie said with a dry chuckle. Heck, if she didn't laugh she was going to cry. "How many women have their own watchdog?"

Lauren shot her a questioning glance.

"Josh came searching for me," Stacie explained. "He wasn't sure Paul was trustworthy."

Anna smiled. "Welcome to the cowboy world, where men think all women need to be protected."

"It was sweet," Stacie admitted, "considering we barely know each other."

Lauren choked on her sandwich and Anna let loose a very unladylike snort.

Stacie pulled her brows together. "What is it with you guys?"

"Puh-leeze," Lauren said. "I saw how you two were looking at each other, how close he was holding you on the dance floor. I couldn't have asked for a better advertisement for the survey unless you were naked and getting it on."

"Oh my God, Lauren," Anna's peal of laughter rang throughout the room, "you are so bad."

Stacie took a sip of coffee, even as her cheeks heated. "Well, anyway, that was our last date."

"Why?" Anna asked. "I saw real chemistry."

"Lots of chemistry," Lauren added, an impish smile on her lips.

Stacie ignored the good-natured teasing. "Josh and I decided on the first date that we weren't—" Stacie paused. To say that they weren't a good match might be a slap in the face to Lauren's survey. "That while we get along great, we don't want the same things out of life. Sort of like Amber and Paul."

"I could put you back in the system," Lauren volunteered. "Match you again."

Stacie shook her head. Talking to Paul about her dreams had only reinforced her desire to find her bliss. While Paul thought hearing about Amber would make her run back to Ann Arbor, the story had the opposite effect.

Regardless of what her brother thought, Amber had been happy in L.A. in a way she'd never have been happy in Ann Arbor. Just like Stacie would never be happy until she found her purpose in life.

Surprisingly Lauren didn't try to change Stacie's mind. Instead she forked a bite of coffee cake. "Remind me to give you the postmatch survey after church."

"You're going to church?" Anna's blue eyes sparkled. "After the comment you made about Stacie and Josh on the dance floor?"

"It's her penance," Stacie said, unable to keep her blood from heating at the thought of her and Josh on the hardwood…naked.

"I promised Pastor Barbee we'd be there and I'm a woman of my word," Lauren said, suddenly all prim and proper. "Service starts at eleven."

"Count me out." Anna sat back in her chair. "I need a breather from the Sweet River folks."

"Don't give me that," Lauren said. "Every time I saw you last night you were smiling."

"I had an okay time," Anna admitted. "But I grew up here. I know what this place is like, and I'm not going to let them suck me back into the fold. Self-preservation dictates I keep my distance."

"Me, too," Stacie said, knowing if she didn't she might end up with a naked cowboy in her bed.

"Well, you can both start keeping your distance… tomorrow," Lauren declared. "The church is having a box-lunch fund-raiser after the service and we're participating."

Chapter 6

The sun shone brightly overhead and the temperature was a balmy seventy-five when Josh joined the citizens of Sweet River on the back lawn of the First Congregational Church.

He'd stayed at the dance way too late last night. Then, when he finally got back to the ranch, sleep had eluded him.

It seemed as if he'd just drifted off when the alarm sounded. He'd been tempted to stay home and do some scraping on the house. But he'd promised Pastor Barbee he'd participate in the box-lunch auction.

The once-a-year event benefited the church's Vacation Bible School program, and the coffers desperately needed replenishing. Last year the weather had been bad and the turnout dismal.

In the tradition of the Wild West, single women made

up a picnic lunch for two and bachelors bid on the decorated baskets of food.

Two years ago Josh ended up having lunch with Caroline Carstens, who'd been back from college for the summer. It had been pure torture. She'd spent the entire lunch talking about her fancy cell phone and her blog. Not his style at all. This year had to be better. If only Stacie were participating…

As quickly as the thought entered his mind, he dropkicked it out of his head. They'd gone to the dance together only as a favor to Lauren. There was no reason for them to spend any more time together.

The auction had already started by the time Josh took a seat on the grassy knoll. The minister—who supplemented his church income by being an auctioneer—was holding up a basket with sunflowers on the side. Josh immediately recognized it. He kept his mouth shut and his hand down. A guy could only take so much, even if it did benefit the church.

The basket was won by the younger brother of one of Josh's friends. He let out a war whoop when the minister pointed to Caroline.

There were only a handful of baskets left when Stacie and her roommates arrived and deposited theirs at the minister's feet.

A murmur went through the crowd and the bidding grew spirited when first Lauren's and then Anna's were brought to the stage. Stacie's was the next one up.

There were many guys who hadn't yet bid, including Wes Danker. Josh wondered which would have the pleasure of Stacie's company.

Pastor Barbee began his spiel, but instead of men shouting out bids, there was only silence.

The minister tapped the microphone, making sure it

was still on. "Let's start with twenty-five. Who'll give twenty-five?"

No one said a word, much less called out a bid. A hush settled over the crowd. Stacie's cheeks turned bright pink.

When Wes turned and cast a pointed glance at him, Josh finally realized what was up. In the minds of the citizens of Sweet River, Stacie was his girl and they weren't about to poach.

But Stacie wouldn't know that. All she knew was that no one wanted to have lunch with her.

Though Josh had vowed to keep his distance, he refused to see her humiliated. He stood. "One hundred dollars."

Okay, so that was overkill. With no one bidding against him he could have had her basket for five. But how would that have looked to Stacie and to the town? Like he didn't value her company. Anyway, that's how it would appear…

A look of relief crossed the minister's face. "Number fifteen sold to Joshua Collins for one hundred dollars."

Stacie turned, looking utterly delectable in a pink-and-white summer dress. He couldn't read her expression from the distance, but she lifted her hand in a little wave.

The remaining picnic lunches went quickly. It was soon time for Josh to claim his basket…and Stacie.

He moved to the front and grabbed the wicker handle before turning to face the pretty brunette. Josh shifted from one foot to the other, feeling as awkward as a new colt. "Together again."

"So it seems."

He noticed her eyes were red rimmed and he remembered the look on her face last night when she'd learned her friend had been murdered. "Look," he said. "We don't have to do this."

"I think we do." A slight smile lifted Stacie's lips. "You saved me from owning the only basket not bid on."

"It wasn't you," he said. "Or your basket."

A doubtful look crossed her face. "What else could it be?"

Out of the corner of his eye he saw the pastor's wife headed their way. To be interrogated—no matter how well-meaning—was the last thing Stacie needed after her emotional night.

"Walk with me." He cupped her elbow in his hand and started back in the direction of where he'd been sitting. They quickly reached the spot, but Josh didn't slow his pace. "You've been marked as mine and guys 'round here don't trespass."

A look of startled surprise crossed her face and she stopped. "Seriously?"

"I know." He placed his hand against the small of her back and urged her across the street toward a small park surrounded by an ornate wrought-iron fence. "Sounds crazy, but…"

Josh didn't know what else to say. While in many places a pretty woman was always considered fair game, that wasn't the Sweet River way.

"I think it's admirable," Stacie said. "You don't see loyalty like that anymore."

This time Josh was the one surprised. "I thought you'd be angry."

A tiny frown marred Stacie's forehead. "Why?"

"For starters," Josh said, "I messed up your chance to meet and have lunch with someone new."

"I didn't want to eat with anyone else," Stacie said in a matter-of-fact tone.

His heart skipped a beat. "You didn't—er...don't?"

"What's the point? Most guys are looking for a wife." She reached over and gave his hand a quick squeeze. "You and I know exactly where the other stands."

The realization should have made him happy. Instead a leaden weight filled his stomach.

Stacie took the basket from his hands and placed it on a nearby picnic table. She flipped the top open and pulled out a tablecloth. "I hope you're in the mood to experiment."

He spread out the blue-and-white cloth while she took out a bottle of wine and two glasses. "Experiment?"

Stacie gestured toward the basket. "The food I packed isn't ordinary picnic fare."

"I like out of the ordinary," Josh said, realizing with sudden shock that it was true. Stacie was different from any other woman he'd known, and he was starting to like the roller-coaster ride he'd been on since he met her.

"Then you're in for a treat."

Josh stared at Stacie's hazel eyes and moist red lips. "I'm sure I am."

The air, which had been light and slightly breezy only moments before, turned thick and heavy. Everything faded and the only thing Stacie was conscious of was Josh: the long, dark lashes that framed brilliant blue eyes, the firm lips that had tasted so sweet...

"What did you make?" His words were like a splash of cold water.

Stacie blinked and pulled herself back to reality—the reality that said kissing Josh the first time had been a mistake, the reality that warned kissing him a second time would only compound the error.

"I've got tomato basil and brie spread, Spanish shrimp and rice salad and raspberry crumb bars. But my absolute favorite is the gourmet tuna salad on wheat." Already anticipating the tangy blend of tuna, capers and almonds, Stacie's taste buds tingled. "Tuna is one of my favorite ingredients. The green olives and Worcestershire sauce take it from ordinary to—"

"Tuna?"

Stacie put down the silverware and napkins and gave him her full attention. "Are you feeling okay?"

"Absolutely," he said. "I'm just not a tuna man."

Of course. This was cattle country. Roast beef and Swiss would have been a safer choice. Not to mention tuna could be bland and tasteless—depending on who did the preparation. But hers was spectacular. She had no doubt that he'd be a huge fan after one bite. "You'll love mine."

"I don't think I made myself clear," Josh said. "I can't stomach the stuff."

His tone left no room for argument or doubt.

Stacie leaned forward, letting her hair swing to cover her face as she rummaged in the basket, not wanting him to see her distress. "That's okay." She told herself not to take his dislike personally. "There's plenty else to eat."

"The smell alone nauseates me," he added.

"I understand." Disappointment caused her voice to be sharper than she'd intended. She lifted her head and softened the words with a smile. "We all have foods we don't like. In fact, this reminds me of a story my mother liked to tell."

Uncorking the wine, Josh filled each glass halfway and handed one to Stacie. He took a seat on one side of the picnic table and she sat opposite him.

Josh took a sip. "Did the story involve tuna?"

Stacie laughed as she pulled out the rest of the food. "Scalloped potatoes."

His eyes lit up. "A favorite of mine."

"Mine, too," Stacie said. "Pretty much every one I know likes them…except my mother. She got sick after eating a big helping one year. After that, her formerly favorite casserole shot straight to the top of her cannot-stand-the-sight-or-smell list."

Josh grabbed a piece of French bread and scooped out a little of the basil and brie spread.

"What was weird was a couple of times every year she'd make it for my dad." Stacie could still see the look of surprise and pleasure on her father's face when he'd see the casserole dish on the table.

"Why did she do that?" Josh added a healthy helping of shrimp and rice salad to his plate. "I'm sure he didn't expect it."

"You're right. He didn't expect it at all." Stacie's lips lifted in a smile. "Whenever I asked her, she'd just laugh and say 'nothing says love like scalloped potatoes.'"

Josh paused, a piece of French bread in hand, a thoughtful look on his face. "She did it to show how much he meant to her."

Stacie took a sip of wine. "I didn't understand when I was little, but as I got older I came to that same conclusion. It was a way of saying 'I love you' without words."

"They sound like a nice couple." Josh took a bite of the French bread with spread and murmured his appreciation.

"They are," Stacie admitted. "Their only fault is an intense desire to make me more like them."

"I understand." Josh's eyes took on a distant look.

"From the time I was small I was pushed toward a career in business, not ranching."

Boy, did Stacie understand what that was like. She'd never bought into her family's rigid definition of success. And because of that, they'd always thought she was a flake.

"My dad has a successful auto dealership in Ann Arbor. My mother is a CPA with her own firm." Stacie shook her head. "My siblings all inherited that entrepreneurial spirit."

"At least you have that in common," Josh commented.

"What are you talking about?"

"Your dream is to own a catering firm," he said. "Doesn't get much more entrepreneurial than that."

"I disagree." Stacie took a bite of the shrimp and rice salad and chewed thoughtfully. "I'd be doing it because it's my passion, not because I want to make gobs of money."

"Success and passion don't have to be mutually exclusive." Josh's gaze lingered on her face. "I have to turn a profit to keep the ranch going."

"I realize that. I just don't want money to be the main focus." Stacie sighed. Sometimes it felt as if she'd never find her bliss. "At least Amber got to live out her dream."

A lump formed in her throat. Stacie glanced down at the food on her plate. Her appetite had vanished.

"Losing a good friend," Josh said in a soft, low voice, "is like losing a family member."

"She was so full of life. And such a good person." Tears filled Stacie's eyes despite her best efforts to keep them at bay. "She didn't deserve to die like that."

She dropped her fork on the brightly colored paper

plate then buried her head in her hands. Tears slipped down her cheeks.

Though she hadn't heard Josh get up he was suddenly sitting beside her. "You're right," he said. "She didn't deserve to die like that."

"I'm sorry. I thought I'd cried myself out last night." Reaching into her pocket, Stacie pulled out a tissue and blew her nose. "I just feel so empty inside."

A family spilled into the park. The kids scurried to the play equipment while the parents plopped an overflowing picnic basket on the table. The man waved to Josh and the woman cast a curious glance at Stacie.

Stacie wiped the remaining wetness from her cheeks with the tips of her fingers. "Let's go before your friends come over."

Josh's gaze searched her face, two lines of worry between his eyes. "There's a place on my ranch. I don't know if it has good cosmic energy or what, but I always feel better after I've been there. Best of all, it's completely private."

Stacie didn't think there was a single place on earth that had the power to lighten her heart. Still, going back to the house and crying in her room held little appeal. "Would you show it to me?"

"Of course," he said, his eyes never leaving hers. A slight smile lifted his lips. "Trust me—when you get there, you're going to say 'Josh Collins, you are so smart. This place is just what I needed.'"

"I suppose you'll expect a kiss, too."

She wasn't sure who was most surprised by the words, but the slow grin that spread like molasses across his face told her he liked the idea.

His gaze dropped to linger on her lips and they immediately began to tingle.

"Kissing," he said softly, "will be entirely up to you."

Chapter 7

After dropping off the picnic basket at Anna's house and changing into a pair of jeans—at Josh's insistence—Stacie hopped into his truck.

Excitement nudged at her melancholy. But it wasn't until she rolled the window down and let the clean, fresh air rush in that a smile touched her lips. It helped that Josh continued to keep the conversation light. Time passed quickly and soon the cross timbers announcing the Double C ranch came into view.

Just as the truck turned into the long lane leading up to the house, Bert burst from a grove of trees into view. The dog ran alongside the truck, barking and wagging her tail, the entire length of the lane.

The minute the vehicle stopped, Stacie jumped out and gave Bert a big hug, receiving a doggie kiss on the cheek in return. When she learned Josh expected her to ride a *horse* to his mysterious location, she almost balked. But the clouds had disappeared and the sun now shone high in the sky. It seemed like a sign. As did the fact that Josh gave her a mare so gentle a three-year-old could ride her.

Brownie only had one speed: slow and easy. Stacie liked the horse more with each plodding step.

Josh's mount, a shiny black stallion named Ace, chomped at the bit, but Josh kept him in check. As they left the yard, Bert and several of the puppies came running.

They were a good ten minutes from the house when a couple of the pups took off in another direction. Worry bubbled inside Stacie as they disappeared from the sight. "Should we go after them?"

"No need," Josh said. "Blue heelers are smart and the young ones are old enough to do some exploring. They'll find their way home."

Stacie cast another look at the ridge where she'd last seen the puppies. "If you're sure…"

"Positive," he said in a reassuring tone, and she knew he'd heard the worry in her voice. "How are you and Brownie getting along?"

"I'm starting to feel like a real cowgirl." And that wasn't a bad thing…as long as it was temporary. Stacie patted the coarse brown hair on Brownie's neck. "You're right. She *is* very gentle."

His smile held a bit of "I told you so," but the words remained unspoken.

"I'd never put you in harm's way," he said instead.

A warmth that had nothing to do with the sun heated her body. "I appreciate that."

"You look like you're feeling a little better."

"I am." Maybe it was the sunny sky or fresh air or being with Josh…whatever the reason, the dark cloud that had hung over her head seemed to have vanished. "But I feel guilty for enjoying the day."

"Why would you feel guilty?"

Stacie urged Brownie across a trickle of water too small to be called a stream. "Amber hasn't even been dead two weeks. Yet for the past hour I've hardly thought of her."

Josh nodded and she could see the sympathy in his eyes. They rode in silence for several minutes before he turned in his saddle. "When I was twelve, my grandfather died. I thought my life had come to an end." Sadness underscored his words. "Granddad loved ranching. He taught me how to rope and ride and most of all to respect the land."

"You must miss him very much." The sentiment seemed inadequate, considering Josh had not only lost a grandfather but a *mentor*.

"At first, a lot," he agreed. "Then one day I realized I hadn't thought of him in over a week. Like you, I felt guilty. Until my father pointed something out to me."

"What was that?"

"There was no chance I'd forget Granddad." A smile lifted the corners of his lips. "He's as much a part of me as this land. Whenever I rope a cow or string a line of fence I think of him. He'll be with me forever. Just like your friend Amber. The memories you shared will always be a part of you."

A flood of gratitude washed over Stacie. Somehow Josh had managed to articulate her fears and worries and give her comfort without making her feel stupid. She paused, searching for words that would convey her appreciation for his compassion without being gushy.

Josh gave an embarrassed laugh, obviously misinterpreting her silence. "I usually don't talk this much."

Without giving her a chance to reassure him, he kicked his heels and Ace climbed the hill in front of them, stopping at the top.

Stacie stared at Josh's back and waited for her horse to follow. When Brownie didn't move, Stacie lightly tapped the mare's sides with her heels. The horse still didn't budge.

Suddenly a series of whistles split the air. Out of the corner of her eye Stacie saw Bert shoot from the bushes and head straight for Brownie's rear hoofs. Seconds later, the gentle brown beauty stepped forward, methodically making her way to the top. Every time the horse's pace slowed, Bert barked encouragement.

Once Brownie stood by Ace, Bert disappeared again. Seemingly mesmerized by the view, Josh didn't even glance her way.

Stacie released the reins and stretched, reveling in the feel of the sun against her face. She'd spent the last ten years in Denver, surrounded by tall buildings and masses of people. And she'd loved every minute.

But now, breathing in the clean, fresh air and gazing at the green and amber-colored grass that stretched like a patchwork quilt all the way to mountains in the distance, she could understand why Josh liked it. A sense of peace stole over her. "Breathtaking."

"It is." Josh's gaze lingered for a long moment on the valley before shifting back to Stacie. "But this isn't our final destination. To get *there,* we need to walk."

He slipped off his horse with well-practiced ease and then helped Stacie off Brownie.

"What about the horses?" she asked. "We can't just leave them here."

"Bert will watch them." Josh's piercing whistle split the air again and the dog came running.

"It's not far." Josh took her arm as he led her down a dirt path. "Watch out for the poison ivy and…" He cleared his throat. "Just stay on the path and you'll be fine."

Stacie couldn't remember if poison ivy had three leaves or four, and she had no idea what else she should avoid. But as she continued to walk, she decided she didn't need to know as long as she kept her feet on the path.

Several black-headed birds circled overhead and the leaves of a large cottonwood rustled in the light breeze, but other than the music of nature, silence surrounded them. Grinning at the fanciful thoughts, Stacie followed Josh down the narrow path.

"This is it." He stopped and stepped to the side, making room for her.

While the view from where they'd left the horses had been amazing, this scenery stole her breath. Miles of bluebells blanketed the meadow below. Off to the right, next to a bubbling brook, a herd of cattle grazed on a carpet of green grass.

"Yours?" she asked, her mind too full to form a more coherent question.

His arms spread out. "As far as the eye can see."

"Unbelievable."

"I hoped you'd like it."

"It doesn't seem like something that could be owned." Stacie struggled to bring her tangled thoughts into some semblance of order. She lifted her gaze to the bright blue expanse. "Any more than one person could claim the sky."

A look she couldn't immediately identify flashed across his face, and she feared he'd taken offense.

She placed a hand on his arm. "I'm not saying this *isn't* yours, just that—"

"No worries." Josh reached up and covered her hand with his. "I've had those same thoughts."

"Really?"

He nodded. "My ancestors settled here in the 1800s. While the deed says I own these acres, I see myself more as a caretaker. My job is to make sure the land will be here, unspoiled, for generations to come."

"For your children," Stacie said. "And their children."

"For them and anyone else." A smile lifted Josh's lips. "You don't have to own a piece of land to appreciate its beauty."

Stacie thought of the vacations her family had taken when she was growing up. There had been so many states, so many places that had filled her with awe. Places she'd like to visit again. Now she had another to add to her list.

"I'll remember this always." She turned to face him. "One day I'll return."

Josh reached out and touched her arm. The scent of jasmine filled his nostrils. Would he ever be able to smell that scent without thinking of her? "You'll always be welcome here, as well as your husband and kids."

Confusion clouded her gaze. "Husband?"

"By the time you get back to Montana, you'll likely be married," he said in as offhand a tone as he could muster. "Probably even have a couple children in tow."

Though his voice gave nothing away, the thought burned like a branding iron to his heart and suddenly he knew why. He wanted her to be happy, of course, but he wanted her to be happy with *him*. Not with some nameless, faceless executive who wouldn't know how to nourish her soul.

Nourish her soul? Dear God, he sounded like one of the valentines Sharon's Food Mart sold every year. As far as him nourishing Stacie's soul, that, too, was laughable. He hadn't been able to meet Kristin's needs so what made him think he could do so for Stacie?

"That's a ways off." Her eyes took on a faraway look. "There's so much I want to do, so many things I want to accomplish first, beginning with finding my bliss."

"You'll find it," he said. "Then you'll meet some-one, fall in love—"

"I can see that happening more to you than to me," she said, an odd look on her face.

"Don't think so." Josh gave a little laugh. "Been there. Done that. Didn't work."

"You were married?"

The shock in her voice took him by surprise. He'd thought Anna had told her.

"I was."

"Does she live in Sweet River?" Stacie asked, and though her tone was casual, he could see the curiosity in her gaze. "Do you have any children?"

"She moved to Kansas City after the divorce." He kept his tone matter-of-fact. "We were only married a couple years. Not enough time for kids."

Back then, he'd wanted a baby, but Kristin hadn't been ready. Now he was glad they hadn't had children.

Stacie touched his arm. "I'm sorry it didn't work out."

"I had my chance." Josh shrugged. "I'll probably have a series of flings and die alone."

Josh couldn't believe the thought had formed in his

brain much less made it past his lips. It wasn't the way he felt...not really.

Unlike some of the men he knew, Josh liked the idea of spending his life with one woman and had always thought he'd make a good husband. Though his failure with Kristin had made him doubt himself for a while, he knew he had a lot to offer the right woman.

"You'll find someone," she said softly. Before he could respond she slipped her arms around his neck, her curves pressing against him. "Your soul mate is out there. In fact, I bet right now she's finding her way to you."

He knew he should push her away, but how could he when he liked having her close? Especially since the "soul mate" in his head had started looking and sounding an awful lot like the woman in his arms. "I don't—"

She brushed his lips with hers, silencing the protest. "Say 'Stacie, you're right. That's how it's going to be.'"

Though Josh didn't like anyone putting words in his mouth, if it would keep her close a few seconds longer, he'd agree to almost anything. "Stacie," he lowered his head and planted kisses up the side of her neck. "You're right."

She moaned and leaned her head back, exposing the soft ivory skin of her neck to his lips.

He trailed his tongue along her jaw line and heard her breath catch in her throat.

"Say 'that's how it's going to be.'" Her breathing had grown ragged, but she managed to get the words out.

"Stacie." He put his hands on her hips and pulled her so close there was no space left between them. "*This* is how it's going to be."

He closed his lips over hers and drank her in. And when she opened her mouth and her tongue fenced with his in a delicious thrust and slide, all desire to pull back fled.

He burned with the need to make her his. To make her love him…

The thought was like a bucket of water on the fire that threatened his good sense. He took a step back, dislodging her fingers from his hair, ignoring her murmured words of protest.

"On second thought, *this,*" he said, trying to contain the tremble in his voice and not completely succeeding, "is a very bad idea."

Stacie let her hands drop to her side, heartbeat pounding and her breath coming in short puffs. She struggled to pull herself together. The last thing she wanted was for him to see how much his kiss had affected her. She resisted the urge to touch her still-tingling lips.

"Beautiful scenery always affects me this way," Stacie said finally when the awkward silence lengthened. "When I was in fourth grade, our Girl Scout troop leader and her husband took a group of us to Mackinac Island. When the island came into view, I was so excited. Unfortunately poor Mr. Jefferis was standing next to me."

Josh's eyes widened. "You kissed your troop leader's husband?"

"I was ten." She swallowed a giggle. "I gave his arm a big ole squeeze."

Josh laughed, his eyes now filled with merriment. "What am I going to do with you?"

Stacie knew what she wanted him to do. She longed to be back in his arms with his lips pressed against hers, but he was right—such intimacy *was* a bad idea. Still, the urge persisted.

She desperately needed to put some distance between

them…at least until she felt more able to resist temptation. Glancing around, Stacie saw a narrow path behind him. She guessed the trail would be an alternate way back to the horses.

"Catch me." As she spoke, Stacie turned and scampered down the path, unable to resist tossing one last taunt over her shoulder. "If you can."

"Stacie, no."

She heard him call out, but didn't slow her steps. The path quickly disappeared. Soon navigating her way through the dense brush and broken tree branches took her entire attention.

She could hear Josh closing in and considered conceding, but instead she pressed forward.

"Stacie, there are snakes—"

The words had barely registered when she stepped on something soft, yet firm. A feeling of impending doom settled over her. Perhaps running off *had* been a mistake.

Then she heard a hissing sound and realized there was no "perhaps" about it.

Chapter 8

The ominous hissing was immediately followed by a stabbing pain in her ankle. Stacie screamed and hopped back, her heart stopping at the sight of a large shiny brown snake with black blotches.

"What happened?" Josh was beside her in a heart-beat, his eyes dark with concern.

Swallowing a sob, Stacie pointed to the five-foot reptile slithering in the opposite direction. "A rattle-snake bit me."

Josh's gaze turned sharp and assessing. After a second he crouched down, gently pushing up the edge of her jeans.

"I don't feel so good." The world started to spin and darkness threatened.

"Lean over," he said, urging her head down. "Take deep breaths."

Bracing her hands on her thighs, Stacie focused on

breathing in and out. After a few seconds the darkness receded.

"My ankle burns." Though her insides felt like a quivering mass of jelly, her voice came out steady.

Josh met her gaze. "I'm taking you home."

He scooped her into his arms and walked with long, purposeful strides back the way he'd come.

Though her ankle burned, it didn't stop a thrill from traveling up Stacie's spine. She'd never been carried by a man before. Never been held in such a protective embrace. It was so... Sir Galahadish.

The second they reached the clearing he gently sat her down and knelt beside her. "I'm going to take a closer look."

Stacie tried to remember what she'd learned about snakebites in the first-aid class she'd taken in college. "Are you going to cut my leg and suck out the venom?"

He looked up from his examination and audibly exhaled. "Just as I thought, it wasn't a rattler."

Though she didn't want to doubt him, the reptile had looked eerily similar to the rattlesnakes she'd once seen on Animal Planet.

"The snake you pointed out looked like a gopher," he continued. "Those snakes have similar coloring to a rattler, but the head and body are slightly different. I didn't want to assume anything until I checked the wound more carefully, but now that I've seen the fang marks, I'm positive it was a gopher snake."

His voice was strong and confident, but a few doubts lingered. "How can you be sure?"

"Rattlesnakes have fangs only on the upper jaw, so when they strike, you see only one or two puncture marks," Josh said in a matter-of-fact tone. "Gopher snakes have upper and lower fangs, so they leave two sets of holes."

Stacie steadied her nerves and glanced down. Four needlelike punctures pierced the skin. "Are gopher snakes poisonous?"

"Nope," Josh said. "No venom."

Stacie felt light-headed with relief. "I was lucky."

"You were *very* lucky."

"I shouldn't have run off like that."

"I should have told you there could be snakes in the brush," he said.

It was sweet of him to try to shoulder the blame. But she was the one who'd run into the wooded area without a second thought, and now she would endure the consequences. "My ankle still hurts a little. Is that normal?"

"I was bit once as a kid," Josh said. "I remember it hurting *a lot.*"

The words had barely left his lips when a mind-numbing pain lanced her ankle. She gasped and then pressed her lips together to keep from crying out.

Concern furrowed his brow. "C'mon." He straightened and then held out a hand. "I'll carry you back to the horses. We'll get your wound cleaned up at the house."

Though he'd carried her from where she'd been bitten, that had been a relatively short distance. The horses were farther away. "I can walk."

"No need to be brave." He laid a restraining hand on her arm.

His chin was set in a determined tilt and Stacie sensed this was an argument she was destined to lose. Still, she hesitated. "I don't want you injuring your back carrying me all that way."

"Don't worry about that." He chuckled and she was

back in his arms in an instant. "I lift calves the same size as you all the time."

For a moment Stacie was taken aback, and then she had to laugh. Who but a cowboy could compare a woman to a cow and have it be charming? All the way down the path, she was acutely conscious of his broad chest and the strength in his arms. To take her mind off the pain—and him—she chattered nonstop about her aversion to snakes, mice and all things crawly.

When they reached the horses, instead of helping her mount Brownie, Josh lifted her onto Ace.

"I can ride by myself," she protested.

"You may feel faint again. I don't want you falling." His tone brooked no argument. In a matter of seconds, he sat behind her.

Stacie worried if Brownie could manage without her. But the following mare kept a brisk pace all the way to the ranch. Of course, Bert's reappearance, along with her missing puppies, may have had something to do with the mare's willingness to keep moving.

By the time Stacie reached the house, her ankle had started to swell. After turning over the care of the horses to one of his ranch hands, Josh insisted on carrying her into the house.

This time she didn't argue. Once inside he deposited her in the recliner with the footrest up and told her to stay put. He returned seconds later with a glass of water and four capsules.

"What are these?"

"Advil," he said. "Eight hundred milligrams. Prescription strength. It'll take the edge off."

At her questioning look, he smiled. "Remember, my mom is a nurse."

Stacie popped the capsules in her mouth and took a big drink of water. "What now?"

"You relax," he said. "I'll clean your ankle with antibacterial soap and then we'll get some ice on it."

Stacie glanced down at her injured foot. If she'd pulled on her pink goats as Josh had strongly suggested, the leather might have protected her skin. But no, she'd insisted on cute tennies without any socks.

"How about I go into the bathroom and wash up instead?" she said. "While I'm doing that, you can get the ice."

The look on his face said he wasn't sold on the idea. "What if you get light-headed?"

"I won't," she said in as strong a voice as she could muster. "I felt funny at first, but that was just the shock of it all. I'm better now."

"Are you sure?"

"Positive."

Josh disappeared into the kitchen and Stacie hobbled down the hall, doing her best to keep her weight off her right foot. By the time she reached the bathroom, her breath came in short puffs and her body started to shake. She placed both hands on the counter and inhaled deeply, willing herself to calm down.

A knock sounded at the door. "How are you doing?"

"Is it okay if I take a washcloth from the cabinet?" she asked.

"Use whatever you need."

Several minutes later, Stacie returned to the living room feeling more in control. Though the burning and aching wasn't any worse, it wasn't much better, either.

Exhausted and finally ready to be babied, she took a seat in the recliner and let Josh fuss over her. With gentle fingers, he treated the puncture wounds with a disinfectant before putting an ice pack, wrapped in a pillow case, on the swelling.

"The ice should stay on for about twenty minutes." He glanced at his watch. "Can I get you something to eat or drink?"

Stacie leaned her head back against the soft leather. Her stomach was still full from the picnic and, even if it wasn't, the thought of food wasn't at all appealing. "I'd rather you stay here and keep me company."

"Hang out with a pretty girl." Josh flashed a smile. "I can do that."

But before he could sit down the doorbell rang. He glanced at Stacie. "Wonder who that could be."

She shrugged, crossing her fingers that whoever it was wouldn't stay long. While she normally held to the motto "The more the merrier," she didn't feel like making small talk.

The bell sounded again and Josh cast a glance at Stacie. "I'll be right back. You stay put."

"Aye, aye, sir," Stacie brought two fingers to her forehead in a mock salute. "But if it's a snake at the door, don't let him in."

Though it wasn't all that funny, Josh laughed and headed to the front door. He wasn't sure who he expected to see on the doorstep, but it certainly wasn't Wes Danker.

As usual, the big man didn't wait for an invitation. He pushed past Josh and whipped off his hat. "You are not going to believe this. The mothership has landed."

Josh had to smile. The last time he'd seen Wes this excited was when Sharon Jensen had started carrying Ding Dongs at the food mart. "What's up?"

"Good times, that's what." Wes paced to the door then back to Josh. "And for not just me—for you, too."

Uh-oh. In the last of Wes's mothership landings, Josh had lost several hundred dollars to the slots at Lucky Lil's in Big Timber. "C'mon, Wes. I gave it a try but I'm not into gambling, no matter how loose the slots are."

"This is no gamble, my friend," Wes said in that loud, booming voice that was as much a part of him as his ten-gallon hat. "This is a sure deal."

Stacie straightened in the chair. Though she knew it was wrong to eavesdrop, she didn't have much choice. Wes had one of those voices that carried. In fact, she was able to make out a few words of what Josh said, as well.

From what she'd heard so far, Wes was selling something and Josh wasn't buying.

"Misty saw you at the dance last night," Wes said. "The little lady liked what she saw. Now I know you and Stacie—hey, don't even try telling me you didn't notice her."

Josh said something that Stacie couldn't make out.

"That's right." Wes's booming voice drifted into the living room. "The hot blonde with the big boobs."

Josh responded in a low voice and both men laughed.

Stacie clenched her fingers together in a fist.

"Her friend Sasha has the hots for me," Wes said, and Stacie could hear the satisfaction in his voice. "She and Misty are both working at Millstead's this summer."

Millstead. Stacie had heard the name before. After a second it came to her. It was a dude ranch south of Sweet River. Most of their summer help came from the area, but according to Anna they brought in outsiders, as well.

"The best part is the girls are just here for the summer," Wes continued. "We can hook up, have some fun and if we get tired of 'em, it's *adios* in September."

Irritation shot up Stacie's spine. She couldn't believe Wes had stopped over on a Sunday night to fix Josh up. Had the big man forgotten his friend had already been matched? She ignored the tiny voice in her head reminding her that Josh was a free agent. That he'd only taken her to the dance because of pressure from Seth. That he'd only bid on her basket because no one else would—

Stacie shoved the thoughts aside and concentrated. Despite sitting in absolute silence, she could only hear a mumbled response. She cursed the ice pack on her ankle. Only a few feet closer and she'd be able to hear every word.

"I'm headed over there now," Wes said. "Want to come along?"

Once again, Stacie heard only mumbling. But when the door closed and Josh returned to the living room without Wes, she exhaled the breath she didn't realize she'd been holding.

"How are you feeling?" he asked. "Do you need more ice?"

She shook her head. "Who was at the door?"

"Wes." Josh waved a dismissive hand. "He wanted to hang out."

"You turned him down?" Somehow Stacie managed to keep her voice casual and offhand.

"Of course." He flashed a smile. "I wanted to stay home and take care of you."

Stacie searched his eyes. Though Josh hadn't gone with the big guy tonight, that didn't mean he wouldn't be joining him another time.

But there was no answer to her unspoken question in his liquid blue depths, only concern…for her.

Warmth spread up her spine. Josh was a good man. Caring, smart and handsome to boot. The thought of him in another woman's arms set her teeth on edge.

"Stacie." His voice broke through her thoughts. "Are you okay?"

She blinked.

He moved to her side and crouched down, placing a hand on her leg, his brows pulled together in concern. "You have a funny look on your face. Is your foot hurting more?"

She stared at the face some lucky woman would one day love. A man *she* could find so easy to love.

A smart woman would let Josh take up with Misty, the dude-ranch girl. A smart woman would realize that such an action would mean someone's heart might be broken at the end of the summer, but at least it wouldn't be hers. A smart woman would never consider voicing the shocking proposal pushing against her lips.

Yet when Stacie opened her mouth, she knew she was headed down a path far more dangerous than the one she'd been on earlier. "I heard what Wes asked you."

Surprise skittered across his face. "I hope you know that—"

"I have my own proposition for you." She spoke quickly before she lost her nerve.

He cocked his head.

"If you're in the mood for a fling," she said. "Have one with me."

Chapter 9

Josh had once been thrown off a bull and had the air knocked out of him. He felt the same way now. Had Stacie really said she was up for a no-strings-attached fling? With *him?* "Beg pardon?"

A sexy little smile lifted the corners of her smooth, soft lips. "We might as well start now."

Dropping his gaze from her mouth to the soft curves visible beneath her pink shirt, Josh processed the request. His mouth went dry imagining how her breasts would feel cradled in his work-hardened hands…how they would taste to his exploring tongue. He went instantly hard.

Though his body had made its answer clear, he'd never done his thinking with that particular part of his anatomy, and he wasn't about to start now.

Just say no, his head urged. He opened his mouth, but the simple word wouldn't come.

"Josh?" A hint of uncertainty—at total odds with her bold offer—crossed Stacie's beautiful face.

He knew he was crazy to hesitate. But for him, being intimate had never been simply about scratching an itch. When he made love to a woman, it was, well, because he cared.

But as his gaze lingered on Stacie, he realized he did care. And if he didn't take her up on her offer, any number of men would happily volunteer to take his place, including his buddy Wes Danker.

For a second, Josh saw red. Friend or not, no other man in Sweet River was going to touch Stacie. Suddenly it became clear to Josh what his answer would be, what it *had* to be.

He took her hand and stared into those beautiful hazel eyes.

"Okay." Even as Josh prayed he wouldn't regret the decision, his heart picked up speed. "Let's fling."

As Josh lowered his bedroom window shade, a frisson of excitement skittered up Stacie's spine and her heart fluttered like a trapped butterfly in her throat. With one simple comment her life had gone from slow—and slightly boring—to runaway-train mode.

She'd asked. He'd accepted. And his burning gaze told her they'd both be naked before another fifteen minutes had passed.

It's just sex, she told herself, *nothing you can't handle.*

Josh turned, his eyes dark and penetrating. "How's the ankle?"

"Good." Which was true as long as she didn't stand on it or move it much. Fortunately, she wasn't planning on being upright too much longer.

He smiled and stepped closer, his eyes filled with anticipation. She wondered how long it'd be until those beautiful eyes filled with disappointment. "Before we get started, I have a confession."

"Sounds…interesting."

Stacie twirled a piece of hair around one finger. When she'd impulsively made her offer, she'd been so caught up in the moment she'd forgotten one very important fact. "I'm not a good lover."

Despite the look of startled surprise on his face, she pressed forward. "I'm a dud in bed. I don't have much experience. And, well, I'm easily distracted."

He moved closer until he stood directly in front of her, the spicy scent of his cologne wafting in the air. "By…?"

She'd never realized before that his eyes had little gold flecks in the blue. Or that his lashes were so long that—

"What are you distracted by?" he repeated.

Right now it was by his nearness, but that wasn't the answer. Stacie could feel her face warm. She'd only wanted to alert him not to expect too much, not get into a lengthy discussion on her sexual inadequacies.

"Usually food," she said, when he continued to stare expectantly.

"You like to eat when you're making love?" He sounded interested, rather than shocked.

"No, silly," she said. "I plan menus."

"After?"

Heat rose up her neck. "During."

His mouth dropped open. "Who were these guys?" He wanted names?

"Obviously they weren't doing their job if you could

plan menus while they were making love to you," he continued.

Making love? Those words were way too strong for a quick fling. "You think having sex is a job?"

"A man's 'job' is to give pleasure to his partner," Josh said. "Trust me. The only thing you're going to be thinking of tonight is how good it feels when we're together."

Doubt must have shown on her face because he chuckled softly. "Guess I'm going to have to convince you."

He pulled off his shirt and tossed it to the floor. Dear God, he was gorgeous. Broad shoulders tapering to narrow hips. Perfectly sculpted chest with a dusting of dark hair.

Every muscle and hard plane was in perfect balance. His wasn't a body toned from regular workouts in a gym, but one hardened from physical labor.

Too bad he wouldn't find her quite so perfect. Her B cups were hardly centerfold material, and while her belly was flat, the only six-pack to be found was in her refrigerator. With trembling fingers Stacie reached for the buttons on her shirt, hoping he wouldn't be too disappointed.

Before she could get the second button released, his hand closed over hers.

"No rush," he said in a deep sexy voice that sent blood flowing through her veins like warm honey. "Fast is fine, but slow is even better."

His fingers were slightly rough, and Stacie found herself wondering what those callused hands would feel like against her breasts.

That was her last coherent thought as he sat beside her and his mouth closed over hers. He caressed her skin with that mouth, planting gentle kisses on her lips, her jaw and down her neck while his hands remained respectfully on her shoulders.

He nibbled her earlobe and then moved back to her tingling lips. She opened her mouth, and when he still didn't deepen the kiss, she slid her tongue into his mouth.

His body shook and for a second she couldn't figure out why. Until she realized he was *laughing*.

She jerked back. "What is so funny?"

His lips twitched. "For two people who wanted to take things slow, we seem determined to move quickly."

"Not you." Stacie's peevish tone reflected her pent-up frustration. "You could take all night."

Josh didn't seem to take offense. In fact, his lips widened in a smile and satisfaction filled his eyes. "Sounds like I'm doing my job."

"What are you talking about?"

"Tell me honestly, have you been thinking of recipes while we've been kissing?"

"No," Stacie shot back. "I've been too busy trying to figure out how to get your tongue in my mouth and your hands on my breasts."

Heat flared in his eyes.

"I like a woman who asks for what she wants." He pushed her gently back on the bed, his fingers moving to the buttons on her shirt, even as his mouth briefly covered hers again. "And I like you."

The words were as slow and unhurried as his touch. Though her body clamored for skin-to-skin action, the knowledge that he wouldn't go too fast and leave her struggling to keep up brought a comforting warmth.

Josh had promised he would make it good for her, and though she hadn't known him long, she believed him to be a man of his word.

When his hand finally closed over her breast and his tongue slid into her mouth, an unfamiliar ache made further analytic thought impossible. And when her clothes joined his on the floor, want became need.

For the rest of the night her world was Josh, and all that mattered was him…and her…and becoming one.

Josh rolled over, the early-morning sun pulling him from his slumber. Most days he was outside before dawn, but today chores could wait. Feeling satiated and content, he stretched, reluctant to let go of the dream that had been last night.

The night had been mind-blowing. They'd tossed aside rational thought and inhibitions and never looked back.

Sensing Stacie stirring, Josh opened his eyes. Surprise shot through him at the sight of his lover propped on one elbow facing him, her dark hair tumbled around her face, her expression way too serious. And considering how late they'd been up, she looked amazingly wide-awake.

"Do you have any regrets?" she asked before he could say good morning.

"There are lots of things I regret." Josh raised himself on his elbows. "Do you have something specific in mind?"

"This," she said. "You. Me. Together. Naked."

After his enthusiasm last night, he couldn't believe she had to ask. But from her serious expression, the answer was clearly important to her.

"No," he said honestly. "Not a single regret."

"Interesting." She sat abruptly up, ignoring the sheet that fell to pool at her waist. "That's how I feel, too."

Josh told himself they were *talking,* which meant his

attention should be focused on her face. Unfortunately his eyes seemed to have minds of their own. His gaze caressed her luscious curves. He'd explored every inch of her body, but seeing her in the morning light filled him with awe.

As if she could read his mind, a tiny smile lifted her lips and she leaned forward, brushing her mouth against his. "You're the sexiest cowboy I've ever met. Not to mention an amazing lover."

He'd been determined to make their lovemaking as good for her as it was for him. It sounded as if he'd succeeded. Puffing with pride, he shot her a wink. "I promised I'd make you forget about those recipes."

Stacie laughed, her cheeks a dusky pink. "You did indeed."

He trailed a finger down the silky softness of her cheek. "It was easy. You made it easy."

He pressed his lips shut before he could tell her it was easy because of how she made him feel. But his emotions were his problem—his issue—to deal with, not hers.

She shifted again and slid the fingers of one hand through his hair, kissing the corners of his mouth. "Are you sure you don't have any more?"

He inhaled the intoxicating scent of jasmine. "More?"

"Condoms."

His body, which had soared to a heightened state of readiness, plummeted as he remembered the handful he'd found forgotten in a drawer had all been used last night. "Out."

"I wish I'd stayed on the Pill," Stacie said with a sigh. "But there was no need and—"

"There are other ways to have fun," Josh said, "that don't carry a risk of pregnancy."

"Like riding horses? Or playing with Bert?"

The innocent look on her face didn't fool him in the least. He laughed aloud. "I was thinking of more…intimate activities."

"I have a friend back in Denver." Stacie's eyes brightened. "She and her boyfriend are into role-playing. I remember one time he pretended to pick her up at the bar. She played the part of a small-town girl in the big city for the first time. I always thought the game sounded like fun."

Josh had never been much of an actor, but the last thing he wanted to do was stifle Stacie's enthusiasm. Or let her thoughts return to planning menus.

The first time they'd made love, she'd been unsure, hesitant in her overtures. Until he'd shown by his actions and his response that he was open to anything she wanted to try. And now it appeared "anything" included role-playing.

"What exactly do you have in mind?" He did his best to inject enthusiasm into his voice.

She brought a finger to her lips. "First we get dressed—"

"Get dressed?"

"Hear me out." She pulled the sheet up, covering her breasts. Apparently she really did want him to listen. "Once we have our clothes on, I go downstairs and start breakfast."

The game was sounding less appealing by the minute. But her enthusiasm continued to build, so he forced an interested expression and offered an encouraging smile. "Then what?"

"You knock on the door and we pretend we're meeting for the first time," she said. "But with one important difference."

Josh prayed the difference was a big one, because so

far this game didn't have much to recommend it. Other than, of course, it made Stacie smile.

"Have you ever been out and met someone so hot you wanted to forego the social niceties and jump him—er, her?"

He paused, remembering the moment he'd first seen Stacie on Anna's porch. "Yes, I have."

"Me, too," she said.

Josh's stomach clenched with jealousy that was as unexpected as it was ridiculous.

"When I saw you, I felt that way," she said softly. "You were so incredibly hot."

It was a nice compliment, but he hadn't forgot how she'd shot him down. "You were disappointed I was a cowboy."

She smiled. "I still thought you were sexy."

"Let me get this straight. I come to the door. I make my move and—"

"I'm ready and willing." She smiled. "But no condoms mean pants stay on."

Even with the restrictions, he could see the possibilities. "I like this game."

She lifted a brow. "Meet downstairs in twenty?"

Anticipation fueled his smile. "It's a plan."

Chapter 10

Stacie stood at the stove in Josh's kitchen, finding it hard to stand still. She couldn't believe she'd brought up this role-playing stuff and gotten Josh to agree to it.

"Ask and it shall be given you." Though the Bible verse from last Sunday's sermon certainly wasn't intended for this situation, being bold *had* worked. Anticipation skittered up her spine.

Everything was in readiness. Coffee perked noisily in the shiny chrome pot, perfectly cooked bacon sat draining on paper towels, and the scrambled eggs were almost done when a knock sounded at the kitchen door.

Setting the burner heat to low, Stacie sauntered to the door, her heart tripping over itself. With suddenly sweaty palms, she opened the door.

"Hello, ma'am." Josh whipped off his hat. "I'm Josh Collins."

She extended her hand. "Stacie Summers. Pleased to meet you."

"Pleasure is all mine." He held her hand for several extra beats and a tingling traveled up her arm.

She took a steadying breath and motioned him inside. Instead of sitting at the table as she expected, he stepped close, crowding her.

"Are you hungry?" she stammered. Her body thrummed at his closeness.

His gaze met hers and she shivered at the hunger in the blue depths.

"Starved," he said in a deep, sexy voice that brought to mind tangled sheets and sweat-soaked bodies.

"Me, too." She moistened her lips with the tip of her tongue. "I'm ravenous."

He reached for her, but Stacie slipped past him, feeling his eyes on her as she walked to the stove. No need to make this too easy or quick. She'd discovered last night that anticipation was half the fun.

She'd just turned off the burner and scooped the eggs onto two plates when she felt his arms slip around her waist.

"It smells good in here," he said, his breath warm against her neck.

"It's the coffee." She spoke extra loud so he could hear her answer over the pounding of her heart. "I ground the beans myself."

"It's not the coffee." He leaned even closer and nuzzled her hair. "You smell like spring flowers."

"I love a man who knows how to give a compliment." She turned in his arms and faced him.

"What I want to know is," Josh's gaze dropped to her lips, "do you taste as good as you smell?"

"I—"

Josh's mouth closed over hers before she could respond. His lips began their delicious assault on her senses and Stacie forgot how to breathe. By the time he stepped back, her knees quivered like jelly and she had to lean against the counter for support.

"Yep. You *do* taste as good as you smell." His gaze dropped to her chest.

Her breasts strained against the thin cotton fabric, already anticipating the feel of his lips.

"Wow." Stacie fanned her face. "It's getting warm in here. Do you mind if I unbutton my shirt?"

His eyes glittered in the fluorescent lights of the kitchen. "Need help?"

"I'm good." Actually she was feeling more wicked than good as she unfastened each button with exaggerated slowness. Finally the shirt hung open.

"You're not wearing a bra."

"I'm not wearing any panties, either," she said, offering him an impish smile. "Course, I'm not taking off my pants."

His smile turned into a grin. "Of course you aren't."

He stepped forward, pushing aside the shirt with his fingers, his hands closing over and cradling each small mound. His thumb scrapped across the tip and Stacie moaned.

Josh lowered his head. "I have to taste—"

His mouth had just closed over one aching nipple when the door swung open with a clatter.

"The horses—" Seth pulled up short. A swath of bright red splashed across his cheeks.

Josh whirled, his muscular body shielding Stacie as she pulled her shirt together.

"Don't you knock?" Josh demanded.

"I saw the light," Seth stammered. "The guys are saddled up and ready."

"Ready for what?"

"You asked for help moving the herd this morning," Seth said.

Josh muttered an expletive and raked a hand through his hair. "I forgot."

"I understand," Seth said, his bland expression fooling no one. "You had other…things…to attend to…"

Stacie ducked her head and fastened the last button, wishing she could sink through the floor.

"Enough, Seth," Josh warned. "Whatever you saw, whatever you *think* you saw, is between Stacie and me. Not you. Not anyone else. Understand?"

"Absolutely," Seth said immediately.

"We're clear then."

"I saw nothing."

Josh blew out a hard breath. "Okay."

Seth's gaze shifted to the plate of eggs and his expression brightened. "Do you mind if I grab some breakfast? I'm starved."

Stacie coasted down the street and shifted Josh's truck into Park in front of Anna's house, the scene eerily reminiscent of high school. Back then she'd feared her parents would be waiting up to give her a lecture. Now it was the thought of seeing her roommates that filled her with dread. If they were back in Denver, a sleepover would be no big deal. But here, everything felt different.

Easing the truck's door open, Stacie stepped from the vehicle and closed the door, being careful not to slam it. She cast an assessing look at the place she temporarily called home. Though the rooms upstairs were dark, lights shone in the kitchen.

That meant one, if not both, of her roommates had already started the day. It also meant if she entered through the back, she'd be asked all sorts of questions. Questions she wasn't sure she was ready to answer.

She glanced longingly at the front door, but in her heart she knew that would only postpone the inevitable. Squaring her shoulders, she followed the sidewalk to the rear of the house and pushed open the screen door.

"I'm home," she called out in a cheery tone.

"Perfect timing." Anna turned from the stove, a large wooden spoon in hand. "The oatmeal is almost ready."

While Stacie was dressed in yesterday's clothes, Anna had on a raspberry-and-cream-colored summer dress with matching sandals. Lauren was more casual. Like Stacie, the psychologist wore jeans and a cotton shirt. But Lauren's shirt was crisp and freshly ironed, not rumpled from a night on the floor.

"You're making breakfast?" Stacie couldn't keep the surprise from her voice. Though Anna was a good cook, she normally stayed out of the kitchen.

"Anna has gone domestic." Lauren glanced up from the *New York Times,* a wry smile on her lips. "I'm not sure what to make of it, but if it means a hot breakfast, I'm all for it."

"I was in the mood for oatmeal," Anna said, "and you weren't around."

"Because she spent the night with Josh." Lauren raised a coffee cup to her lips, but didn't take a drink. Instead she peered at Stacie over the rim, curiosity lighting her eyes. "How was he, by the way?"

"Lauren!" The words shot from Anna's mouth before Stacie could respond. "You don't ask about a man's sexual prowess. At least not right away."

Lauren choked on her coffee, but quickly brought herself under control. "I was asking how he was doing, not how he was in bed. Although, if someone wanted to share…"

"Josh is busy." Stacie moved to the cabinet, took out a cup and poured herself some coffee. Though she normally added cream and sugar, this time she left it black. "He and Seth and some other guys are taking the cattle to another part of his land today."

Stacie didn't quite understand the purpose of the cattle move, but she knew it was an all-day event. That's why she'd volunteered to drive herself home. And if talking about bovines meant she didn't have to discuss her sex life, she'd chatter about the brown-and-whites all day.

"Cows remind me of dogs," Stacie said. "When they look at you with their big brown eyes, it's almost as if they can read your mind."

"You sound like Dani." Anna shook her head, but a smile lifted her lips. "Lauren and I had dinner with Seth and her at the Coffee Pot last night. She's getting so old. I can't believe she'll be seven soon."

Though Anna hadn't been keen on returning to Sweet River—even for the summer—she seemed to be enjoying the opportunity to reconnect with her family. Every time she talked about her brother and his young daughter, her eyes sparkled.

If only Paul and I could be so close, Stacie thought wistfully. But then, Seth accepted and supported Anna's dream of owning her own clothing boutique, so there was no tension between brother and sister.

Stacie fought a pang of envy.

"Seth is planning a big party for Dani," Lauren added. "We'll be invited."

From cattle drive to birthday party. Could this conversation get any crazier?

"There was a write-up in the Denver paper yesterday you should read," Anna said, changing the subject once again. "About a cooking contest."

"Who's sponsoring the contest?" Stacie asked, her interest piqued.

"Remember Jivebread? That catering firm in Denver that's so popular?" Anna asked.

"Of course." Stacie's heart skipped a beat. The firm, known for innovative recipes and eclectic cuisine, was her dream company. She'd interviewed with them a couple times, but both times lost out to more experienced chefs.

"They're looking for innovative recipes," Anna continued. "The winner gets five thousand dollars and the chance to work with their catering team for one year."

"That would be a great opportunity." Stacie kept her tone casual. "Who's doing the judging?"

Anna leaned back and grabbed a newspaper clipping from the counter. She took a sip of coffee and glanced down. "Abbie and Marc Tolliver."

Stacie groaned. Anyone else and she might have stood a chance. But with those two she was dead in the water.

Lauren glanced up from her coffee. "Is that a problem?"

"Big problem." While Stacie didn't want to be negative, she had to be realistic. "I entered a recipe in the Best of Denver competition a couple years back. Marc and Abbie were the final-round judges. They didn't like my entry at all."

While their criticism of the dish had some validity, and she'd learned from their comments, her recipe style hadn't changed much since then.

"That doesn't mean they won't like the one you submit this time," Anna said with a touching loyalty.

"Perhaps Stacie's passion has changed." Lauren took a sip of coffee and cast Stacie a pointed glance. "From recipes to men. Or more specifically, to one certain cowboy."

"My passion hasn't changed," Stacie said firmly, her gaze shifting from one roommate to the other. "Working for Jivebread would be a dream come true. Whatever is happening between Josh and me…well, it isn't anything permanent. If I got that job I'd be outta here in a heartbeat."

Anna opened her mouth for a brief second, but instead of responding, she busied herself filling the bowls with oatmeal and placing them on the table.

"Seth mentioned he was helping Josh today." Lauren tilted her head. "Did he see you before you left?"

Oh, he'd seen her all right. Stacie didn't need to close her eyes to remember Seth's startled expression.

"Our paths crossed," Stacie drawled. "I think he was as surprised to see me as I was to see him."

"So, he knows you spent the night," Lauren said.

Stacie laughed, though right now she was finding it hard to see the humor in the situation. "Let's just say I have no doubt he knows exactly what's going on between Josh and me."

Anna dropped into the seat opposite Stacie. "What *is* going on between you and Josh?"

"Chemistry, Anna, chemistry," Lauren interjected before Stacie could answer. "Mixed with common values, it's a potent combination."

"Yeah, but I thought Stacie didn't like cowboys," Anna said, her eyes clearly puzzled.

"I didn't," Stacie said, starting to understand how a trapped animal felt, "I mean, I don't."

Lauren lifted a perfectly tweezed brow. "You don't like him, yet you slept with him?"

"I don't like the lifestyle," Stacie clarified. "But I like Josh."

"You know he was married before." Anna's expression gave nothing away.

Stacie focused her attention on sprinkling raisins over her oatmeal. "He told me."

Anna pushed her bowl aside and leaned forward, resting her forearms on the table. "Did he tell you Kristin was a city girl who made it clear to everyone in this town that being with Josh wasn't enough of a reason to stay? He didn't go out socially—even with the guys— for almost a year after she left."

There was a warning in Anna's tone that came through loud and clear. But it was the censure that raised Stacie's hackles.

"Say what you mean, Anna." Stacie held on to her rising temper with both hands.

"I don't want to see him hurt, Stace," Anna said, her eyes filled with concern. "I know he's hot. And a person would have to be blind not to see the sparks that fly whenever you're together. But he's also vulnerable."

And I'm not?

"I like him," Stacie said. "And he likes me."

Lauren added an extra dollop of brown sugar to her cereal. "Would you consider staying in Sweet River?"

"No," Stacie said. "But that's no secret. Josh knows I have to complete myself before I can be a partner to any man."

"Complete yourself?" Anna laughed. "Honey, you've been spending way too much time with Lauren."

"What she's saying makes sense," Lauren said before Stacie could respond. "There would be more happy people in this world if women and men gave themselves permission to pursue their dreams."

"Thank you, Lauren," Stacie said.

"Hey, I'm not saying Stacie should give up her dream." Anna sounded affronted that they'd even suggest such a thing. "I've just seen the way she looks at Josh."

"Don't forget the way he looks at her," Lauren added.

"Can't deny it," Stacie admitted. "There is that attraction. But it's purely sexual. And that's the way we both like it."

Chapter 11

Josh stood in front of Anna's house the following morning. Moving the cattle yesterday had taken until sundown. By the time he'd gotten back to the house, all he'd wanted to do was collapse into bed and sleep.

His lips curved up in a smile. He might have been dead in the saddle yesterday, but the night he'd spent with Stacie had definitely been worth it.

Josh had never been with a woman with such a capacity for giving and receiving pleasure.

Though he and Stacie had known each other only a short time, a bond of trust had formed between them. A trust that had allowed them to explore each other's bodies with boldness and passion not normally seen so early in a relationship. He hoped she didn't have any regrets. He sure didn't.

He yawned and glanced at his truck. He'd risen early and had one of his ranch hands drop him off in town.

With an extra set of truck keys in his pocket, he could pick up his 4x4 and head home without disturbing anyone.

The trouble was he didn't want to jump in the truck and leave. He wanted to see Stacie. Wanted to talk to her. Most of all he wanted to make sure she was cool with what had happened. Once Seth had arrived, it had been impossible for them to talk privately.

He stared at the house. Was it only wishful thinking, or was there a light on in the back? Josh moved to the curb when the front door opened. The woman who'd taken hold of his dreams stepped onto the porch, her arms filled with four large white boxes.

Her attention was focused on closing the door, a tricky maneuver with her hands occupied elsewhere.

Josh started up the sidewalk. He increased his pace when the boxes started to tip. He sprinted up the steps when the top two slipped from her arms.

As a former wide receiver for the Sweet River Rockets, Josh had caught the winning toss in the state championship game his senior year. That experience served him well today as he stretched out his hands and pulled the boxes into his arms.

"Touchdown… Collins," the announcer's voice in his head called out.

"Josh." Stacie's voice jerked him back to the present and stopped the victory dance before it could begin. "What are you doing here?"

Her voice was shaky and slightly breathless.

"I came to pick up the truck," he said, feeling out of breath himself. His gaze dropped to the boxes in his arms. "And to carry these."

She returned his smile and he felt himself relax. Why had he worried that seeing her again might be awkward? This was Stacie, a woman he liked…a lot.

"I'm sorry you had to come all this way for your truck," she said.

"I'm not," he said, thinking how beautiful she looked in the early-morning light. "It gave me a chance to see you again."

A hint of pink colored her cheeks. "Yes, well…"

"Where you headed?"

"The Coffee Pot," she said. "Merna buys cinnamon rolls from me Tuesday through Saturday."

He heard the satisfaction in her voice, but forced himself not to read too much into it. Stacie had made it clear she'd be leaving Sweet River by the end of the summer to search for her bliss. "I didn't know you worked for Merna."

"There's a lot about me you don't know," she said with a little laugh. "Now if I could have my boxes back, I need to scoot. Merna insists the rolls be in her hands by seven."

"I'll give you a lift." Josh gestured to his 4x4. "And I'll carry these in for you. Maybe even buy you a cup of coffee."

Stacie hesitated and for a second Josh thought she might turn him down. Then she flashed a brilliant smile and sashayed past him, heading straight for his truck.

Stacie knew something was different the moment she opened the front door of the Coffee Pot Café. For six-fifty on a Tuesday morning, the place was hopping. Normally at this time there were only a couple grandpa types sitting by the window playing checkers. Today, the tables were occupied by card-playing retirees of both sexes.

Merna hurried to greet them, coffeepot in hand.

"Thank goodness you're here. Everyone's been asking for cinnamon rolls."

Stacie felt a warm flush of pleasure. The whole-wheat sourdough rolls had been a big hit. She was sure that was why Merna had asked her to start making some specialty breads and muffins on a trial basis.

Helping out at the Coffee Pot had turned out to be a great job. Not only did she get to practice new recipes, but she got a paycheck for doing what she loved.

"What's with the crowd?" Stacie asked as Josh placed the boxes on the counter.

"Pitch tournament," Merna said. "Started at six-thirty."

"So early?" Stacie couldn't hide her surprise. She'd always thought people retired so they could sleep late.

"Everyone here has gotten up before dawn most of their lives." Merna's tone reflected genuine fondness for her customers. "In fact, they were crowded around the door when I arrived at six."

"Anticipating Stacie's fabulous cinnamon rolls, no doubt." Josh shot her a wink.

"The rolls—oh my goodness—we need to get them on plates immediately." Merna turned to the woman coming out of the kitchen. "Shirley, could you help me get these dished up?"

"I'll help, too," Stacie said.

Merna shook her head. "You did your part making them."

"It was no trouble." Stacie glanced at Josh and smiled. "I love to bake."

"Yes, but because of the rolls, you and Josh had to get up early. I remember what it was like when my Harold was alive. Mornings were our best time to cuddle."

For a moment, the words hung in the air. Stacie willed her cheeks not to warm.

"Josh didn't spend the night, Merna." Stacie kept her tone even, being careful not to protest too much and give credence to Merna's comment. As far as anyone knew, she and Josh were just casual acquaintances. That's how she wanted it to stay.

Josh was already known around town as the cowboy one city girl had left in the dust. Stacie refused to make it two.

Josh bided his time while he parked the truck in Anna's driveway. Stacie had been different on the drive back, more reserved and determined to keep the conversation general.

He first noticed the change in her demeanor when Merna had made the comment about them sleeping together. Josh didn't like the fact people were gossiping, but this was a small town and it came with the territory. There wasn't anything he could do to stop it.

"Thanks for the ride," Stacie said in that pleasant voice women used when giving a guy the brush-off. "I'd better go."

She reached for the door handle and stepped out, not even giving him a chance to open it for her.

He jumped out and caught her on her way around the truck. The bare skin of her arm was warm beneath his fingers.

She paused and the look of longing in her eyes gave him hope that he still had a shot.

"Will you go with me to a baseball game Saturday night?" Josh couldn't remember the last time he'd felt so unsure of himself, but he pressed forward despite his unease. "Sweet River is playing Big Timber. Should be a good game."

He thought he saw a spark of interest at the mention of baseball, but it fled so quickly he decided he'd been mistaken.

"Thanks for the invitation." She played with her watch, twisting it back and forth. "But I don't think it's a good idea."

He felt as if he'd taken a sucker punch to the gut. But he warned himself not to jump to conclusions. What wasn't a good idea? The baseball game? The day of the week? Or dating him?

"Is it me?" Somehow he managed to keep a smile on his face. "Or don't you like baseball?"

She hesitated and he knew she was dumping him.

"We decided our first time together that dating wasn't a good idea," Stacie said.

"We did." Josh wasn't sure what had brought about her abrupt change of heart. And what about her offer of a fling? Was she taking that back, too?

The look in her eyes gave him that answer. If she wanted to change her mind, that was her prerogative. But that didn't mean he understood.

As he walked her to the front porch, he found himself talking about the dry spell the area had been experiencing. They'd discussed the weather on this porch the first time they'd been together. It only seemed fitting they'd discuss it on the last.

"I don't understand why you didn't go with Josh when you had the chance," Anna said. "The guy is a baseball fanatic."

Stacie walked beside Anna down the sidewalk, wishing her friend would drop the subject. In the past four days they'd had this discussion more times than she could count. "He's out of town this weekend...remember?"

"But he wouldn't be in Billings today if you'd agreed to go with him," Anna pointed out. "He would have waited until next Thursday, when he'd already be in town for the cattle auction."

"I didn't have a choice." Stacie heaved an exasperated breath. "Our relationship was starting to become front-page news in this town. I didn't want people talking, especially when I left, saying he couldn't satisfy me just like he hadn't been able to satisfy Kristin."

"But—"

"You told me not to hurt him," Stacie reminded her friend. "That's what I'm trying not to do."

Anna's gaze grew thoughtful. "Did Josh say the gossip bothered him? Or that he didn't want to date you anymore?"

Stacie gritted her teeth and counted to ten. "No. It was my decision."

"Because you were afraid he'd break up with you?"

"Oh, for goodness sakes, Anna, drop it." Couldn't her friend see she was just trying to do what was best for Josh? If she didn't care, she'd ignore the fact that somebody was going to get hurt. "Let's talk about something else. Tell me about Sweet River's baseball team."

From the time she'd been old enough to pick up a Wiffle ball, Stacie had loved America's favorite pastime. Though she hadn't been blessed with the natural talent for sports like her siblings, she'd always been a passionate spectator.

"The team is coed, which is cool," Anna said, going along with the change in topic. "It's made up of former high school and college players from the area. The town really gets behind them. Tonight they're playing their rival, Big Timber."

That told Stacie the stadium would be packed. The realization reinforced that she'd been right to turn down Josh's offer. Although, she thought wistfully, going with him would have been fun. Anna had little interest in the sport. Still, when Stacie had mentioned that she'd like to attend the game, Anna had good-naturedly agreed to go with her.

The closer they got to the ball field, the more people they saw. Even after years away, Anna knew almost everyone. And Stacie discovered she had her own fan club.

"I swear," Anna said, after another person stopped them, "your cinnamon rolls might be the hottest things ever to hit this town!"

Stacie had spent so many years with little reinforcement of her cooking skills, she loved the compliments. "I'm happy people like what I make. And I'm so grateful to Merna for giving me the opportunity to do what I love. Sweet River is lucky to have such a nice café."

"I sure hope that continues," Anna said cryptically.

"What are you talking about?"

"Rumor is Merna may sell and move back to California."

"She hasn't mentioned that to me." Though Stacie wouldn't be around to see the place sold, she found the news distressing. She knew what the café meant to the community. It wasn't just a place to eat, but a place for citizens to congregate and connect.

"Maybe Shirley will take over." Stacie thought aloud. "She runs the place when Merna's away."

"She'd be the logical successor," Anna agreed. "But

maybe she doesn't have the money. Or doesn't want to shoulder all the responsibility."

"Is that why Merna's selling?" Stacie asked. "Because she needs money?"

"I heard Merna's daughter in California is going through a divorce and wants her mom with her."

"I can't believe she hasn't said anything to me."

"It may not happen," Anna said, seemingly unconcerned. "It's not like people are busting down the doors to buy businesses in Sweet River."

"I guess—"

"Don't worry. I'm sure it'll be at least another couple months," Anna said. "You'll have a job until you're ready to leave."

Stacie realized that Anna had misinterpreted her concern. She didn't care about herself. She worried what was going to happen to Al and Norm, who played checkers there every morning. And to the ladies who came in on Thursday for lunch and stayed to play bridge. Not to mention, where would the kids who stopped in after school go?

"Nice evening for a ball game."

Stacie turned. It took her a second to recognize Pastor Barbee. Wearing a blue T-shirt and ball cap, he bore little resemblance to the minister who preached from the pulpit every Sunday. His wife had also gone ultra-casual in a powder-blue jumpsuit.

"I thought you'd be here with Joshua." Mrs. Barbee glanced around as if expecting the cowboy to magically appear.

Stacie gestured to her friend. "I'm here with Anna."

Anna smiled, lifting a hand and wiggling her fingers.

"You two girls stay out of trouble," Pastor Barbee said in a hearty voice.

"Good luck finding Joshua," Mrs. Barbee called out as she and Anna continued down the sidewalk.

Anna grinned. "Small-town living at its best."

The two laughed and continued toward the ball field. With each step Stacie's excitement grew. "I can't believe Lauren didn't want to come."

"I don't think Lauren has ever been to a baseball game." Anna chuckled. "Not her childhood activity. Too lowbrow for her father."

From the little Lauren said about her dad, Anna was probably right in her assessment. The couple of times Stacie had met the respected researcher and university professor, he'd been polite, but a bit scary in his intensity. Definitely not the kind of guy she'd picture with hot dogs and beer at a baseball game.

"Maybe one day she'll give it a try." Stacie looped her arm through Anna's and gave it a quick squeeze. "I'm glad you came with me."

"There it is," Anna said when they turned a corner.

A wave of nostalgia washed over Stacie. The ballpark reminded Stacie of her high school baseball stadium with the sections of wooden bleachers flanking home plate. Only these bleacher seats were painted a bright robin's-egg blue.

Anna tugged on her arm. "Let's get some food."

They'd barely eaten their kraut dogs when Anna started complaining that her stomach hurt. After two urgent trips to the restrooms Anna found an old friend to give her a lift home.

Stacie had been determined to see her sick roommate safely home, but her friend wouldn't hear of it. So before the first pitch had even been thrown, Stacie found herself sitting at the top of the stands...alone.

She took a sip of ice-cold beer and glanced around

the stands, amazed at the number of people she recognized. She'd just finished checking out the Sweet River bench when she saw Josh.

Her breath caught in her throat. What was *he* doing here? Though Stacie told herself to look away, her gaze remained riveted on him. He didn't see her, so she took her time looking. He was standing at the end of a bleacher talking to an older gentleman.

Like many Sweet River fans, Josh wore a blue shirt in support of the local team. The fabric accentuated the obvious width of his shoulders. She couldn't help remembering how the muscles in his back had flexed when she'd caressed him.

She swallowed hard against the sudden ache in her chest. Not seeing him, not talking to him, had made the past four days unbearable. But keeping her distance was necessary. If they'd stayed together any longer, they'd be considered a couple. Expectations by the locals would rise only to be dashed when she left town. She would not have the town laughing at Josh or gossiping about his inability to satisfy a big-city girl.

Still, what would it hurt to be polite and say hello? She'd half risen from her seat when she caught sight of Wes Danker returning from the concession stand with two pretty girls close behind. One of the young women had a mass of dark, curly hair and a bright smile. The other was a well-endowed blonde.

Misty.

Stacie sank down, bile rising to her throat. Had Josh called the blonde when she'd turned down his date? Was that why he'd returned early from Billings? Was Misty Josh's new fling?

A twinge of something that felt an awful lot like

jealousy stabbed Stacie's heart. The kraut dog—Anna's nemesis—turned to a leaden weight in her stomach.

Wes gestured to the empty seats and Josh stepped aside to let the three pass. Stacie noticed Misty went last, ensuring she would be sitting by Josh.

"Is that seat taken?"

Stacie pulled her gaze from Josh to find Alexander Darst standing in the aisle. Instead of wearing shorts or jeans and a T-shirt like most of the spectators, her first "match" wore dress pants and a shirt open at the collar. The attorney's only concession to the informal event seemed to be leaving his tie at home.

Stacie smiled. "It's available."

"I wasn't sure I'd make the opening pitch." Alex maneuvered past her and sat down. "I got caught up with some work at the office."

"Today's Saturday."

Alex shrugged. "Only time the client could make it."

Stacie didn't know why she was surprised. Her brother worked weekends. Back in Denver, many of her high-achieving friends routinely put in sixty-plus-hour weeks. But Stacie realized one of the things she loved about Sweet River was its slower pace. Oddly enough, the kind of place that used to drive her crazy had become her new gold standard. Who'd have guessed?

"Do you like baseball?" she asked Alex.

"Not particularly." He settled next to her. "But every person in these stands is a potential client. I decided it was time to get out and mingle. What about you?"

"I came with my friend Anna," Stacie said. "She wasn't feeling well and had to leave. I love baseball so I stayed."

"Lucky for me." He flashed a smile.

Stacie wondered how she could have ever thought he

was good-looking. Though his hair had obviously been cut by a stylist and his dress pants were hand tailored, his features were too perfect, his body a little too lean.

He also had an annoying habit of talking continuously. She listened to him ramble through eight innings, sneaking a peek now and then at Misty and Josh. But when Misty leaned her head against Josh's shoulder, Stacie had seen enough.

She pressed her lips together and pulled a sheet of paper and a pen from her purse. Although the game was nearly over, she started recording strikes, balls and errors.

"What are you doing?" Alex asked.

"Keeping stats," she said between clenched teeth, resisting the urge to glance down at Josh and Misty. "My brothers played ball and my father used to keep the books for the coaches. He taught me how to do it."

"Sounds like you and your dad are close."

She could hear the envy in his voice, and with a start she realized it was true. She and her father *had* been close. Until he'd decided to try to ruin—er, run—her life. "We were… I mean, we are close."

"You're lucky," he said. "My father had expectations I could never seem to meet."

Something in his tone caused Stacie to really look at Alex. The sadness lurking in his eyes surprised her. "I bet he's proud of you now."

"He wanted me to go into corporate law," Alex said. "I wanted to live in a small town and do a little bit of everything."

"How did you end up here?" She couldn't remember if he'd told her on their "date."

"We came to Montana on vacation when I was a small boy. I loved the mountains and the wide-open spaces in between. When I got out of law school, I tried it his way. I practiced in Chicago until I moved here."

"How do you like being a Sweet River resident?" She waited for him to start raving.

"A little disappointing," he said instead.

"How so?" Stacie asked.

"The people in this area are cautious." He paused and appeared to choose his words carefully. "Many of them choose to make the trip to Big Timber for their legal needs rather than come to a stranger."

Stacie pulled her brows together. She understood what he was saying, but it didn't make sense. "I've been here less time than you, but I've found everyone to be more than welcoming."

"That's probably because one of your friends is from here," Alex pointed out. "And aren't you dating a local?"

"He and I were—we are—just friends." Stacie didn't elaborate. Talking to this man about Josh didn't feel right. "Are you thinking of moving back to Chicago?"

"No," Alex said, then more firmly as if trying to convince himself: "No. I'm sure, given time, business will improve."

Alex seemed sincere and Stacie found herself wanting to help him. "Have you ever thought of maybe… I don't know…dressing more…casually?"

She softened the suggestion with a smile.

"Wear jeans and a T-shirt to the office?" Alex shuddered. "I couldn't. It wouldn't be professional."

"I'm not talking about the office," Stacie said. "I'm talking about now, at a sporting event. You don't wear dress pants and Italian leather shoes to a ball game, not if you want to fit in."

"I suppose—"

"And another thing, the Clipper is a barbershop on

Main Street, a block from the Coffee Pot Café. Give them a try. If you patronize local merchants, maybe they'll support your business."

She half expected Alex to scoff at her suggestions. Instead he appeared to be seriously considering them.

"You like it here," he said at last.

"What?"

"You like it here…in Sweet River."

"Of course," she said. "It's a great place."

"Have you decided to stay?" His gaze was curious. "I know when we went out you couldn't wait to get back to Denver, but you seem more settled now."

"I've—"

The crack of a bat split the air and Stacie and Alex rose to their feet along with the rest of the crowd. It was bottom of the ninth, Sweet River at bat and trailing by one run. With a runner on base, this was her team's chance to bring home a victory.

"Go. Go!" Stacie yelled.

The runners rounded the bases. When the batter slid into home plate, the crowd roared and Stacie jumped up and down, hugging everyone in sight. When Alex hugged her, she hugged him back. Joy sluiced through her. She was on top of the world until her gaze dropped to the field and she saw Josh staring up at her, a look of stunned disbelief on his face.

Chapter 12

Josh's heart stopped beating then started up with a sputter. Now he understood why Stacie had dumped him. It made sense she'd pick a guy who looked like he'd stepped off the cover of *GQ* rather than a cowboy with dirt on his boots.

The first time they'd met she'd made it clear she didn't like cowboys. But he thought she'd changed her mind. *Obviously not.* He clenched his teeth.

"Hey, Collins." Wes poked him in the ribs. "We're going to Earl's to celebrate the V."

Josh shifted his gaze to Wes and the two women. He'd gotten back early from Billings and had called his friend to see if he was going to the game. Wes hadn't mentioned anything about bringing Sasha and Misty along.

Though Misty seemed like a nice person, she wasn't his type, and the last thing Josh wanted was to prolong the evening. But the pleading look in Wes's eyes stopped the refusal pushing against his lips. Something told him if he said no, the girls might go their own way. It didn't matter to him, but he knew it mattered to Wes.

"I'll go," Josh said. "For a little while."

"It's karaoke night." Misty slipped her arm though his. "Wait until you hear me sing. I'm really good."

Josh's first impulse was to pull back from the possessive gesture. But he sensed Stacie watching him, so he smiled at the buxom blonde instead. "Tell me more about yourself. We didn't get a chance to talk much during the game."

Actually there had been ample time, but he'd been too busy brooding about Stacie to pay Misty much attention. The blonde was a country girl. That much he remembered from Wes's brief introduction. Grew up on a ranch close to Cheyenne.

"Did I tell you me and Sasha filled out one of those surveys for that professor lady?" Misty tightened her hold on him, forcing her breast against his arm. "We have so much in common, what with us both being country folk. I bet they match me with you."

Josh didn't know what to say. Misty was right. She should have been the perfect woman for him. There was only one problem—she wasn't Stacie.

Misty chattered happily on the way to Earl's Tavern, a cowboy bar around the corner from the Coffee Pot Café. Wes found a parking spot not far from where Josh had left his truck.

As he walked past the café, Josh couldn't help remembering how good things had been between him and Stacie just four days ago. Until that morning he'd helped her deliver—

"I love their cinnamon rolls," Misty said, interrupting her story about her barrel-racing days. "Sasha and me come here on our day off just to get one of those rolls."

"They're humongous," Sasha added. "And super yummy."

Wes cast a pointed glance at Josh as if waiting for him to comment. But as far as Josh was concerned the less said about those damned cinnamon rolls, the better.

"Josh knows the woman who makes 'em," Wes said. "She—"

The big man was picking up steam and would have said more, but Josh shot him a quelling glance. The last thing he wanted to talk about, to think about tonight, was Stacie Summers.

"Anyway," Wes said, quickly switching gears, "I like 'em, too." He patted his belly. "Some might say I like them a little too much."

The girls giggled.

For a moment, blessed silence descended. Until Misty started talking about the time she'd made it to the semifinals on the national rodeo circuit.

By the time they reached the tavern, Josh was ready to bolt. Wes must have sensed it because he motioned to a large round table toward the back of the bar.

"Why don't you three grab that one so we're sure to have a seat," Wes said. "I'll order the pizza and beer."

"We have to sign up for karaoke." Misty slanted a sideways glance at Josh. "Everyone says I sound like Shania."

Josh forced a weak smile. Once they were out of earshot he turned to Wes. "She's driving me crazy. I've got to—"

"Tune her out," Wes said. "Just give me fifteen minutes. That's all I'm asking."

Josh glanced longingly at the door.

"Then, if you want, you can leave," Wes said. "I won't try to stop you."

"I'll give you fifteen minutes, Wes," Josh warned. "Then I'm outta here."

Josh headed to the back table. Wes was right about one thing: the place was filling up quickly. After only a few minutes, every table was taken and Misty had moved on to how she'd gotten her job at the dude ranch.

Josh listened politely, but his thoughts kept returning to the town's new attorney.

Misty paused in her story just long enough to take a breath and Josh realized one of the things he'd really liked about Stacie was that she wasn't in love with hearing herself talk.

Wes arrived before Misty took another breath, but he wasn't alone. "Guess who I found looking for a table? I told them they could join us."

Even before Josh looked up, the scent of jasmine told him who he'd find standing there. It took everything he had to force a smile to his lips and resist the urge to throttle Wes.

Josh stood and extended his hand to the man. "Josh Collins," he said by way of introduction. "I have a ranch about forty miles from here."

The man returned Josh's strained smile with a friendly one of his own. "Alexander Darst. I'm the new attorney in town."

"Good to finally meet you." The first thing Josh noticed was the lack of calluses on the man's hands. The second was his size. The guy was on the smaller side— built the way Stacie had once told him she liked her men. His heart twisted.

"Nice to see you again, Josh," Stacie said in a soft voice that sounded lyrical next to Misty's nasally whine.

Josh shifted his gaze, surprised at the absence of her usual heart-stopping smile. Until he reminded himself that her happiness wasn't his concern. Not anymore. Not since she'd kicked him out of her life and taken up with a city dude.

He settled for giving her a nod of acknowledgment. But old habits died hard, and when she rounded the table to take the open seat next to him, he found himself pulling out her chair.

"Thanks," she said.

When her gaze met his, he looked away, afraid of what his eyes might reveal.

Thankfully the pizza came, along with a pitcher of beer and a couple of extra glasses for Alex and Stacie.

Alex hesitated. "I wonder if they serve wine—"

Josh wasn't sure what the glance Stacie sent the attorney meant, but Alex shut his mouth, grabbed the pitcher and filled Stacie's glass and his own.

Though the fifteen minutes Josh had given Wes were up, there was no way he could leave now. Not without it looking like he was running from Stacie. So he tried to keep his attention on the conversation and off her. It wasn't easy. When she was near, his body operated on a heightened state of awareness.

"On deck, Misty and Sasha," the DJ called out.

Misty squealed and jumped up, jerking Sasha to her feet. "Wish us luck."

"Good luck," Josh said, relieved when the two headed to the stage.

It didn't take more than a couple seconds for him to realize he had a problem. While he was happy that Misty was gone, when she'd been at the table he could focus all his attention on her. Now Wes and Alex were talking investment strategies, leaving him no choice but to make conversation with Stacie.

"What did you think of the game?" Stacie's smile was hesitant, and for the first time Josh realized this was as awkward for her as it was for him.

"It was good." Josh turned in his seat to face her. "What did you think?"

"The come-from-behind ending was super exciting." Her fingers tightened around her glass of beer. "I was jumping up and down and hugging everyone in sight."

The words hung in the air. Josh stilled. Was this her way of telling him there was nothing between her and the attorney? But if that were true, why had she gone to the game with him in the first place?

You're reading too much into a simple comment. He's the type of guy she's been looking for, not you, he told himself.

"I was surprised to see you with Darst." Josh forced his expression to remain neutral, his tone offhand, as if he were talking cattle prices with another rancher. "When did you two start dating?"

"Dating?" Stacie made a face. "I'm not dating Alex. He's a nice guy, but not for me."

Josh's heart did a series of flip-flops. He cleared his throat. "You were at the game with him. You're with him now."

"Are you and Misty on a date?"

"No. Absolutely not."

"You were at the game with her," Stacie pointed out. "You're with her now."

"Wes brought her along." Josh wondered when he'd been switched from offense to defense. "I came with them to get a beer, but Misty and I are definitely not together."

"I went to the game with Anna," Stacie explained, her tone as matter-of-fact as his. "But she got sick and went home. Alex came late and happened to sit beside me."

"You hugged him," Josh said.

"I hugged everyone around me. I was happy we won." Stacie met his gaze. "But I didn't hug any of those people like I hug you. I don't hug anyone that way."

Though the bar was dimly lit, there was no mistaking the emotion in her eyes. Josh found himself more confused than ever.

"You dumped me," Josh said. "Everything was great between us. Then, all of a sudden, you decide you didn't want to see me again."

"That's not how it was," she said, glancing at Alex and Wes, as if making sure they weren't listening.

"That's how it felt." It was as close as Josh could come to baring his soul.

The women finished their karaoke rendition of "That Don't Impress Me Much" and the room erupted into applause. Josh put his hands together and clapped with the others. Misty was right about one thing. She *could* sing.

Still, he groaned when they started back to the table. His groan turned to a silent cheer when Misty and Sasha stopped to flirt with a group of rowdy, admiring cowboys.

"We need to talk," Stacie said. "But not here."

Though Misty was occupied for the moment, Josh knew it would be more difficult to get away once she came back. He hadn't asked Misty on a date, so as far as he was concerned he was a free agent. But Stacie, on the other hand…

"What about Alex?"

Stacie lifted her chin. "I already answered that question."

Josh knew the clock was running out. He could hold on to his pride and tell Stacie there was nothing to discuss. But he still had questions. And she was the only one with the answers.

He rose to his feet and Stacie stood, as well. When Wes and Alex paused mid-conversation, Josh reached into his pocket, pulled out a couple of bills and tossed them on the table.

"I'm taking Stacie home," Josh said, keeping his tone casual.

Wes's gaze turned speculative. "I guess I'll see you later."

Josh nodded and turned his attention briefly to the attorney. "Good to meet you, Darst."

Alex's gaze shifted from Stacie to Josh. "Likewise."

When Josh walked out of Earl's Tavern, it was with a lighter step than when he'd entered. Stacie was at his side and he was taking her home.

The only question that remained was would they end up at her house? Or his?

Stacie had hoped that she and Josh could sit on one of the metal benches scattered on Sweet River's Main Street. But too many people still mingled on the sidewalks to make a private conversation possible.

She could take him back to Anna's house, but they'd face the same problem there. Because her reason for breaking up with Josh centered on her concern for his reputation, being seen together—even if they were just talking—wasn't a good idea.

"Could we go for a drive?" Stacie asked. "I know gas is expensive but—"

"My truck is parked around the corner." His expression gave nothing away.

Stacie hurried to the vehicle. Not until she was safely in the cab and they were on a road headed out of town did she relax. She cast Josh a sideways glance. "You have questions."

"A few."

Okay, so he wasn't going to make this easy. In a way she didn't blame him. The past four days had been hard on her, but she'd at least known why it was best they remain apart. He hadn't a clue.

And that was *her* fault.

Shame rose inside her. When Merna had made her speculative comment, it had been a wake-up call. People could end up hurt—*Josh* could end up hurt—by their fling.

"I probably seem like a flake." She gave a humorless laugh. "Hot to cold in sixty seconds."

"I don't understand what's going on in your head," he said in a low voice. "That's why I'm here. So I can understand."

"It's because of you," Stacie blurted out, her heart aching at the hurt and confusion in his voice and knowing it was all because of her. "I did it because of you."

His fingers tightened around the steering wheel and a tiny muscle in his jaw jumped. "Is it because I'm a cowboy? Because I'm not the kind of man you want... even for a fling?"

"No." Stacie blinked back tears, realizing just how much her actions had hurt him. "It was because I didn't want to see you hurt. I don't want people talking about you after I'm gone, calling you the man city girls always leave. Don't you understand? I couldn't bear that."

Several stray tears slipped down her cheeks. She quickly brushed them aside, hoping he hadn't noticed.

"Are you telling me this is all about *gossip?*" His voice grew louder with each word.

"I don't want anyone to laugh at you." Stacie's heart rose to her throat and shattered in two. "Not ever. And certainly not because of me."

"You don't want to hurt me." It came out as a statement rather than a question.

"Never."

"Then take back your goodbye." The muscle in his jaw jumped. "I can deal with gossip."

"When I leave, it's going to be hard." Stacie couldn't resist anymore. She reached over and took his hand. "Painful. Really, really painful. For both of us."

When the words slipped from her tongue, she knew Anna had been right. She wasn't just worried about Josh being hurt by the gossip. She was also worried about herself. Worried that she wouldn't be able to leave him when the time came.

But she wanted—no, *needed*—to find her bliss.

"I'm willing to take that risk," he said quietly. "The question is…are you?"

Josh turned off the highway onto a country road, but Stacie paid little attention. Her head was swimming. Could she do it? Could she spend two more months with this man and then walk away?

"The baseball game would have been more fun if we'd been together," Josh said in a persuasive tone. "We enjoy each other's company. Why should we both be alone these next couple months?"

Still, Stacie hesitated. "The gossip won't bother you?"

Josh chuckled. "Do I look like the kind of guy who pays attention to that stuff?"

"No," she said, then more firmly: "No, you don't."

"Well?"

She opened her mouth, but the sound of barking dogs stopped her. Bert and her pups ran alongside the truck as it drove down a familiar lane.

"This is your place."

"Last I checked."

"Why are we here?"

"I said I was taking you home." He pulled the truck to a stop and his lips hitched up in a lazy smile. "I didn't say *whose* home."

Dear God, she adored this man. "If you're expecting me to sleep over you need to know I didn't bring any pajamas."

He grinned. "Not a problem."

A surge of emotion blinded Stacie with its intensity. She didn't just adore this man, she *loved* him. With that realization came a certainty that she was right where she wanted—and needed—to be, at least for now.

The next month felt like a dream. Sometimes Josh wanted to pinch himself to make sure it was real. He'd never been happier. He and Stacie spent every free moment together.

One day she even rode with him to look for stray calves. They'd ended up making love under the noonday sun and the bright blue sky.

Today he was meeting Stacie for lunch while in town picking up supplies. He'd already gotten what he needed from Sweet River Grain and Feed and he had thirty minutes to kill. He turned onto Main Street and parked in front of the bank. A half hour was more than enough time to accommodate a quick side trip to see his dad.

There had been a message on his answering machine last night from his father asking him to stop by the next time he was in town.

Josh waved at the teller as he headed to the back of the bank. His father's door was open and Bill Collins looked up when Josh entered the office.

A smile of welcome split his father's tanned face. "Come in, son. Shut the door so we have some privacy."

Josh found the request unusual. The last time they'd shut the door had been when Josh told his dad Kristin had left him.

"You're looking good." His father nodded approvingly. "Happier than I remember."

"Things are going well at the ranch." Josh glanced at the clock on the wall, taking note of the time.

"I've heard things are on the upswing in your personal life, too." His father motioned for him to take a seat in the leather wingback in front of the desk.

Josh dropped into the chair. He shifted, unable to get comfortable. "You could say that."

"Your mom and I would like to meet your new girlfriend," his father said. "Especially since things seem to be getting serious."

"We're not serious." Josh gave his dad the same answer he gave everyone who asked. "Stacie and I are just good friends."

"That's not what we've heard."

Josh kept his smile easy. "I'd have thought you'd lived in this town long enough to know not to listen to gossip."

"Rosalee told your mother Miss Summers frequently spends the night."

Josh's smile froze on his face. Rosalee Barker was the woman he employed to cook and clean. She'd worked for his parents for years before semi-retiring. Nevertheless, she worked for him now and he thought she could be trusted to keep his privacy. "Rosalee just lost herself a job."

"Don't be angry." His dad held up both hands. "Rosalee only told your mother. You know she's not going to say anything."

"Mom told you," Josh pointed out.

"We know you wouldn't be with this woman if you didn't care for her." His father's brows pulled together. "What I don't understand is why you're being so secretive. It's not like you."

"This isn't high school, Dad." Josh kept his tone light. "You don't need to meet everyone I date."

"We like to meet the ones who are important to you," his father said smoothly. "Come over for dinner tomorrow night around six. We'll keep things nice and casual."

"Not a good idea."

"Why not?"

"I know how it'd go. You'd start asking about our future." Josh could just imagine the look on Stacie's face if his mother began talking about her desire for grandchildren. "Since we don't have a future, that would be awkward. Stacie will be leaving Sweet River before long. That will be the end of our relationship."

"You don't plan to keep in touch?"

"What would be the point?" Frustration made Josh's voice harsher than he'd intended. He'd considered that option, but he knew it would only be postponing the inevitable. "She doesn't want to live here. That's the bottom line."

"Does she know you love her?" His father rose to his feet and walked to the window.

"What makes you think I love her?"

"You're my son," his dad said, his gaze still focused outside. "I know you."

Josh wanted to deny his feelings for Stacie, but he couldn't. "What would be the point in telling her? Stacie needs to choose her own course in life."

Bill Collins turned. "In business, you need *all* the facts to make a good decision."

His dad made it sound simple, but Josh knew how much finding her bliss meant to Stacie. Telling her he loved her would be the equivalent of emotional blackmail.

He wasn't going to do it. Not even if it meant losing the woman he loved.

Chapter 13

Stacie parked the Jeep on the shoulder of the long lane leading up to Seth Anderssen's house. Obviously this was more than a child-blowing-out-candles-and-opening-gifts party.

She glanced over at Lauren. "I can see why Seth insisted on such a big cake."

"I hope I look okay." Lauren snapped the vanity mirror shut. "I didn't want to be too casual, but now I'm worried I went the other way."

Stacie didn't immediately respond. She wasn't sure what to make of Lauren's behavior. Her roommate had changed outfits five times before leaving the house and she'd been fussing with her makeup since they'd pulled out of Sweet River.

"You look amazing." While Lauren's sleeveless linen sheath was simple, the periwinkle-blue color said this professor could be fun, too. "Very professional."

Lauren's face blanched. "Professional?"

Stacie blinked. Lauren's tone made her compliment sound like a bad thing. "I thought that was the image you were trying to project."

Her roommate had been counting down the days until the party. Stacie had assumed it was because a lot of Seth's single friends would be there. While she didn't expect Lauren to actively recruit survey participants during Dani's special day, she *had* expected her to be in full businesswoman mode.

"What was I thinking?" Lauren's face fell. "I *am* overdressed."

Sensing whatever she said wouldn't be right, Stacie opted for silence. She focused on pulling the keys from the ignition and dropping them in her purse.

"Take a good look at me. I want you to be completely honest," Lauren said. "Am I overdressed?"

Reluctantly, Stacie shifted her gaze. She studied her friend with a critical eye, determined to give a fair appraisal. "The pearls *may* be a bit over the top, but then again I don't know what is de rigueur for these events. Remember, this is all new to me, too."

Like Lauren, Stacie had debated what to wear. Knowing everything in Sweet River tended to be casual, Stacie had opted for pants and a top made of gold silk and embroidered with little designs. The outfit reminded her of Chinese pajamas. Anna said the color made her hazel eyes look more amber than green.

"I must change." Lauren's voice sounded shrill in the car's silence. "I can't go in there looking like this."

For a second Stacie thought her roommate was kidding. After all, Lauren was the quintessential academic. Logic over emotion. Then Stacie took a closer look. Dear God, were those really *tears* in the beautiful blonde's eyes?

Stacie's heart twisted at Lauren's distress. Finding males for her research was obviously taking its toll on her friend. Stacie turned in the seat and offered a reassuring smile. "Why would you change? You are fantastic in that dress. The color makes your eyes look violet, and the style suits your fabulous figure."

Lauren dabbed at her eyes with a tissue. "Do you think Seth will be impressed?"

"Does it matter?"

Lauren's cheeks turned a dusty pink. "He's a handsome man. A woman likes to look her best."

Stacie paused, the puzzle pieces finally falling into place. She gave a whoop. "You have the hots for Anna's brother."

The pink dusting Lauren's cheeks darkened to a deep rose. "I do not have the 'hots' for him." Her tone was a touch indignant and classic Lauren. "But I do like him as a person. And in case you've forgotten, Seth is the number-one reason I was able to get enough subjects to complete my research."

The flush on Lauren's cheeks and the sparkle in her eyes told Stacie that her friend's feelings went beyond gratitude. But the tilt of Lauren's chin said this wasn't the time to press for deeper emotions.

"He'll think you look beautiful," Stacie said.

Lauren's stiff shoulders relaxed. She took a deep, steadying breath. After retouching her lipstick and powdering her nose, she reached for the door handle. "I'm ready now."

Thank you, Jesus.

Though they'd discussed what would happen once they got to the ranch, Lauren had been so stressed during the ride that Stacie wasn't sure if any of what she'd said had registered. "Don't forget I need help getting the cake inside."

Lauren glanced down at her spiky heels. "Why don't I carry the salad and send someone back to help you with the cake?"

"That's fine," Stacie said. "I'll wait."

When Lauren disappeared around the bend in the drive, Stacie moved to the back of the Jeep to ready the cake.

"I can carry it for you."

A warmth flowed through Stacie's veins like warm honey. She turned and there he was, standing in the gravel drive, his dark hair tousled by the breeze. Her heart did a happy dance in her chest. "Josh. I thought you were in Bozeman."

Josh smiled. "I came back early. I couldn't wait any longer to see you."

Her heart fluttered and suddenly she found herself drowning in his eyes. She'd dated her share of men, but no one who'd touched her heart. Until this cowboy.

She'd told herself over and over the past three days that she needed to take a step back from the relationship. It wasn't good to miss someone so much.

With that in mind, she tore her gaze from his and popped the hatch. After lowering the end gate, she tugged the cardboard box toward her.

Josh moved to her side. He leaned over her shoulder, clearly curious. "What's in the box?"

"A 'Cinderella and Her Castle' cake." Several years ago Stacie had done a stint as a baker's assistant at a wedding shop in Denver. It had felt good to use those skills again. "Want to see it?"

"You know I do," he said, his warm breath tickling her ear as he planted a kiss on her neck.

A delicious shiver of wanting washed over her. But she forced herself to ignore the sensation and instead focused on lifting the top off the box.

A low whistle escaped Josh's lips. "You made that?"

"I did indeed." Stacie surveyed her masterpiece, feeling like a new mother showing off her firstborn.

He peered closer. His eyes widened. "The castle sparkles—"

"Edible food glitter."

"The turrets with the flags?"

"Sugar cones, construction paper and toothpicks."

"Wow." Admiration filled his gaze. "You are one talented lady."

Like any pretty girl, Stacie had received her share of compliments over the years. But this was different. This wasn't about looks. This was about talent.

Who'd have thought a *cowboy* would be the one to understand her so well? "Thank you, Josh."

"You *will* find your bliss." His tone left no room for doubt. "You're too creative and talented not to."

Stacie carefully replaced the lid and pulled the box closer, wondering why she didn't feel more excited at the prospect.

"How'd you end up doing the cake? Last I heard Merna was making it."

"Seth said Merna had caught that flu that was going around." Stacie struggled to remember his exact words. "He'd already tried a woman in Big Timber, but she was booked."

"You came to his rescue."

"What can I say?" Stacie said with a laugh. "I'm a nice person."

"Yes, you are." His gaze wrapped around her, holding her close. Familiar warmth washed over her.

"I've missed you," she said softly, ignoring the warning flags popping up.

Josh opened his arms. "Come here."

Stacie didn't hesitate. Josh had been out of town on some ranch business for three long days, and she'd missed him terribly.

She laid her head against his chest and listened to the beat of his heart. Strong and steady, like the man himself. Only with him did she feel safe…cherished…loved.

"You're shivering." He leaned back and held her at arm's length, his brow furrowed in worry. "Do you feel okay?"

She slid a finger down his cheek. Though she knew every inch of his body, right now she felt as if she could explore it forever. "Like I said, I missed you."

Josh captured her hand and planted a kiss in her palm, his gaze never leaving hers. "Maybe I should go away more often."

"Don't you dare."

"Come home with me tonight," he said suddenly.

Instead of answering she slipped her arms around his waist and tugged him close, inhaling the clean, fresh scent of him. "You showered with my favorite soap."

He chuckled, rubbing his hands down her back. "Showering isn't as much fun without you there."

When he lowered his voice and gazed into her eyes, she was tempted to give him anything he wanted. But she'd come with Lauren. It wouldn't be right to make her friend drive home alone. Still, she found herself tempted. She reached up on tiptoes and brushed a kiss against his lips. "I'll see what I can arrange."

"I'll make it worth it for you."

A languid heat filled her limbs and an overwhelming need to be close to him rose inside her. Her heart skittered and Stacie knew she had to get the situation under control or she'd end up doing something foolish. She took a deep breath and focused on the box. "If you take that side, I'll—"

Josh reached around her and lifted the entire box without any trouble. "I'll carry. You open the door. Deal?"

She cleared her throat and found her voice. "Deal."

On the walk to the house Stacie found herself distracted by the intoxicating scent of his cologne and the heat emanating from his strong, work-hardened body.

How could she ever have believed the starving-poet look was sexy? Such a man could never have handled the cake in such an efficient manner. Or, for that matter, rescued her from the clutches of a vicious serpent...

"My snake bite is all better." She climbed the steps without the slightest twinge of discomfort and held the screen door open for him. "If not for the fang marks, I'd think that day had been just a bad dream."

"Not all of it was bad." Josh paused for a moment in the doorway, his gaze raking over her body. "I got to see you naked for the first time."

He flashed a smile and stepped into the house, leaving her to stamp out the flames of desire his words had reignited.

An hour later, when she took her seat at one of the tables Seth had set up, the embers still smoldered. She tried to focus on the food, but it wasn't easy. Not with Josh beside her.

Seth had furnished barbeque beef for the potluck while the guests were to bring a variety of dishes. Since this was Stacie's first party in Sweet River, she'd been determined to bring something exciting and different. Thankfully, several nights earlier, a strawberry and feta salad had come to life in her head.

She'd reworked the ingredients multiple times, intent on getting the balance of flavors and textures perfect. Once she was satisfied, she'd had her roommates do a taste test. Anna raved about the toasted almonds. Lauren, who didn't even like feta cheese, had given the dish an A+.

"Anyone know who brought the salad with the strawberries and almonds?" Seth glanced around the table. "It's really good."

"That would be me." Lauren's cheeks turned a becoming shade of pink when Seth focused his attention on her. "Actually Stacie made it, but I brought it into the house."

"A team effort," Seth said, a teasing glint in his eyes.

"With her doing 99.9% and me doing the rest," Lauren responded in an equally light tone.

"Each member of a team is important," Seth said.

Stacie listened to the banter in amazement. If she didn't know better, she'd think Lauren was flirting with Anna's brother. Could scholarly Lauren really have the hots for a man who rode horses and worked with his hands?

The answer was like a rolling pin up the side of her head. *Absolutely not.*

"You're right, Seth," Anna chimed in. "This salad is fabulous. Like I told Stacie, if she enters this recipe, she'll win the contest for sure."

"Contest?" Josh's fork paused midair.

Stacie shot her roommate a warning look. But Anna must not have seen it because she leaned forward, her voice loud enough that everyone at the table could easily hear.

"I read about it in the *Denver Post*." Excitement reverberated in Anna's voice. "Best recipe wins five thousand dollars *and* a chance to work for Jivebread."

"Jivebread?" Seth grabbed two corn muffins from a basket on the table. He kept one for himself and lobbed the other across the table to Josh, who caught it easily. "Never heard of it."

"It's one of the top catering firms in Denver," Anna explained. "Working there has always been Stacie's dream."

Josh lowered his fork and though Stacie didn't glance his way, she could feel his eyes on her.

"I think she's got an excellent chance at winning," Lauren added. "*If* she enters by next week's deadline."

The baked beans that had been sliding quite nicely down Stacie's throat came to an abrupt halt. She swallowed hard.

"Why wouldn't she enter?" Seth said. "This salad is her ticket to the top."

Her roommates had said the same thing at least a hundred times. Stacie knew they didn't understand her hesitation. Heck, she didn't fully understand it herself.

The entry fee was reasonable. And even if Abbie and Marc hadn't liked her previous recipes, that didn't mean they wouldn't like this one. This truly was, or could be, her chance to grab the brass ring.

Stacie ignored Josh's questioning glance and focused on the food on her plate. Thankfully everyone at the table seemed eager to talk and the conversation flowed to the next topic.

Seth told stories from his little girl Danica's childhood. Lauren updated everyone on the number of surveys she'd processed to date. And Anna brought out some new clothing designs she'd "just happened" to bring along for everyone to ooh and aah over.

Dressed in a frilly pink "princess" dress, Dani flitted from room to room, her blue eyes sparkling and an infectious smile on her lips. When the seven-year-old wasn't playing with her friends or bestowing wishes with her "magic wand," she was begging her dad to let her blow out her birthday candles.

"Fifteen minutes." Seth promised. His smile widened as his gaze lingered on the sparkly tiara Anna had placed on his daughter's blond head. "Our guests are still eating dinner."

"But Daddy, I want my cake and ice cream now. Pleaaase—"

"Danica." Seth's firm tone left no room for argument. "One more word and I'll make it twenty."

The child studied him for a long second and then heaved an exaggerated sigh worthy of any princess.

Anna pushed back her chair and stood. She held out a hand to her niece. "Fifteen minutes is just enough time for one game of musical chairs."

Danica's expression immediately brightened. "I'll get Madison and Emily and Tyler and Jessie." She took off running, still spouting names.

Lauren rose to her feet. "I'll help."

"I'll take you up on that offer," Anna said to Lauren before slanting a glance at her brother. "Just make sure you have the cake ready to cut in fifteen."

Seth appeared not to hear, but seconds later he disappeared into the kitchen, leaving Stacie and Josh alone at the table.

"I probably should help," Stacie said, making no move to get up.

"You've done your part." Josh placed his hand over hers and gave it a quick squeeze. "Relax and enjoy the evening."

"I am enjoying it," Stacie admitted.

Josh shifted, turning in his chair to face her. "You sound surprised."

"I didn't have any idea what this would be like." Stacie's lips lifted in a rueful smile. "I never expected so many people to attend a child's birthday party."

"In this part of the country, any occasion is a reason for a party." Josh took a sip of iced tea. "My parents would have been here, but my dad wasn't feeling well."

Recently there had been times when Stacie had wondered about his parents; what they were like, whether she'd like them, whether they'd like her. Though it didn't matter, she *was* curious.

His mother had given the blue heeler to her son, so she was obviously an animal lover. She and Stacie would have that in common. And despite any misgivings, his father had supported his son's decision to be a rancher, which told her she'd like him, too.

"I'm sorry to hear they won't be here," Stacie said. "It would have been nice to meet them."

"They were looking forward to meeting you," Josh said. "They've heard so much about you."

Stacie stilled. "From you?"

Josh shook his head. "Everyone but me."

She lifted a questioning brow.

"Word on the street is that Anna's friend has taken up with their son," he said, answering her unspoken question.

"I hope you set them straight," Stacie said. "Made sure they understand we're just good friends."

"I did mention you and Lauren and Anna will be moving back to Denver soon," Josh said.

"I'm not sure about *soon,* but you're right, that time will be here before we know it." Stacie tried to summon some enthusiasm. Two months ago she'd have given anything to return to Denver. But that was before Josh. "I'll have to find another apartment. Another job—"

"You'll have a job," Josh said. "Once you win the contest."

"To win, I have to enter."

Josh grinned. "That's usually the way it works."

"I'm not sure I'm going to enter." Stacie traced an imaginary figure eight on the lace tablecloth with one finger. "Every time I think of mailing the entry I get this scared feeling in the pit of my stomach."

Josh searched her eyes—for what, she wasn't certain—but whatever he found there must have satisfied him because he accepted her explanation without comment and changed the subject. "Do you like porch swings?"

Stacie smiled. "Love 'em."

"Good," he said. "'cause that's where we're headed."

She followed his lead and stood, but she hesitated when he offered his hand.

Though she knew Seth had kept his mouth shut after their first night together, the fact that she and Josh were spending so much time together had caused some raised eyebrows. From the knowing glances being cast their way this evening, the gossip mill appeared poised to grind out innuendoes and rumors at breakneck speed.

Yet, something in Josh's eyes told her she'd hurt him more by ignoring his hand. She wrapped her fingers around his and let him lead her to the porch swing. She took a seat on the far right. He plopped down in the middle and without either of them saying a word, they began to swing.

The back-and-forth motion was soothing, almost hypnotic. And when Josh slipped an arm around her shoulders and tugged her close, a feeling of complete and utter contentment stole over Stacie.

Billowy clouds wrapped the sky in a thick blanket of gray, muting the normal nighttime sounds. Laughter and conversation drifted through the screen door, but seemed far away. She and Josh were alone in the moment.

In the past, Stacie would have been bored and eager to get back to the party. But she wasn't as restless as she used to be. Sitting in the twilight with Josh at her side was enough.

"Tell me why you're hesitating," he said in a low tone that invited confidences. "What's holding you back from entering that contest?"

This was it. Her opportunity to tell him what being in Sweet River had meant to her. Her chance to make him understand that she loved small-town life, her work at the café and most of all…him.

But she hesitated. Though she was pretty sure he loved her, he'd never said the words and she couldn't bring herself to go first. So she played it safe and told the story he already knew, the one she'd been telling for years.

"When I started tenth grade, my parents started telling me how important it was to have a plan for my future." Stacie chuckled. "But to have a plan, you have to know what you want to do. I knew I didn't want to work with numbers like my mother. Or own an auto dealership like my dad. And I certainly didn't want to follow my oldest brother and go to law school."

They swung in silence for several long seconds.

"I wanted to do something creative, something fun," Stacie said. "I told them I wanted to find my bliss."

"What did they say?"

"They didn't *say* anything," Stacie said. "They laughed."

"You didn't let that dissuade you."

"In a way I did," Stacie said with a sigh. "I got a BA in business. I put my dreams on hold for four years."

"Then you were free to pursue your dreams."

"Yes. But my bliss hasn't been as easy to find as I thought," Stacie admitted.

Until I came here and met you, she thought.

The expression on Josh's face changed, and for a second she feared she'd spoken aloud.

"What about Jivebread?" he asked.

"That type of place would be my ideal job. The company prides itself on its unique cuisine. If I worked for them I'd be encouraged to develop new recipes, as well as prepare and serve the food."

"Sounds…busy."

"I'm sure it is," Stacie said. "But like with anything, if you enjoy what you're doing, it doesn't seem like work."

She thought of the time she spent making her rolls and breads for the Coffee Pot. The hours she'd put in helping Merna get her accounting and ordering systems organized. It had been a labor of love.

"I'd have thought you'd be working for them by now."

"I applied several times. I got the interview, but I didn't have enough relevant experience. I even offered to start at the bottom. Still no cigar." Stacie remembered how upset she'd been. But if she'd gotten that job, she wouldn't be here with Josh now.

"So this contest would be your ticket in."

Stacie reluctantly nodded. "*If* I win."

Josh lifted an eyebrow. "You have doubts?"

"The last thing Paul said to me before he left was that a smart person knows when to shut the door on a dream." She knew Paul was trying to tell her she should stop searching for her bliss. But over the past couple of weeks Stacie's heart had also been telling her that she could quit. The bliss she'd longed for couldn't be found working for Jivebread in Denver. It was here, with Josh. "I've been thinking that maybe I should just find a normal job, get married and forget about Jivebread."

"What are you saying?"

"Maybe I should stay here in Montana…with you."

Chapter 14

For a moment, Josh stared, unable to believe this wonderful woman wanted to stay in Sweet River with him. His heart pumped hard in his chest.

"Ah, Stacie." He pulled her to him, needing to feel her body against his, needing the reassurance that she was with him now and that's where she wanted to stay.

This was what he'd hoped for ever since he'd fallen in love with her. He wanted her to choose to live in Sweet River. Not because she was scared to face the outside world or because she didn't have other options, but because she loved the land and people as much as he did.

She snuggled close. "Who needs Jivebread anyway?"

An icy chill formed a tight fist of doubt around Josh's heart. He rubbed his hands up and down her back, telling himself that she wouldn't regret her decision to live here. He'd make her so happy she'd forget about her dreams.

She'd forget about her dreams.

The realization was like a kick to his gut. That was the lie he'd told himself when he'd married Kristin. Her major in college had been broadcast journalism, and everyone agreed she was born to be in front of a camera.

But the year they'd graduated, jobs in her field had been scarce. The world she'd envisioned had failed to materialize. He hadn't realized it at the time, but he'd been her consolation prize.

He'd had reservations when she suggested they get married, after all. Every time he'd brought her home she couldn't wait to get back to the city. But she convinced him—and he hadn't been that hard to convince—that once Sweet River was her home things would be different.

Trouble was, it hadn't been different. She'd hated the land, the people and, in time, him. And she'd blamed him for cheating her out of her dream. In a way, Josh understood. He'd known how much her chosen career meant to her, yet he'd let her give it up.

Wouldn't a man who truly loved a woman do everything possible to make sure she was happy? Wouldn't he encourage her to follow her dreams even if those dreams didn't include him? Wouldn't a man in love help the woman he loved find her bliss?

According to her friends, Stacie had wanted the position at Jivebread for years. Yet, like Kristin, she professed a willingness to give it all up…for him.

It hadn't worked for Kristin. Why would it work for Stacie?

"I'd like it if you stayed here. Heck, who am I kidding, I'd love it." Josh brushed a kiss against her hair, fighting the raw emotion rising inside him. He took a moment and cleared his throat. "But you should enter the contest anyway."

Stacie lifted her head from his chest and he could see the confusion in her eyes. "What would be the point?"

"The salad you brought to Dani's party was a culinary masterpiece," Josh said. "It deserves a chance to shine."

You deserve a chance to shine, he thought.

Her gaze lingered on his face. "Why is having me enter that contest such a big deal to everyone?"

Because everyone knows that getting that job is what you need, what you want, what you deserve, he wanted to say.

"Humor us. Humor me," he said instead, keeping his tone light. "Put the entry in the mail."

"I'll do it." She wrapped her arms around his neck and smiled. "But in exchange, I get to see you naked."

Josh fulfilled his part of the deal and Stacie mailed the entry the next day. In the ensuing weeks she forgot about it. Putting the contest out of her mind wasn't hard when every day seemed to bring something new and exciting.

With Merna's blessing, Stacie started a gourmet dinner night at the Coffee Pot. Though Merna warned her that once the café sold the event would likely end, Stacie decided to have fun with it. The five-course menu was a big hit with the dude-ranch guests, as well as the locals. A food critic from the *Billings Gazette* proclaimed her brisket with apricots and lemon juice "the best in the state."

Lauren's dissertation research continued to bring like-minded individuals together. Sasha and Wes were both matched, but not to each other. Misty was paired with a rancher who lived outside of Big Timber. Stacie knew that relationship was destined for success when she heard they'd sung a karaoke duet at Earl's Saturday night.

Stacie continued to spend most of her free time with Josh. The only downside was she barely saw her roommates. That's why she'd asked Anna to pick huckleberries with her this morning.

The excursion was the perfect opportunity for some serious girl talk. Not to mention that when Anna started reciting all the uses for the berries, Stacie's mind had immediately began flipping the pages of her mental cookbook.

She could already taste the pan-seared chicken breast with huckleberries, blue cheese and port sauce. The dish would make a fabulous entrée for the Coffee Pot's next gourmet night. Of course, she'd be sure to set aside enough berries to make a pie, and maybe even use some to make compote for her increasingly popular buttermilk biscuits, which now rivaled her cinnamon rolls.

As her mind explored all the possibilities, she plucked berries and placed them gently into a basket. In the distance birds cawed and the leaves of a large cottonwood whispered in the breeze. A feeling of contentment stole over Stacie. She couldn't remember ever being so happy.

She had her cooking, her friends and Josh. Though she hadn't thought it possible, every day she loved him more. Only one thing troubled her. "Do you know Josh has never told me he loves me?"

"Buckets of blood." The curse shot from Anna's mouth, and she slowly straightened, hand pressed against her lower spine. "I feel like a ninety-year-old granny with rheumatism."

Stacie had to smile, both at her friend's long-suffering expression and at the phrase. Anna had done nothing but complain since they started picking. Even if you ignored the fact that her chartreuse sling-backs were totally unsuitable for a day in the woods, the country girl was clearly out of her element—even if she'd spent her childhood in this kind of life.

"Did you hear what I said?" Stacie asked when Anna started mumbling something about a hot tub and massage.

Anna stopped and turned, shading her eyes with her hand. "Your back hurts, too?"

"My back is fine," Stacie said. "My problem is Josh."

"I thought you two were doing great." Anna's brows pulled together. Stacie could hear the surprise in her voice.

"He hasn't said he loves me," Stacie said, embarrassed by the admission yet not sure why. "Don't you find that strange?"

"Why would you even expect it?" Anna asked, her expression clearly puzzled. "You said it was just a physical thing between the two of you."

Stacie shifted uneasily from one foot to the other.

Anna's gaze narrowed. "Is there something you're not telling me?"

Stacie could feel her face warm. "The physical thing didn't work."

"What?" Anna's mouth dropped open. "Josh can't—?"

"No, no, nothing like that." Stacie hesitated to explain. "I went into this with the best of intentions. I just couldn't keep it strictly physical." Stacie heaved a sigh. "I guess I'm not a fling kind of girl."

Anna chuckled. "That doesn't surprise me at all."

"I love him, Anna. Truly. Deeply. Completely." A

lump rose and lodged in Stacie's throat. "I'm just not sure how he feels."

Her friend didn't appear at all shocked by the admission. She brought a finger to her lips. "What did he say when you told him you love him?"

Stacie rolled her eyes. Had the sun affected Anna's brain? "Women don't say 'I love you' first."

Anna laughed. "What century are you living in?"

"I have it on very good authority that the man should declare his love first."

"What good authority is that?"

"My mother."

"The same mother who told you not to sleep with a guy because no one wants to buy the cow when the milk is free?" Anna's lips twitched. "You didn't seem to have any problem not following that suggestion."

Anna shot her a leer that was so over the top that Stacie couldn't help but chuckle.

"Some of her advice may be a bit dated," Stacie admitted. "But what if I say 'I love you' and he just stares at me? What if there's a horribly awkward silence?"

"What if he takes you into his arms and says he loves you, too?"

"You're probably right." Stacie had told herself over and over that her fears were unfounded and foolish. With his every look, every gesture, every touch, Josh declared his love. "I'm making a big deal out of nothing."

"What are you going to do about it?"

"I'm—"

"I thought I'd never find you two." Lauren stumbled through the brush. Sweat dotted her brow and her white cotton shirt had twigs stuck to it. "I finally called Seth and he told me this used to be a favorite spot of yours."

Although Anna didn't act surprised, Lauren was the

last person Stacie expected to see this morning. Stacie shot Lauren a curious gaze. "I thought you told us you were too busy analyzing your data to pick berries?"

"Hey, don't look a gift horse in the mouth. Put her to work." Anna gestured to the bushes brimming with berries. "Grab a basket, Lauren, and start picking."

"I didn't come for the berries." Lauren pulled a thin white envelope out of her bag and offered it to Stacie. "I came to give you this."

Stacie placed her basket on the ground and wiped her hands on her jeans. "What is it?"

"It's from the contest." Lauren shoved the paper into Stacie's hand.

Stacie stared at the return address. As she focused on the Jivebread logo, her heart tap-danced in her chest. The light-as-a-feather envelope turned suddenly heavy in her hand.

"Open it," Anna urged.

Stacie took a deep breath. How many years had she dreamed of working for Jivebread? Of working in a state-of-the-art kitchen with any ingredients she could imagine at her disposal. Of working with other professionals who understood the thrill of creating with food. A shiver traveled up her spine, but she stopped the rising excitement by reminding herself that dream was before Josh. "I'll look at this later."

"Aren't you curious?" Lauren's gaze remained focused on the envelope. "Don't you want to know what it says?"

"Yeah." Anna crowded close, leaning over Stacie's shoulder. "The past three weeks have been pure torture. I can't wait another minute."

It was Stacie's letter. She could take it back to the house. Open it only when she was good and ready. But

Stacie knew her roommates wouldn't give her a moment's peace until she did.

With a resigned sigh, Stacie slipped open the envelope and pulled out a sheet of crisp parchment paper. A check fluttered to the ground. She read the words silently once. Then read them again just to be sure.

"How did you do?" Anna asked.

"What does it say?" Lauren added.

A sense of wonder flowed through Stacie's veins. She lifted her gaze. "I won."

Chapter 15

By the time the three women arrived back at the house, Stacie felt drunk with compliments. After years of honing her skills, her talent had been recognized by professionals. That was an even better gift than the five-thousand-dollar check.

She and Anna placed baskets of huckleberries on the back porch and then formed an impromptu conga line behind Lauren and danced their way to the dining room.

"This is just so cool," Anna said for the tenth—or was it the hundredth?—time. "And to think you almost didn't enter."

"I'm glad we pushed you." A self-satisfied smile tipped the corners of Lauren's lips.

Stacie didn't bother to correct her friends, but she knew it was *Josh's* encouragement that had made the difference. It was as if he knew winning the contest would give her a much-needed boost in self-confidence. And the money, well, she already had a plan for it...

"Time for a toast," Anna declared, uncorking the bottle of champagne Lauren had picked up on their way back into town.

Lauren grabbed three crystal wineglasses from the antique china cabinet. She'd just finished filling the glasses when the doorbell rang.

"I wonder who that is?" Stacie asked.

Lauren and Anna exchanged glances.

"Surely you didn't think we were going to have a celebration of this magnitude with just the three of us?" Anna asked with a smile.

Lauren pulled two more glasses from the cabinet.

Stacie gave her friend an assessing look. "Who did you invite?"

Lauren filled the extra glasses, a tiny smile hovering on the edge of her lips. "I called Seth on my way home and asked him over. Josh was with him, so he's coming, too. I told them we had some celebrating to do."

Disappointment sluiced through Stacie. She knew Lauren meant well, but she'd wanted to tell Josh the news herself. "Oh."

"I didn't tell him *what* we were celebrating," Lauren hurriedly added. "That's your news to share."

"Anybody home?" Seth's voice rang through the old house followed immediately by the clatter of boots on hardwood.

"Back here," Lauren called out.

Josh stopped next to Seth at the dining-room entrance. His gaze skipped over Anna and Lauren to settle on Stacie.

Even with her hair pulled back in a ponytail and a

patch of dirt on one knee, she was the most beautiful woman he'd ever seen.

"Hey." Josh returned Stacie's smile, and then crossed the room to drape an arm around her shoulders. He found it increasingly hard to be near her and *not* touch her.

She lifted her face and Josh brushed a kiss across her lips, resisting the urge to linger. There'd be time for that later. "I didn't think I'd be seeing you until this evening."

"This is a special occasion." Lauren picked up two of the champagne glasses, handing one to Josh and another to Seth.

"It better be." Seth sounded gruff, but Josh knew his friend hadn't hesitated when Lauren had asked him over. "We were in the middle of branding when you called."

"Hold your spurs, cowboy," Anna said. "We wouldn't have asked you to come if it wasn't important."

Seth turned to Lauren. "Did you get all your survey participants? Is that what this is about?"

"Actually this is about me." When Stacie met Josh's gaze, it was as if she were speaking to him alone. "I won the contest."

"Congratulations," Seth said. "I knew that recipe was good."

Josh heard the pride in her voice, felt the excited tremble in her shoulders. The bliss she'd searched for all these years was now in reach, and he was happy for her. But the thought of losing her now filled him with regret and pain. He somehow managed to smile. "That's wonderful."

"This doesn't change anything," Stacie said in a low tone obviously meant to reassure him.

"I know that." He gave her shoulders a squeeze.

"This calls for a party," Seth said.

"My thoughts exactly." Lauren's eyes snapped with excitement.

"We'll have it here at the house," Anna mused aloud, and Josh could almost see her mind kick into high gear.

"It'll be a send-off the likes of which this town has never seen." Lauren lifted her glass.

"But I'm not—" Stacie began.

"To Stacie." Seth raised his glass. "To continued success."

Josh joined in the toast. If he was honest with himself he'd admit this was the worst news he'd ever received, far uglier than Kristin's request for a divorce. But he kept his thoughts to himself and managed to talk and laugh as if this were the best news he'd ever heard.

It was funny. He'd never known he had a talent for acting...until now.

Stacie wasn't surprised when Josh made up an excuse to cancel their date. She'd seen the look of surprise in his eyes when she'd made her announcement. She'd felt him pull away even as he stood beside her.

She'd wanted to reassure him that this changed nothing between them, but he left with Seth before she had the chance. He hadn't even kissed her good-bye.

"This party is going to be fabulous." Lauren glanced up from the list of names she and Anna had been compiling since the men left.

"I'm so glad you'll be back in Denver before us." Anna added another name to the list before looking up. "That way we'll have a place to live once Lauren's work here is done."

"This is a dream come true." Lauren heaved a happy

sigh. "I remember you talking about working for Jive-bread and now it's happening. When do you start?"

"Anytime during this next month," Stacie said automatically, recalling the instructions in the letter. "It's up to me. Assuming I want to work for Jivebread."

"Of course you do," Anna said.

"Actually, I don't." Stacie pulled a chair back from the table and took a seat opposite her friends. "I'm not moving back to Denver. I'm staying here in Sweet River with Josh."

Anna's pencil paused midword. Lauren opened her mouth then shut it. Finally Anna leaned forward, resting her forearms on the table.

"This is what you've been searching for your entire life." Anna took a deep breath then slowly released it. "I adore Josh, but opportunities like this only come around once. If you walk away now, it's gone. How can you think of giving up your dream for a guy who hasn't even told you he loves you?"

Lauren raised an eyebrow. "Really?"

"He does love me." Stacie shoved back her chair and stood. She'd thought her friends would understand. "Just because he hasn't said it doesn't mean—"

"You want that job," Lauren said. "I can see it in your eyes."

"Of course I want it," Stacie explained. "I just want Josh more."

"I realize you've fallen in love with this area and with Josh—" Anna spoke slowly and deliberately "—but how are you going to feel when Lauren and I are back in Denver, the snow is piled high and ranch life isn't quite what you envisioned?"

"I love Josh," Stacie repeated, more forcefully this time. "And I love it here."

"Would you stay if he didn't love you back?" Lauren asked.

The very suggestion that Josh might not return her feelings tore at Stacie's heartstrings. Could she stay in Sweet River loving him, knowing he didn't love her back?

She shook her head. "I think it would be too hard."

"You know what you have to do." Lauren's eyes were clear and very green.

Stacie met Lauren's gaze, but couldn't make herself speak.

"Before you make your final decision, before you throw away something you won't be able to get back," Lauren said, her gaze as pointed as her words, "you need to find out how he feels about you."

Josh grabbed a bottle of beer from the refrigerator and took it to the living room. He clicked on the television, but minutes later muted the sound, irritated by the sitcom laugh track.

What a difference a few hours could make. This morning he'd jumped out of bed, anticipation fueling his steps. After he helped Seth, he'd looked forward to the evening with Stacie. Instead, one piece of mail had changed her life and his…forever. Stacie would soon be gone and he doubted he'd ever see her again.

Unless I tell her I love her, he said to himself.

Part of him wanted to hop into his truck, head straight back to Anna's house and tell Stacie he loved her more than he'd ever thought possible. But the other part refused to let him act on that impulse. If Stacie stayed in Sweet River, it had to be *her* decision, not one he influenced with three little words.

Josh took a long sip of beer, wishing it were strong

enough to stifle the pain in his heart. But then again, there wasn't enough alcohol in the world to accomplish that impossible task.

The bottle found its way to his lips once again when the sound of a truck engine blended with Bert's barking. Josh glanced at the clock. Ten o'clock. Late for company to stop by.

Moving to the front window, Josh pushed back the curtain with one finger. His shoulders tensed at the sight of the Jeep.

By the time the bell rang he was in the foyer. He pulled open the door. "What a surprise."

"I don't see why." Stacie's chin tilted upward. "We had plans."

The wind lifted her hair from her shoulders. Thunder rumbled in the distance. Droplets of rain splattered the porch.

Josh opened the door wider and motioned her inside. When he touched her arm to move her aside so he could shut the door, her trembling caught him off guard.

"Are you okay?" He glanced out the front door but didn't see anything unusual. "Did something happen?"

"Hold me, Josh," she said. "I need to feel your arms around me."

If she'd asked him if he loved her, he had a noncommittal response ready. If she pressed, he'd end up telling her the truth. And then he'd insist she pursue her dream before committing to him. But her simple request caught him off guard. Before he could consider the full ramifications of his actions, he'd already wrapped his arms around her and pulled her close.

They fit together perfectly.

Like we were made to be together, he thought. Josh shoved the fanciful thought aside but couldn't keep from reveling in the feel of her body against his. The scent of jasmine filled his nostrils and he knew he'd never be able to smell that scent without thinking of her.

He wasn't sure how long they stood there, the house silent except for their hearts beating in perfect rhythm. The light from the living room cast a warm glow. It was as if they were alone in their own world.

Stacie rested her head against his chest. "Tonight I want us to play a game of 'Let's Pretend.'"

Josh opened his mouth to turn her down, but those words wouldn't come. "What do you want to pretend?"

"That for now, *for right now,* there's only you and me." Stacie met his gaze. "I need to be close to you."

The desperation in her eyes told him that she knew that tonight could be their last time. Making love would be a way of saying goodbye. For him, it would also be his way of showing his love.

His feelings were strong and deep and true. Whatever he'd felt for Kristin had been a pale imitation of what he felt for the woman standing before him.

"Okay." He lifted his hands and tilted her head back, brushing tears from her cheeks with the pads of his thumbs. "Okay."

She smiled tremulously as he captured her hand and led her to the bedroom.

"Oh, Josh." Stacie breathed the words.

For a second, he wasn't sure what had made her eyes shine until he saw the bed. This morning, in anticipation of the evening ahead, he'd scattered red rose petals across the sheets. While he'd never been a romantic guy, lately he'd found himself looking for out-of-the-ordinary ways to make Stacie happy.

She touched his arm. "You are so sweet."

"And you are so beautiful." Josh's lips moved lightly

across her mouth then trailed down her cheek to bury in the warm fragrance of her neck.

Though he was starved for her, he forced himself to take his time. He sipped from her lips, rather than gulped. He moved his hands gently over her curves, asking rather than demanding.

Slow and easy, he told himself. Memories of this night would have to last a lifetime.

The moon cast a golden glow through the open window. As they kissed, her sighs of pleasure mingled with his.

"You have on way too many clothes," he muttered.

Stacie laughed and quickly rid herself of her jeans and shirt. Seconds later she stood naked before him, hands on hips. "Now who's the one who's overdressed?"

Josh winked. "Not for long."

He jerked his shirt over his head and tossed it aside. His jeans and boxers had barely hit the floor when he gently pushed her down on the bed and lay beside her.

Stacie ran her hands over his biceps then trailed them over his chest. They'd made love numerous times before, but somehow this felt new. "So strong, so—"

"Soft." He cupped her breasts in his palms, his fingers brushing the tips. Her nipple puckered and tingled as he continued his exploration, skipping his hands over intimate dips and hollows.

Stacie sighed. His touch was gentle and caring. The silky thickness of his hair brushed against her breast. Stacie slid her hands across his shoulders, up through his hair. It had never been clearer. A lifetime with this wonderful man wouldn't be nearly long enough.

"Joshua." She put everything she felt, all the love and longing in her heart, into that single word.

His lips closed over hers once more, his tongue

plunging into her mouth with a hunger at odds with the gentle pressure of his hand between her legs.

She responded fully, without reservation. Her passion, her need for him, grew with each kiss, each tender caress. Finally she couldn't stand it anymore. She needed to have him fill her so completely that nothing could come between them. "I want you. Now."

A second later he thrust inside her, and Stacie groaned with pleasure. His strokes lengthened, quickened. Wrapping her arms around him she moved her body in an age-old rhythm. She loved the way he felt inside her, rubbing her intimately, filling her.

Stacie rode the building pressure until their bodies were damp and sweaty. Still she clung to him. He was the sexiest man in the world to her, and he was all hers. And when the combination of emotion and physical sensation sent her crashing over the edge, it was right that she was in his arms when the world exploded.

When Stacie returned to earth, a smile of pure pleasure lifted her lips. "That was incredible."

Without taking his eyes off her, Josh lifted her hand to his mouth and pressed a kiss in the palm. "*You* are incredible."

She leaned her head against his hand. The raw emotion rising inside her refused to be contained. "I love you, Josh. I love you so very much."

Josh froze. His smile disappeared and his eyes grew shuttered. The awkward silence she'd envisioned never occurred because he jumped up so quickly you'd have thought the barn was on fire.

"I'll make us something to eat." Snatching his clothes from the floor, Josh exited the bedroom without a backward glance.

For several seconds, Stacie lay motionless, stunned.

He didn't love her. A fling, that's all she was to him. She blinked back the tears that flooded her eyes. She would not cry. She. Would. Not. Cry.

Though her chest was so tight she could barely breathe, Stacie dressed quickly. She stopped only to swipe at tears that seemed determined to fall.

She could hear Josh clanging pans in the kitchen when she reached the front door. She thought about saying goodbye. But she was too busy for meaningless conversation with her summer fling. She had a move to Denver to arrange.

Chapter 16

Josh sat in the pew next to his parents and wondered what craziness had made him agree to attend Sunday services. Granted, his mother was being honored for her years as Sunday School superintendent, but he could have come up with a believable excuse.

He'd been working hard, too hard if you listened to his father. But there was a lot to do on a ranch this time of year. And Josh had discovered when he pushed himself physically, by the time he got home he was too exhausted to do much more than collapse into bed. Which was exactly how he wanted it.

No time to think. No time to miss Stacie. No time to wonder if he'd made the biggest mistake of his life.

He'd hoped the pain would lessen with each passing day. Instead it had grown worse. He remembered the sweet love they'd made, the look in Stacie's eyes when she'd told him she loved him, the strength it had taken not to say the words back.

Because he did love her. More than he ever thought possible. In fact, he'd give up everything to be with her now....

Whoa. The thought took him by surprise, but he couldn't deny the joy had gone out of his life when Stacie left. Like his father always said: all the treasures in the world don't mean much without someone you love by your side.

When Kristin left, Josh felt she'd failed to live up to her promise. She'd told him she wanted to live in Montana, and then, after they were married, she'd changed her mind. What he hadn't realized until this moment was that he'd failed her, too.

Not once had he seriously considered giving up his life on the ranch to move to where she could find work in her field. If he'd loved Kristin the way a man should love his wife, he'd have gone to the ends of the earth with her...

"Wasn't that a wonderful sermon?" his mother whispered as they stood for the closing hymn.

"Yeah," Josh said, "it was great."

Truth was, he only heard bits and pieces of the sermon. Something about pursuing the life you want, not letting yourself be constrained by a spirit of fear...

He knew the life he wanted, and it was with Stacie. Yet, he'd let her walk out of his life without a word of protest. Technically there was no reason she couldn't have her bliss and him, too. But for that to occur, he'd have to give up the land and the life he loved so much.

He'd never considered leaving for Kristin. But for Stacie...

Could he do it? Could he walk away from his legacy and not look back? Did he really love her that much?

Though it was late when Stacie returned to her hotel room, she headed straight for her laptop.

She kicked off her shoes while the computer booted up. In the three weeks she'd been in Denver, reading e-mail from Sweet River had become her reward at the end of long, stress-filled days.

The work at Jivebread had exciting moments, but Stacie felt detached from the customers she served. Not like in Sweet River, where she cooked and baked for the people she cheered alongside at baseball games and worshipped with on Sunday.

She'd called Anna and Lauren last Friday at a particularly low point. They'd been surprised she was having so much difficulty acclimating. Go out with coworkers, they'd urged. Check out a new movie. Join a gym.

Stacie hadn't been able to make them understand that she didn't have the heart to do any of those things. Heaving a sigh, Stacie scanned her in-box.

She read the e-mails from Lauren and Anna first. Anna had finally been matched. Lauren was ecstatic. Anna was reserving judgment until she met the guy.

Stacie opened the e-mail from Merna next.

Dear Stacie,
I can't believe it's been almost a month since you left. Every day at least one person asks when you'll be back. The owners of the dude ranches are pressuring me to restart the gourmet meal night. I'd like to, but I don't have your talent for planning or preparing that kind of food.
You asked if I'd found a buyer for the café yet. Unfor-

tunately the answer is no. Earl Jenkins has expressed interest, but he wants to turn it into a bar. Just what Sweet River needs…another watering hole! lol

I really don't want to sell to him, but my daughter needs me. If I go much longer without an offer, I may not have a choice.

I hope all is well with you.

Love, Merna

Stacie sat back in her chair and massaged the bridge of her nose. She couldn't imagine Sweet River without a café. She shifted her gaze back to her in-box. A new message from AlexD caught her eye. She opened it next.

Dear Stacie,

I hope you don't mind that I got your e-mail address from your roommates. I wanted to let you know how grateful I am for the advice you gave me at the baseball game. When you told me I should become more involved and visible in the community I was skeptical. But you were right. I picked up a few clients by frequenting the barbershop. But when I joined a dart league at Earl's, business really took off. I realize a dart league sounds rather pedestrian, but I'm enjoying it.

I was surprised to hear you'd left Sweet River—you and the town seemed perfectly suited—but I wish you only the best in your new endeavor.

Sincerely,

Alexander Darst, Esq.

"I sometimes wonder why I left, too," Stacie murmured. But even as the words left her lips, she knew the answer.

Shoving Josh's image from her mind she returned her attention to the lengthy list of unopened mail.

A message from her brother had sat unopened for several days. She started to click on it, but the growling in her stomach reminded her she hadn't eaten since lunch. So she clicked on the MP3 file of Pastor Barbee's sermon instead. Turning up the volume, she headed for the refrigerator.

The sermons had shown up in her in-box every Monday since she'd left Sweet River. She wasn't sure how the church had gotten her e-mail address, but it didn't really matter.

While she'd been tempted to erase the first, once she listened she'd been hooked. When Pastor Barbee preached all she had to do was close her eyes and she was back in Sweet River, surrounded by the people and the land she loved. Just thinking of the meadows filled with flowers and the smell of fresh-mown hay brought a tightness to her throat.

Shoving the emotion aside, Stacie opened the refrigerator and pulled out some carrots and celery while the sermon continued. The reverend had chosen a verse from Timothy, something about not having a spirit of fear. As his words continued to fill the room, it was as if he were speaking directly to *her*. She'd left the only place that'd ever felt like home because she was scared. Scared of living near the man she loved, knowing he would never be hers. Scared she'd see him on the street and not know what to say. Scared of hurting even more than she did now.

By the time the sermon concluded, Stacie's head was spinning. She forced herself to concentrate and opened her brother's message. After skimming the paragraphs of family news, she read the rest more carefully.

...I'm so proud of you. Accepting the position with an up-and-coming company like Jivebread was a smart move. Though you never came out and said it, I know you were tempted to stay in that backwater town in Montana. I'm relieved you gave up the notion of finding your "bliss" and made a good business decision instead.

Stacie closed the e-mail, unable to read any more. Didn't Paul realize Jivebread *was* her bliss?

But if it's my bliss, shouldn't I be happy instead of miserable?

There was so much to like about Jivebread, so much to appreciate about Denver. But the truth was the Mile High City was no longer home to her.

With or without Josh, her heart, her bliss, was back in that small town in Montana. Now she had to decide if she had the courage to do something about it.

Chapter 17

Traffic had been backed up on I-25. Unfortunately, when Stacie turned onto E470 it didn't improve. By the time she reached the Staybridge Suites on Tower Road, she was thirty minutes late for a dinner with a sorority sister she didn't remember.

Anna had told her that Josie Collier was in the process of moving to Denver after a heart-wrenching breakup in another state and needed a friend. Stacie had thought it might help cheer her up to eat at one of the bistros that had been popular during their college days. But Anna—acting as the intermediary—said Josie preferred to stay in and make dinner.

The extended-stay hotel where her former sorority sister was staying was similar to the one where Stacie had been living. The lobby was warm and homey with overstuffed leather chairs and a large stone fireplace.

She took the elevator to the third floor, following the signs to Suite 312.

Though Anna had insisted she didn't need to bring anything, Stacie refused to arrive empty-handed. She'd picked up a bottle of chardonnay when she learned through Anna that Josie was planning to serve fish.

Stacie stood at the door for a long moment, tension knotting her shoulders. This had been such a busy week with many loose ends to tie up. She really didn't feel like spending an evening making small talk with a woman she didn't remember.

But she reminded herself, it was the kindness of the strangers in Sweet River that had made such an impression, and this was her chance to pass such caring forward.

Plastering a smile on her face, Stacie gave the door a hard rap.

It swung open almost immediately and Stacie's breath caught in her throat. She blinked once. He didn't disappear. She blinked again. Still there.

Dressed in jeans and a chambray shirt, Josh Collins was thinner than she remembered. Lines of tension bracketed his mouth and the hollow look in his eyes was at odds with his bright smile. But he was still the handsomest cowboy she'd ever seen.

"Josh." Her voice sounded breathless to her ears. "What are you doing here?"

He took the bottle from her hands with hands that trembled slightly. "We'll open this later."

"We'll?" He was staying for dinner? Stacie's heart fluttered in her throat like a trapped butterfly as he motioned her inside. "This was supposed to be girl time." She glanced around the room. "Where's Josie?"

"Have a seat." He placed a hand on her arm and gestured with his head to a chair in the living room area. "I'll explain."

Her skin burned beneath his touch. Dear God, didn't he realize how hard this—

No. She stopped the thought before it could fully form. His unexpected appearance wasn't a disaster, but a blessing. When their paths crossed in the future, the initial awkwardness would be out of the way. They needed to have this conversation no matter how painful. But she really didn't want an audience.

"Where's Josie?" Stacie repeated in a voice loud enough to rouse the dead, but the woman still didn't appear.

"She doesn't exist." A sheepish look stole across his face. "It was a name Anna made up. Josie Collier. Josh Collins. Get it?"

Stacie stared at him for a long moment, confusion warring with a rising irritation. "What kind of game is this?"

"I wasn't sure you'd see me if I called," Josh said. "So I enlisted Anna's help."

"Meaning you got her to lie to me," Stacie said, her voice heavy with disappointment.

"I needed to talk to you." His gaze searched hers. "To tell you how I feel."

Stacie crossed her arms and cleared her throat. "You made your feelings—or shall I say lack of feelings— very clear the last time we were together."

"You walked out without a word."

Stacie lifted her chin. "You never came after me."

He hooked his thumbs in his belt loops and rocked back on his heels. "I wasn't going to be the only reason you stayed. I'd learned the hard way that sometimes love isn't enough. But I let you go and I'm an idiot."

By now Stacie was totally confused.

"I'd have stayed in Sweet River, if you'd asked," she found herself confessing when he didn't elaborate further.

"I wanted to," he said, and the regret in his voice took her by surprise. "But I knew what that position at Jivebread meant to you. I didn't want you to stay and later have regrets…like Kristin."

Now, finally, she understood. He'd deliberately made her think he didn't love her like she loved him. Stacie wanted to rail at him for the pain she'd endured. Tell him he had no right to make decisions for her. Tell him that he was wrong, that she could have remained in Sweet River and had no regrets. The trouble was she wasn't sure that was true. It had taken moving back to Denver to convince her that Sweet River was definitely where she belonged. She clasped her hands together to still their trembling. "Why are you here now?"

"I'm moving to Denver." He stepped closer and took her hands in his, resisting her attempts to pull away. "I've come to ask for another chance. I thought my bliss was the Double C, but when you left I realized my happiness is wherever you are."

"You'd move here?" She must have misheard. "You can't be serious. What would happen to the ranch? And to Bert?"

He smiled. "I kinda hoped she could come with me. As for the ranch, one of my hired men has agreed to manage it for me. I'm thinking we should be able to get back every couple months to check on things."

Stacie shook her head, hoping the action would help her tangled thoughts make sense. "But what would you do here? In case you haven't noticed, there aren't any ranches or cattle nearby."

He shrugged, seemingly unconcerned. "I'll find something. What's important is we'll be together."

Stacie opened her mouth and then shut it. She frowned and slanted a glance in the direction of the kitchen. Was that a haze in the air? She sniffed. Then sniffed again. "Is something burning?"

An expletive shot from Josh's mouth, he sprinted to the stove. Stacie followed close behind. When he opened the oven door, smoke billowed out. Using a towel as an oven mitt, he pulled out a charred casserole.

By the time he'd placed it on the stovetop, Stacie had opened the window. She glanced over his shoulder and wrinkled her nose. "What is it? Or should I ask... what *was* it?"

Josh stared down at the crispy black contents with a crestfallen expression. "It *was* a tuna casserole."

"But you hate tuna."

He met Stacie's gaze. "I didn't make it for me."

Their gazes locked and her heart turned over. A warmth that had nothing to do with heat from the stove spread through her body. She finally understood why Josh had come. "You love me. Really and truly love me."

She couldn't keep the wonder from her voice. It all fit. Coming to Denver. Volunteering to give up his life in Sweet River. And now, the pièce de résistance: a tuna casserole.

"Of course I love you." Josh took her hands in his, his expression serious. "That's why I'm here. I love you and I want to marry you. If you'll have me."

It may not have been the fanciest proposal, but she could hear the sincerity in his voice, see the love in his eyes. The cowboy had put his heart on the line. The next step was hers.

The joyous answer rose from the deepest depths of Stacie's soul. "I'd be honored to be your wife."

The smile he shot her was blinding. "We're going to be very happy."

His hands slid up her arms. Though Stacie longed to melt against him, she took a step back. They would soon be starting a life together and she wanted no secrets between them.

"We *are* going to be happy," she said, "but you don't have to move to Denver for that to happen."

He cocked his head and she could see the puzzlement in his eyes.

"I'm moving back to Sweet River," she said. "Today was my last day at Jivebread."

A look of stunned disbelief crossed his face. "I don't understand," he said. "Working there was your passion—"

"My heart is in Sweet River." She gazed up at him. "It's where I belong. I was planning to return before you came to get me."

"Are you sure?"

"I've never been more sure of anything in my life," she said.

"I love you," he said, his voice husky and thick with emotion.

The words were music to her ears. Stacie knew that no matter how old she got or how many years passed that she'd never grow tired of hearing them. "Say it again."

"I love you." He pulled her close and planted kisses down her neck. "I love you. I love you."

She laughed with pure joy and Josh grinned. "Want me to show you how much?"

Though she couldn't wait to see what he had in mind, Stacie couldn't resist teasing. She widened her eyes. "You're going to make me another tuna casserole?"

"Another time," he promised. "For now, this will have to do."

As his lips closed over hers, Stacie had no doubt that this would do quite nicely indeed.

Epilogue

One year later

Stacie walked hand in hand with her husband down the main street in Sweet River, contentment draped around her like a favorite coat. "You remember what today is, don't you?"

A startled look skittered across Josh's face. "Our anniversary isn't until next month," he murmured to himself. "And it's not your birthday…"

"It's been a whole year since I moved back from Denver." What a wondrous day that had been, sunny and warm, but with a hint of fall in the air. When Josh had pulled into the lane leading to his house, she'd felt like a lost lamb who'd finally found her way home. "It's gone so fast."

"What do they say?" Josh grinned and shot her a wink. "Time flies when you're having fun?"

Stacie chuckled. It had been a fabulous, fun-filled

twelve months. She and Josh had married less than a month after she returned in a simple but elegant ceremony in Anna's backyard. The quick wedding had given the town folk lots to talk about—and Lauren's research project a boost she hadn't anticipated.

Soon after, Stacie had become an entrepreneur like the rest of her family. She'd used the money she'd won in the contest as a down payment on the Coffee Pot, making her father and brother Paul proud.

Merna moved to California to be with her daughter. Shirley agreed to stay on and manage the café, giving Stacie time to bake and plan menus. Giving her time on the ranch with Josh. Giving them time to make the baby they both wanted.

Stacie's hand stole to her belly, which wouldn't be flat much longer. Tonight, before they met Josh's parents for dinner, she planned to tell him the good news.

"We like the new sign," Pastor Barbee commented as he and his wife strolled past the café, headed in the opposite direction. "Very eye-catching."

Stacie smiled at the couple. She'd worried how the community would react to changing the café's name to Bliss. So far she'd heard only positive comments.

Josh gave Stacie's hand a squeeze, his gaze focused on the sign he'd put up himself yesterday. "You've finally found your bliss."

Stacie let her gaze linger on the man who'd brought such joy to her life. Familiar, known, increasingly beloved, this cowboy was everything she'd ever wanted and more. Her heart overflowed with happiness and she leaned her head against his arm. "Yes, indeed. I've definitely found my bliss."

* * * * *

Teresa Southwick lives with her husband in Las Vegas, the city that reinvents itself every day. An avid fan of romance novels, she is delighted to be living out her dream of writing for Harlequin.

Books by Teresa Southwick

Harlequin Special Edition

The Bachelors of Blackwater Lake

Finding Family...and Forever?
One Night with the Boss
The Rancher Who Took Her In
A Decent Proposal
The Widow's Bachelor Bargain

Montana Mavericks: Six Brides for Six Brothers

Maverick Holiday Magic

Montana Mavericks: The Lonelyhearts Ranch

Unmasking the Maverick

Montana Mavericks: The Baby Bonanza

Her Maverick M.D.

Montana Mavericks: What Happened at the Wedding?

An Officer and a Maverick

Montana Mavericks: 20 Years in the Saddle!

From Maverick to Daddy

Visit the Author Profile page at
Harlequin.com for more titles.

THE RANCHER
WHO TOOK HER IN

Teresa Southwick

To my female friends. Your support and love
inspire me every day.

Chapter 1

It wasn't often a woman walked into the Grizzly Bear Diner wearing a strapless wedding dress and four-inch satin heels.

If Cabot Dixon wasn't seeing it for himself, he'd have heard pretty quick because people in Blackwater Lake, Montana, talked and this was something to talk about. The bride had parked a beat-up truck out front and she was a looker. The woman, not the truck. From his seat at the diner counter he had a view of Main Street and had watched her lift the floor-length cream satin skirt in one hand, probably to avoid tripping because it was way too late to keep it from getting dirty. Then she marched inside, as opposed to down the aisle.

He was sitting on a swivel stool, and she slid between the two beside him to talk with Michelle Crawford, the diner's owner, who was openly staring.

"I'm here about the Help Wanted sign in your window."

The bride was even prettier up close, with light brown, blond-streaked hair and a figure that could back up traffic for miles. And that wasn't all. Her voice had the barest hint of huskiness that could stop a man's beating heart for a second or two.

There were a few customers in the diner and everyone continued to stare when the newcomer added, "I could use a job."

"Okay." Michelle slipped him a help-me-out expression, obviously wondering if he would jump in, considering he was the one looking to hire.

When he'd put the Help Wanted sign in the diner window, she'd promised to run interference and weed out the applicants who weren't really serious so he didn't have to come all the way into town from the ranch every five minutes. Frankly, he was looking forward to seeing Michelle handle this one on her own. Because there was no groom in sight, the lady clearly was a runner. It would appear that, unlike his ex-wife, she'd cut out *before* taking vows and getting pregnant.

Cabot glanced at her flat belly in the tight, unforgiving, dropped-waist gown that wouldn't hide even an extra ounce of fat, let alone a bump. He couldn't swear there was no baby on board, but it didn't look likely. Her bare arms were super toned and she had great shoulders, slender but strong. She was a little lacking in the chest department, but her cute nose and even better mouth made up for it.

The bride rested her palms on the red Formica counter. "I've never waitressed before, but I'm a fast learner and a hard worker—"

Michelle held up a hand. "Let me stop you right there. I'm not hiring, just handling the interviews for the rancher who is." She glanced at him. "The ranch is about ten miles outside Blackwater Lake."

"I see." The woman looked momentarily thrown, and then she nodded. "I admit I didn't read anything on the poster after the *help wanted* part and that doesn't speak well about my attention to detail. But I'm a bit distracted just now."

Cabot figured that was the truth. The wedding dress was a big clue.

"Well—" Michelle gave him another jump-in-any-time look. "The job is for a summer camp counselor. The owner runs a program for kids at his ranch, and duties include activities, sports and whatever else comes up. General pitching in as needed."

"I can handle that," the bride said. "I love kids."

"I'm not sure you're what he had in mind."

"Who?"

"The rancher who's looking to hire," Michelle responded. "You're probably overqualified."

"I just want to work." Cabot saw something vulnerable and fragile in her expression. "These days a lot of people are taking jobs they're overqualified for and happy to have them."

She was right about that, he thought. Although the job he needed to fill was more suited to a young college kid or recent graduate, he'd posted the sign in the diner window later than he usually did. Camp was starting soon and most people who wanted summer work had already lined something up. That meant he couldn't afford to be as picky as usual.

Michelle folded her arms over her chest and looked the woman up and down. "Even your average employee doesn't go formal to apply for work."

"So you noticed the wedding dress." The bride's tone

was deliberately casual, as if she always showed up for a job interview in a long white gown. "I guess I stand out like a fly in milk."

"Pretty much," Michelle agreed.

The woman was plucky, Cabot thought. He'd give her that. Taking a sip of cold coffee, he listened intently, interested to hear what she had to say.

"The truth is, I ran out on my wedding."

"Really? Could have fooled me." Cabot knew he should have stayed out of this conversation but just couldn't resist. "So you broke some poor guy's heart."

She met his gaze and took his measure. "And you are?"

"Cabot Dixon. Couldn't help overhearing. So, why did you run?"

"Not that it's any of your business, but he's a lying, cheating, scumbag weasel dog."

"That sounds bad," he said. "But I have to ask— couldn't you have said something to him before he showed up for the wedding?"

"Probably I should have. My sister warned me, told me he hit on her, but I was stubborn and didn't believe. Then I caught him kissing one of my bridesmaids at the church. It seemed like an excellent time to let him know the marriage probably wasn't going to work out." She clenched her teeth and a muscle jerked in her delicate jaw. "I hate it when my sister is right."

"Jerk," Michelle said, the single word dripping with disgust.

Cabot had to agree.

"I gave him back the ring with a fervent wish that he'd choke on it, but dealing with the rest just then was—" The bride sighed and the movement did amazing things to a chest that suddenly didn't seem so lacking. "I grabbed the truck keys and left. Drove all night and this looked like as good a place as any to stop."

"It is a good place, honey." Michelle patted her hand and gave him a glance that begged him to take over.

"What's your name?" he asked.

"Katrina Scott. Kate." She glanced between him and Michelle. "Why do you keep looking at this guy?"

"I keep looking at this man because he's Cabot Dixon, the rancher who put the Help Wanted poster in my window. Take over anytime." Michelle settled a hand on her hip and met his gaze. "In my humble opinion, Kate is just your type." To the bride she added, "He's a sucker for hard-luck cases."

"I know you mean that in the nicest possible way," he said to Michelle.

"Maybe I did. Maybe I didn't." She smiled at the bride and said, "My work here is done. By the way, I'm Michelle Crawford. It's nice to meet you, Kate. Welcome to Blackwater Lake, Montana."

"Thanks." After the other woman left, Kate turned to him. "You could have said something about being the rancher in question before I spilled my guts."

"You were on a roll," he said.

"Just so we're clear, I'm not a hard-luck case. And I don't suppose there's a chance that you could overlook or forget everything I just said?"

"Probably not."

"I didn't think so." She sighed.

"So Katrina. Like the hurricane."

"I came first and I'm pretty sure my parents named me after a Viking queen or at the very least a Swedish princess."

He laughed. She was quick-witted. He liked that. But Michelle was probably right about her being overqualified. He would guess her to be in her late twenties and likely on a career path that had been interrupted by running out on her wedding. Although by the looks of the ancient truck out front, she didn't have much money.

"Nice dress."

"Thanks. I plan to burn it." She smoothed a hand over the curve of her hip.

The gesture drew his attention and suddenly his mouth went dry. This was a pretty strong reaction and he didn't much trust the feeling, but there was no reason to read anything complicated into it. He was a guy and she was a pretty woman. That was all. But she was looking to work for him and he was looking for a reason to turn her down.

"You need a job."

"It would help me out."

She had pride. He understood and respected that.

Cabot pushed his empty plate and coffee cup away. "Like Michelle said, it's really a nowhere job."

"Just where I want to be."

"The kids' activities include sports—basketball, baseball, soccer."

"I'm athletic." He noted conviction in her voice, not so much in her expression.

He couldn't tell about athletic, but she looked as if she was in great shape. "I'm offering minimum wage, and that's not much more than gas money for a college kid who's willing to work."

"I'm obviously not a college student but definitely not afraid of hard work. And money buys gas whether you're in school or not," she said. "I'm sensing hesitation on your part and just want to say that you're not seeing me at my best right now."

He had to disagree with her on that. What he saw

was pretty darn nice, although she did look tired. She had dark circles under her eyes. Green eyes, he noted. Beautiful, big green eyes.

"When was the wedding supposed to be?" he asked.

"Yesterday."

The skirt of her dress had deep creases, as if she'd been sitting for a long time. Behind the wheel of a crappy old truck.

"Where did you sleep last night?"

"I didn't."

He'd guess she was running on fumes. "Do you have a place to stay here in Blackwater Lake?"

She shook her head. "Not yet. Maybe you could recommend something."

Glancing out the window, he assessed her ride. The paint was old and chipped, and rust showed through in some places. It had seen better days. He figured she probably couldn't afford to pay for a room.

"Blackwater Lake Lodge is the only place in town, but it's expensive."

"That's okay. I'll be all right."

Again, that was probably pride talking. Sleeping in the truck wasn't a good idea, but she likely had no other choice. She was here without a lot of options. And somehow he felt she was now his problem, which he didn't like even a little bit. Bottom line was the camp needed an extra pair of hands and the duties weren't rocket science. He couldn't afford to be too choosy.

He stood up. "The job comes with room and board. Meals included."

She blinked those big green eyes at him. "Are you hiring me?"

"Subject to approval by Caroline Daly. She manages the camp for me and also does the cooking."

"Wow. I don't know what to say."

He didn't, either. If anyone had told him he'd be hiring a runaway bride that day, *crazy* would have been the first word that came to mind.

The thought made him irritable. "Do you want the job or not?"

"I want it."

He looked at the dress then met her gaze. "Do you have anything else to wear?"

"No."

"You'll need stuff. I can give you an advance—"

"That's okay. I can handle it."

"Okay." He wasn't going to argue. "Michelle can tell you where the discount store is and give you directions to the ranch. Like she said, it's about ten miles outside of town. When you've got what you need, meet me there."

"Thank you, Mr. Dixon."

"It's Cabot." He looked at his watch and shook his head. If he didn't leave now he'd be late picking Tyler up from school. "I have to go."

"Okay." She held out her hand. "It's nice to meet you, Cabot. I promise you won't regret this decision."

Time would tell. He shook her hand and the electricity that shot up his arm made him regret not letting Michelle handle the interview solo. But the diner owner was pretty close to dead on about one thing. He was a sucker for hard-luck cases. At least he wasn't a romantic sucker anymore.

When a wife walked out on her husband and infant son, it tended to crush the romance out of a man.

A few hours later, as Kate Scott was driving to the ranch, she figured a rush of adrenaline was the only explanation for the fact that she hadn't passed out and run off the road into a ditch. She'd never been this tired in her life. As an athlete she was trained to eat well, get enough sleep and take care of her body. In the past twenty-four hours she'd done none of the above. Candy bars and coffee were nothing more than survival snacks. That was what happened when you drove from Southern California to Montana in nineteen hours.

But the adrenaline rush in the diner had been unexpected. It had a lot to do with Cabot Dixon, she thought as she drove Angelica, her brother's ancient truck, through his gates and beneath a sign that announced Dixon Ranch and Summer Camp.

Serenity was the first thing she noticed. It was all about rolling green meadows crisscrossed by a white picket fence. Majestic mountains stood like sentinels in the distance. As the truck continued slowly up the long drive, she passed a huge house. It looked a lot like a really big wooden cabin with dormers and a double-door front entry. The kind of place *Architectural Digest* would have on the cover for an article about mountain homes for the wealthy.

Following the instructions Michelle Crawford had given her, Kate drove past a real working barn, then a smaller barnlike building with a large patio and scattered picnic tables. That must be where camp meals were served. Beyond that were six spacious cabins. Michelle had told her the first five housed campers and senior counselors, and the last one, a much smaller cabin, would be where she'd stay for the summer. *If* she got the cook's approval for the assistant-counselor position.

She parked by cabin number six and turned off the truck's ignition before blowing out a long breath. What a relief to just be still. It felt weird. Not good; not bad. Just…strange. She couldn't remember the last time she hadn't had a million things going on at once. Training, practice, competition and product endorsements made for twenty-hour workdays. Now she had…nothing.

Sliding out of the truck, she noticed a little boy running toward her. Oh, to have that much energy, she thought.

The dark-haired, dark-eyed kid skidded to a stop in front of her. He looked about seven or eight. "Hi. I'm Tyler, but most people call me Ty. Not my teacher, though. She believes in calling kids by their given name."

"I'm Kate Scott. Nice to meet you, Ty." His features and the intensity stamped on them were familiar. "I bet your last name is Dixon."

"It is." His long-lashed eyes grew bigger, as if she'd read his mind. "How'd you know?"

"You look like your dad."

"That's what folks say."

And when he grew up, he'd probably be just as dropdead gorgeous as his father. It hadn't escaped her notice that Cabot Dixon was one fine-looking man, which had probably sparked the unexpected blast of adrenaline at the diner. She hadn't been too tired to notice that he wasn't wearing a wedding ring.

She'd felt only a little shame about the spurt of gladness following the observation. Shame because mere hours ago she'd been on the verge of getting married and now she was scoping out commitment symbols, or lack thereof, on the handsome rancher. It felt wrong to ask this little boy about his mother, so she didn't.

She looked around and saw the lake just past a grassy area beyond the cabins. "This is a nice place you've got here, Ty."

"It's not mine. It's my dad's." His expression was

solemn, as if he'd been taught to tell only the absolute truth. "He told me to come down and let you know he and Caroline will be here in a few minutes." The boy thought for a moment, as if trying to remember something, and then his expression changed. "Oh, yeah. And I'm s'posed to welcome you to the ranch."

"Thanks. That's very sweet of you. I'm here for the camp-counselor job—to do whatever I'm told to do, which could be dishes. And I'm fine with that."

Ty nodded sympathetically. "I have to do that all the time."

"Even grown-ups have to follow orders."

"Not my dad." She heard pride in his voice. "He gives 'em."

"I guess you can do that when you're the boss," she agreed. "I appreciate the welcome. Thanks."

Thin shoulders lifted in a shrug. "My dad would say that's just the way it is here in Blackwater Lake."

For a second Kate felt as if she'd ridden a twister to the land of Oz. This was a place where folks made a person feel welcome because it was just a small town's way. That was unbelievably refreshing.

"Well, a stranger like me thinks it's pretty cool to get a friendly welcome."

"Where are you from?" He looked up, and a ray of sunshine slicing through the tree leaves made him squint one eye closed.

"I've been all over."

That was vague but still the truth. She trained wherever there were facilities for skeet shooting. Then there were competitions all over the country, all over the world, not to mention the Olympics. Winning had opened the door to lucrative product-endorsement deals, and fitting in those location shoots with everything else was stressful and challenging.

Ted, her too-good-looking-for-his-own-good manager and weasel-dog ex-fiancé, had pushed hard to get it all in and now she knew why. Marrying her would have punched his meal ticket for life. The sleazy jerk had been using her. She'd been stupid to accept his proposal and move forward with wedding plans, but at least her instinctive judgment about the man had been right on target. She'd never once been swept off her feet when she kissed him.

"My dad said you're pretty." The kid was staring at her, obviously trying to decide for himself if it was true.

"He did?"

Ty nodded uncertainly. "Caroline asked if you were as pretty as Michelle said. That's Mrs. Crawford. She owns the Grizzly Bear Diner."

"I met her." And obviously word about the weirdo in the wedding dress was spreading. "Your dad said I'm pretty?"

He thought about that. "He just said 'yes' when Caroline asked if you were as pretty as Mrs. Crawford said."

That was something, anyway. Kate would have figured if he thought anything at all, it was mostly questioning her sanity for asking for a job while dressed for her own wedding.

"That was very nice of your dad. Thank you for telling me, Ty."

"It's the truth. My dad says you should always tell the truth. People get hurt when you don't."

She was curious about the moral and personal lesson that was in there somewhere. Maybe she'd find out, and maybe she wouldn't. And maybe she was better off not wondering about it at all.

"Here comes my dad and Caroline." He pointed, then raced back down the road to meet them.

Kate watched the man stoop down to his son's level and put a big hand on the small, thin shoulder. He smiled and affectionately ruffled the boy's dark hair before Ty continued running toward the house. One picture was worth a thousand words, and the one she'd just seen said Cabot Dixon loved his boy a lot.

She waited and watched the two adults walk toward her. Now that she'd seen the ranch, something about it pulled at her, and she wanted very much to stay for a little while. It wasn't hiding out, she assured herself. Just taking a much-needed break.

Kate had always thought she was different from other women, so it was surprising to realize that she was having a clichéd reaction as Cabot approached. She found something inherently sexy about a tall, well-built man in worn jeans, white long-sleeved cotton shirt, boots and a black cowboy hat. What was it about a cowboy? He stopped in front of her and again she could *feel* adrenaline obliterating her exhaustion.

A quirk turned up one corner of his mouth. "I sort of miss the dress."

"It's carefully packed away."

"I thought you were going to burn it."

"Something to look forward to." Kate glanced down at the new sneakers, jeans and red scoop-necked T-shirt she'd purchased at the big discount retail store in Blackwater Lake. "This is more practical. And comfortable."

"Amen to that." Caroline looked to be somewhere in her fifties. She was tall with stylishly cut and discreetly streaked blond hair.

"Kate, this is Caroline Daly." Cabot looked from her

to the other woman. "Caroline, meet Kate Scott, Black-water Lake's own runaway bride."

"It's a pleasure." Caroline held out her hand.

Kate gave it a firm squeeze. "Very nice to meet you. And, just so you know, I had my reasons for leaving that toad at the altar."

"Cabot told me." Sympathy brimmed in her blue eyes. "He also said you need a job."

That wasn't technically accurate, but she did need to keep busy. She didn't know any other way to be. "I could use work."

"Have you ever been involved with kids?"

She'd mentored some of the girls in her sport and roomed at the Olympics with a younger archery competitor, but she had never coached. Then Ty's words echoed in her mind. *My dad says you should always tell the truth. People get hurt when you don't.*

"I've never worked with kids. But I was one once," she said hopefully.

"Funny how that happens," Cabot said wryly. "I don't know what I'd do without Caroline. Not only is she a good cook and outstanding camp manager, she's great with kids. Probably has something to do with being Blackwater Lake High School's favorite English teacher and girls' basketball coach."

"Wow. That must keep you busy." Kate had had tutors in high school and had never attended traditional classes with other kids. Sacrifices were required at the level she competed and she'd never regretted it. Not until she found Ted kissing another woman on the day of their wedding and realized he'd been playing her for a fool.

Caroline waved a hand as if it was nothing. "I like

to be busy. I like to cook. Mostly I like the kids, and being around them keeps a person young."

"So that's your secret to looking so youthful," Cabot teased.

Kate tapped her lip and studied the older woman. "Not a secret so much as embracing an attitude. In addition, I think you just have some good genes, the kind of DNA that makes forty the new thirty."

Caroline grinned. "You're just saying that so I'll give Cabot the okay to hire you."

"Busted." Kate shrugged. "But seriously, you look timeless."

Caroline seemed pleased at the compliment. "If I were you, Cabot, I'd hire this young woman. Now I've got to get home and fix dinner for my husband. We own the sporting-goods store in town," she added. "Food has to be on the table at a certain time so someone at the store can cover for him."

"I see." And if her husband looked through the outdoor magazines that were probably displayed at the checkout counter, there was a good chance he'd seen her picture in an ad for camping and outdoor equipment.

"'Bye, Caroline. See you next week when the kids get here," Cabot said, watching her walk down the dirt road to her car parked in front of his house.

When he looked back at her Kate asked, "So, what's the verdict?"

He reached in his jeans pocket, pulled out a brass key that probably unlocked cabin number six and handed it over. "I'm willing to give you a chance."

"Thanks." Relief swept through her and took the last of her energy with it. Suddenly she was so tired she could hardly stand. Not even close proximity to this handsome hunk of cowboy could generate enough adrenaline to hold back a yawn. She shook it off and said, "Sorry. That's not what I usually do at an interview."

"The first part was bizarre enough, what with the dress. And now it's technically over since you got the job." Sympathy softened his dark eyes before he shook it off. "Caroline's a good judge of character."

"And you're not?"

His mouth pulled tight for just a moment. "I wanted her opinion since she has to work with you. I just sign your paycheck."

A dozen questions raced through her mind, but the one she really wanted to ask was *Does that mean I'll never see you?* The deep disappointment generated by that thought was bewildering; she'd spent barely ten minutes in this man's presence.

"I like her," Kate said. "Caroline."

"Me, too. A lot. So don't make me regret giving you the job." He turned and started walking away. Over his shoulder he said, "Get some sleep. You're going to need it."

A shiver skipped over her as she stared at his broad shoulders. They tapered to a trim waist and a backside that would earn ten out of ten points from any female judge. But she'd learned her lesson about looks being shallow and superficial. She didn't know Cabot Dixon from a rock. It was entirely possible that he used women and threw them away. Just like the man she'd almost married.

Still, the attraction was just strong enough to make her hope that when the summer was over she didn't regret taking this job.

Chapter 2

Two days ago when Kate had arrived in Blackwater Lake after driving for nearly twenty-four hours, doing nothing had seemed like heaven. Now she was rested, restless and bored. She sat in her one-room cabin that was comprised of a small stall-shower bathroom, full bed and kitchenette that had a four-cup coffeemaker, frying pan and microwave. She was grateful to have four walls, a roof and the small cozy space they made, but the smallness was starting to close in on her along with the realization that she'd run away from everything and everyone in her life.

A walk before dinner seemed like a really good idea. After, she would head up to the big house and talk to Cabot about doing chores to earn her keep until camp started.

She left the cabin and, as a precaution, locked the door. The ranch was remote and quiet and she didn't have much to steal, but you could never be too careful. The beauty of Blackwater Lake lured her down to its edge, where she drew in a deep breath of sweet, clean air. Blue water sparkled where rays of sunshine kissed it, and on the other side, tree-covered mountains stood guard over the serenity.

"So this is what peace looks like," she whispered to herself. It felt as if a louder tone would violate Mother Nature's sensibilities, and that seemed like a sin.

When she'd looked her fill, she went the other way, past her cabin and the ones that campers and seasoned counselors would occupy in a couple of days. She was looking forward to that, to being busy. With too much time on her hands it was difficult not to obsess about how stupid she'd been to accept Ted's marriage proposal.

What a huge mistake she'd nearly made. And how anxious her parents had sounded when she'd called to let them know she was okay but refused to say where she was now. She needed time by herself, and God bless them, they understood. They had handled canceling the wedding and reception and were returning gifts. She had planned to take the summer off for a honeymoon and settling into married life. Now she had time off to figure out where her life went from here.

The sound of a deep voice followed by childish laughter carried to her. Then she heard a muffled slap. As she made it to the top of the hill, she saw that in front of the big log-cabin house Cabot was playing catch with Tyler, who had his back to her. When the boy missed his father's underhanded toss, the baseball rolled downhill toward her. He turned to chase it and stopped short when he spotted her.

"Hi, Kate." His smile was friendly and he seemed happy to see her.

"Hey, kid." She stopped the rolling baseball with her foot, then bent to pick it up.

She couldn't remember the last time she'd played any sport involving a ball. Once she'd started going to the shooting range with her father and showed an aptitude for skeet, her life had changed. Practice and competitions dominated her life. Before that she'd gone to traditional school, where organized peer activities were possible, but she'd never participated. All the family moves because of her father's military career had made her reluctant to join anything. Then she found her best event. The sport, and being good at something, had made her happy. Until finding skeet shooting, she'd never fit in anywhere.

"Are you going to stare at that ball all day or throw it back?" It wasn't clear whether Cabot was irritated or amused.

"Sorry." She drew her arm back and tossed the ball at Ty. At least that had been her intention. It went way to the right of the mark and rolled away from him. "Sorry," she said again.

"It's okay." Ty ran after it.

"Athletic? Really?" One of Cabot's dark eyebrows rose questioningly. "You throw like a girl."

"At the risk of stating the obvious, I *am* a girl."

"Yeah. I noticed."

Nothing in his tone or expression gave away what he was thinking, but Kate remembered that Cabot had said she was pretty. It had been indirect, an answer to a question from someone else, but he'd agreed. That was something and she would take it. Her ego had recently taken a hit, even though it was stupid to care what Ted thought. If she'd been enough, he wouldn't have been hitting on someone else on the day of their wedding.

Ty ran back with the ball clutched in his hand. "Wanna play catch with us, Kate?"

"I don't have a glove."

"You can use mine," Cabot offered. "It's probably a little big but should work okay."

She could have said no, but that eager, friendly, freckled eight-year-old face wouldn't let her. Ty was a sweet kid and his father had taken a chance on a stranger and given her a job. The world wouldn't end if he fired her now for misrepresenting her skills, but she didn't want to go back to Los Angeles and the glare of the spotlight waiting for her there. At some point she'd have to, but not yet.

"Okay, Ty. But you might be sorry. I'm not very good."

"My dad and I can give you pointers."

"I'd like that."

When she moved close to Cabot and smelled the spicy scent of the aftershave still clinging to his skin, the sport of baseball slipped right out of her mind. Everything about him was sexy, from the broad shoulders to his muscled legs covered in worn denim. She liked his white, cotton, long-sleeved snap-front shirt and decided he wore the cowboy uniform really well.

She took the seen-better-days leather glove he held out and put her fingers inside, finding it still warm from his hand. It seemed intimate somehow and tingles tiptoed up her arm, put a hitch in her breathing.

"Ready, Kate?" Tyler called.

"Yes." She dragged her gaze from the man and turned it on his son. "Go easy on me."

"I will. Don't worry. Just keep your eye on the ball." Obviously Ty had heard that advice before.

She did as he suggested, but as it came at her, she didn't know whether to hold the glove out like a bucket or lift it and close her hand around the ball. In the end she jumped out of the way and let it fall.

"That's okay," Ty called. "Good try."

Probably he'd heard that from his father, too. Children were a reflection of their environment, and she had to conclude that Cabot Dixon was providing a very positive one. The revelation made her like him a lot.

She picked up the ball, then straightened to meet Cabot's gaze. Amusement glittered there and his silence said what her mother had always told her three children—*if you can't say something nice, don't say anything at all.*

She put the ball in the glove, testing the feel of it. After several moments, she prepared to throw it back. "Get ready, Ty. I can't guarantee where this is going."

The boy set his sneaker-clad feet shoulder-width apart and held up his glove as a target. "Right here."

The body movement to make it go there was so different from sighting a moving clay pigeon. She was also pretty good with a bow and arrow. During Olympic training, she'd made friends with one of the female archers who had given her pointers in their downtime. Right now she had to command her arm to throw this ball at just the right velocity and close to the vicinity of the kid's glove.

She threw and it went way to the side, out of his reach, forcing Ty to chase after it again. "I'm sorry."

"I like to run," he called out cheerfully.

"Hmm" was all Cabot said.

She wasn't sure whether she was just a little embarrassed or totally humiliated for being proved a fraud. When Ty returned, he moved closer and tossed the ball underhand, like his father had. She turned her hand up but misjudged and it fell at her feet.

"Hey, kiddo, I'm really sorry. This isn't my best sport. Playing this with me isn't much fun for you, is it?"

"It's okay." He shrugged. "You'll get better with practice."

They kept at it for a while, and Kate figured Tyler had also learned patience from his father in addition to encouragement and liberal praise. She actually caught a few and was getting the hang of throwing more accurately. Finally shadows started creeping in and Tyler announced he was getting hungry.

"It's about that time," Cabot said. "Ty, you go on in and wash up for supper."

"Okay, Dad. See you later, Kate."

"'Bye." She watched the boy run up the steps and into the house, then handed the glove back to Cabot. When he started to turn away, she said, "Can I talk to you for a minute?"

"Sure." He folded his arms over his chest. "What's on your mind?"

"I want to do something to earn my keep until the kids arrive for camp." Because that sounded a little like a come-on, she felt it necessary to put a finer point on the statement. "Chores. Like housekeeping maybe. Cleaning. Doing dishes. Cooking."

"You know your way around a stove?"

"I'm not the best, but I'm definitely competent in the kitchen."

"I already have a housekeeper." He looked as if he'd rather be kicked in the head by a horse than let her into his house. "Although I do my own cooking. You'll earn your keep soon enough. Making dinner for us isn't necessary."

"It is to me. I don't take something for nothing. Cooking a meal would be a way for me to give back."

She was still processing the fact that he had a house-keeper, which made her pretty positive that he was a bachelor. That along with the fact that she hadn't seen a woman at the house or another vehicle besides his truck.

Surely the women around here would be interested in a man as attractive and sexy as Cabot Dixon. The fact that he was single didn't speak well of Blackwater Lake females. Although, by definition, a relationship required two interested parties, which could mean he was unreceptive to being part of a couple. Could be he'd learned the hard way, just like she had.

If Kate had paid attention to her instincts, she wouldn't have gotten herself in this mess. But when she took in the beauty of his land, as messes went, this was an awesome place to be in one.

Something wouldn't let her drop the offer and she was pretty sure the determination was driven by her need to prove she had other skills. That he shouldn't be sorry he'd hired her.

"Do you love cooking?" she asked.

"Not really."

"Wouldn't you like a break from it? Hang out with Ty for a change? Maybe play a game with him?"

"He's used to hanging out on his own." But his mouth pulled tight at the words.

"Sometimes it's good to shake up the routine when you can." She'd certainly done that, and only time would tell whether or not it was a good thing.

"Look, Kate, I really appreciate the offer—"

Before he could say "but," she interrupted and started

past him toward the front steps. "Okay, then. Lead the way to the kitchen and I'll get started."

Kate half expected him to stop her either with words or physically. Instead he mumbled something, and she didn't try very hard to understand what he'd said. Then she heard footsteps behind her.

She took that as a yes and walked into his house.

It was weird to see a woman in his kitchen.

Cabot remembered the last time a female, other than his housekeeper, had stood in front of the granite-topped island. His wife, Jen, had said she was leaving him and her infant son. She'd hated the ranch and right that second Cabot had hated it, too.

Now Katrina Scott was here and he hated to admit that she was stirring up more than fried chicken and macaroni and cheese. She was scraping off a patch on the ache in his gut, the yearning for that time when he'd had a whole and complete family. How stupid was it that this woman did that to him? She'd freely admitted running out on a life like that. Although, if he was being fair, the cheating jerk had deserved it.

But here she was, cooking. He'd planned chicken for dinner, but his method involved a boxed coating and the oven. Hers involved flour, egg, oil and a frying pan. His mouth watered at the aroma. She'd rummaged through the fridge and pantry, coming up with all the ingredients necessary for macaroni and cheese. He'd kept her company, just making small talk, because it didn't seem right to leave her in here alone.

Ty ran into the room. He'd been watching TV in the family room, which was an extension of the kitchen. It was a big, open place where he'd once pictured a bunch of kids playing while he and Jen watched over them from the kitchen. That dream went out the door with her.

"Is dinner ready? I'm starving," the boy said.

Kate moved to the stove and checked the chicken sizzling in a pan. "This is done."

After turning off the burner, she lifted the golden-brown pieces to a platter and set it on the island beside a warming tray. Turning, she went to the oven, opened the door and took out a casserole dish using protective mitts. She was better with them than the baseball glove, and the thought almost made Cabot smile.

"The mac and cheese is bubbling nicely. I'd say it's done." She set the dish on the hot tray beside a pot containing cooked green beans. "Dinner is ready."

"Ty—"

"I'm already washed up."

"Okay, then. You're all set, men. Enjoy your dinner. I'll see you tomorrow."

Cabot was just about ready to breathe a sigh of relief as she started to leave. He felt edgy around her and was looking forward to letting his guard down and relaxing. "Thanks for cooking."

"Wait," Ty said to Kate. "You're not eating with us?"

"No, sir," she said. "I'm on the payroll and not doing anything to earn it. That's why I cooked. I certainly wasn't looking for an invitation to stay."

"But, Dad, we should invite her." Dark eyes, eager and innocent, looked into Cabot's.

Apparently his son wasn't getting his vibe about wanting her gone. "We shouldn't take up any more of Kate's time. She probably has things to do."

"She just said she wasn't doing anything and that's why she cooked dinner," Ty pointed out. "You always tell me to be polite and neighborly."

Cabot looked at Kate, giving her a chance to jump in and say she couldn't stay. The expression glittering in her green eyes said she knew he was squirming and she didn't plan to do anything to help him out. If he had to guess, he'd say she was enjoying this.

He always did his best to be a good example to his son, which basically left him no choice. "Would you like to stay for dinner, Kate?"

"I'd love to," she said brightly.

"Cool. I'll set the table. It's my job." Ty proceeded to get out plates and eating utensils and set them on the round oak table in the nook.

"Don't forget napkins," Cabot reminded him. He looked at Kate. "What would you like to drink? Water, iced tea, beer, wine?"

"Beer," she said after thinking about it.

For some reason her choice surprised him. "You look more like a wine woman to me."

"Beer sounded good. I don't drink normally when I'm in—" She stopped short of saying what she was in. Then she added, "I just don't drink much."

He wondered about the slip but let it pass. The less he knew about her, the better off he was. After pouring milk for Ty and grabbing two longnecks from the fridge, the three of them sat down to eat.

"This is my favorite dinner." Ty took a big bite out of the chicken leg he'd picked off the platter. "This is really good. Way better than the Grizzly Bear Diner."

"I'm glad you like it," she said.

Cabot took a bite of his piece and found the crunchy, juicy flavors unbelievably good. After trying the mac and cheese he decided she was two for two. Green beans fell into a category of not good, not bad. Just something he had to eat because of that being-a-positive-role-model-for-his-son thing.

"Don't you think this is the best dinner, Dad?"

He looked at the boy, then Kate. "It's really good."

"Thanks." She looked pleased.

"How did you learn to cook like this?" he asked.

"My mom taught me. I spent a lot of time hanging out in the kitchen with her."

"Why? Didn't you have any friends?" Ty asked.

"Ty," Cabot scolded. "That's nosy and rude."

"It's all right," Kate said. "You're very perceptive, Ty. I actually didn't have any friends."

"Why?" Ty started to say something, then stopped.

Knowing his son, Cabot figured he'd been about to ask if there was something wrong with her. His son was developing a filter between his brain and his mouth. Maturity was a wonderful thing.

"When I was growing up," she said, "my dad was career army and we moved every couple of years. It got hard to make friends and leave them, so I just stopped. I hung out at home mostly."

"Wow." The boy set his picked-clean leg bone on the plate, his eyes growing wide. "I wouldn't like moving away from C.J. He's my best friend. And I've never lived anywhere but here."

"The ranch has been in the family for several generations," Cabot explained.

Kate looked wistful. "I've never had roots. You're lucky, Ty, to have a long-standing connection with the land and community."

"It's a blessing and curse," Cabot said.

"How so?" She scooped up a forkful of macaroni and delicately put it in her mouth.

"When you're the only son of a rancher, you pretty

much know what your career is going to be when you grow up. What's expected of you. There's not a lot of choice."

"Did you want to take another career path?" she asked.

"I majored in business in college because it was expected that someday I'd run this place. What I didn't expect was having opportunities in the corporate sector. That life pulled at me some. But when it's a family business, the situation becomes a lot more complicated."

Kate glanced at Ty, and it was clear that she wanted to ask how he fit into the scheme of things, considering Cabot's mixed feelings. When his boy grew up, would he be expected to take over the ranch? Cabot hoped he would be more flexible than his own father and let his son decide what he wanted to do with his life. He didn't plan on pressuring Ty and saddling him with expectations of taking over the operation. Being stuck on the land near a small town in rural Montana could be limiting.

It was a great place to grow up, but there was a big world out there, and once upon a time it had tugged at Cabot. Now he just didn't think much about it. He was doing his best as a father, rancher and businessman who was exploring the responsible use of mineral rights on the land. Pretty much he was content with things now. Until meeting Kate, that was.

"So, I've been looking over the camp curriculum," she said, changing the subject.

Cabot was grateful to her because taking over the ranch wasn't something he wanted to discuss in front of his son. The years were going by too fast, but a decent amount of time was still left before any decisions needed to be made.

"Caroline takes care of that."

"You don't have input?"

"I could, but I mostly just stay out of the way."

Kate looked surprised at that. "I see."

"You look surprised. Is there a problem?"

"No. It's just that you're so patient and comfortable with Tyler, I'd have thought you were more involved with the camp and the visiting kids."

"I don't have a lot of time for it." Guilt pricked him because he could make more time if he chose. "What do you think of the activities?"

"There sure are a lot of them." She looked thoughtful. "Arts and crafts. Water sports, which makes sense with the lake right here. Archery. Horseback riding. I like that the kids can choose what activities they want to participate in."

Cabot hadn't made any changes since he'd taken it over from his father. And he didn't get involved very much after the kids arrived, leaving it to Caroline to run things day to day.

"They're encouraged to try as many activities as possible," he said, recalling his manager's recommendations. "But it's still their choice what they do."

Kate nodded thoughtfully. "I noticed there was a course in wilderness survival."

"Presenting the basics is wise, although it's up to the staff to make sure the kids' survival is never in question."

"Very funny." She took a sip of beer. "Seriously, though, are basics enough? You always hear stories in the news about someone getting lost in the woods, stranded with their car, driving off the road. Last winter there was the case of a family who got stuck when they went to play in the snow."

"What happened to them?" Ty asked.

"The father did everything right. They stayed with

the vehicle, burned the car's tires to stay warm, and everyone huddled in the car at night to share body heat when the temperature dropped below freezing."

Cabot's attention perked up at the body-heat part. His definitely cranked up at the thought of keeping her warm. It was an image that popped into his mind without warning or permission. Once there it seemed disinclined to leave.

"It took a couple of days, but they were finally found not too far from their home." She looked at Cabot. "By the way, I'm certified to teach wilderness-survival techniques."

In spite of the fact that she was doing a good job on her beer, it was hard to believe this girlie girl could hold her own in the wild. "You're serious?"

"Don't judge me by the way I handle—or mishandle—a baseball. I can build a fire without matches and find food in the woods."

"Why?"

"Why not?" she shot back.

He waited for more details, like why she would go out of her way to acquire that kind of skill, but she stared him down without saying more. It made him curious, but he didn't ask. She probably had her reasons for not sharing more personal details. It was typical of all the strays who had a need to use his spare cabin.

All he knew was that she'd been engaged to a guy, then ran out when it was time to commit. Her story was that he'd cheated, but Cab didn't know for sure. What he did know was that there were too many similarities to his ex, and that was plenty of reason to keep his distance.

But obviously he was cursed. Otherwise he wouldn't be attracted to a woman who had run away from something.

Chapter 3

It was a spectacular night.

At about nine o'clock, after cleaning up the pots and pans she'd used to cook dinner, Kate sat on the wooden bench on the small front porch of her little cabin. The inky-black Montana sky glittered with stars, a sight that took her breath away. The absence of Los Angeles nuisance light revealed the beauty a person couldn't see in the big city.

Being away from L.A. was having unexpected effects on her. She hadn't been this relaxed in a very long time. Dinner with the Dixon men had been partly responsible for that. Fried chicken, mac and cheese and beer were probably the world's most comforting foods. But the best part was that no one wanted anything from her. She'd had to make a federal case to get her boss's permission to cook.

Cabot Dixon was a brooder, which only added to his

appeal. He didn't have a poker face, either. That was for sure. When he'd talked about missed career opportunities, she'd seen resentment and resignation in his expression. But when she'd gone into Blackwater Lake to shop for food and toiletries, everyone she'd talked to had said he had made the Dixon ranch more successful than his father or grandfather had. So it might not be his first choice for making a living, but he was darn good at what he did.

The scrape of boots coming down the dirt path startled her in the still night. Adrenaline kicked up her heart rate; she was all alone out here. As a tall form moved closer, lights mounted on the cabins revealed that it was Cabot.

"Evening," he said, not slowing his stride.

He was going to walk right on by. If he'd said nothing, a case could be made that he hadn't seen her, but he clearly had and didn't want to talk to her.

Kate knew she should let him go, but for some reason his remoteness kicked up her contrary streak. She didn't like being ignored. On top of that, she was curious about why he was out here. Surely he didn't exercise. He was lean and muscular, walking proof that his job kept him fit without having to add a workout routine.

"Hey, wait up." She stood and hurried after him.

"What?" he asked over his shoulder.

Kate caught up to him, but it wasn't easy. His long-legged stride made it a challenge. "That's what I'd like to know. Why are you out here? Is something wrong?"

"Nope. Habit. I do a nightly inspection of all the ranch buildings."

"Where's Ty?"

"In bed." Cabot glanced down at her. "He's old enough to be left by himself for a few minutes."

"I wasn't judging," she protested.

"Maybe not out loud, but I could hear you thinking about it."

Just a little. Possibly.

When he got to the grassy area by the lake, he turned right on the dirt path and headed for the barn and corral. He wasn't saying anything, and she felt the need to fill the conversational void.

"It's a beautiful night."

"Yeah."

"Do you ever get used to it? Take all this for granted?"

"Probably."

The least he could do was throw her a bone, she thought. But she didn't discourage easily. A person didn't win Olympic gold medals by giving up when the going got tough.

"The lake is spectacular during the day, but with the moon shining down, it just takes your breath away." Or maybe she was breathless just being near him and trying to match his strides. "The mountains are gorgeous, too. And the air." She drew in a deep breath. "So clean and fresh."

"You're not wrong about that."

"This is a lovely piece of land you've got here."

He glanced down again. "Sounds like you love the outdoors."

"Who wouldn't?"

"My ex-wife, for starters."

Their arms brushed and she could almost feel the tension in his body, the annoyance he felt at letting that slip out.

But he had let it slip. "You were married."

"A lifetime ago."

"What happened?" That was nosy and probably rude, but he knew about *her* past. Turnabout was fair play. This was the opening she'd been waiting for, and she didn't plan to let it drop.

"She didn't like it here. Wasn't happy being a wife and mother."

"That pretty much sucks."

"Pretty much," he agreed. But there was a harsh edge to his voice.

"Must be hard on Ty—not having a mom, I mean." Moments of silence dragged out after the comment, and she didn't think he was going to answer.

"He asks questions," Cabot admitted. "And I answer as honestly as I can."

"What do you say?"

"That the two of us are a different kind of family. But there's no way a kid can understand why his mother didn't want to stay for her own son. Hell, *I* don't understand."

Anger had given way to wistfulness in his tone and that made her wonder if he still had feelings for the woman who'd walked out on him. "Is there a chance that Ty's mom will come back?"

"Always, I suppose."

Kate was a little surprised when he didn't add that it would be a cold day in hell before he took her back. "What if she did?"

His mouth pulled tight for a moment, but when he answered, his voice lacked any emotion. No anger, regret or sadness. Just matter-of-fact. "If she showed up at the front door tomorrow, Ty wouldn't have to wonder where his mother is."

"Do *you* wonder?"

"No. I know where she is." *And she doesn't want to*

be here. He didn't say it, but the words hung in the air between them.

"Where is she?" That question *was* out-and-out nosy. Every time he answered something, more stuff popped into her head to ask him. At some point he was going to tell her to mind her own business, but until he did she couldn't seem to stop herself from inquiring.

"Helena."

Montana's capital. "So it's not that she doesn't like Montana."

"Nope. Just the ranch and small-town life."

"Does Ty know how close she is?"

"Nope. She hasn't shown any interest in seeing him and I wouldn't put him through that unless she did." He slowed his pace. "There's no point in it. Rejection hurts."

"Yeah." She'd been rejected very publicly. She was realizing that she didn't love her ex-fiancé because he hadn't crossed her mind all that much since she'd arrived in Blackwater Lake and, more specifically, since she'd met Cabot. But at first it had hurt. The humiliation was no fun, either. And she was a grown-up. Ty was a little boy. "Are you ever going to tell him?"

"If he wants to know."

"That seems wise," she agreed.

"You're judging again." This time there was a smile in his voice.

"In a good way."

"It's not wise. Just common sense," he claimed. "If you tell a kid he can't do something, that's exactly what he wants to do."

"Is that the voice of experience talking?" she teased.

"Maybe. Maybe not. I think of it more as human nature."

They had come full circle, past his house. She'd expected he would go inside and let her see herself back, but he didn't. Cabot walked her to her front door and stopped.

"Good night, Kate. Two more days until the kids get here. Get some rest. You're going to need it."

"See you," she said.

She watched him turn and walk back up the hill, a solitary man in the dark. Walking with him had been both exhilarating and enlightening. He had been married but was now divorced. She'd wanted so badly to say that he and his son were better off without a shallow, selfish woman like that having any influence on their lives. Only an idiot would run away from the child she'd borne and a man who loved her.

It was the running part that gave Kate pause. *She'd* run. Granted, the guy she'd left might be a good match for Cab's ex—in the shallow-and-selfish department. But still, she'd run. Did he put her in the same category as his ex-wife?

The thought troubled her, which was both annoying and not very bright. She'd just escaped from complications with a man and shouldn't let herself lose sleep over what this man thought. They'd only just met.

And she hoped to be wrong but couldn't shake the feeling that he might be pining for the woman who'd left him.

On the first day of camp Kate helped the other four counselors greet and sign in the kids, then assign cabins and settle them there. The other employees were all first- or second-year schoolteachers and this was their summer job. She was the only oddball without training.

It was late afternoon when she walked into the camp

kitchen. The dining room was a log-cabin-style building, and the food-preparation area was situated behind the larger room where picnic tables would seat the campers for meals. A patio jutted off, and if they wanted, the kids could eat out there with a spectacular view of the lake. Without children around, it could be the perfect spot for a romantic dinner if you were with a man who looked like Cabot Dixon, one who might lean toward a little romance after a walk under the stars. He didn't seem to lean that way, but maybe she just wasn't his type.

And the fact that she would even wonder about this meant she probably needed serious therapy.

"Hi, Caroline." She greeted the manager/cook who was cutting up vegetables on the long stainless-steel counter in the center of the room. A six-burner stove stood behind her, and different-sized pots hung from a rack suspended from the ceiling.

The tall blonde looked up and smiled. "Did the kids scare you off?"

"No." But Kate grinned at the teasing. "They're a terrific bunch and I really enjoyed meeting them. But Jim told me to take a break while they divide the campers into color groups for activities."

"Jim Shields is a good teacher and really terrific at what he does here."

Kate knew Caroline worked with him at Blackwater Lake High School, where he taught math and was the boys' volleyball coach. "I came to see if you need any help in the kitchen."

"You don't want to put your feet up? Catch a power nap?"

"Working with children might not be my best skill, but I can take it. I'm sturdier than I look."

"What *is* your best skill?" the other woman asked.

Kate couldn't blame her for being curious. She'd shown up in a wedding dress and given no other information about herself besides the fact that she'd left her cheating weasel of a groom at the altar. But this peace and quiet felt good after so many years of nonstop media interest and craziness. It would end if the details about her came out. She wanted serenity for just a little bit longer.

"If you don't mind, I'd rather not say."

"Suit yourself." Caroline put down the knife in her hand. "I can use some help. Hamburgers and fries are the traditional first-night meal here, and I insist on fresh, not frozen, potatoes. You can cut them up. Real thin."

"Okay."

"When you finish that, would you slice some carrot and celery sticks? I always like to have those available."

"Got it."

Kate saw that the potatoes were already peeled and soaking in a pot of water. She got to work, and after checking the thinness of her fries, Caroline said nothing for a few moments. Finally Kate couldn't stand the silence. It was against all the laws of nature for two women to be in a kitchen together and not talk. Usually about men. And she knew exactly which man she wanted to talk about.

"How long have you managed the camp for Cabot?"

"Ten years now."

Tyler was eight, which meant this woman had met his mother. After the little bit Cabot had said, Kate had a lot of questions. "So what was Cabot's wife like?"

Caroline glanced up quickly from the tomato she was slicing. "Why do you want to know?"

"He told me what happened and why."

"Interesting." She looked up again. "He doesn't usually talk about it."

Should she feel special that he'd told her the story? A question for another day. "I guess I'm just curious what you thought of her."

"It's hard to answer that. There is my impression when he was first with her and my feelings about what she did to him by running away." She sighed and rested her wrist against the cutting board. "She was a very pretty little thing. Long black hair and violet-colored eyes. Seemed sweet and head over heels for Cabot. No one saw that she was unhappy or that she would do what she did. Folks were shocked, and some blamed it on postpartum depression. But she never came back to set things right. Cabot was stunned and dazed. The thing is, he didn't really even have time to process his feelings because he had an infant to care for and a business to run. Maybe that was a blessing."

Kate remembered his wistful tone when he'd talked about his wife. "Do you know how he feels about her now?"

"No," Caroline said. "As far as I know, no one knows."

Kate had been hoping for something specific, a tidbit to explain why he hadn't shown the least bit of interest in kissing her. It wasn't that she'd wanted him to get romantic, because that would complicate her peace and quiet. But she kind of wanted him to want to and be fighting it just a little. Crazy. Except that she was still feeling the effects of her fiancé cheating on her and the lingering questions about why she was found lacking. Maybe her self-confidence had taken a bigger hit than she'd realized.

"Does he have a girlfriend?" That would explain the lack of interest.

"Not that I'm aware of. And this is a small town," Caroline said pointedly. "If he did, everyone would know."

"He must have needs."

Caroline gave her a sharp look. "You're awfully curious."

"I'm sorry. That was really nosy. I didn't mean to be inappropriate. But he's an exceptionally good-looking man. It's hard to believe he's been unattached for so long."

Kate figured if he had an itch that wasn't getting scratched and he'd still not been tempted by her, that would make her feel even more pathetic.

The other woman nodded, apparently understanding the curiosity. "Cabot likes women, if that's what you're asking. No one knows for sure, but the assumption is that he 'dates' discreetly. The last thing he'd want is talk linking him to anyone getting back to his boy. He'd never put up with that."

"Anyone can see he cares about Ty," Kate agreed. "He seems like a wonderful father."

"And then some." Caroline looked thoughtful. "Because of what happened, he's got a deep empathy for wounded people and goes out of his way to protect them."

That actually was a segue into something else she was curious about. "I have another question."

"I bet you do."

"Clearly I have no right and I'd like to believe it's not prying. Maybe inquisitive—"

"You think?" She saw humor in Caroline's blue eyes.

"Yeah. But I can't help it. I'm curious about the cabin where I'm staying."

"Why?"

"It was empty and available. Stocked with basics—including coffee and toiletries, like a hotel room. As if it was ready. Like people in areas that are prone to natural disaster keep emergency supplies up to date."

"*Natural disaster* and *emergency* pretty much describe Cabot's reasons for keeping it prepared."

"I don't understand."

"Folks call it the 'stray cabin.' Cabot has a soft spot for the three-legged dog or a blind cat. People, too. He keeps that place for anyone who's in need. Like the soldier returning from the war who needs quiet to deal with post-traumatic stress disorder. Or the homeless guy who lost his job and just needs a temporary place to stay while he gets back on his feet. Then there was the abused woman who left her husband, and Cabot made sure she was safe until the crisis was over."

"Very noble of him."

"Also, there's the occasional runaway bride," Caroline added drily.

"Not that I don't think he's an incredibly decent man, or that I'm ungrateful for his help, but I'm not a charity case," Kate assured her.

"Okay."

The tone was on the patronizing side and Kate felt obligated to share just a few big details. "In some circles I'm fairly well-known."

"That doesn't mean you don't need a little help."

"Not really," Kate assured her. "I can take care of myself. In fact, it will be news when I surface and I'll have to make a statement."

"You mean running out on your wedding wasn't statement enough?" Caroline asked.

"You know why I did it. And there are lots of reasons for running. That doesn't make me like his ex-wife."

"If you say so."

"I do." She winced at the words that she would have said if she hadn't run out on the wedding.

Kate would love to know what Cabot had said to this woman about her. If she had to guess, there was some comparison between her and the woman who'd done him wrong. Some judgment that lumped her in the same, unsympathetic group of females who were selfish and irresponsible.

"Look, Caroline, I did run out on my wedding. In hindsight, probably I should have faced everyone at the church and announced the wedding wasn't going to happen and explained why I was backing out of it. At the very least I'm guilty of avoiding the public humiliation, but I'm not a liar."

"I believe you, Kate."

"Then I hope you'll accept as fact that I like the anonymity here in Blackwater Lake and the chance to work with kids for the summer. It's something I never really considered doing, but I think it will be challenging and fun. I'm grateful for the chance."

"No matter what your circumstances are, that's Cabot's goal. The stray cabin is his way of giving someone a chance."

Kate nodded and continued slicing potatoes. Her goal in the conversation had been to extract information, but now she had more questions than answers. It wasn't clear whether she was more bothered about being put in the same category as the woman who'd upended his life or that he was treating her as if she needed a handout.

Still the most persistent question of all was why she even cared what he thought.

Chapter 4

Kate hadn't known what to expect from this job, but after her first full day and most of her second, she was pleased with her showing. More important, she was enthusiastic about doing it again tomorrow.

She was there as backup for the other experienced counselors, an extra pair of hands during games, crafts and competitions. Another pair of eyes to watch over the kids and make sure all went smoothly didn't hurt, either. If one of the adults got sick or needed help, she could fill in. The kids were funny, energetic, exasperating and so much fun to be around.

With school out, Ty was participating in camp activities. Caroline had explained this was child care for him so that his father could work. The boy had joined in on some of the events and had hung back on others. Swimming was his strongest skill; he was like a fish. He was not a shining star at basketball, football or baseball, and his lack of confidence showed in his facial expressions and body language. Tyler Dixon simply tugged at her heart.

It was now late afternoon. Everyone was taking a little breather before dinner. She'd checked with Caroline to make sure no help was needed for the evening meal. After getting the all clear, she'd decided to take a walk by the lake.

Even though she saw it every day, the beauty of Blackwater Lake still astounded her. It would never happen in a million years, but she wondered whether or not she would take the view for granted if she lived here.

She stopped at an outcropping of rocks at the water's edge, breathed in the pine-and-flower-scented air and watched the sunlight turn the gently moving surface of the lake into a sparkling blue carpet. If not for her pesky attraction to Cabot Dixon, her soul would be at peace for probably the first time ever.

She hadn't talked to him for a couple of days, since that night he'd explained he walked ranch inspection every night. From the window of her tiny cabin she'd seen him pass by, but he didn't look over, obviously not even tempted to drop in and see her. She wasn't accustomed to serenity, but she also wasn't used to being ignored. Or being considered a "stray." It had been so hectic she hadn't had time to process what Caroline had told her about the cabin being available to Cabot's charity cases. She wasn't a three-legged dog or blind cat. Or an abused woman. It rankled some that he'd pegged her that way.

"As a rule a man's a fool. When it's hot he wants it cool. When it's cool he wants it hot. Always wanting what is not." She shook her head at the silliness of the ode to human nature that her mother had taught her.

"Kate—"

She whirled around, startled because she hadn't heard footsteps behind her. Ty stood there. "Hi. Wow, you were really quiet."

"You weren't." His freckled face was solemn. "Do you have an imaginary friend?"

"No. I was just talking to myself." She studied him. "Do *you?*"

"I used to. Then C. J. Beck—I mean, Stone—and me got to be best friends."

She was no shrink, but it wasn't much of a stretch to assume that this little boy was lonely. His father was busy running a business and his mother was somewhere in Montana but made no effort to see her son. No two ways about it. The situation just totally sucked.

"Do you want to walk back with me?" she asked.

He looked up hopefully. "Would it be okay?"

"I'd like that very much." She pointed to the way she'd come. "It'll be time for dinner pretty soon."

Ty fell into step beside her. "Can you have dinner with me and my dad again?"

"I'd like that," she said cautiously. "But you'd have to ask your dad if it's okay first."

He kicked a rock on the lakeshore. "I just know he'll say no."

Kate figured the only reason Cabot had allowed her to dinner that one time was because she'd just pushed ahead and didn't give him a tactful out. "Does your friend C.J. come to dinner?"

The boy thought for a minute. "Not very often. I usually go to his house."

"I'm sure your dad has his reasons."

"He works all the time," Ty agreed. "And C.J. has

a mom and dad now. When there's school I go to his house a lot and either his mom or dad brings me home."

"That's nice."

"Yeah." He picked up a rock and threw it into the lake. "He got adopted."

"Oh?" Did C.J. have different biological parents? Her response was designed to elicit more information if Ty wanted to tell her.

"Yeah. Dr. Stone—Adam—got married to his mom and then adopted him."

"I see. Does he like Adam?"

"Yeah. But he calls him Dad now."

"That's really nice." She looked down, and it was impossible to overlook the brooding expression and longing on the small face.

"He's got a mom and dad."

"Do you miss your mom?"

He thought about that. "I was a baby, so I don't remember her."

If she read between the lines, he was saying you couldn't miss what you never had. But you could certainly envy what someone else had. "I always had a mom and dad around, so I don't really know what you're going through. Guess it's hard to only have one parent, huh?"

"Most of the kids at school have two parents," he said. "I wish my dad would get married so I'd have a mom."

Uh-oh. She was afraid there was an ulterior, matchmaking motive to another dinner with them. Oh, God, what to do? She didn't want to reject him, but wasn't it more cruel to let him hope that she and his father would ever become romantically involved?

"Ty, are you hinting about me and your dad getting—close?"

He looked up. "Maybe. I think he likes you."

Kate wasn't so sure about that. "Why do you say that?"

He shrugged. "Prob'ly 'cause he looks at you funny."

Prob'ly he did that 'cause he wished he'd never laid eyes on her or offered her the "stray" cabin, she thought. "I'm flattered that you believe he's attracted to me. But you know it takes two people to like each other for anyone to even think about marriage."

"Yeah, I know." He kicked a well-worn sneaker into the wet dirt at the lake's edge. "Do you like my dad?"

She'd walked right into that one. No way could she answer honestly, that she thought Cabot Dixon was the hottest cowboy she'd ever seen and one look into that handsome face made her heart beat way too fast. But there were too many stumbling blocks. He needed someone who would love the ranch and stay there. She thought it was the most beautiful place she'd ever seen, but she had to go back to her regularly scheduled life and numerous commitments. Letting this child go on hoping for a relationship felt heartless, and she couldn't let him continue.

She put a hand on his shoulder. "Ty, your dad is a great guy. He's a wonderful father and works very hard to take care of the ranch and you. But—"

"What? You like him."

"I do. But my stay here is temporary and you're talking about forever."

"Do you have to go?" His voice was wistful.

"Yes. I'm just taking a break here." She squeezed his thin shoulder. "Do you understand?"

"Yeah."

The tone said quite clearly that he didn't like it, though.

They were just passing the archery range, an open field where targets were secured on bales of hay. In the summer-camp compound, bows and arrows were stored in an equipment shed. Kate had dabbled in the sport because almost every shooting range where she practiced hitting clay targets also had an archery section. And she'd become friendly with some of the members of the Olympic team. Her roommate had come close to a gold medal but had to settle for silver. Today Kate had given some of the kids pointers to improve their form and accuracy. It had felt good to make a difference.

Ty glanced over at the field and frowned. "I'm no good at that."

"It's a difficult skill to learn and takes a lot of practice to master it."

"Dustin and Maddie are really good."

"They're older and have been to camp for the past several years," she said. One of the other counselors had filled her in on them.

"I'll never be as good as them."

Kate looked down at the boy's expression and recognized it from looking in the mirror twenty years ago. Because of all the moves her family made, she used to be him, on the outside looking in. The loneliness was consuming. Her parents had noticed and that was when her father started including her on his outings to the skeet-shooting complex. She'd wanted to try it and then amazed everyone with her raw ability. The rest was history.

But her parents were a team. Cabot was a single father and couldn't be faulted for not noticing his son's isolation. She suspected Ty wouldn't say anything because on some level he knew his dad was juggling so many things and didn't want to be a burden. Or risk that another parent would think he was too much trouble.

Unlike her, he was growing up in the place where he'd been born, but he still battled loneliness. This boy got to her, and suddenly the words were coming out of her mouth. "I could help you with archery. Privately."

"Really?" Excitement shone in his eyes when his gaze jumped to hers.

"I'd be happy to. Although you should know it's not my best event."

"Horseback riding is my best event," he said, clearly engaged now.

"Good for you. I'm afraid of horses."

"Really? They're easy compared to archery," he said, more carefree and a little cocky now. "I could help you get over it."

"I bet you could." And it would boost his self-confidence. "Let's make a deal. I'll teach you about archery and you help me with horses."

Tyler took the hand she held out and said, "Deal."

Would Cabot's average charity case be able to do that?

Cabot made sure Ty was sound asleep before starting his nightly inspection of the ranch buildings. It hadn't taken his son long to be out like a light; camp activities kept him busy and wore him out. Caroline had texted him that everything was fine before she went home for the day. As he walked down the hill all seemed quiet.

The program was a good one because he hired the best people to run it. His son was busy in a positive way and well supervised during the summer off from school. That meant Cabot could take care of business without worrying about him getting into trouble.

Earlier Ty had come in happy and excited after having dinner with the campers and said this year he was going to learn how to shoot a bow and arrow really good. That was a direct quote. And Kate was going to teach him. Why the heck would she know how? Maybe she'd had a class in college, but that would have been a while ago. Just showed Cabot how little he knew about the runaway bride.

He walked past the camp cabins, where he could see dim lights and hear quiet talking from inside. The crickets were louder than the kids, which told him the situation was normal. Moving on, he passed the cabin where Kate was staying and felt the same knot in his gut that he had every night when he forced himself not to look over and see if she was on the porch.

If he did and she was, the temptation to talk to her could be too much to resist. And if he didn't resist, there was a better-than-even chance he would make a move on that spectacular mouth of hers and live to regret it.

No, ignoring her was the smartest play and that was what he did.

Cabot came to the end of the dirt path, where a patch of grass bordered the lake. The moon was nearly full tonight, and he spotted a lone, slender female figure at the water's edge. Because the counselors were with kids and Caroline had gone home, he knew whom that body silhouetted against the moonlight belonged to.

Kate Scott.

Fate was putting another temptation in his path, but her back was to him. She didn't know he was there, which meant slipping away quietly was an option. He started to turn and his boot scraped a rock, a small sound that echoed loudly in the quiet night.

She looked over her shoulder. "Cabot?"

So much for slipping away quietly.

"Evening, Kate." He walked across the grass to stand beside her.

The sun had gone down. How was it possible that her lips looked even more appealing? Moonlight was sneaky that way.

"You're on routine inspection?" No greeting and her tone was cool, clipped, as if there was a chip on her shoulder about something.

"Yeah. Everything's quiet."

"No three-legged dogs creating havoc or blind cats bumping into trees?"

"Not that I've seen." Definitely a chip on her shoulder, and he had no idea what was on her mind.

"That's a relief."

He wasn't going to bite. Staying neutral and unengaged. "Nice night."

"Beautiful," she said, glancing up at the stars. "The sky is like diamonds on black velvet."

He followed her gaze. "Never thought about it like that, but could be."

"Tell me something."

"Okay," he said, bracing himself.

"I can't imagine ever taking all of this for granted. But I can't help wondering. Does it ever get old?"

"What? The scenery?"

"It's not just scenery. The lake. The mountains. Trees and flowers. Meadows. Everything."

"It never gets old, but I guess you get used to it. Every once in a while it's good to have a reminder of what's around you. See it all through someone else's eyes."

"That's what I figured."

Why did he have the feeling that he'd somehow let her down? And why should it matter if he did? He could see that she was brooding, and this time he couldn't stop himself.

"You okay?"

"Peachy."

Yeah, he could tell. But if she didn't want to talk about it… "Ty tells me you're going to give him pointers on using the bow and arrow."

"Yes. We have a bargain."

"Oh?" He couldn't wait to hear the terms of this deal.

"I'm going to work with him to improve his archery skills and he's going to teach me about horses."

There was a clue about her. "So, you've never been around horses?"

"No." Eyes narrowed, she met his gaze. "Do you have a problem with that?"

"Why should I? Lots of people don't know the first thing about horses."

"That's not what I meant and you know it." She huffed out a breath. "I was talking about the bargain with your son. Do you mind if I work with Ty? It seems important to him."

"I have no objection." He paused a moment, then said, "Where did you pick up archery skills?"

She stared at him for several moments, looking injured and insulted at the same time. For the life of him, he couldn't figure out what he'd done to tick her off.

Finally she said, "I'm not who you think I am."

"And who do you think I think you are?"

"A stray."

The light was beginning to dawn. "So you heard you're in what everyone calls the 'stray cabin.'"

"Yes. And it has to be said that I'm not some down-on-her-luck loser. Unless you're talking about my choice in men."

"Okay. But from my perspective, you showed up in a wedding dress, driving a truck that's seen better days and jumped at that Help Wanted sign in the diner window. Seems like a no-brainer that you needed a job."

"You ever heard the saying about judging a book by its cover?" She faced him squarely, hands on hips, agitation making her eyes shine and a muscle jerk in her delicate jaw.

His fingers itched to cup her cheek in his hand, turn her face up to his and smooth out the tension in her jaw. He'd known talking to her was a bad idea, and there was no satisfaction in being right.

"Yeah. I've heard the saying. And I'll take your word for it that what you're telling me is true." He started to turn away. "Night, Kate."

"Just a minute. I'm not finished." She put a hand on his arm to stop him.

Cabot felt the heat of her fingers clear through to his gut. It got his attention in all the wrong ways and all the right places. "Okay. What else have you got?"

"I jumped at this job because I needed a time-out from my life. I wanted time to process what happened. How things went so badly. Get my head on straight and be able to do that in private."

They were standing so close that he could feel the heat of her body and smell the sweet floral scent of her skin. The combination smoldered inside him and he wanted to *feel* her everywhere. He needed to get away *now.*

"All right, Kate. If you say that's all there is to it, then I'll go with that."

Again he started to turn away and she stopped him. "I get that you have no proof what I'm saying is the truth. It's just words. So, donate my paycheck to the three-legged dog of your choice. Better yet, give it to your favorite charity. Wait—I know." She pointed at him. "Build another stray cabin with it. Makes no difference to me."

Cabot's willpower had been forged through crisis and disaster. In the years since his wife had walked out, he'd learned when to take someone on and when to walk away. It was all about survival. And right now his head was telling him to hit the road as fast as he could. The problem was other parts of him were telling him something else.

His self-control couldn't stand up to the force that was Kate. It felt as if he would burn up and blow away if he didn't kiss her. So he did the only thing he could.

He pulled her against him and lowered his mouth to hers.

Chapter 5

Kate tasted surprise and irritation on his lips and completely understood what he was feeling. It went double for her, along with the perversely conflicted inclination to stay like this for a good long time.

Then the full effect of it hit her like a meteor suddenly slamming into Earth. She'd never expected to feel that kind of power just from kissing a man. His mouth was soft and warm, chasing away the mild coolness of the beautiful summer evening. He brushed his fingers over her neck, scattering tingles through her body like sparks from a campfire and just as potentially dangerous.

Telling him to stop never crossed her mind. She realized that from the first moment she'd seen him, this was what she'd been hoping for. And maybe, just maybe, this was what it felt like to be swept away.

She slid her hands over his solid chest, linked her

wrists around his neck and toyed with his hair. Maybe that was some kind of a signal because he traced the seam of her lips with his tongue, and when she opened for him, he entered her. He explored and caressed the sensitive interior of her mouth, making her want to feel his touch everywhere.

Her breasts pressed against his chest and seemed to swell in anticipation of more intimate pleasure to come. Raising on tiptoe to meet his mouth more firmly, she couldn't seem to get close enough. The sound of his harsh breathing combined with hers and drowned out the chirping crickets.

He kissed her mouth, her neck, her cheek and gently nipped her earlobe, sending more tingles zinging over her arms and down her spine. Her pulse raced and her blood simmered and sizzled in her veins.

His mouth began the sensuous task of reversing the path he'd just blazed when childish laughter echoed from one of the nearby cabins. Cabot froze for several seconds, then moved his lips away from hers.

"Damn—" His voice was ragged and full of self-censure.

"What?" she managed to ask. "Is something wrong? I don't get—"

He dropped his hands from her waist and stepped back, giving the night air space to come between their bodies and cool the heat they'd just generated. "This was a bad idea."

Define "bad idea," Kate thought. She'd only recently refused to go through with her wedding. But fighting the moonlight was more than she could manage. She was breathless from the feel of his mouth. Most of all she was deeply missing his body so close to hers and the feel of his lips taking her somewhere she'd never been before.

Bad idea? The words finally penetrated the sensuous haze fogging up her head and she wanted clarification. "What do you mean it was a bad idea?"

"This is all my fault. I take full responsibility."

He was making it sound as if kissing her was wrong. It sure hadn't felt wrong to her.

"I agree that you started it," she said. "But if a line was crossed, I think a case could be made for sharing accountability equally. But I'm not seeing the problem here."

"I wish I wasn't seeing it," he muttered.

"So, enlighten me."

Cabot dragged his fingers through his hair and she felt a great deal of satisfaction in the fact that his hand was shaking. "For starters, two weeks ago you ran out on your wedding."

"Yeah." That had just crossed her mind, too. And something else. She'd never felt like this when "the jerk" had kissed her. Proof that she'd never been in love with him. And, although she didn't really want to focus on this aspect right now, it was also proof that her judgment in men was questionable. "What's your point?"

"When a woman tells you she's taking a time-out, a break to get her head on straight, it crosses a *bad* line to kiss her. That wasn't smart of me."

She disagreed, and every sensually deprived nerve ending in her body was protesting, too. In spite of the intensity tightening his features, or maybe because of it, she felt compelled to argue.

"Sometimes a kiss has nothing to do with IQ or rational thought and everything to do with pure instinct."

"I'm not going to do this with you. Nothing good can

come of debating the pros and cons of what just happened. And I say that because there's something more important going on here."

Admittedly her thought-processing mechanism was scrambled at the moment, but she couldn't think of anything that trumped chemistry and attraction. "I'll bite. Why are we making a federal case out of this?"

He angled his head toward the cabins. "What if any of the kids wandered down here and saw us?"

"They're not supposed to do that without a counselor present."

"Right. And kids have never broken rules before." His tone dripped sarcasm. "Parents entrusted their children to me and it would be a violation of that trust if one of their kids came across me kissing one of the counselors. An employee," he added.

"I see where you're coming from," she admitted. "But witnessing a kiss between a man and woman who are both single would hardly scar a child for life. Although, darn it, you do have a point."

"I'm glad you understand because it's not a chance I'm willing to take." He moved another step away from her. "I'm sorry, Kate. As you said, I started it. My fault entirely. And I promise you that it will never happen again."

Maybe just one more time, she thought. An experiment to see whether or not she'd really been swept away or just treading water.

But he turned and walked back the way he'd come, and the sight of his retreating back proved the wisdom of "show, don't tell" when making a point. He could stand there and say until hell wouldn't have it that the kiss was wrong and would never happen again, but leaving her in the dust said loud and clear that he took that pledge seriously.

How much of his action was motivated by sense of duty? How much was provoked by his sense of violated trust because his wife had broken her word to stay? And how much was prompted by the reality that he might still be in love with her?

Kate would probably never know the answers to those questions because Cabot Dixon impressed her as the sort who would maintain his distance because he always kept his promises.

In a man, that was both a blessing and a curse. And that frustrated her.

This wasn't Kate's first time sitting around a campfire, but it had never been part of her job before. Tonight they were bidding farewell to the kids who were staying for only a week. Others would be with them for another seven days and some were staying all summer.

The circular fire pit was made up of well-charred cinder blocks from past send-offs. It was located in an open area away from trees, shrubs and structures and not far from the lake, which offered them a view of the moon shining on the water.

Gotta watch out for that moonlight, she reminded herself. It could make a person do crazy things, like kiss a cowboy.

Kate was relieved that she wasn't leaving the camp until the end of the summer. But for the boys and girls who were going home, she felt a little sad.

Adults and children would sit around the fire on logs permanently placed there along with folding chairs that could be moved around as needed. The group had finished a final meal of salad, sloppy joes and chips, then filed out of the dining room and down to the fire pit. Two little girls, blonde Emily and dark-haired Hannah, had moved beside her and each grabbed one of her hands.

Kate was surprised. She'd interacted with all the kids and was friendly but firm. No one had been clingy until now. Probably that was a sign they were sad to leave.

"Hey, Em. Hannah." She smiled at the girls, who were ten and eleven, respectively. "How was dinner?"

"Good," they both said.

"I can't wait for s'mores." Emily skipped along, always full of energy until lights-out.

Hannah, tiny for her age, moved her short legs as fast as she could to keep up. "I just want a toasted marshmallow. Gooey and sticky. The boys usually just let them catch on fire."

"Ew," Kate said. "That's like eating ashes."

"Oh, they don't eat them," Emily explained. "It's the only way they're allowed to play with fire."

"I guess that's the way boys are," Kate agreed.

But Cabot was a man, and she figured cowboys had a different way of playing with fire.

The moon overhead was a reminder of Cabot starting a fire inside her. She hadn't seen him since he'd kissed her by the lake; the residual embers from that searing kiss refused to go out.

"I wish this wasn't my last night." Hannah's voice was wistful.

"Me, too. Next year I want to stay longer," her pony-tailed friend agreed. "I'm going to miss you, Hannah."

"Where do you live?" They reached the fire-pit area, and Kate looked around for two seats together for the girls. "Close enough to visit?"

"No." Emily shook her head. "I live in Dallas and Hannah is from Seattle."

"That's too far for a sleepover," Kate admitted. "You could exchange email addresses and phone numbers and keep in touch."

"That's what we decided," Hannah told her. She pointed to an empty space on one of the logs. "Why don't you sit between us over there?"

"Maybe after s'mores," she said. "I have to be up and around to help anyone who might need it. You girls go ahead and sit. Save me a place if you can."

The fire was already a healthy blaze, snapping and popping, bathing the area in a golden glow as it kept the shadows at bay around the circle. A quick glance told her all the campers were gathered around, although she didn't see Tyler. She'd noticed during the week that he wasn't always there for meals with the other kids. He could come and go; his presence or absence likely was based on his father's work schedule.

Caroline had a cardboard box containing metal skewers, graham crackers, chocolate squares and marshmallows. She was going to supervise making s'mores and was probably packing a fire extinguisher for anyone who decided to play with fire. Kate and the other counselors were going to handle simple roasting.

She'd thought kids plus fire would equal chaos and had stressed about keeping the campers safe and happy. But the activity was completely organized. The counselors knew what they were doing. On the first day everyone had been divided into groups, and tonight the kids waited for their color to be called before taking a turn at roasting a marshmallow or putting together s'mores.

She assisted a boy in getting his marshmallow firmly on the skewer, then managed to convince him it was beautifully toasted before it went up in flames. S'mores she left to Caroline and the other adults experienced in that process.

The last group was almost taken care of when she heard her name called. She turned and saw Ty running toward her.

He stopped, nearly out of breath, and said, "Hi."

"Hey. Where were you? I didn't see you at dinner and worried you wouldn't get a chance to say goodbye to the kids."

"Dad took me to town and we went to the Grizzly Bear Diner. I needed new shoes and this was the only time he could take me. Mine are too small." He looked down at the old, ratty sneakers. "But he wouldn't let me wear the new ones tonight."

"I don't blame him. It's pretty dusty out here."

He looked up, his big eyes full of childish innocence and wonder about why that mattered. "They're just gonna get dirty tomorrow."

She laughed and ruffled his hair. "I guess it's just a dad thing that he'd like them to stay new for at least twenty-four hours."

"Guess so."

"Don't you want a s'more?" she asked.

"Nah. I had a Grizzly Bear burger and I'm stuffed."

"Maybe later," she suggested.

After everyone who wanted a s'more had been taken care of, Hannah and Emily ran over to her and grabbed her hands with their still-sticky fingers. Their freckled faces were streaked with chocolate. "Come sit with us now," they both pleaded.

She looked at the little boy. "Let's make room for Ty."

"Okay." Hannah grabbed his hand. "Come on."

So the four of them sat together on the log and somehow Ty ended up next to her on one side, with Emily on the other. Hannah sat beside the little boy. When they were settled, Kate glanced up and saw Cabot on the other side of the pit watching her. Just like that it wasn't the fire making her warm, but more memories of the man who'd held her close.

That night had been chilly and clear, just like it was now. But with the fire throwing so much light, the stars were hard to see, unlike when she'd been in Cabot's arms. That setting couldn't have been more romantic if it had been created for a Hollywood movie.

Her pulse was hammering now just like it had then. Her breasts tingled, remembering the feeling of being held close and tight to his wide chest. It was disconcerting to realize she'd never reacted so strongly to a man's kiss before. And the glaring intensity in his expression right now was a clue that he'd felt something, too, and wasn't any happier about it than she was.

"Okay, kids, it's time for awards." Jim Shields, the tall, good-looking chief counselor, was standing by the pit in the center of the area. "First is Red Group, the overall winner of the Color War."

The kids in that group cheered and high-fived, then lined up to receive a ribbon.

"Greens, you came in first for water sports."

Another round of applause went up as the children got in line to receive their first-place prizes.

"Next is yellow for arts and crafts. This is probably the most artistically talented group of campers I've ever had the pleasure of working with."

Everyone clapped and cheered the artistic accomplishments of the yellow group. They were a little quieter than the others but no less pleased. Kate realized that no child would leave camp without an acknowledgment of their skill and participation in whatever activity they'd chosen. No one would be made to feel insecure or less than anyone else.

"Last, but certainly not least, we have the blues. And it's not about being sad that you're going home tomorrow." That got a laugh. "This group has excelled in animal care. The horses, cows, goats, lambs, dogs and cats are really going to miss you guys. Come on up."

After the children had taken their ribbons and found a seat again, Jim looked around at everyone sitting on the logs or in chairs. "This year we decided to give out a new and special award for our newest counselor. Kate, come on up."

She wasn't unaccustomed to being in the spotlight or under public pressure, but not with a man looking on whom she'd kissed in the moonlight a couple of nights ago. It didn't help that this man was also her boss.

She shook her head, trying to decline, but someone who might have been Caroline started a chant. "Kate! Kate! Kate!"

Sighing, she stood and walked over to the chief counselor. "I don't deserve an award."

"Wait until you hear what it is." He grinned, then looked out at the gathering. "Kate takes first place in the klutziest-counselor category. For tripping over the soccer ball instead of kicking it."

Her knees were still skinned from that humiliating episode. "Not my finest hour."

"Also for trying to do a header at soccer practice and almost knocking herself out."

"Soccer is not my best sport," she admitted.

"Neither is basketball—" Laughing and hooting erupted as the kids called out teasing comments. "Enough said on that."

"No one is perfect."

"This award is also for being a good sport about it all. And doing your best even though it wasn't pretty."

"Thanks." She took her ribbon, and for some reason her gaze drifted to Cabot.

His mouth was pulled tight and hard, but she remembered his lips being soft and arousing. He was either recalling their kiss or planning on terminating her employment for lack of ball skills. At least she was good for the kids' self-esteem. She'd made them all look good because she was so bad.

When she went back to her seat, Emily and Ty made room for her. She noticed that the ribbon said Number One Goofball and she laughed. Her Olympic teammates would think this was hilarious.

"My parents would be so proud," she said.

"Really?" Ty looked up at her, eyes wide.

"They'd think it's funny. I do, too," she told him.

"I'm not sure what my dad would think." He glanced over at the man on the other side of the circle, standing a little off to himself.

"I think all you have to do is your best and he'll be proud of you." Right now all he looked was wary.

"I'm not so sure," Ty said.

"Why do you say that?"

The small shoulders lifted in a shrug. "I guess maybe I'm not doing my best at some stuff."

"Like what?" she asked.

"Well…" He thought for a moment. "He tells me not to mope when the kids leave every week. That some stay on for a little longer, but sooner or later they all have to go. And I try not to be sad, but I guess I can't help it."

"I suppose it's pretty hard not to be," she said, giving

him a quick hug. "But did you ever think about the fact that when you're sad, that makes your dad feel bad?"

"I guess I never did think about that." He looked thoughtful. "But I like it when all the kids come in the summer."

"It's great for them, too. A chance to see what it's like to live on a ranch." She tapped his nose gently. "And there's stuff to keep you busy while you're out of school and your dad is working and can't spend time with you."

"Yeah." He nodded.

"The experience is sort of like life," she said. "People come into our lives for a short time and we learn that we'll go on and be fine without them."

"Kind of like what happened with my mom."

"Exactly." When Kate answered, she forced a cheerful note into her voice that was the opposite of what she felt.

She could have smacked herself for reminding him about that. When she looked over at Cabot, he was still watching—and frowning. It dawned on her that this reaction could be about his son seeking her out and sitting by her. Talking to her.

He was standing guard over his child. And good for him. Cabot knew she wasn't staying after the summer any more than these campers were, and he was afraid Ty was getting attached to her. She wouldn't like and respect him nearly so much if he didn't give a flying fig about his son.

She sympathized with Cabot and his concerns. If anyone knew how it felt to make friends and then lose them, it was her. And she'd had to learn to work it out. That was part of growing up.

But it didn't feel right to push this vulnerable little boy away. Plus, she'd made a deal with him to work at improving his skills with a bow and arrow. Cabot wasn't the only one who took promises seriously. That meant spending a little more time with him than she normally would.

All she could do was try to protect this boy, too. Remind him that when summer was over, like the kids who came to camp, she would be leaving, too.

She had a life waiting for her and it wasn't here.

Chapter 6

No matter how hard he tried, Cabot just could not get the picture of his son talking to Kate out of his mind because the two of them made a really nice picture. She seemed good with Ty—and he clearly ate up the attention. The problem was Cabot knew how it felt when someone stole your heart, then left it behind. He didn't want the boy he loved more than life itself to hurt that badly at such a tender age.

Cabot wasn't stupid. He knew sooner or later the kid would get his feelings stomped on. It happened to everyone. But if it was up to him, that would happen later rather than sooner.

"This is the barn." Speaking of the devil, he could hear Ty now.

It was late afternoon and Cabot was standing in the barn rubbing down his horse after a long workday. The jet-black pony was tired and hungry and Cab knew just how he felt. He'd take Ty up to the house for dinner and some quality father-son time. They didn't get enough of it.

"These are the stalls. Don't be scared," Ty said, coming into view where the gate was open wide.

And right behind him was Kate.

Cabot's pulse jumped at the sight of her and that was damned annoying. She was all tanned arms, big green eyes and sun-streaked brown hair. In her purple Camp Dixon T-shirt, ponytail and no makeup, she hardly looked older than the kids he paid her to supervise.

"Hi, Dad. I didn't know you were here."

"Hey, son." Would the kid have brought her here if he'd known? "I finished up early."

"Hello, Cabot." Kate stuck her hands in the pockets of her jeans. "I had a break and Ty offered to help me get over my fear of horses."

"It's not her best event, Dad."

"I see." Kind of an unusual way to phrase it, he thought.

But Cabot didn't put too much time into analyzing that. He was dealing with a fatherly pang over how grown-up the boy sounded—protective. The way a guy should be with women. His dad had drilled it into him that men were bigger and stronger. Along with that came a responsibility to look out for anyone smaller and weaker. He was trying to instill the lesson into his own son, and it looked as if the message was taking.

"I hope I'm not intruding," she said.

"Nope. This is a good time," he told her.

Ty moved into the stall beside the horse. "This is Blackie."

Kate's mouth quirked up at the corners. "I wonder why."

"Because he's black—" Ty saw her expression and grinned. "You were teasing."

"I definitely was," she confirmed.

Cabot continued to drag the stiff-bristled brush over the horse's flank. "This is a real good time to get acquainted. He's tired out from working all day. In the morning after a good night's sleep, he's frisky and full of energy. Not as quiet as he is now."

Kate was staying by the stall's opening, deliberately not moving closer. Apprehension darkened her eyes nearly to brown and tightened her mouth. "But he'd still be as big."

"Blackie's just a little guy," Ty told her. "Dad likes to ride him on the line 'cause he's fast and has quick moves if any of the cattle take it into their head to make a run for it."

Cabot hid a smile at the way the boy repeated to her what he'd been told. Good to know he was actually listening when his old man said something. Sometimes he wondered. "It's a cowboy's job to be smarter than the animals, to anticipate their moves and be ready to counter."

"Come over and touch him, Kate," Ty urged. "Don't be afraid. Blackie won't hurt you."

"He's right," Cabot told her. "This pony is as gentle and sweet as they come. I won't let him get out of line with you."

Ty met his father's gaze, then looked at the woman hanging back, and a gleam stole into his dark eyes. "Dad, I just remembered something I forgot to do."

Without further explanation, the boy turned and ran past Kate and out of the barn before Cabot could say "hold your horses."

He glanced at where his son had disappeared, then at her. "I apologize for him. Can't imagine what that was all about."

"Really?" Amusement danced in Kate's eyes. "You don't know?"

"Do *you?*"

"I have a pretty good idea."

"Care to share?" he asked.

"Of course. It's something I suspected at the campfire the other night, but his behavior just now confirmed my suspicions."

"Of what?"

"Tyler wants a mom. Like his friend C. J. Stone."

"Technically," Cabot told her, "C.J.'s mom got married and gave him a dad."

"So he's told me." She leaned a shoulder against the fence, still keeping her distance. "The point is, he wants the parent he doesn't have in order to get a complete set. And he seems to have picked me."

"Well, that's not good," he muttered.

"I'm going to try not to take offense at that." She gave him a saucy look. "And it has to be said that I'm not completely without maternal skills."

"That's not what I meant. It came out wrong." He rested his hand on Blackie's back. "Let me rephrase."

"I get it. My job is for the summer only. I'm here temporarily," she said for him. "Believe it or not, I actually agree with you. It's not good. No one, especially me, wants that child to be disappointed or hurt when his expectations aren't met."

"Amen," he agreed.

"But I'm pretty sure when he saw you here, he decided to play matchmaker and leave us alone. Let nature take its course, so to speak."

Cabot remembered the last time they were alone. Nature had taken its course all right. He'd kissed her. Surprised the heck out of himself when he'd done it and no matchmaking had been required. He'd chalked it up to the heat of the moment when she'd been giving him a piece of her mind. But she wasn't telling him off right this minute and he still wanted to kiss her.

The light wasn't all that good here in the barn, but he would swear her cheeks turned pink. He'd also swear she was remembering that moonlit night, too. He'd managed to pull together his self-control and walk away, but thinking about her all the time was taking a toll.

"So, you're saying that he's trying to push us together?"

"I think so, yes." She nudged the hay with the toe of her sneaker, not quite meeting his gaze. "Far be it from me to give fatherly advice, Cabot, but I hate the thought of Ty being hurt. I'd talk to him myself about why things with us can't be the way he wants, but it would be better coming from you."

He appreciated her sensitivity to his son and found himself admiring her straightforward manner. No games. No pretense. Just state the problem and a solution. Practical and appropriate.

"I agree. And I'll have a chat with him to explain."

"Good. That makes me feel a lot better." She smiled at him as if he'd hung the moon.

Cabot felt the pull of that smile clear down in his gut. He had a finely honed mistrust of women in general and this one in particular. In spite of that, being with her was like enjoying the first day of spring after a long, cold winter.

"Don't worry about Ty. He's tough."

"He's a charmer, that's for sure. You've got a terrific kid there."

"I know." Giving him that boy was the only thing he

was grateful to Ty's mother for. Other than that, she'd left a trail of emotional destruction in her wake.

"Speaking of kids… I should get back."

Her body language said she was going to bolt, but Cab wanted to hang out in her sunshine just a little longer. So he said the only thing he could think of to get her riled. "Coward."

"I'm sorry?"

"You're going to cut and run without getting close to this horse?" Now for the challenge. "What would Ty say?"

"Probably that I'm a coward." She shrugged. "I'm okay with that."

"Blackie will feel rejected."

"I'm okay with that, too."

"I'm really disappointed in you, Kate." He pointed at her. "And don't tell me you're okay with that. This is a working ranch and some of the camp kids want to spend time with the animals. Consider it part of your job description."

Her mouth pulled tight and she glared in his general direction, then finally nodded. "Feel free to check the 'uncooperative' box on my employee evaluation."

He didn't say anything, just watched her inch forward. Then she stopped, keeping him between her and the horse.

Cabot stepped aside. "If he wanted to, a horse can hurt you with his hooves and his teeth, so a side approach is pretty safe."

"Good to know."

"Just put your hand on his neck."

"What if he decides to bite?" She looked up at him nervously.

"He'd have to move his head and you'd have plenty of time to react," he assured her.

Her hand was shaking when she lifted it and he covered it with his own. Setting her palm on Blackie's long neck, he showed her how it was done.

"Just rub him, like you would a dog or cat."

"If he were that small, I wouldn't have a problem." But she didn't pull away as he gently moved her hand up and down the long neck.

"He's not really soft," she observed.

No, but *she* was, Cab thought. He'd settled his other hand at her waist and it took every ounce of his willpower not to explore the curves that were just inches away from his fingers.

"His coat is coarse." He heard the ragged edge in his voice. Blackie nickered softly, as if he sensed the reaction.

"Is he okay?" Kate asked, tensing.

"Fine. Just his way of letting you know that he likes it." Cabot couldn't see her face, but he could still feel her tension. "You doing okay?"

"Yeah. This isn't so bad."

Just as she said that, Blackie threw his head back and shifted to the side. Startled, Kate let out a squeak that was not quite a scream, then turned as if to run. Cabot's arms automatically went around her, pulling her close. At least he told himself it was automatic. Then he shifted, putting himself between her and the horse.

"You're okay," he crooned. "That wasn't a predatory move. He was just shifting his weight to be more comfortable. Like we do when we're standing."

In a reclining position, he could think of a lot they could do. And the warmth of her body, the softness of her pressed against him and the scent of her skin made him want that more than his next breath.

Kate clutched at him. "I'm sorry. It's just that was unexpected."

"I know. Don't worry about it," he said easily. "You'll get comfortable after a while."

"Yeah." She blew out a breath and snuggled just a fraction closer. "I'm sure that's true."

The same thing could be said about the two of them, Cabot thought. Spending time together could make him drop his guard and that was all kinds of bad. He put his hands on her arms and set her away from him.

"You okay?" he asked.

"Fine. Feeling a little silly," she said, "but fine."

"Good."

He was feeling silly, too, but for different reasons. It was stupid, but he wanted to kiss her, in spite of the fact that she worked for him and he'd made a promise to her that it would never happen again. Didn't take him but a couple of days to nearly break his word, and that was a big black mark on his integrity.

Kate must have seen something in his expression because she said, "I'm not being a coward, but Caroline might need some help in the kitchen. It's really time I get back to the job."

"Right."

She backed up toward the stall's open gate. "Thanks for trying to help me with my large-animal phobia."

"No problem."

"See you, Cabot." She turned and walked away, taking the feminine floral scent with her.

It had been on the tip of his tongue to say he would help her anytime, but he stopped those words from coming out of his mouth. She was here at the ranch for a paycheck. And his job was to work harder at not making another mistake with her.

Kate took her dinner tray out to the patio overlooking Blackwater Lake. The dining room was loud with excited kids chattering about the day and banging plates and glasses while they did. It was a kid-friendly environment and that was appropriate. But it was also crowded and there weren't any seats left. Outside only two seats were available, and she took one of them.

These children were the quieter, more artistic ones, so it was less noisy here. Peacefully beautiful. A strange feeling came over her…contentment. She hadn't felt it for a long time; possibly she never had, given her nomadic childhood.

She looked at the redheaded girl beside her. "Hi, Amanda."

After a shy smile the child said, "Hi."

"Are you enjoying your dinner?" She directed the question to the four children at the table—two boys and two girls.

"Chicken nuggets are my favorite." Dylan was a dark-haired, freckle-faced nine-year-old.

"Good." Again she glanced around, trying to draw all of them out. "How do you feel about carrot sticks?"

"I'd rather have ice cream." That was Ryder, a charming blond, blue-eyed heartbreaker in training.

"Me, too." Kate laughed. "But veggies are important."

"That's what my mom says." Lisa pushed her black-framed glasses up on her nose.

"Yeah, moms are like that." She took in the lake, mountains and trees and breathed deeply. "Don't you love it here?"

Before anyone could answer, the sound of two voices carried from the dining room behind her.

Caroline was saying, "It's about time you joined us to see how your summer-camp program is working out."

"I have good people running it for a reason. If there's a problem they can't handle, and by that I mean you, I'll hear about it." That deep voice definitely belonged to Cabot.

"That's a given. So what did we do to deserve a visit from you?"

"Just wanted to check on Tyler and see how he's doing with the other kids."

"And?" Caroline asked.

"He was so busy talking, he didn't even know I was there."

"That's the way it should be."

"I know."

"And now you're stuck eating dinner here." Caroline waited for a response.

"I wouldn't put it like that," he said.

"I would." Humor mixed with a dash of challenge was in the woman's voice. "Looks like the only seat left in the house is right there beside Kate. Enjoy your chicken nuggets."

"Thanks."

Kate held her breath and listened to the scuff of boots on the wooden deck as he approached. Then a shadow blocked out the light when he stopped beside her.

"I understand this seat isn't taken."

"It is now."

She looked up at him because it was the polite thing to do. With the waning sunlight behind him and the shadow of his black Stetson distorting his features, it was impossible to guess what was going through his mind. But his lips were pressed together and a muscle jerked in his jaw.

That was all it took to figure out that he wasn't happy about this forced proximity, either.

She slid over to make more room for him. "Kids, this is Mr. Dixon. He owns the ranch and the summer camp."

Then she introduced the four children by name and each of them said hello.

"Are you a cowboy?" Dylan asked.

"Yes."

"What do cowboys do?" Lisa wanted to know.

"Let's see…" He took a bite of one of the nuggets and chewed thoughtfully. "I help the other cowboys take care of cows. Make sure the herd stays together—it's safer for them that way. Move them somewhere else when the food supply is running out. Watch over the ones who are going to have babies and help if necessary."

"Is it hard?" Amanda's sky-blue eyes widened.

"Can be," he answered. "Animals need looking after three-hundred-sixty-five days a year. They don't take the summer off or Christmas vacation."

"But you get to ride a horse." Dylan clearly thought that made it the best job in the world.

"His horse's name is Blackie," Kate informed them. "Because he's black. I got to touch him."

Just then Cabot's arm brushed hers and sparks resulted as surely as if flint and steel had rubbed together. Not more than two hours ago he had held her in the barn; steadying hands had pulled her against him.

Kate was sure he'd been about to kiss her…and then he hadn't. She'd wanted him to, and the warmth of his body beside hers right now rekindled the wanting. Just because this wasn't the time or place didn't mean she'd get over the feeling anytime soon.

Cabot was watching her. "You're not eating."

That was because she could hardly breathe, let alone bite, chew and swallow. "I guess I'm not all that hungry."

An awkward silence stretched between the two adults as the kids made observations about cows, horses and what they wanted to be as grown-ups. Kate found that not talking was worse than carrying on a conversation with him. Every time either of them shifted even a fraction of an inch, their bodies touched. In the absence of any distraction, the contact was magnified and the reaction compounded.

She had to say something. "So, I've been reading up on Montana plant life."

"Oh?" He looked at her.

"Yes. I thought the bearberry was interesting. At first I thought it was the politically correct name for a bear's—you know."

"Yeah. I get it." Surprise, surprise. He actually smiled at that.

"Turns out I was wrong. Not only is it edible either raw or cooked, but also Native Americans added it to venison or salmon. They also dried it into cake and ate that with salmon eggs."

"Sounds tasty." Amusement sparkled in his eyes.

"Apparently it isn't all that tasty, but it can be useful as an emergency food if chicken nuggets aren't available."

"Good to know if I'm stuck in the wilderness."

"Speaking of that…" She realized he wasn't making this talking thing easy. But she was nothing if not determined. "If one ever does get stuck, fire is probably the number one tool of survival."

"I'm aware of that."

"It's useful to stay warm, cook food, sterilize if necessary and signal for help." She figured he knew all of this but wanted to let him know she wasn't without skills.

"That's what matches are for."

"What if they get wet?" she challenged. "Do you know nine ways to start a fire without them?"

"Do *you?*" Skepticism was written all over his face.

"Of course." She held up a hand and started to tick off the ways. "Friction-based using a fire board and spindle. The wood you choose is important. Cottonwood, juniper and walnut are best. You make a hand drill. Build a tinder nest with dry grass or twigs, put a V-shaped notch in the board and insert a stick, then start spinning." She held up another finger. "Flint and steel are obvious. Make sparks. Fire good."

"That's basic," he commented.

"Then there's the lens-based method." She thought this next one would get his attention. "Every little boy has melted his plastic action figures this way. You can use a magnifying glass, binocular lens or eyeglasses and let the sun reflect through it until your tinder ignites."

"Again, basic."

"You can also use a balloon. Or a condom," she added, dropping her voice so the children present couldn't hear. They were still chattering among themselves.

"You're joking."

She held up her hand. "I swear."

"How?"

"Fill it up with water—not too full or it will distort the sunlight's focal point. Make it as spherical as possible. You want to create a sharp circle of light, then hold it an inch or two from the kindling. The other one, not the balloon," she said, making sure the kids weren't listening, "you can try squeezing in the middle to form two smaller lenses."

"Is this your normal, run-of-the-mill party talk?" He looked both impressed and uncomfortable.

At least he was now participating in the exchange. "Actually, it is." When you were the public face of an outdoor-equipment brand, a girl needed to know what she was talking about. "I've used all nine techniques with success."

"I'd like to see that." He shook his head and actually laughed.

Kate felt as triumphant as if she'd won a national championship. Not only that, she thought he was more carefree and incredibly handsome with a smile on his face. "You should do that more often."

"What?"

"Smile. Laugh. It looks good on you," she said.

Just like that the laughter disappeared. He looked uncomfortable, as if he'd somehow broken an unspoken rule. "I don't know what to say to that."

"It was just an observation." But she was incredibly sorry she'd said it out loud.

He stood up, as if he couldn't get away from her fast enough. "Speaking of observing, I'm going to see what Ty is up to."

"Right. Of course. That's why you came to dinner in the first place."

"See you." He picked up his hardly touched food and walked away.

Kate sat there, her head spinning at how quickly her casual words had changed his attitude. Was he not supposed to have fun? Was it somehow against his code of honor? Maybe this was about the woman who'd walked out on him, some misplaced loyalty to vows taken, even though she'd broken them first.

Or he still had feelings for the mother of his son.

It was as if he'd forgotten any of that for just a few minutes with her, and then after he'd violated his personal code of honor, he couldn't get away from her fast enough. Her feelings wanted to be hurt, but in reality it was just as well he'd left.

She was here for a break from men as much as she was from the rest of the chaos that was her life. It made absolutely no sense on any planet for her to get involved with a handsome cowboy she would walk away from when summer was over.

Chapter 7

Just before lunch the next day, Ty asked Kate if it was
a good time to work on archery. The other kids were
busy with activities he'd chosen not to participate in.
She carved out a half hour for him right then, partly
because of her promise, but mostly because the vul-
nerability on his face tugged at her heart. She had no
idea why Ty was so determined to improve his skill,
but probably it had something to do with getting his father's attention to make him proud.

Hopefully Cabot had talked to the boy about the
fact that she and his father would never be a couple.
She and Ty were alone on the archery range, standing
at a line about ten feet from a bale of hay fitted with a
target. The boy had picked out the bow and a quiver of
arrows from the equipment shed. It seemed to be the
right size for him.

Kate stood at the line beside him. "The first thing you need to do is set your stance."

"Kind of like baseball when you're batting."

"If you say so." She smiled down at him. "It's pretty clear that I know very little about that sport. You could tell by the way I couldn't catch or throw the ball."

"You were kind of bad. Sorry," he said.

"Honesty is always best." She ruffled his hair. "If I wanted to and had time, practice would improve my baseball skills, although it will never be my best event."

"What is?"

Kate didn't want him to have information about her Olympic sport and share it with his father. It would be too easy for him to look her up on Google and find out that in some circles she was pretty recognizable. For now she wanted to be anonymous and enjoy the peace and quiet. Soon enough she would have to resume the craziness of her life but not yet. Vagueness was the way to go with his question, followed closely by a distraction.

"Like archery, my best event involves a target." Of course, the ones she aimed at were moving and made of clay. "Some of my friends were very good at it and taught me the basics. So, like I said, the first thing is your stance." She positioned him facing the target, leaving no time for more questions about her sport. "Put your feet shoulder-width apart with your weight evenly distributed."

"Like this?"

She checked him out. "Looks good. Now move your left foot back about six inches."

"Okay."

She nodded approval. "Next step is to grip your bow

with your thumb and index finger, then slide the notch of your arrow onto the bowstring. That's called 'nocking.'"

"Sounds weird." Ty looked up quizzically and squinted into the sun.

"It's just a fancy word for loading the arrow to point it at the target."

"Okay."

"Relax your fingers. The palm of your hand should never apply pressure. Think of it as hanging your bow on hooks on the wall and keeping it steady. Your other hand is going to do the hard work."

"Okay." He held it as instructed, then looked up. "Now what?"

"Lift your bow and point the arrow at the target. Keeping your hand as still as possible is the most important fundamental in shooting." Any kind of shooting, she thought.

When her father had first taken her shooting as a way to help her adjust after another move, he'd been surprised at how steady she was. And that had continued, but only in her event. Life was far less controllable.

An image of Cabot Dixon drifted into her mind along with the memory of sitting next to him at dinner last night. Her senses had soaked up the whole experience until he'd had the presence of mind to walk away.

"Kate?"

"Oh, sorry. Lost my concentration." *Steady as you go,* she reminded herself. She stood behind him and nudged his bow hand to align it with the target.

He tightened his fingers and the arrow fell off. Frustrated, he looked up and said, "That happens a lot."

"Because you're holding it too tightly. Relax." When he was ready again, she said, "Raise the bow and draw back the string. Then find your anchor point."

"What's that?"

"It's the place on your face where the hand is placed consistently with the bowstring at full draw and is most comfortable for you."

"How will I know where that is?" he asked.

"Practice. For now, put it by your jaw and we'll see what happens. You're all lined up with the target. Just keep loose and release the arrow with your fingers. Try not to move any other part of your body."

He did as instructed and the arrow fell short of the target. His body language screamed discouragement. "That happens a lot, too."

"Try again," she urged.

He did and the same thing happened. Kate checked his stance and finger position, then helped him pull back the bowstring a little farther. She made sure his fingers were loose, then directed him to release. It hit the hay bale just below the mark.

"Better," she praised.

"I still didn't get a bull's-eye."

"That takes practice, kiddo. This sport is different from baseball, where speed comes from your shoulder and accuracy is in follow-through with your arm. Archery is about focus, steadiness and aim. And how you set yourself up. How far you pull back the bowstring gives your arrow oomph, and follow-through is best when you can hold your position toward the target."

Ty continued to practice, and she helped him make adjustments until one of his arrows hit the target's outer ring.

"Did you see that?" His face glowed with excitement.

She grinned at him. "Excellent shot."

"Wow, I'm better already, thanks to you. I can't wait to tell C.J."

"He'll be very impressed," she agreed.

"Maybe I can show *him* how to do it."

"That would be great and would help you, too. But your dad or another adult should supervise," she suggested.

"I know. That's what he always says." Ty took another shot, and the bowstring snapped against his tender inner arm. "Ow."

"Let me see." She went down on one knee to check him and saw a small red mark but nothing serious. "That happens a lot. If you want to practice a lot, there's a guard you can get to protect you and keep it from hurting." She could see that his arms were shaking. It was time to call it quits. "I think that's enough for today. Why don't you pick up all the arrows?"

"Okay." He did as asked and put them back in the quiver, then returned to where she stood. "Next time C.J. comes over, could you supervise us?"

"That's up to your dad and Caroline. I might have things to do for the camp kids."

"I'll ask them," he said. "C.J. likes coming to my house to get away from his baby sister."

Kate laughed and started walking back toward the cabins. "She's annoying?"

"He says she cries a lot and is stinky." He shrugged. "I think she's kinda cute, but I don't tell him that."

Not macho, she thought. "What's her name?"

"Sophia Marie."

"Pretty name."

"I guess." He slung the bow over his shoulder. "Seems to me it would be cool to have a sister or brother."

"It has pros and cons," she commented.

"Do you have a sister?"

She nodded. "And a brother."

"Do you like them?"

"Yes." Although she'd heard her brother was a little peeved at her for taking his truck in her wedding escape. Pointing out that he also had a luxury car apparently hadn't appeased him, according to her mother. She'd asked her mom to tell Zach that she promised he would have it back by Christmas so he could get a tree, which, as far as she could tell, was his only reason for hanging on to the thing. "But brothers can be annoying, too."

"Well, I'd like one. Or a sister."

It was hard to know what to say because she was pretty sure that his dad was not on board with that. "Kids are a lot of responsibility, and your dad has a lot going on with you and the ranch."

"Do you like babies?"

The question didn't come completely out of the blue because the conversation was headed in this direction. Like she'd said at the beginning of his lesson, honesty was always best. "Yes. I think babies are cute, although I haven't had much experience with them."

"Do you want one?" His expression was hopeful.

Again she had to tell the truth. "Someday. When I fall in love and get married."

Ty stopped and looked up. "Do you like my dad?"

Oh, kiddo, she wanted to say. *Please don't make me break your heart.* Obviously Cabot hadn't talked to him yet about not trying to get them together.

She went down on one knee so their gazes were almost level. "Ty, I do like your father, but not in that way."

But he got serious points for being a spectacular kisser.

"What way?"

"Well, he's my boss." She thought for a moment. "And I think we're friends." Probably. Although the attraction was confusing. "The thing is, you have to remember that I'm only going to be here for the summer. When camp is over, I'll be leaving."

"Do you have to?"

Her heart was twisting in her chest. As gently as possible, she said, "Yes."

"Then can you help me practice archery a little bit every day so I can get better?" he asked.

"That would be great. And this seems to be a good time for it. We'll call it a standing date—unless," she cautioned, "Caroline has something for me to do."

"Cool." He sighed. "I sure hope that before you have to go, I can make archery my best event."

And she hoped that when she went, leaving this boy didn't break her heart.

Wearing a slicker in the rain, Cabot walked from the house down to the camp building where meals were served. He could never decide if this weather was more miserable in the summer or winter. Either way it was nasty. Because of it he'd assigned to the hired help only the chores that couldn't be put off and then instructed them to get inside ASAP. He was on his way to get a status report on how the campers and counselors were handling being cooped up inside.

It was about three o'clock when he walked into the empty dining room. Looking out the sliding glass door to the patio, his gaze was automatically drawn to the picnic table where he'd sat beside Kate. A reluctant smile curved the corners of his mouth as he remembered her explaining how to start a fire with a condom. The smile disappeared when he realized that putting Kate,

condoms and fire in the same thought was dangerous.
The problem was that he was having a devil of a time
getting her *out* of his thoughts.

"Damn it," he muttered.

He couldn't have just let her get back in that beat-up
old truck and keep on driving. Not him. The stray guru.
He had to go and hire her.

Shaking his head, he walked past the steam table
and stainless-steel counter where the kids lined up to
fill their plates buffet style. Behind this room was the
kitchen. In the back was a storeroom and small office,
which was where he found Caroline now, working at
the battered and scarred old desk. On top was a laptop
computer, upright file holder and a coffee mug with the
words *Camp Dixon* on it that held pens, pencils and a
bright yellow highlighter.

He stood in the doorway. "Hey, Caroline."

Dragging her gaze away from the computer screen,
she looked up, reading glasses resting low on her nose.
"Cabot, I hate this weather. And I'm pretty sure the
camp counselors are hating it even more than I am."

"Days like this make me wish my job was in an office."

"Then you'd have to wear a suit and tie." Blue eyes
took his measure.

"Yup." He almost never thought about what his life
might have been like if he hadn't been obligated to take
over the ranch responsibilities. But on days like today...
"Today it might be worth it. The rest of the time, probably not." He had begrudgingly taken over the ranch
and was a single father to Tyler, but he was the boss and
didn't have to ask anyone for permission to come and
go. "Guess every job has its pros and cons."

"Yes, they do." As the rain pounded on the roof, she

added, "We need to remember to be grateful for this drenching. Some parts of the country are in a terrible drought."

"True enough," he said.

He'd heard stories from his father and grandfather about hard times when the land was parched and grass for the cattle to graze on was scarce. Hopefully that wouldn't happen on his watch. Not that he could control it any more than he could control his damned attraction to Kate.

"Tomorrow when the sun is out, I'll be grateful. Today I really feel like complaining."

"Is the weather responsible for this mood?" Caroline removed her glasses and set them on the desk, topping a stack of file folders. "Or is it something else? Or *someone?*"

Whether or not that was the case, Cabot knew it was always best to let her say what was on her mind. "Why don't you share your theory about my disposition?"

"Clearly it's not PMS." Her tone was wry.

"Got that right." Probably things would be easier if that was his problem.

"Seriously, though, it seems to me that your grumpiness can be traced back to the day Kate arrived in town."

Cabot wasn't sure she was right about that, but he could put a finer point on the observation. He'd started to feel really jumpy after realizing Ty had ideas to push Kate his way. That wasn't going to happen; only bad could come of it. So far there hadn't been an opportunity to have a father-son chat about the situation, but he would make it happen soon.

"You're not completely wrong about that," he admitted.

The blonde leaned back in the chair as she studied him. "Do you like her?"

"What is this? High school?" He tried to make light of the question. "You've been hanging out with teenagers too long."

"Maybe. But unlike some people I could name, I'm not living under a rock. *And* I don't deflect questions that I'm uncomfortable answering."

He leaned a shoulder against the doorjamb. "Remind me to warn Ty not to try and put anything over on you when he lands in your class eight or nine years from now."

"That's the thing. Adults are just big kids. Human nature doesn't change even when maturity sets in. And your nature is all about turning your back on emotions."

"Okay. Now I forgot the question."

"No, you didn't. But I'll remind you anyway because now I'm even more curious. Do you like Kate?"

"Define 'like.'"

Her eyes narrowed. "Don't make me send you to the principal's office."

"Okay." He held up his hands in surrender. "Let's just say I've noticed that she's not hard on the eyes."

"I'll take that as a yes." She nodded, looking pleased. "It hasn't happened to you since your wife left, and that scares the crap out of you."

"Watch it, Caroline. I'm a guy. Nothing scares me."

"No," she agreed. "Unless you're talking about personal feelings and commitment. And who could blame you? The only thing more scary to a guy than talking about feelings is being solely responsible for an infant, the way you were when your wife left. I've got news for you, Cabot. If a woman has no experience with a baby, she's just as scared as you were with that little boy."

"What about the maternal instinct?" He'd often wondered what Ty was missing out on without having his mom.

"I'm not sure. I just know being scared isn't gender specific when it comes to babies."

"You?" He didn't believe she was afraid of anything.

"Oh, yeah. When Jake was born, I'd never held a newborn before, let alone been primarily responsible for keeping one alive." She shook her head ruefully at the memory. "And I had a husband to help. God bless Nolan. The night we brought our son home, the baby was crying. I was crying. Nolan told me to go to bed and he'd make sure the little guy was okay. And he did."

"Good man."

"No argument here. But you didn't have anyone when Jennifer walked out. And you had a ranch to run, not a nine-to-five job. No one can blame you for not ever wanting to be that vulnerable again."

"So, you're not going to tell me to get over it and take a chance? Get back up on the horse?"

"I'd be lying if I said I don't want to. Part of me does." She sighed. "But mostly I don't want to see you hurt like that ever again."

Cabot would second that motion. "Then why are we having this conversation about whether I like Kate?"

"Because I've seen the way you look at her. Ty, too. The Dixon men both have a crush on that runaway bride. That alone should make you take off in the other direction."

"So, you don't like her."

"I didn't say that." Caroline folded her arms over her chest. "I actually like her quite a bit. She's a hard worker. Funny. Very pretty. But—"

"What?"

"She's got secrets. And not about that jerk she left at the altar."

"And you know this—how?"

"When you've worked with teenagers as long as I have, you learn to spot that in a person. Not saying the secret is a bad thing. Or a good thing, for that matter. Just that she's hiding something. I wanted to give you my take on that."

"Okay. Consider it shared." He started to turn away, then remembered why he was here. "How are the kids? Rain can put a damper, no pun, on outdoor activities."

"Jim and his staff have it covered. They're showing videos, playing board games and doing crafts. Indoor stuff. The usual."

"At least they have an extra pair of hands with Kate here to fill in when someone needs a break."

"True—" She stopped. "Except, now that I think about it, she should be back by now."

"Where is she?"

"I sent her into Blackwater Lake with a short list of a few things I needed for the breakfast menu. But that was a couple of hours ago."

"Maybe she came back and is with the other counselors and the kids," he suggested.

Caroline shook her head. "She'd have dropped the groceries off here first. No. I hope nothing's wrong."

"Don't borrow trouble."

"Can't help it. I'm wired that way." She shrugged. "Just have a feeling."

"I'll go look for her."

"Thanks, Cabot. That would make me feel better."

"Don't mention it."

He left Caroline at her desk and trudged back up to the house, where his truck was parked. He got in out of the rain and, after fishing the keys out of his pocket, turned on the ignition. The engine roared to life and he backed out of the space, then headed slowly up the road. Worry nagged at him—partly for Kate's safety, but partly something else.

The first thing he'd learned about her was that she'd run away. Caroline had just reminded him about that. It crossed his mind that she might have run out now, and the thought tied him in knots. That realization proved his control over this attraction thing wasn't nearly as tight as he'd wanted to believe.

Only one road could take him into town, so if she was stuck or out of gas, he couldn't miss her. Proving his point, a couple of miles from the ranch he spotted a lone figure walking toward him. A closer look told him it was Kate and she was soaked.

He stopped the truck beside her and hit the button to roll down his window. "Hop in."

She nodded and walked around the front of the vehicle. It was bad enough that she was shivering, which made him want to strip off her clothes and hold her close to warm her. But she was wearing a white T-shirt that might as well be invisible because it was wet and nearly transparent. Thank God she was wearing a bra, although he could make out the size and shape of her breasts.

He put the truck in Park and released his seat belt, then slipped off his slicker. When she was in the passenger seat, he said, "Put this on. It will help a little. I'll have you back to your cabin in ten minutes."

"O—okay." She slid her arms into the too-big coat and pulled it closed.

Everything that made his mouth water was covered,

but some sights you couldn't un-see or convince your-self that you didn't want to see more.

"What happened?" There was nothing the least bit gentle in his tone and he was really sorry about that.

"T—truck broke down halfway to town—" An at-tack of shivers stopped her. "No idea what's wrong with it. But do you realize there's not a lot of traffic on this road?"

"Yeah."

"I forgot my cell phone. So I finally decided to walk."

"Now you're soaked to the skin." He burned all over just from saying the word. "You should have stayed in the truck."

"I did that, but clearly there's no traffic on this road. I finally decided to walk back for help because I thought Caroline might need the things on the list."

"She can work around them," he snapped. "No one's going to starve."

"I don't know why you're so crabby."

Worry did that to a man. And she wasn't the first female that day to wonder about his mood. "Let's just call it PMS."

"Oo-kay."

At least that shut her up for the rest of the drive. When they got back to the ranch, he drove her straight to her cabin. "Get dry clothes on."

"Really? You think I require an order for that?" She shot him a look. "Because I look like I enjoy being soaked?"

No. Because he couldn't handle much more of know-ing that underneath the slicker he'd given her there was a wet T-shirt that clung to her breasts.

"You'll be more comfortable when I take you into

town to get that stuff for Caroline and arrange to have your truck fixed."

"Give me five minutes," she said and hopped out.

He blew out a long breath and rubbed the back of his neck. The quicker she put on dry clothes, the sooner he would stop thinking about getting her naked. Possibly he would even stop aching to touch her bare silky skin.

Maybe, but not likely.

Chapter 8

Cabot's crabby mood didn't improve on the way to Blackwater Lake. Kate had made several attempts at chitchat, but his one-word answers didn't invite conversation. It probably didn't help that she'd kept him waiting longer than five minutes. The lure of a hot shower had been a temptation she couldn't ignore. It was one thing to get soaking wet in the rain and quite another to do it under a hot spray. She'd been freezing, and that was the quickest way to warm up. Now her hair was pulled into a ponytail and she was wearing dry jeans with a camp T-shirt. No makeup. Because Cabot was driving her to town, she'd been tempted to put on mascara and lipstick, but there hadn't been time. He didn't look like a man who wanted to be kept waiting.

On the road they passed the sad truck. She had no idea why her brother had such an attachment to the thing, including naming it Angelica, but he was a man. Who knew why they made certain choices?

Case in point… She glanced over at Cabot. Why didn't he let one of the ranch hands drive her into town to pick up things for Caroline and take care of her dead truck? Clearly Cabot didn't want to be here, so why had he chosen to come?

Darned if Kate knew. She just wanted to take care of business and get back to the kids. They were much less complicated and a lot more fun.

"We're going to stop at McKnight's Auto Repair."

For groceries, she wanted to say. But he wasn't in the mood for jokes. She was in the mood to poke the bear just a little, though. "Aren't you going to tell me it's the best place in town?"

"It's the *only* place in town." He glanced over. "But Tom McKnight is honest and good at what he does. He taught his daughter, Sydney, everything she knows. Between the two of them, I don't think there's anything they can't fix."

"Is Sydney McKnight the son her parents never had?"

"Well, her mother died when she was born. And since she has two older brothers, I'd have to say no to the son thing."

Wow, she'd never known her mom. Kate couldn't imagine growing up without her own mother. The woman had been her anchor every time the family moved when the army reassigned her dad.

"Maybe she's competing with her brothers for her father's attention."

"Don't tell me. You were a shrink in your other life."

"No." At least she'd gotten him talking. "I'm just

wondering why a woman would choose a career working on cars."

"Family business."

Hmm. Apparently he wasn't the only one pressured into taking over. "Why didn't her brothers go to work in the garage?"

"Ben McKnight is an orthopedist who works at Mercy Medical Clinic. His brother, Alex, owns a construction company."

"So Sydney was forced into it." She looked at Cabot and saw a muscle in his jaw jerk.

"I can't picture Tom McKnight laying a guilt trip on any of his kids. He's salt of the earth and just wanted them to do whatever would make them happy." He met her gaze for a moment. "I also can't see Syd doing something she doesn't want to."

"You must know her pretty well."

"Yeah."

And they were back to one-word answers. In the silence, Kate's thoughts turned to the female mechanic and how *well* Cabot knew her. If Kate had to put a finer point on the feeling squeezing her chest, she would call it jealousy. That was stupid, so she decided not to define what she was feeling.

But she couldn't stop wondering. Caroline had said he discreetly dated, and Sydney was certainly handy. But, seriously, a female mechanic? Grease, dirt, engines? What kind of woman would want to...?

That was where she stopped herself. People could say the same thing about her and why she would want to take part in skeet-shooting competitions. The saying about glass houses and throwing stones came to mind.

And then they were driving down Main Street in the town of Blackwater Lake. Every time she saw it, the charm of the place pulled her in a little deeper. They passed the Grizzly Bear Diner. Beside it was Potter's Ice Cream Parlor and Tanya's Treasures, a souvenir and gift store. The Grocery Store came up on the left and again she felt as if the combination of businesses and residential areas made up a magical village surrounded by evergreen trees to protect it from encroaching civilization.

"There's McKnight's," Cabot said. "Just up ahead on the left."

As they got closer, Kate decided it looked pretty much like any other garage she'd ever seen—an office connected by an overhang to the work area, where vehicles were elevated on hydraulic lifts so the mechanic could easily look underneath. A tow truck took up a parking space and sported the business name and phone number on the side door. The building was white with royal-blue trim, and a sign visible from the street declared in bold black letters McKnight's Auto Repair.

The rain hadn't stopped, so Cabot pulled up and stopped beneath the overhang outside the office. "I'll introduce you."

"Okay."

As she slid out of his truck, a man somewhere in his late fifties walked out of the office. He was tall, handsome and distinguished looking with a full head of silver hair.

Cabot walked over to him, hand extended. "Hi, Tom. How are you?"

"Great. Good to see you, Cabot." His gaze settled on her.

"This is Kate Scott."

She smiled. "Nice to meet you, Mr. McKnight."

"Call me Tom." He was friendly and easygoing, and then something that looked a lot like recognition slid into his eyes. "Aren't you the runaway bride I heard about?"

Kate was relieved that he'd referenced her first day in town and not recognition for her accomplishments in the sporting world and her outdoor endorsements. "That depends on what you heard. If it was good, then I'm the one."

The older man laughed. "Nice to meet you."

"Kate had a problem with her truck," Cabot explained. "It died on the road from the ranch into town."

"Sorry to hear that," Tom said. "We'll get it towed in and have a look. See what we can do."

"I'd appreciate that. It's pretty old but has a lot of sentimental value." At least that was her guess. Why else would her brother hang on to it? He could easily afford a new truck to have around for the convenience of transporting stuff that wouldn't fit into his expensive sports car.

"If anyone can get it going, Syd can. That's my daughter," the older man explained.

The door behind him had opened and a young woman came out just in time to hear what he'd said. She had a bottle of water in her hand. "What can I do?"

This stunning woman was Sydney McKnight, girl mechanic? Kate had stereotyped her until this very second. She'd expected a bigger woman, someone less delicate. For several moments, she stared and sincerely hoped that her mouth hadn't dropped open.

"I was just saying you can fix pretty much any car— old, new and in-between."

"Thanks, Dad." She took a sip from her water. "Hey, Cabot. Haven't seen you for ages. How's Ty?"

"Great. No offense, Syd, but I'm glad I haven't seen you on a professional call."

Kate literally felt the tension drain from her body. If they hadn't seen each other for ages, that meant this beautiful woman wasn't dating him. They acted more like brother and sister. Either that or the two of them were very good liars, but she didn't believe that was the case.

"Who's this?" Sydney asked, looking at her.

Kate had a feeling she already knew. Still, she stuck out her hand. "Kate Scott, the infamous runaway bride."

"Nice to meet you." The other woman grinned and squeezed her fingers.

She was wearing a light blue shirt with the business logo and her name embroidered on it tucked into the waistband of navy work pants. Steel-toed boots completed the ensemble. Sydney made it look almost chic. She was petite and curvy with dark hair pulled into a ponytail. Wisps and curls had escaped to charmingly frame her delicate face and make her big brown eyes look even bigger. They were snapping with intelligence and curiosity.

"Nice to see you, Syd." Cabot started toward the office. "If it's all right with you, Tom, I'd like to get the paperwork going on Kate's truck."

"We'll get it taken care of," the older man said to her.

"Thanks." She started to follow him into the office.

"Got this covered," Cabot told her.

"But it's my responsibility to take care of it."

"Stay here and talk to Syd."

"I'd like that. After I make arrangements for the truck. Cabot?"

The men had disappeared inside. Her words had not slowed them down.

"You just got the equivalent of don't-worry-your-pretty-little-head." Sydney was amused.

"I noticed. You know, sometimes it's annoying," Kate observed. "But with cars and bugs and a few other things, not so much. Men can be handy to have around."

"I know what you mean." Sydney sized her up. "So, was it those other things or the annoying part that made you run out on the wedding?"

"I guess there's no point in expecting that the run-away-bride label will ever be forgotten here in Blackwater Lake?"

"Not likely. I'm pretty sure the story will take on legend status in the annals of Blackwater Lake folklore." Sydney's gaze was penetrating. "Why did you run?"

"He was a cheating weasel. I walked in on him kissing one of my bridesmaids at the church on the day of."

Anger mixed with understanding in the other woman's eyes and turned them a darker shade of brown. "Why do the backstabbing bastards steal from our pool of friends? Why can't they just go swimming with a perfect stranger?"

"Is that a rhetorical question?"

Syd looked thoughtful for a moment, then nodded solemnly. "Yes."

"It happened to you, too, didn't it?"

The other woman shrugged. "Even Blackwater Lake has its share of jerks."

An understanding expression in Sydney McKnight's eyes convinced Kate she'd been through a similar experience.

"Whoever he is, I hope he rots in hell," Kate said vehemently.

"If only." Her mouth pulled tight for a moment before letting go of the bad memory. "Have you met many people in town yet?"

"No. I've been busy." *And reverting to the learned*

childhood behavior of not getting close to anyone because I won't be staying.

Sydney tapped her lip, studying her. "You look really familiar. Have you ever been to Blackwater Lake before?"

Kate shook her head. It could be that the other woman had seen her in a magazine or TV ad. She was, after all, the face of a well-known outdoor-equipment company. But if the cat wasn't out of the bag yet, she would like to keep it there for a little while longer. Not being recognized was a lovely change.

"I guess I just have one of those faces. Or, as they say, everyone has a twin." Kate shrugged.

"Maybe," Sydney said without much conviction. "The thing is, I'd like to get to know you better. We should have a girls' night out."

"Sounds good." And she meant that. It wasn't often you met someone and clicked, but she felt that with this woman. "The counselors at the summer camp rotate an evening off during the week."

"Dad and I do that, too. And since he started dating someone, I can't just ask him to cover for me."

"You think he'd mind, just one night?"

"No. He just doesn't know I know that he's got a woman. First one since my mom died."

Because she'd brought it up, Kate felt she could ask. "Cabot said you never knew your mother."

"That's right. She died giving birth to me." The emotion in her voice was no more than if she'd just said the sun was hot.

"It's all right, Kate. I never knew her. It's hard to mourn someone you didn't have a relationship with. Plus, it was a long time ago."

"Sorry." Kate hadn't been aware that her thoughts

showed so clearly on her face. Then it sank in that Syd was in her mid to late twenties and the picture came together. "You mean your dad hasn't gone out with a woman in all these years?"

"If he did, no one knew. And he's not covert-operations material, although he really believes he's covered his tracks this time and no one is the wiser." She grinned a little wickedly. "I'm curious about how long he can keep up the charade. When it's out, I can tell him how much I just want him to be happy."

"That's hilarious and sweet in equal parts." Kate grinned at her. "Men think they're so cool about this stuff."

"Or hot." Sydney's eyes narrowed. "So we're clear, now I'm talking about the way that handsome rancher looks at you."

"Cabot?" She could see him through the window at the service desk inside. "Either you're imagining that or it's because he's irritated with me."

"Anger and affection are flip sides of the same coin and touch somewhere in the middle."

"Did you get that out of a fortune cookie?" Kate teased.

"No. I think I heard it somewhere." Sydney grinned. "But, seriously, the sort of looks he was giving you could burn up the sheets."

Kate made light of the comments, but that didn't stop her from wondering. Since he'd apologized for kissing her, his vow not to do it again had been in jeopardy only that one time in the barn, when Ty had schemed to get the two of them alone. But that didn't stop her from hoping.

She really wanted another opportunity to see if she

was simply inventing the passion she'd felt in his kiss or if there was a real possibility of getting swept away.

"I really like Sydney McKnight." Kate hauled herself into the passenger seat of Cabot's truck, then slammed the door shut.

"She's good people." He put the key in the ignition and, unlike her vehicle, it roared to life.

The two of them had made arrangements for McKnight's Auto Repair to tow her truck from the side of the road to their shop. After they looked it over to diagnose the problem, she'd get a call about the estimate for repairs. Hopefully Angelica was fixable and parts for the old girl were available. Then she thought about how Cabot had described Sydney.

She's good people.

Kate had been curious about the female mechanic before meeting her and was even more interested now. How had he meant that? Sydney was a very pretty young woman, and if a guy liked cars, she would be a hot ticket. She would be even if a guy didn't like cars. Although Kate figured her boss as more of a horse guy, her female radar was shooting out signals like crazy. Signals that felt suspiciously like jealousy even though the two of them seemed nothing more than friends.

"How well do you know her?" Kate asked.

"I don't know." He checked traffic on Main Street, then pulled out of the lot and stopped at the signal. "She was born and raised here. So was I."

That was the opposite of helpful when what she wanted was details. Was there ever anything romantic between them? Like had they ever gone out? But she couldn't ask that.

And yet the words came out of her mouth. "So, did you two ever go out?"

The light changed and he accelerated. "No."

"Why not?" She wasn't going to let him out of answering that easily.

"I was friends with her brothers."

"Which would make her like a little sister."

"Yes."

He was going to have to stop being so stingy with details so she could find out what she wanted to know more quickly and efficiently. "Do you think she's pretty?"

"I've never given it much thought." He turned right into the grocery-store parking lot and found a space.

After sliding out of the truck, Kate fell into step beside him. "So, think about it now."

"Why?" He scowled at her. "You're like a dog with a favorite bone."

"I'm curious about your type."

"Given my lousy track record with women," he said grimly, "if I had a type and decided to be involved with someone, I'd look for the exact opposite."

"So you would ignore a woman you're attracted to and gravitate toward one you don't like?"

"Always a good rule."

Hmm. He was systematically and thoroughly ignoring *her,* so apparently that was a compliment.

He grabbed a grocery cart and rolled it past the glass doors that automatically opened for them. "You got that list Caroline gave you?"

"Yes. It's a little damp, but I think I can still read what she wrote."

They moved quickly through the store, grabbing pancake mix, syrup, cereal and a few other things. Fortunately the place stocked the large industrial sizes, but that was probably because ranches were in the area and the owners liked to buy in bulk. To stock up for emergencies, she'd been told, like getting snowed in.

At checkout the clerk scanned everything and gave Cabot a total, which he put on a credit card. When the items were bagged and in the cart, he wheeled it out to the truck, then put the bags in the rear seat while she got in the front. He stowed the cart so it wouldn't roll into another car, then slid into the driver's seat. After starting the engine, he looked over his shoulder to check for other vehicles. When the coast was clear, he backed out and headed for the exit.

"So, about Sydney—"

"You better be talking about Australia." His face wasn't visible because he was looking away to make sure there was a break in traffic, but his voice was full of irritation. "What's with you, anyway?"

"I'm curious. Sue me." She was enjoying this more than she should be. "She's an above-average-looking woman and you're not hard on the eyes. Just saying…"

"Just *stop* saying." He glared at her. "Syd is way too smart to hook up with me. Besides, she's had her own romantic disaster—"

"What happened to her?"

"No, you don't. I'm not getting sucked into gossip. Not spreading it."

"But where's the harm? I'm leaving at the end of summer."

"Doesn't matter. In the spirit of discretion and setting a good example, my answer is that if you want to know what happened to Sydney, you'll have to ask her."

"All right," she said. "I'll do that. We're going to get together soon. So there."

"Okay, then."

Kate was surprised when after driving a short way down Main he pulled into a parking space in front of Blackwater Lake Sporting Goods Warehouse. "Why are you stopping here?"

"I need a couple things. Might as well get them while we're in town." He looked at her. "You in a hurry to get back?"

"Caroline might need me."

"She'll call if she does." He ended the conversation by getting out of the truck.

"Okay, then." She followed him inside.

A friendly-looking middle-aged man stood at the cash register just inside the door. He glanced up from something he was reading when they walked in and smiled. "Hey, Cabot. Haven't seen you in a while."

"Nolan." He shook the other man's hand. "Been pretty busy."

"How's Ty?"

"Great. Getting big." He must have sensed her waiting for an introduction. "Nolan Daly, this is Kate Scott."

"You look familiar," he said, trying to place her.

"I guess I just have one of those faces." She shrugged, then changed the subject. "You're Caroline's husband. I really like working with her at the camp. It's very nice to meet you."

"Caro told me about you. How do you like it here in Blackwater Lake?" Like his wife, he used reading glasses and perched them on the end of his nose.

He didn't say anything about her being a runaway bride. Maybe it was possible to live that down. "It's a really nice place. I love the lake and mountains. I can truthfully say that I've never seen anywhere prettier."

"You traveled much?"

"Actually—" she met Cabot's gaze "—I have. All over the world. I'm an army brat, after all."

"You like what you're doing at the summer camp?"

She knew the store owner was really asking what she did for a living before running out on her wedding. Fortunately the phone rang and she didn't have to give him an answer.

Cabot looked at her. "I'll go grab what I need."

"Do you mind if I look around?"

"Suit yourself. Meet you back here in fifteen minutes."

She nodded and they parted ways. Kate headed to the women's outdoor-clothing section. She browsed through fleece jackets and knit shirts displayed on racks. One of the brands was a company she'd done some modeling for, lending the name of an Olympic medalist to their product.

"Cute," she said to herself, holding up a pink, long-sleeved V-neck shirt.

Next she looked through a rack of knit hats. If she were staying in Blackwater Lake for winter, she would need one, but not for California, unless she went skiing in the mountains.

They had a good selection of running and hiking shoes and boots. Warm socks were on display nearby. She didn't realize how much time had passed until she glanced at her watch.

"Uh-oh." She hurried back to the front, where Cabot was flipping through one of the outdoor magazines displayed in a wire rack by the cash register. All she could see was his profile, but as she moved closer, it looked as if his jaw was clenched.

He must have heard her approach and looked up. "See anything?"

"Why?" She thought there was something weird in his tone.

"I sure did." He held up the magazine. On the cover was a picture of her in a bikini, holding a fishing rod. "You're not who I thought you were."

Chapter 9

Cabot watched Kate's eyes narrow and knew some sassy words were coming his way. Oddly, he was looking forward to it.

"I told you I wasn't who you thought, but you insisted on believing what you wanted. I never lied to you about needing a break to get my life together."

"You also never gave me any details about the life you needed a break from."

Looking away for a moment, she pressed her lips together. "I had my reasons."

"It's about time you share them." He could almost feel Nolan behind them watching this unfold, listening to every word.

"Okay. The short version is that I've won several Olympic medals for skeet shooting. That led to product-endorsement contracts. In certain outdoor-enthusiast circles, I'm somewhat well-known."

"I knew you looked familiar." Both of them turned toward Nolan Daly, who was looking a little starstruck.

"You know her?" Cabot asked.

"Yes. Katrina Scott. Can't believe I didn't put the name and face together when we were introduced. Except the Kate part threw me off and maybe that picture of you on the magazine cover was a distraction."

Cabot knew what he meant. The photo of her in a bikini revealed curves that he'd only felt through her clothes. That was temptation enough, but putting that memory with the visual might be his undoing. "How do you know her?"

The man set his reading glasses beside the bagged merchandise on the counter. "I follow the major shooting competitions, and this young lady has quite the reputation. Second-youngest woman ever to medal when she was just a teenager. And she did it again at two more games."

Cabot met her gaze. "Impressive."

"Thank you."

Nolan reached over the counter and picked up one of the magazines from the display. "Miss Scott, would you mind signing this for me?"

"It's Kate, and I'd be happy to, Mr. Daly."

"Nolan, please. It's a real honor to meet you."

She smiled. "The pleasure is mine."

"Wait until I tell Caroline about this," he said. "She has no idea who you are. An Olympic medalist here in Blackwater Lake, right under our noses."

"I've really enjoyed the peace and quiet here."

Cabot heard the regret in her voice and noted her use of past tense. The peace and quiet would be over now that she'd been outed. She was an Olympic medalist, not an Academy Award–winning actress who could manufacture emotions. She was telling the truth. It wasn't his proudest moment when the realization hit that he'd wanted her to be a stray, someone who needed his help. Someone he'd never compromise with messy complications.

Now he couldn't hide behind that to resist her. He was his father's son; wanting Kate was proof that he did possess the Dixon DNA that predisposed him to be attracted to women who would leave.

"Well…" Cabot put the magazine away, then picked up his purchases off the counter. "We better be going."

"Nice to meet you, Kate."

Her smile looked a lot like the cover-girl one—it didn't reach her eyes. "Nice to meet you, too."

"Come in again."

Cabot put the bags in the backseat of the truck while Kate climbed inside. When everything was stowed, he got in beside her.

"Want to get a bite to eat before we go back?"

"Why?" It was a tie as to whether her tone or expression was more wary.

"Because you're hungry?"

"I can eat with the kids. And we have to get the groceries back to Caroline."

"There's nothing she needs tonight, and all of it is nonperishable." He turned the key in the ignition. "I'd like to talk to you."

Technically he didn't have to buy her a meal to do that. They'd had a number of conversations, one that had ended with a kiss, and there hadn't been food involved at all.

"What about Ty?" she asked.

He glanced at his watch. "He's getting picked up

right about now for a sleepover at C.J.'s. So, what do you say?"

"You're the boss." At least for now. She didn't say that out loud, but her tone clearly implied it.

He debated the pros and cons of going to the Grizzly Bear Diner. The two of them together would trigger talk, but that was going to happen anyway, what with this trip to town.

"What's wrong, Kate?"

"So many things, so little time." She glanced over at him. "Mostly it's about the fact that word about me will spread and everything will change. It was nice when I knew that someone liked me for me and not because I have a certain celebrity."

Cabot couldn't say that his feelings hadn't changed at all. He'd been attracted the first moment they'd met and still was. If only the truth had neutralized his interest in her.

After parking in the lot behind the diner, they went inside and were seated right away at a booth in the back. The place, decorated with pictures of bears on the walls, wasn't crowded yet. It was late for the lunch crowd and early for dinner. A waitress handed them menus, then said she'd give them a few minutes.

Kate's expression was guarded. "There's no reason for you to get angry and defensive."

He pushed the menu aside because he always ordered the same thing. "Who says I am?"

"Like I said before, I never lied to you."

"If anyone is defensive, it's you," he pointed out.

"I'm trying not to get fired."

"Clearly you really don't need the money, so why do you care?" He studied her, the bruised look and big eyes. "The cat is out of the bag. The word will be all over Blackwater Lake in a day. Two, tops. What difference does it make if folks know your story?"

"The difference is that the campers have no idea who I am and don't care. I forgot what it felt like to be judged on my work and not like someone who's been in the news." She met his gaze. "Don't get me wrong. I'm not complaining. I've been lucky and I'm not one of those people who gripe that the crown is too tight, the jewels too heavy. It took practice, dedication and sacrifice to achieve what I have. Also a lot of hard work. And luck. I'm grateful for everything. It's just that circumstances presented themselves and along came a chance to be anonymous."

"Circumstances? Meaning running out on a wedding?" He deliberately brought that up, trying to rekindle resentment and remind himself she was a runner. That should be enough to make him avoid her, but apparently he needed more.

"Yeah, the wedding that didn't happen." She opened the menu but didn't look at it. "He's a sports agent and contacted me after my repeat medal performance. I was a media darling and he convinced me to sign while I was hot."

Past tense? To Cabot's way of thinking, she was still hot, but that wasn't what she meant. "And?"

"He got me lucrative endorsement deals and magazine shoots. In the outdoor-equipment business I'm a spokesperson, and I'm well paid for it. He got a piece of that, but apparently it wasn't enough. The marriage would have given him financial security that his percentage didn't. But, also apparent to everyone but me, he was unwilling to give up the other women."

"I see." Creep, he thought. Her expression tugged at him. Was it anger, hurt or both?

"Cabot, there was bound to be media hype after I walked out on the wedding. I'd just seen him kissing someone I considered a friend. I was emotionally raw and just plain tired. Instinct made me run, but eventually it turned into an opportunity for the story to cool off and for me to get out of the fast lane for a while." Sincerity was all over her face. "Now I just want to finish what I started. Make it to the end of the summer with the kids. I love working with them."

"Okay." He believed her. "For the record, I never planned to fire you."

"Then why did you bring me here?" she asked, looking around the diner.

"So I can say that I'm the guy who bought you your first Grizzly Bear burger." He shrugged. "Claim to fame."

She laughed and nodded. "Okay, then."

It wasn't okay, but it was the best he could do. She was right. He didn't have to bring her here. After that kiss he'd been doing his best to avoid her and was at a loss as to why he'd invited her to dinner.

If he was being honest with himself, part of the reason was that he wanted to postpone taking her back to her cabin, then going into his empty house alone. The other part was a risk, pure and simple.

He couldn't shake his inconvenient and unwelcome attraction to her, and the avoidance strategy wasn't working. Maybe it would be better to confront the situation, go with it and get her out of his system once and for all.

After two glasses of wine at the Grizzly Bear Diner, Kate was rocking a little buzz as she rode back to the ranch in the passenger seat of Cabot's truck. She'd had a really nice time with him, which she hadn't expected. She'd figured he'd be tense and disapproving after finding out she wasn't a stray he needed to take under his wing, at least not financially. Emotionally was a different story.

He'd taken her in and given her refuge, a quiet place to nurse the bruises of public humiliation. She would always be grateful to him for that.

Word would spread in Blackwater Lake about who she was, and she didn't mind too much, proving that she was strong enough now to deal with the mess she'd left behind. When the summer was over, she would take care of that. For now, she was enjoying the heck out of being here and working with the kids. She wasn't looking forward to this pause coming to an end.

"So," she said, glancing over at him. "I had a much better time at the diner today than the day I first walked in."

"That was an interesting moment for Blackwater Lake." Just enough moon shone in the truck windows for her to make out his grin.

Desire hit her—sudden and irresistible. Without the chip on his shoulder, he'd been funny and charming, different from the guarded man she was accustomed to seeing. And she'd been attracted to that man with the chronic brooding expression, maybe because of it. But this guy who smiled and laughed, the one who spread around charm like butter on toast, really cranked up the fascination factor.

"It must be nice to go out and know everyone and they know you."

"It has pros and cons."

"Like what?" she asked.

"You don't always appreciate folks knowing your

business, but if you ever need a hand, it's usually not necessary to ask for it."

"I like that." Cozy and calm, she leaned her head against the high seat back. "Bad stuff happens, but it's probably a comfort to not feel alone when it does."

"Did you run because you felt alone?" She heard a rasp in his voice, just a hint that he might be a little irritated about what had happened to her.

"I didn't mean to sound pathetic. And my family is supportive, but sometimes protecting them means going it alone. Without anyone to share the burden."

"What did you think of the Mama Bear Burger?"

His question lightened the mood, as if he knew she was going to a pensive place and made a deliberate effort to pull her back from the edge. That was so nice. And sensitive.

"Please don't tell Caroline because she does amazing things with a ground-beef patty—"

"I hear a 'but.'"

She laughed. "*But* I've been to some gourmet hamburger places in L.A. and Las Vegas that were good. But that Mama Bear has to be one of the best I've ever had."

"I know you told Michelle that, but you can be honest with me. We're alone now."

Yes, they were, and it was best not to dwell on that too much.

Michelle had stopped by their booth tonight. She'd said it was customer service, to make sure everything was okay, but Kate was pretty sure the move had been motivated by curiosity. The woman hadn't laid eyes on her since the day Kate had walked in wearing a wedding gown and Cabot had hired her on the spot. Now they'd come in together for dinner. Who wouldn't want more information?

"This is the honest truth—it was a straight-up juicy, thick patty without sauces and distractions that mask the flavor. I loved it. And those big, fat fries are my favorite. Trust me on this—I know my potatoes. I'm a connoisseur."

"Ty likes the fries, too. And the Bear Cub chicken fingers."

"It's a very cute place. Great atmosphere. And quite a nice wine selection."

"It will be a while before he'll be able to have an opinion on that."

There was that devastating smile for the second time, and again she felt the difference in him. He was more relaxed, not pushing back against the natural give-and-take between them. Maybe she should have given him details about herself sooner. But he probably wouldn't have believed her.

Maybe he didn't care enough to look her name up on Google. Or maybe he cared too much.

Tingles danced through her, and she was pretty sure it had nothing to do with the wine. The sooner she got out of this truck, the better. He'd made it clear that there was a line between boss and employee that shouldn't be crossed. She didn't want to slip up and jeopardize this budding friendship.

"He's a great kid," she said. "You've done a wonderful job with him."

"I appreciate you saying so. It hasn't been easy—no two ways about that. But he is, without a doubt, the best thing that ever happened to me."

Kate wondered yet again how a woman could turn her back on her own baby. And walk away from a good man like Cabot Dixon. He was honest, hardworking and capable of deep feeling—not like anyone she'd ever met, and she figured it was doubtful she would run across his like again.

Just in the nick of time, before any of that could come out of her mouth, Cabot drove underneath the sign that said Dixon Ranch and Summer Camp.

The headlights picked out puddles still scattered over the dirt road from the earlier rainstorm. He pulled to a stop by the big house and turned off the engine. A lot had happened since her soaking earlier that day, and things felt different, a sign that she needed to get back to her cabin ASAP.

"Thanks for taking me into town and helping deal with my truck."

"Anytime."

"I'll grab those groceries and drop them by the kitchen on the way to my cabin."

But before she could open the truck's rear passenger door, Cabot was beside her. "Leave them."

"But Caroline needs the stuff for breakfast."

"I'll make sure she gets it." He moved close and his breath stirred wisps of hair around her face.

"Cabot, we shouldn't— You said—"

He touched a finger to her mouth, instantly stopping the flow of words. "I was wrong."

The softness of his voice did nothing to diminish the intensity of his tone. And then he kissed her.

Kate sighed and, in spite of her protest, relaxed against him. With his arms around her to cushion her, he backed her against the truck, making the contact of their bodies closer. They were a surprisingly good fit; it would only be better if they were horizontal.

He proceeded to kiss the breath out of her and didn't stop the resistance-shattering assault even as she moaned against his mouth. He traced her lips with his tongue, and she opened to him without hesitation. Boldly, he dipped inside and showed her what he would do if he made love to her.

Finally he came up for air, the sound of his heavy breathing harsh in the clear night air. "Kate, I want to take you upstairs to my bed—"

And she wanted badly to say yes, but...

Cupping her hand to his cheek, she felt the scrape of stubble on his jaw. Absurdly she thought how fast his beard had grown in the hours since he'd shaved that morning. It was sexy and stoked the heat of desire building inside her.

"Cabot," she finally managed to say, "this isn't smart."

"Probably not. But then, no one has ever accused me of being too smart." As he turned his mouth into her palm, the words caressed the sensitive skin.

She sucked in a breath. "I'm trying to be strong."

"It's not that I don't appreciate what you're saying, but right this minute I'd rather not talk."

"Are you sure you want to start something?"

"I'll tell you what I'm sure about. We're just a man and woman who want each other. Nothing more."

"Nothing less," she whispered. "Safe."

"Yes." He regarded her with impatience and heat swirling in his eyes, but he said nothing else to sway her one way or the other. No pressure.

And there didn't need to be. She wanted him, too. "I wish I could say you're wrong."

His smile was full of satisfaction and he simply held out his hand. She put her fingers into his palm and let him lead her up the front steps and into the house.

Cabot turned on a light just inside the entryway, revealing the need in his eyes. Without letting go of her hand, he guided her up the stairs to the second door on the left—his bedroom. He flipped the wall switch and the room lit up.

A four-poster pine bed was straight ahead with a matching dresser and armoire on adjacent walls. A doorway to the left was probably the bathroom, and French doors opened to a balcony that from this orientation would have a spectacular view of the lake and towering mountains. It was a big room and definitely a *man's* space.

"This suits you," she said.

"*You* suit me." His voice was hoarse with desire.

A woman wasn't living here now, but his wife must have once upon a time. And no doubt after her abandonment he'd brought women here, on those nights his son was having a sleepover at a friend's house. But Kate couldn't deal with any of that. Didn't want to. For so long she'd done everything by the book, followed the rules, thought all decisions to death. Her life had been structured every minute of every day.

All she wanted now was something spontaneous and just for her. She had to believe that sometimes it was all right to be selfish.

"Earth to Kate…" Cabot leaned over and gently kissed her with no other parts of their bodies touching.

It was so sweet and provocative at the same time that she ached to be as close as a man and woman could get. She stood on tiptoe and wrapped her arms around his neck, and the movement was like tossing a match on dry leaves. She was ready to ignite, and tension in his body was a clear indication that he felt the same.

Cabot tugged at her shirt as she undid the snaps on his. She toed off her sneakers, and he yanked his boots, then tossed them aside. The harsh sound of their mingled breathing filled the room as the rest of their clothes joined the growing pile.

He tugged her to the side of the bed and tossed back the comforter, blanket and sheet in a single, powerful move. Then he grabbed her to him and turned his body so that she fell on top of him when they tumbled together onto the mattress. The power position lasted all of a nanosecond as he rolled her onto her back and nestled beside her.

The feel of his bare skin was intoxicating and the dusting of hair on his chest teased her breasts. He kissed her mouth, cheek, jaw and neck as his hand slid past the curve of her waist, over her hip and down her leg.

Then he turned his attention to the inside of her thigh. The featherlight touch sent a shaft of heat straight to her feminine core and he never stopped kissing her. Men were notorious for not multitasking well, but he seemed to be doing all right. His fingers inched higher, and anticipation flowed through her, waiting for him to touch the most sensitive of places. When he did, she nearly whimpered from the exquisite torture of it all.

"You're so soft," he whispered against her neck. "And you smell good, like flowers."

He smelled good, too, and the strength in his arms and chest were undeniable, but he held her as if she were a delicate, pricey piece of porcelain. That was such a turn-on.

"Cabot—" She arched her hips against his hand, letting him know without words what she craved.

She was nearly to the point of begging when he shifted slightly and reached into the nightstand drawer to pull out a small, square packet. Later she would be grateful he'd remembered protection, but right this second, all she could say was "Hurry."

"Doing my best." He sounded as if he were on mile twenty-six of a marathon.

Moments later she had his full concentration again. He moved his hand over her abdomen, then lower, sliding one finger inside her. She'd anticipated the touch but not the reaction, as if a bolt of electricity had zapped her into another dimension. She pulled her heels high on the bed, nearly shattering with the power of it.

Then he shifted, taking his weight on his forearms, and entered her—slow, smooth, steady.

He stroked once, gently, letting her grow accustomed to him, then followed up with a hard thrust. His technique was flawless, delivering the maximum amount of attention until that pleasure was too much to take. Release exploded, creating a shuddering wave, and he held her until it had rolled all the way through her.

Then he began to move again, once, twice and third time was the charm. He groaned and his body grew tense, then trembled as spasms of satisfaction exploded through him. And she held him close as feelings of exquisite tenderness welled inside her.

She couldn't move and dozed in his arms until he nudged her awake, vowing that he'd been in too big a hurry before, but this time it would be slower. It was until it wasn't and neither of them could wait, but the thrill was no less than before.

And somewhere in the middle of the night he made love to her again. It was without a doubt the best night of her life, and she promised herself that she'd hang on to the glow as long as possible because when morning came she would surely have regrets.

Chapter 10

Cabot woke before dawn as usual, but having a soft, curvy, warm woman in his arms was definitely a different way to start out the day. And it was a little unsettling because of how easy it would be to get used to waking up like this with Kate every morning. For a short time in his life he'd had that. Then everything had changed.

The thought of going to hell after he died didn't bother him much since he'd spent quite a bit of time there while still on this earth. Putting himself in a situation where it could happen to him again wasn't especially appealing. Although that wouldn't be an issue because Kate's mornings on the ranch were limited to the end of summer.

He tried to move without waking her, but she stirred, then opened her eyes. He saw uncertainty at first. Then it cleared and the realization of where she was along with apparent memories of what they'd done last night made her full lips curve into a smile. His expectation had been that she would regret going to bed with him. He didn't know whether or not to be relieved that she didn't.

"Good morning." He raised up on his elbow.

"Yes, it is." She had the look of a thoroughly satisfied woman.

But he still had to ask. "Are you okay?"

"Fine." Her forehead wrinkled in confusion. "Why?"

"I just get the feeling you don't do that sort of thing, so I wanted to check."

"You were wondering if I'd hate myself in the morning?"

"Well…" He shrugged. "Yes."

"I don't."

"To put a finer point on it…do you hate me?"

"Of course not." She reached out and put a hand on his arm. "I'm a consenting adult and I definitely consented to what we did."

Willing participant was more correct, he thought. "Okay."

"You don't look convinced. Are you thinking this is a rebound move for me?"

"Actually, that hadn't crossed my mind." Mostly because in the heat of the moment he'd lost his mind, what with blood flow diverted to points south of his belt. But he should have considered that. "Now that you mention it, is that what happened?"

Without hesitation she emphatically said, "No. And I'll tell you why I know that."

"I'm listening." For some reason he really wanted to be convinced that she was telling the truth.

"I had nothing to rebound from." She raised up on

one elbow, and when the sheet slipped, she pulled it back up to cover her bare breasts.

"Oh?" Cabot forced himself to look into her eyes, even though every ounce of testosterone in his body was coaxing him to look lower.

"I wasn't in love with him."

He remembered her shell-shocked expression in the diner while still wearing the wrinkled wedding gown. The dress she'd put on to get married just a few weeks ago. "How can you be so sure?"

"I know myself, Cabot. There were doubts that I ignored or was too crazy busy to deal with. Once I tried to discuss it with him, but he blew me off and said it was just wedding jitters. Maybe I wanted to believe that, but there's something I'm quite sure of."

"What's that?"

"I didn't miss him. What he did didn't hurt me. If I'd been in love with him, no way would I be here in your bed right now."

"Okay." He believed her and hoped like hell that wouldn't prove to be a mistake.

"In fact," she said, "I think he did me a big favor by cheating on me."

"That needs some explaining. I know men and women process situations differently, but I don't think I could be as philosophical if I caught my fiancée cheating." He was pretty sure about that because there was every indication that his wife had been unfaithful before walking out, and he hadn't been philosophical at all. *Mad as hell* more accurately described his reaction.

Kate's expression was still full of sunshine. "It was a favor because clearly I didn't love him, and the marriage would have been a complicated, messy and costly mistake to undo."

"I know all about that," he said.

That comment took the sun out of her eyes and filled them with questions. "There was just enough passion in your voice to make it sound as if you still have feelings for your wife."

"*Ex*-wife." He shook his head. There was no doubt in his mind that he was over her. And had been for a long time. "The fallout from what happened is something you never forget."

"I see." She glanced at the clock. "I'd better get going. Caroline will be here and ready to cook pretty soon, and she'll need the groceries."

They had just enough time for one more go-around, except his words had efficiently and effectively slammed that door shut. But maybe that was for the best. This thing between them had the potential to be complicated and messy—at least for him. Probably only for him. Which made it *his* problem and character flaw.

"Okay," he finally said.

"I'll go make coffee before I leave."

"That's not necessary."

She shrugged. "It's not a problem."

"Okay, then. Sounds good."

Cabot knew she could find her way around the kitchen without help. So he threw the covers back and walked into the bathroom for a quick shower. Afterward he shaved and combed his hair, then went downstairs, fully expecting her to have left. But she was cooking potatoes, eggs and toast and looking very much at home doing it.

Sliding his arm around her waist and pulling her in for a kiss would feel so natural, and it took every ounce of his willpower to resist the urge.

Instead he said, "You didn't have to go to all this trouble, but it sure smells good."

Apparently her earlier comment about messy, complicated mistakes was forgotten because she slid a sassy look over her shoulder. "Tastes even better than it smells."

His mouth was watering, but it had very little to do with food and a lot to do with her.

Then the phone rang, loud, unexpected and startling. Calls this early weren't unheard of but still unusual, and his first thought was that something had happened to Ty. He grabbed the phone from its charger on the counter and looked at the caller ID. The number wasn't provided, which meant this had nothing to do with his son.

He hit the talk button. "Hello?"

The caller identified himself as a law-enforcement officer from Helena and he was sorry to inform him... Cabot heard the words, but they didn't sink in. This was surreal. He took down a number in case he had further questions, then thanked the officer for letting him know and hung up.

Kate was staring at him. "Who was that, Cabot? You look as if you've seen a ghost."

If he'd been able to manage it, he would have laughed at that. The saying was so close to the truth. He met her gaze and thought how ironic that he'd just been remembering the cheating woman who'd run out on him.

"My ex-wife is dead. She was killed in a car accident last night."

And he had to figure out a way to tell his son that there was now no hope of him ever meeting or having a relationship with his mother.

Kate had regrets about Cabot, but sleeping with him wasn't one of them. She did regret learning that he still had feelings for his ex. He'd denied it, but she'd seen the look in his eyes when he'd told her the news.

It was a very effective way to destroy the romantic buzz she'd had when she woke up in his bed. A horrible start to the morning after such a magical night.

Because of that, Cabot had been on her mind ever since. Working with the camp kids had distracted her some, but now she was walking to the archery range for her prearranged practice session with Ty and had nothing but time to think. She'd wanted to stay with Cabot earlier, just in case he needed or wanted to talk, but both of them had responsibilities. If there was any good news, it was that Ty's sleepover had allowed his dad some space to collect his thoughts. And Kate was sure there was more to what he was feeling than just concern for his son.

From the compound of camp cabins she followed the dirt path around a curve by the lake and in the distance saw the bales of hay with targets tacked on. It surprised her that a man was standing beside one. The figure looked a lot like Cabot, but Tyler was nowhere in sight. She hadn't seen him by the storage area retrieving his archery equipment, either.

Kate hurried over to her boss and stopped in front of him. The brim of his Stetson shaded his eyes although not his face, but there wasn't much to see. It was wiped clean of emotion.

"Cabot," she said. "What's going on? Is Tyler coming to practice?"

"In a few minutes."

"Have you told him yet…about the phone call?"

He shook his head. "C.J.'s mom brought him home from the sleepover a little while ago. He was anxious to get back to practicing with his bow and arrow after being stuck inside, what with the rain yesterday. I gave him a couple of chores to do when he got home. I wanted to talk to you first."

"So he doesn't know about his mother." She nodded. "Don't worry. I wouldn't have said anything before you got a chance to tell him what happened."

"I didn't think you would. That's not what I was going to say."

If that wasn't it, then what in the world? Another thought came to her. "You don't want me around him." She met his gaze. "I've explained to him that I'm not staying after the summer."

"That's not it, either." For the first time a corner of his mouth quirked up. "You can keep guessing why I'm here if you want. Far be it from me to stifle that fertile imagination of yours, but I'd really like to have this conversation with you before he gets here. And it might be a little quicker if you just let me tell you."

"Okay." More words wanted to come out, but she forced them back.

"I can't decide whether or not to tell him." He rubbed a hand over his neck. "Since you already know about it, I thought—"

"You could use me as a sounding board."

"Yes."

"Anytime you're ready," she encouraged him.

"The thing is, Ty doesn't have any memory of his mother. He's seen pictures of her, but he's only in one of them—she's holding him when he was an infant. On a day-to-day basis, she's had no influence on him whatsoever, good or bad."

"I see."

"If I tell him the news, there's no way it could have a good impact."

Kate figured he was making a case for not saying anything. "What about the emotional ramifications?"

"What do you mean?"

"Well…" She thought carefully about how to phrase this. "He's talked to me about his friend C.J.'s family, the fact that his mom's husband adopted him."

"And you're interpreting that to mean that he misses his mom?"

"It's hard to miss what you never had. So maybe not *her* exactly, but the idea of having a mom."

Cabot folded his arms over his chest. "Are you saying you think I should tell him?"

"I would never presume to tell you how to raise your son. No one can make that decision but you." When he shifted, the sun hit her in the eyes and she put a hand up to shade them. "But let me play devil's advocate."

"Okay."

"Let's say you keep this information to yourself. What if Ty is somehow holding out hope of his mom coming back? And what if next year, or the year after, or when he's eighteen or twenty-one, he brings up the subject of looking for her? If you don't say anything and he finds out she's been gone for years and you let him believe, by omission, that there was a chance she'd return—" She just looked at him, letting him draw his own conclusions about the consequences.

Cabot's mouth pulled tight for a moment. "Neither of my choices is very good."

"I know." He could turn his son's world upside down now or risk Ty finding out later and lose his trust.

"And she continues to be a thorn in my side—"

That could mean a lot of things, but when Kate felt her chest tighten, it was clear that she was putting a deeply personal spin on the words. It never would affect her one way or the other; she knew that. But she had to ask anyway.

"Were you hoping that she would come back?"

He looked completely disgusted with himself. "A part of me wanted to put the family back together, give Tyler a traditional home."

Was that all about having a family, or did it mean he was still in love with his ex? Again it was none of her business, but what was the harm in asking? He'd get mad? She'd lose his friendship? He'd never kiss her again? Soon she would go back to Los Angeles and wouldn't see him at all, mad or not. And as far as friendship? That shelf life was limited to however many days she had left on the ranch.

So she had very little to lose if she took her curiosity out for a spin. "Cabot, can I ask you a question?"

"What if I say no?"

She shrugged. "I'll ask anyway. You don't have to answer."

"Fair enough."

"Here goes." She blew out a breath. "Were you still in love with your ex-wife?"

"You asked me that earlier."

In his bed. She remembered. "You didn't really give me an answer. Were you?"

Before he could respond, the sound of running feet drifted to them, quickly followed by Ty's voice.

"Kate? Here I come." Excitement and boyish exuberance filled his tone as he rounded the curve.

Cabot's expression turned somewhere in the tortured range when he saw his son. He still hadn't said what he planned to tell the child.

"Hi, Kate. Dad! Are you here to watch me practice?" He had a quiver of arrows on his back and the bow in his hand.

"Ty—" The man took a knee in front of his son.

The little boy frowned. "But what about the cows you were supposed to move 'cause they ate up all their food? Are they gonna be hungry?"

"No." Cabot smiled. "The other hands can do it without me this one time."

"Because you wanted to see me shoot my bow?"

Kate watched expressions chase across Cabot's face and knew he was reading the same feelings into the boy's words that she was. His son was feeling the downside of being raised by a busy, hardworking single dad.

"I'd really like to see you shoot." He braced a forearm on his knee and met his child's gaze. "But first there's something I have to tell you."

"What?" Ty's anxious tone said he was getting a serious vibe.

Kate was glad Cabot had decided to tell his son, but maybe he wanted to do it alone. "I'll just go back and see if Caroline needs any help."

Cabot glanced up. "If it's all the same to you, Kate, I'd appreciate it if you'd stay."

"All right." She stood a little to the side, giving father and son some space. If there was anything she could do to make this easier, she'd do it in a heartbeat.

"What's wrong, Dad? Am I in trouble?"

"No, son. But I got some news this morning that you have a right to know. It's about your mom."

"The lady in the pictures you showed me?"

"Yes."

"Is she coming to see me?"

As Kate watched Cabot's face, she saw that the slight hope in Ty's voice took a huge toll on the father's heart.

"No, she's not," he said quietly, then reached out and put a big hand on the boy's shoulder. "She was in a car accident. I'm sorry, son, but she was hurt really bad and didn't make it."

Tyler blinked. "She's dead?"

"That's right. I'm really sorry to have to tell you this."

"I know."

Cabot was studying the boy carefully. "This is a lot to take in, buddy. How are you feeling?"

"I'm not sure." He shrugged his thin shoulders. "I guess I thought someday she'd want to see me."

A muscle jerked in Cabot's jaw. "It's natural you'd feel that way."

"Now she never can." The boy's tone was wistful but not miserable.

"No, she can't."

"Daddy, am I s'posed to be sad?"

"Is that how you feel?" Cabot asked.

"Maybe." Ty shrugged. "A little, I guess. But not too much. Is that bad?"

"No, buddy. Whatever you're feeling is just fine. There's no right or wrong about it."

"Okay."

He gently pulled the boy into his arms. "I love you, son."

"I love you, too, Dad."

Tyler stepped away, a thoughtful expression scrunching up his face. "Do I have to go home?"

"You can if you want." Cabot stood and ruffled his son's hair. "Is there something else you want to do?"

"I'd really like to practice with Kate." He glanced at her, then back to his dad. "And it would be cool if you stayed to watch."

Cabot smiled down at his son. "Then that's what we'll do."

"Cool."

Tyler chattered to his father about nocking an arrow, the best stance for a beginner and how he needed to buy a guard so the bowstring snapping his arm wouldn't hurt. Then he took his mark and started shooting one arrow after another, most of them hitting the target circle, although no bull's-eye yet.

Cabot stood to the side, watching, encouraging, approving. And talking to Kate in between.

"That went well," she said in a voice low enough that Ty couldn't hear. "You were so good with him."

"Didn't feel that way."

She understood that. How was there anything good about telling your child he would never get a chance to meet his mother? But the patience, sensitivity and concern this man had shown were pretty awesome. "It was the right thing to do. Telling him, I mean."

"It doesn't feel right, either." Anger swirled in his eyes. "There's nothing right about what she did. She left him twice. Once by walking out and then by dying."

It was time to change the subject. "So, what do you think about your son's skill with the bow and arrow?"

"He's really come a long way." He smiled over at the boy, who was busy retrieving the arrows and replenishing his quiver. "You must be a pretty good teacher."

"Don't sound so surprised."

"Seriously?" He grinned. "I saw you on that magazine cover in a bathing suit, holding a fishing rod."

"Don't let the bikini fool you. I was in that magazine because I conduct seminars on survival techniques."

"Everyone in town is talking about the cover girl in our midst. You know Caroline knows the truth about you, too."

"She does. Nolan told her," Kate confirmed. "We talked about it this morning."

"I talked to her, too," he said. "And she thinks you should expand the camp-survival class we already have and teach it."

Kate could not describe how exhilarating the feeling of being good at something, and getting recognized for it, felt. She wanted to hug him and just barely managed to hold back. "I'd love that. Sounds like a plan."

It was probably good to have a plan, and someday soon Kate needed to get one. For goodness' sake, she'd slept with the man. That was not something she did lightly. She wasn't a one-night-stand kind of girl, which meant she was developing feelings for him.

For so many reasons she shouldn't be, not the least of which was that he might still care about a woman who had treated him and their child badly. Sydney had said anger and love were flip sides of the same coin, and Cabot was clearly furious at Ty's mother for her double abandonment.

Cabot might mourn the loss of hope in reuniting his family. But Kate mourned the loss of any chance to tell that woman off, to say to her face that she was a terrible person for throwing away her beautiful son and a good man.

Kate had run from a man who wasn't even in the same league as Cabot. If she didn't stop herself, she could end up falling for the rancher. And leaving Blackwater Lake would be a lot more traumatic than what she'd been through just before she'd arrived.

Chapter 11

Cabot sat in the dining-room-turned-classroom and watched Kate teach a group of twelve kids basic survival skills. Not only did she seem to know her stuff, but also she looked really good up there talking about it. Hard to believe the summer was already more than half over. It had been an eventful one, including getting closure with his ex. In the past two weeks he'd been watching his son carefully, looking for emotional aftereffects from the news about his mother's passing. Ty didn't seem to have any issues.

Cabot was glad he'd told the boy everything and also grateful for Kate being a sounding board and gentle presence when he broke the news. With the archery range close by, Ty had an activity to distract him. And the kid was getting pretty darn good with a bow and arrow.

What pleased Cabot most was Kate saying how

well he'd handled the situation. He hadn't known her long, but in all that time he'd never seen her hold back, whether her opinion was good or bad. So he took her words as a compliment.

She was standing in the front of the room with a dry-erase board propped on a chair. He'd come in quietly after her presentation started and sat off to the side and near the door, a place where he could observe her and see kids' expressions to determine if they were understanding the material presented. As far as he could tell, no one had noticed his entrance. The kids in attendance ranged in age from nine to thirteen and were mesmerized by what Kate had to share. This class was mandatory for any child signed up for the overnight campout, but Kate had expanded the basic program and Cabot wanted to monitor the new material.

"Before hiking or walking an area, always do your research," she was saying. "Know your surroundings. Learning about local plants and animals could save your life."

A blond boy raised his hand and said, "How?"

"Food. So you know which berries are safe to eat, for instance."

"What about animals?" This was from another boy, a redheaded, freckle-faced kid who looked as though he could stir up mischief without a firm hand to rein him in. "Or bugs."

Kate's expression didn't change. She must've known that he wanted a creeped-out-girl reaction and wasn't going to give him one. "They can be a good source of protein. I hope it never happens, but if you get hungry enough, you'll be grateful for that grasshopper."

"Ew." This was a collective reaction from the rest of the kids in the room.

Kate grinned. "Okay, listen up and you won't get lost in the woods long enough to have to eat bugs." She looked around. "Now, then, always make sure to tell someone where you're going and how long you'll be gone."

"That's what my mom always says," the redheaded boy chimed in.

"Parents know best. It would be a good idea to pay attention to them, Aaron." She looked at Ty and sympathy lurked in her eyes. "Next, remember to bring a cell phone or CB radio, some communication device in case you're lost or injured. Bring survival gear like a knife, matches in a waterproof container, a whistle, signal mirror."

When she met his gaze, Cabot knew she'd seen him come in and was now remembering the night she told him about how to make a fire without matches. By using a condom. He smiled to himself, thinking how much he preferred using it the way they had the night of the rainstorm. That had been a couple of weeks ago, and there'd been no opportunity to get her alone since. Not for lack of wanting to.

His gaze dropped to her tanned legs, beautifully showcased in her denim shorts. Memories of them wrapped around his waist kept him awake nights. The rest of her was equally as tantalizing. This wasn't the first time in his life he'd been relieved no one could read his mind, but it was quite possibly the most inappropriate setting for what he was thinking. A lot of kids were in this room, including his own son.

"All of those things are what you should have if your day in the woods is planned. Now we're going to talk about what to do if you lose sight of the group."

"Like if you're the last in line and everyone else in

your family walks away?" The little dark-haired girl's voice shook a little.

"That's right, Gina." Kate walked over and squatted beside her. Obviously she'd heard the anxiety, too. "Did that happen to you?"

Gina nodded solemnly. "I stopped to look at a flower and they kept going. Then I couldn't hear them anymore."

"That must have been scary." She put her hand on the little girl's arm. "What did you do?"

"I bet she started to cry," Aaron said.

Kate looked at him, anger briefly flashing in her eyes, but when she responded, her voice was calm and even. "Crying when you're sad or scared is a perfectly normal reaction for anyone."

"I did cry a little," Gina admitted, giving the boy a blistering look. "But I just stayed still and they came back for me."

"That was exactly the right thing to do." Kate stood and walked back to the front of the room, then took a stack of papers from the chair. She handed them to his son. "Would you pass these out for me, Ty?"

"Sure." He hopped up and smiled at her as if he thought she hung the moon.

Cabot was starting to feel that way, too, but he was doing his darnedest to fight it.

"Hi, Dad. I didn't know you were here." Tyler gave him a toothy grin and handed him a paper.

"Thanks, son. I slipped in after Kate started and didn't want to interrupt."

"It's really good," his son said. "I gotta finish handing out papers. Are you gonna stay till it's over?"

He hadn't planned to, but the eager expression in the

boy's eyes changed his mind. That and the opportunity to just watch Kate. "Yeah, I'll be here."

"Cool." Ty made sure everyone in class had the handout.

Kate wrote a word on the dry-erase board and underlined it. "The number one thing to do when you're lost is STOP."

"Why is it capitalized?" Gina asked.

"So you can remember. *S*—sit down. *T*—think. *O*—observe. *P*—prepare for survival by gathering materials."

"Like what?" Aaron sat up in his seat and actually looked interested.

"Rocks to make a circle for a fire. Dry twigs to burn. Tree branches for a shelter. Berries just in case you get hungry." She looked around, waiting for questions, and when there weren't any, she continued. "You need to orient yourself. First use a piece of brightly colored clothing or a pile of leaves to mark your location. Then figure out your directions—north, south, east, west."

"How?" Ty asked.

"We all know the sun rises in the east and sets in the west. If it's late afternoon and the sun is on your right, you're facing south." She assessed their expressions and figured, as he did, that they didn't quite get that. "Don't worry. We'll practice."

"Then what do you do?" Aaron wanted to know.

"Stay in one place. This increases your chances of being found and reduces the amount of energy your body uses. That means you won't need as much water and food to keep you going."

Interesting stuff, Cabot thought. He took all of this for granted because he'd grown up with land all around and spent time in the wilderness with his father. At the time it felt like a lecture, but now that he had a son, he was grateful for everything he'd been taught. Unlike his father, Kate was patient and much more fun to watch. She seemed to keep the kids' attention even as she gave them practical information.

"If it's hot out, find shade. And, boys, don't be tempted to take off your shirts."

"How come?" Ty asked.

"You can easily become dehydrated and sunburned."

Cabot got a mental image of Kate in that bathing suit on the magazine cover. If they were alone, he sure wouldn't mind seeing her in that bikini for real—and then take it off her in the shade. And if he didn't STOP, he was going to have to give himself a time-out.

Almost as if she could read his thoughts, Kate took the pen and wrote *Fire* on the board. "Another way to prepare is to start a fire. We'll do a whole class just on safely doing that."

"Cool," Aaron said.

"No—hot," Ty countered, looking pleased with himself when Gina laughed.

"Signal your location," Kate continued. "Make noise—whistle, shout, sing, bang rocks together. If you're in an open area visible from the air, make something searchers can see." She drew a triangle, then wrote *SOS* inside it. "Do something like this in a sandy area or use leaves and tree branches."

Cabot could see the kids were shifting in their seats and looking around, getting restless. At this point they wouldn't retain anything.

"What do you say we call it a day?" Kate apparently had noticed, too. "We'll go over the rest of the material tomorrow. I think it's getting close to lunchtime."

The kids nodded and stood. Aaron started toward the door with Gina. "I wonder if bugs are on the menu."

"Gross," she said, wrinkling her nose.

"How about caterpillars?"

Kate heard and walked over to him. "Never eat brightly colored bugs. And always cook them to get germs off. Grasshoppers are okay. They're quite good, actually."

Gina had hurried out the door ahead of him and didn't hear the remark, but Aaron sure did. He didn't say "ew," but Cabot would swear he turned just a little green.

He and Ty moved to the front of the room and Kate joined them there. Cabot tipped his hat to her. "Nicely done, Miss Scott."

"Which part? The information? Or the bug-cuisine part at the end?" She used a rag to wipe off the board.

"Both."

"Did you really eat a grasshopper?" Tyler asked skeptically.

"Yes."

"Really?" Cabot asked.

"I wouldn't lie." She made a cross over her heart. "In the grown-up version of this class, you have to eat a bug to pass."

"Then I think I'd get an F," Ty said. "Gina's right. That's gross."

"Was it?" Cabot asked. "Gross, I mean?"

"Let's just say that if you're really hungry, it's better than nothing."

"So, and I quote, listen carefully and never get lost in the woods long enough to have to eat bugs."

She laughed. "I'm glad to know someone was paying attention."

He had been when he hadn't been having fantasies about her shapely legs wrapped around his waist.

"I was listening," Ty said. "But if you were there, you could just tell me what to do."

"If I was where?" she asked.

"The campout. Are you going?" He was looking up at her hopefully.

"No one has said anything to me about it." She glanced at Cabot. "I just took over the survival basics from one of the other counselors."

"My dad takes the kids who sign up for it in advance," Ty explained. He looked at his father as something occurred to him. "You never come to camp activities except for that. How come you're here today?"

Cabot almost winced. He knew his son wasn't being critical, just making an observation and asking for an explanation about the change. But it made him think. Maybe he should show up more. Not because he had news about his son's mother or to keep an eye on a new teacher.

"I wanted to see how Kate's new class on wilderness training went." Mostly.

"It was good." Tyler nodded emphatically. "I liked the bug stuff."

And maybe he has a little crush on Gina, Cabot thought. Wasn't it too soon for all of that? He wasn't looking forward to navigating his son's teenage years by himself. But you played the hand you were dealt.

"I'm glad you enjoyed the lesson." Kate smiled at the boy.

"Dad, I have an idea."

"I thought I smelled smoke," Cabot teased. "But that was you using your head."

Ty rolled his eyes. "Kate should go with us on the campout."

"Not as the cook." He met her gaze and saw her grin.

"Don't knock it till you've tried it."

"It's really fun, Kate," the boy persisted, looking up at Cabot. "Please say it's okay for her to go with us."

Obviously it meant a lot to his son. Cabot wouldn't mind, either. She was good with kids and good company. But it wasn't part of her job and she probably wouldn't want to rough it.

"You don't have to," he said. "But there's always room for one more, and an extra pair of eyes on the kids is always welcome. You can do hands-on instruction on the trail about edible plants and animals."

"If you're sure about this, I'd like very much to go."

"Yay," Ty said. "I'm going to tell the other kids that Kate is coming with us on the campout." He ran out of the dining room.

"You know you can't bring that fishing rod. The one you were holding on that magazine cover. Hiking in means traveling light."

"I left it at home anyway."

Was she blushing? he wondered. The next question was why she would be. Millions of people probably saw her in that bikini, but she was blushing for him. Which kind of made him feel good.

But Cabot wasn't at all sure this was a "yay" sort of deal. It could very well be a bad idea.

Kate gathered up pencils and paper in the dining room so that tables would be cleared and set up for the lunch crowd. To her surprise, Cabot stuck around to help her. He'd watched her closely during the presentation, which was both intimidating and thrilling. She'd given talks to outdoor enthusiasts lots of times, but there'd never been a man in the audience whom she'd been to bed with.

"Where does this go?" he asked, pointing to the dry-erase board. "In the equipment shed?"

She nodded. "I can get that. It's not heavy. You must have more important things to do."

"Not just now. I'll give you a hand." He picked it up and headed toward the door where the kids had exited moments before. "You have a shed key?"

"Yes. All the counselors do." She followed him out onto the porch.

At the bottom of the stairs, Aaron, Ty and Gina were standing around talking. The redheaded boy said, "The sun is almost straight up in the sky. How can we tell which way is south?"

"Kate said she would show us," Gina answered.

"Better not get lost before she does," Ty told him. "It's pretty scary when you don't know which way to go."

"If you were listening," the other boy retorted good-naturedly, "you would know that it's best not to go anywhere if you're lost."

"STOP." Ty held up his fingers to count off the letters. "Sit down. Think. Observe. Prepare."

Standing in the shadowy doorway where the kids didn't notice them, Kate glanced up at Cabot. He looked impressed and very proud of his son.

"What if you can't find any food right where you are?" Gina wondered.

"Mark your spot and keep it in sight so you can move around a little and hunt," Aaron told her.

"I didn't think that kid was listening," Cabot whispered.

"Neither did I. But good for him."

Gina said, "We should find a bug and cook it."

"I thought that grossed you out." Aaron raised his eyebrows. "Why should we do that?"

"To eat it," Ty said.

"I dare you to eat it," the other boy shot back.

"It won't kill you," Gina told him. "Kate said so."

Cabot leaned down and said quietly, "Apparently your word is gospel."

The feel of his breath on her ear raised shivers that raced down her arms. Her voice was a little ragged when she answered, "Before they strike out on their own, we better schedule a follow-up class quickly to clue them in on what is and isn't edible."

"Yeah." Cabot moved out of the doorway and down the steps, stopping beside the trio.

"Hi, Dad," Ty said, spotting him. "Hey, Kate. We want to build a fire without matches and catch a bug to cook it."

"Hmm." Laughter sparkled in her eyes, but she managed to stay as serious as the kids. "It is almost lunchtime. If you're too hungry to wait, you could do that. But remember, bugs might spoil your appetite. And Caroline is making mac and cheese."

Aaron looked relieved to have an out that would allow him to save face. "Maybe we can do it on the campout."

"Are you going?" Gina asked Aaron.

"Yeah."

"Me, too," Ty piped up. "And Kate is. You can show us then, right?"

"If you're still interested," she answered.

"Let's go skip rocks on the lake until lunch is ready," Ty suggested.

"Okay." Gina looked at him. "Can you show me how again?"

"Sure. Aaron's really good at it, too. We'll both help you." He looked up at Kate. "Is that okay?"

She could see from where she stood that there was a counselor with a group of kids by the water. They would be supervised. "Sure."

"'Bye, Kate. Last one there is a rotten egg. See you later, Dad."

Before Cabot could answer, the three were racing away to see who could reach the lake first.

"What I wouldn't give to have that much energy," Kate commented.

"I know what you mean." He looked down at her, admiration in his gaze. "You did a good job communicating that information to them."

"I'm glad you think so." Maybe her preoccupation with him hadn't thrown her off as much as she'd feared.

"As you know, it's required for the kids signed up for the campout, but you made it fun and interesting even for the ones who are staying behind. You really had their attention."

That reminded her. Ty had been transparent in his eagerness for her to go along on the campout. She needed to talk to Cabot about his son. But first they had to stow the board and other supplies.

"We should put that away," she told him.

He nodded and they walked around the building to the equipment shed. She reached into the pocket of her denim shorts to get the key and unlocked the dead bolt. She flipped the light switch just inside the door.

The windowless space was well organized with an area for office supplies to the right. Bins held soccer balls, basketballs and footballs. Hooks on the wall held bows and quivers of arrows. Paddleboards stood upright to the left. The equipment was kept under lock and key because kids were unpredictable. You didn't know when they might take it into their head to try something. This way they needed permission.

"The board goes over there with the office supplies," she told him. "Just stand it against the wall beside the shelf with the computer paper."

Cabot did as requested and they turned off the light, then locked up the shed.

Kate shoved the key back in her pocket and turned to find Cabot standing just behind her with a funny look on his face.

"What's wrong?" She brushed a hand down her ponytail. "Is there a spider in my hair?"

"Are you afraid of spiders?"

"Of course. Anyone in their right mind is afraid of them." She shuddered. "To quote every girl in that room, 'ew.'"

He laughed. "So all that about catching and eating bugs is just talk?"

"You did notice that I kept stressing that it's only as a last resort?"

"Yeah. But I think the kids are really intrigued by the thought of doing it."

She nodded. "But I'm really hoping they forget about eating bugs by the time we go on the campout."

The "we" part of that sentence reminded her why she was now included and what she wanted to say. "Cabot, I need to ask you something."

"Okay." He slid his fingertips into the pockets of his worn jeans. "Shoot."

"Have you talked with Ty? About me, I mean? And not getting attached?"

"Not yet."

"I didn't think so." It was important that he understood why she was asking. "I reminded him that I won't be staying. But a little bit ago when he asked me to go along on the camping trip, I got the feeling it hasn't sunk in for him just yet."

"I saw that," he admitted. "And I think you're right."

She had hoped to be wrong, but the man was Ty's father and he'd noticed, too. "I think he needs to hear from both of us, especially you, that you and I will never be romantically involved."

"I know." His mouth pulled into a grim line. "But I just had to break the news about his mother. It seemed like waiting a little longer was a good idea."

She nodded. "The reality of losing her for good could be part of the reason he's still pushing me at you. On some level he feels that loss and wants to replace her."

"Maybe. I'm no shrink, but getting this out in the open is probably a good idea. Warning and preparation are both important. I know how it feels to be abandoned. And to be blindsided by it."

"Because of what your wife did to you."

"She's not the only one. My mother did the same thing when I was a little older than Ty."

"Oh, Cabot…" Kate simply stared at him. She couldn't believe this man had been left twice. No wonder he was so guarded. "That's awful. I'm so sorry."

"I'm over what happened, but I do know how it feels to be left behind." If possible, he looked even more grim. "I got through it by being angry. But my dad never got to that point. He never stopped loving her, making excuses for her behavior."

"And waiting for her to come home."

He nodded. "Until the day he died, at the sound of a car door unexpectedly closing, I saw hope live and die in his eyes. I'm pretty sure that didn't do anything good for his health." He shrugged. "One day his heart just gave out."

Kate read between the lines. As far as she knew, it wasn't even a medically approved cause of death, but she would bet that his father had died of a broken heart. And being the good son that he was, Cabot had taken over the ranch even though he'd been considering another career. So a woman's rejection had led to a turning point that had totally changed the course of his life. That would leave a mark on anyone—inside, where no one could see it.

"I'm really sorry, Cabot." What else could she say? "But not all women do that."

"Couldn't prove it by me." He met her gaze. "But I'll have that talk with Tyler and make sure he understands that you're not staying."

"Okay. Thanks. It would ease my mind because I'd never do anything to hurt him."

He nodded, lifted his hand in farewell and walked away without a word. That silence spoke volumes. He didn't trust her even though he'd known from the beginning that she wasn't staying. It was only ever going to be a summer job. Still, she couldn't blame him for protecting himself. What he'd just told her underscored his deep resistance to commitment.

He was dedicated to his son, but everyone else in his life was only provisional. He rescued people because it was safe and didn't put his emotional well-being at risk. But that begged the question—why had he slept with her?

The only answer she could come up with was that he'd done it because she was leaving and nothing could come of it. For him, even the most superficial relationship came with safeguards and conditions. Attraction had been simmering between them since the day they'd met, but he wouldn't let himself act on it until he learned she didn't need rescuing. And the only reason he'd let down his guard then was because she was temporary.

But what if she wasn't? She would give almost anything to be able to stick around permanently, just to see how he would handle her presence. See if he would run.

Chapter 12

Three days after giving her talk on wilderness survival, a couple of workshops on starting a fire safely and identifying edible forest plants, Kate followed Cabot into the woods with six children and camp counselor Diane Castillo, making it two children per adult. The whole merry band had just arrived at a clearing by the lake. Logs had been arranged in a square with a circular black scorched spot in the center where previous fires had burned. It was weird being off the trail; she'd been following her boss's broad shoulders for several hours and would miss the view now that they were stopped.

"This is a good spot." Cabot slid his heavy pack from said shoulders and set it on the hard-packed dirt in the open area away from the trees and a short distance from the edge of the lake.

Aaron, Gina and Ty were there with three other kids

from the camp—David, Samantha and Rob. All of them looked around, their eyes widening with excitement.

All except Ty. He set his lighter pack down beside his father's. "We always camp here, Dad."

"Because it's a good spot."

"What makes it a good spot?" David was about twelve and wore wire-rimmed glasses—very Harry Potter. He'd never been on an overnight campout before. "Shouldn't we be under the trees? For cover?"

"Not a good idea for two reasons." Cabot helped the boy slide off his pack. "Number one, this is a safe place to build a fire. There's no nearby brush, bushes or trees to catch fire if a breeze suddenly kicks up. Number two, we won't damage a fragile ecosystem on this hard, rocky ground."

"Cool," David said, taking in the terrain around them.

"Any more questions?" Cabot asked.

Samantha, a quiet little brown-haired girl, raised her hand. "Why did you pick up trash when we were walking here?"

"I should have explained that while we were on the trail, but I wanted to make sure we got here in plenty of time to set up camp and have some fun."

"I can tell her, Dad," Ty volunteered. At a nod from his father he continued. "We need to leave everything in the woods the way we found it. Take only pictures, leave only footprints. That means don't do anything that harms the earth or the animals."

"That's right." Cabot ruffled the boy's hair. "Potato-chip bags, aluminum cans and other paper don't occur in nature."

"When we find it," Ty added, "we pick it up for someone else who forgot to or doesn't know any better."

"If we take care of the land, it will take care of us," his father added.

Kate smiled. Ty had been well trained by a man who had a soul-deep connection to the land that had been in his family for generations. He was already training his replacement for the family's ranching business and other interests, not just by what he said but by everything he did. This might have been Cabot's plan B as far as a career path, but he was awfully good at it. Whether he would admit the obvious or not, this life was in his soul.

"Okay, we have some work to do."

As Cabot was assigning two kids to each adult, Ty insisted on being paired with Kate. She met his father's gaze and knew there'd been no father-son chat yet. Now certainly wasn't the time for it, and selfishly she was glad. Ty was a great kid and she sincerely enjoyed hanging out with him.

They broke into groups and set up tents, gathered rocks for a fire pit and arranged dry wood inside it for later. They positioned provisions in an area not too far from where the cooking would be done, and everyone refilled their water containers. Now it was time to have fun.

"Who wants to go fishing?" Cabot asked.

"We don't have fishing poles. They were too bulky to bring with us," Aaron reminded him. All the kids had been instructed about what to pack and what not to.

"I can take care of that." Cabot grinned at their clueless expressions. "Let's go."

Kate smiled as the children eagerly followed him without question. The trust in him was obvious. Kate could understand that. She trusted him, too, which seemed odd after her fiancé's betrayal, but it was a fact.

Cabot showed them how to find a long stick and tie a piece of string to the end of it with a hook attached. From his backpack he'd also taken a container of bait. Aaron did his best to be macho, but in the end Cabot patiently put a worm on the boy's hook. He was there to help whoever needed it. The other boys didn't and looked awfully superior about it.

Kate knew that would just get worse when they grew into men and were smack in the middle of learning about girls. How she wished it would be possible for her to watch Ty grow up, evolve into the heartbreaker he showed signs of becoming. Girls were going to love him, and he would return the favor. If his father's experiences didn't taint the boy's attitude about dating.

As Cabot led the group down to the lake's edge, Kate expected any second to hear a rousing rendition of "Heigh-ho, heigh-ho, it's off to work we go." Diane stood beside her, observing everything. She was black-haired, olive-skinned and in her early twenties. A single teacher who lived locally, she taught at Blackwater Lake Elementary School. She'd been working at the summer camp even before graduating from college and starting her teaching career.

"I've never seen him quite this involved before."

"Who? Cabot?"

Diane nodded. "It's interesting."

"Doesn't he always come along for this outing?"

"Yes." The other counselor met her gaze. "And he's always good with the kids. Patient, but distant. Something's different about him. As if his mind isn't somewhere else, distracted by a dozen different things. He's really in the moment."

"How do you mean?"

"I guess it always felt as if he was just going through

the motions because Tyler wanted him here." Diane shaded her eyes with her hand and watched Cabot talking to the children by the lake. "Today he's really taking his time with the kids."

"It's obvious that he cares deeply about the environment."

"Yes, he does." Diane looked at her. "But I'm not sure it's only about the environment."

Kate's heart stuttered and she wondered about the meaning of those words. "You're not talking about me."

"What do you think?" She shrugged. "He looks at you a lot when he thinks no one is watching him."

"You're imagining it." Kate wasn't sure whether she wanted the statement confirmed or denied.

"I don't think I am." The other counselor met her gaze. "I've been working summer camp for six years. Female counselors have come and gone. I've seen him socialize in town and at church, talking to women, both locals and tourists."

"What's your point?"

"I've never seen him look at anyone the way he looks at you."

That was flattering and disconcerting in equal parts. But Kate wondered if Diane had ever seen him look at his wife. "It's probably just because he thought I was a flake who ran away from her wedding."

"That could be why he looks angry about it, but I'd say the expression on his face is more about what he wants."

If Cabot was that transparent, Kate figured her face and feelings were like an open book. Protesting would only lend weight to what the other woman had said and there was no point to that. She and Cabot had acknowledged the attraction and also their understanding that it would end soon.

She looked at the other woman and said, "I honestly don't know what to say to that."

"I understand. And I'm sorry. It was inappropriate to bring it up. I just feel protective of him. And I'm surly today." Diane sighed. "You know, I should go down there and help supervise the kids, but I'd sure love to put my feet up for a few minutes. I hate to play this card, but I've got my period and the cramps are killing me after the hike."

"I can go." Did she sound too eager? Kate wondered.

"Would you mind?"

"Of course not." It was scary how much she didn't mind. Being with Cabot made her happy. And what was the harm in enjoying the feeling while she could?

Kate walked down the slight bank and stopped beside Cabot. "Need any help?"

When he glanced down, something smoldered in his eyes. "Everything is quiet right now, but if anyone actually catches anything, it could get exciting."

"And if they don't, you know someone is going to ask about eating bugs."

"I wish I didn't have pasta in my backpack as an alternative because I'd really like to see you herd grasshoppers." He grinned. "It would be even more interesting to see you cook up a batch."

"That's not my best event. I'd much rather clean fish."

"Have you ever done that before?"

"Do bears poop in the woods?" She laughed at his pained expression. "Companies pay me to advertise their products, which requires me to be competent while engaging in outdoor activities, including but not limited to catching and cleaning fish."

"So that rod you were holding on the cover of that magazine wasn't just a prop?" Again his eyes darkened with intensity.

It seemed to her that they'd been over that already, but whatever. "As difficult as it might be to believe, I actually know what to do with it. And don't look so surprised."

"Can't help it. I find myself unable to picture you putting a worm on a hook or gutting a trout."

"Why?" She wasn't asking because she was annoyed. Being underestimated had happened all her life. In his case, for some reason she just wanted Cabot to say the words out loud, right here in the outdoors.

He shifted uncomfortably. "All right. I admit it's tough to imagine you doing it because of the way you look."

"How do I look?"

"You know."

"Not really." She shrugged. "I have no idea what you mean."

"I'll spell it out for you. You're so beautiful it's hard to picture you grimy and wet and smelling like fish. Go ahead. Call me a chauvinist, opinionated, closed-minded pig."

"I don't have to. You just did that for me." She laughed, pleased beyond words that he thought she was pretty. "Seriously, is it such a stretch that I could be capable in the outdoors? Or that I love it?"

"Yes." He met her gaze with a stubborn, determined set to his mouth.

Kate was sorry she'd made him say it because she got more than she'd bargained for. The truth was he didn't want to believe she could embrace the wide-open spaces because that was his world and would give him a reason not to let her into it. He'd made that mistake with his wife and wouldn't make the same one again.

Funny how differently they responded in this situation. He was counting on her crumbling under the pressure and inconveniences of being in the wilderness, but his deep respect for the land had only made her like him more. Because her family had moved often, she'd never felt connected anywhere. Until now. The first time she'd seen Blackwater Lake—the town, mountains and lake itself—she'd fallen in love with it. After spending time here, nothing about that had changed.

She wasn't anything like the woman who'd walked out on Cabot, the one he still had feelings for.

The shame of it was that if he could let go, Kate had a feeling they could have something special. But that was impossible because he was still holding on to the past with both hands.

Normally when Cabot was sitting with a tin cup of coffee between his hands out under the stars by a campfire, he felt completely at peace, but not tonight. The kids had been bunked down for about an hour. David and Rob shared a tent. Gina and Samantha had paired off in another. Ty was with Aaron. When they'd given the flashlights-out order, there'd been a lot of hollering back and forth, but that had faded to quiet conversation. He'd expected the girls to go on the longest, but his son held that record. Now all was quiet.

The two female counselors were in the last tent and he had one to himself. That was the source of his restlessness. He was wishing pretty hard he was sharing a tent with Kate. But that wasn't possible and no amount of stargazing or fire-watching could change what was.

She was really something. He knew no one had named that terrible hurricane after her, but it would be fitting. Katrina Scott had blown into town wearing a white gown she hadn't gotten married in and proceeded to turn his life upside down.

He was certain she'd been bluffing when she'd looked him in the eye and challenged him to donate her paycheck to his favorite charity. But she'd been telling the truth, and he wasn't sure whether or not that was a good thing. She had a life and didn't really need his help. That should have been a relief, but it bothered him and he wasn't sure why.

The dying embers kept the tin pot of coffee warm. He reached over and lifted it out to fill his cup. Caffeine wouldn't keep him awake, but thoughts of Kate sure would. She was so near yet completely out of his reach.

That was when he heard movement behind him from Kate's tent. He had a better-than-even chance it wasn't Diane because his luck just didn't run that good.

"Is this log taken?"

Kate's hushed voice tied his gut in a knot. He struggled with the stupid happy feelings pouring through him and tamped down the urge to pull her into his lap.

"I guess I can share." He slid sideways. "I thought everyone was asleep."

"Everyone but you and me." She rubbed her hands together and held them toward what was left of the fire. "Are you standing guard to make sure the fire is out? In the wilderness-survival rules, it says someone has to watch for forty-five minutes in case there's wind and sparks that could compromise nearby trees and brush."

"Rules were meant to be broken." In addition to the

faint glow of the dying embers, a propane lantern illuminated the clearing. He could see the teasing laughter in her eyes. "I'm pretty sure if I douse what's left of this fire with what's left of the coffee, then stir that up to smother any sparks, it will be enough to keep the wilderness safe and only take about thirty seconds." His mouth quirked up. "Or maybe I'll get wild and throw dirt on it for good measure."

"Oh, no." She faked a horrified look, then laughed. "Knock yourself out."

"How come you're still awake?" He'd hoped for a neutral tone, but it was ragged with what he recognized as longing.

"Couldn't sleep," she answered.

"Not even after that hike?"

"Nope. You know how sometimes it's a challenge to shut your mind off?"

Sadly, he did. Maybe she'd caught it from him, and by that he meant he had a bad feeling that he was on her mind just like she was on his. But that thought was going to stay safely in his head.

He changed the subject. "Nice night."

"Beautiful." She sighed. "I've spent a lot of time outdoors, and this is one of the prettiest spots I've ever seen. Thanks for letting me come along."

"It was Ty's idea," he reminded her. "But I'm glad you like it."

"I do. And, it has to be said, you are very impressive, sir."

"I'm glad you think so," he said, "but I can't say I know why you do."

"Oh, just teaching the kids about respecting nature. Leaving the land the way they found it. And you showed them by example that it's still possible to have fun."

"You think they did?"

"Absolutely." She shifted and their shoulders brushed.

Talk about sparks, he thought. No one could see them, but he sure as heck felt them all over just from that small touch. And he had on a denim jacket. This wasn't good at all.

"So," he said, "you're pretty impressive, too. Nice job cooking that trout Tyler caught."

"I'm glad someone liked it. The kids sure turned up their noses, but at least they tried."

"It was delicious, in my opinion. But I've learned that mac and cheese goes over better than fish when you're talking about what kids will eat." When she didn't respond, he glanced over and saw that she was looking pensive. "What's wrong?"

"Nothing. It's just—" She caught the bottom corner of her lip between her teeth. "You seemed to enjoy yourself today, too."

"I did."

"Diane said that's a change."

He thought for a moment about past outings and realized the other counselor had known him a long time and would see differences. Finally he said, "Maybe."

The way Kate was looking right now told him that the counselor had said more than that. Kate's husky voice was inviting him to confirm, deny or explain.

He didn't want to do any of the above, even though Diane was right about him. He hadn't been aware that his attitude showed, but today was the most fun he'd ever had on one of these campouts.

In fact, he'd spent a lot more time hanging out with the camp kids in general this summer, and that was all about Kate. A subconscious need to see her had him visiting the activities more often and reminded him how much he enjoyed interacting with the campers. He'd wanted more kids of his own before that option left along with his wife. That taught him a man couldn't count on a relationship being solid and, without a guarantee, he wouldn't be responsible for more kids growing up in a single-parent home.

Kate rubbed her hands together again.

"Are you cold?" He was only too happy to change the subject.

"No. It's chilly, but my sweatshirt is fine." She folded her arms across her middle. "Should we be worried that the kids high-fived about not taking showers?"

"They're okay until tomorrow." He chuckled. "It's just one night. They're kids. I'm pretty sure none of them will need therapy."

"Good. Just saying…" She laughed, then rested her head on his shoulder.

It felt good—too good. Made him ache to put his arm around her, hold her hand, do those intimate things a man did with a woman he cared about. He couldn't say anything without his voice giving all of that away, so he let the silence stretch out between them.

Finally she said, "I can't believe how fast this summer has gone."

When it was over she'd leave. She didn't say that, but Cabot could read between the lines. "Yeah, it did go fast."

She sat up straight, turning off the intimacy. "When you said it was Ty's idea for me to come along—"

"I know. I'm sorry I haven't talked to him yet. I will when we get back tomorrow."

"He's your son, Cabot. No one knows him better. If

you think it was best not to burden him, I'm sure you're right about that."

"So are you. He's getting attached and there's probably no way to stop that. But a reminder is a good idea. A warning would be smart."

"Maybe." She sighed. "But I'm a grown-up. I'm warned. And I don't think I'm ready to face the world yet." She met his gaze. "There was a lot of publicity when I ran out on the wedding and completely disappeared. When I resurface, that will make news, too."

"You can handle it. You're strong." He kind of wished she wasn't and would stay in his spare cabin just a while longer.

"Having the time to decompress has been great. I will have to give interviews, and I've had a lot of time to think about what I'm going to say."

"Will you tell the truth?"

"You mean that my fiancé is a lying, cheating toad?"

"Yeah, that." He grinned.

"You bet I'm going to." She looked up at him, a softness in her eyes. "But now I can talk about what happened from a position of strength, not an emotional meltdown."

"Good girl."

"The thing is," she said, "it's beginning to sink in that my feelings about wanting to stay aren't about hiding from all of that."

He knew he was going to be sorry, but he had to ask. "What, then?"

"I like Blackwater Lake and just don't want to leave."

Again he had the sensation that she was waiting for him to say something, but he couldn't go there. "We all have to do things we don't like. What will you do when you go back to your regularly scheduled life?

Train for another Olympics? Continue competing? Endorsements?"

"I still have contracts. But I'm not sure about competing." She sounded disappointed, as if he hadn't said what she'd wanted him to. She looked at him. "Will you miss me?"

"That goes without saying."

"What if I *want* you to say it?"

The words and pleading in her voice were like a punch to the gut. It was a willpower test, and he would do his best to meet the challenge because if he didn't there would be hell to pay.

Ignoring the question, Cabot stood. "I think it's time to turn in. We have an early day tomorrow and should get some sleep."

"Okay. I understand." Without another word, she got up, too, and walked back to her tent, disappearing inside.

Cabot made sure the embers of the fire were completely put out. He wished there was another chore to keep him busy because he knew when he got in his sleeping bag sleep wouldn't be coming his way.

No, he would be trying to figure out a way to get the look on Kate's face out of his mind. He felt as if he'd drop-kicked a kitten. But what was he supposed to do? Acting on his feelings, even though he was pretty sure she would willingly respond, was a very bad idea.

She was leaving soon. Too soon. He would never forget how hard it was when a woman you cared about walked away. The fewer memories of Kate he had to deal with, the better.

Chapter 13

Four days after returning from the campout, Kate was sitting on her bunk in the stray cabin. She'd read the same page in her book three times without comprehending what it said. With a sigh, she set it aside. Obviously even a steamy romance novel couldn't distract her from what was on her mind.

Cabot. Now, there was a hero. A living, breathing three-dimensional man with positives and even negatives that only made him more appealing.

In the wilderness she'd learned that this summer he had been hanging around the camp more than usual. Until now, that was. She hadn't seen him at any of the activities since they'd returned.

She'd come to the conclusion that he was keeping his distance from her because she'd flat-out said she wanted him to say that he would miss her. He hadn't.

The silence spoke volumes. Ty had been as cute and sweet as always, but his father was missing in action.

Looking around her small cabin, she felt a pang of regret. Oddly enough, this minimal space was more appealing than her spacious condo in California. This felt like sanctuary, a haven from her crazy, busy life. It sounded weird and overly dramatic, but this time in Blackwater Lake had repaired and replenished her soul. She loved it here.

But her time-out was coming to an end, and it would be good to repair something else. Family relationships. She'd spoken to her parents only a few times to let them know she was all right. She hadn't talked to her brother or sister at all and it was time to fix that. After pulling her cell phone from her shorts pocket and scrolling through her contacts list, she found the number she wanted and highlighted it before pressing the call button. She waited while it rang, expecting to get voice mail. A smile curved her lips when she heard her older brother's familiar voice.

"My truck better be in one piece."

She laughed at his fake growl. Obviously he'd checked his caller ID. He was a big softy with her and they both knew it. "Hi, Zach."

"You better be in one piece, too." He paused, and then she noted real concern in his voice when he asked, "Are you okay, Kate?"

"Yes. And so is Angelica." She paused for a moment, then meaningfully added, "Now."

"What did you do to her?"

"Nothing. She just stopped one day. In the rain, which was inconvenient." Although the silver lining was that she'd ended up spending the day with Cabot and the night in his bed. The sensuous memory made her shiver and brought on a yearning that was never far away.

"Kate? Are you there?"

"Yes. What?"

"Why did my truck stop? What's wrong with her? You know how much she means to me."

"Stand down, Zach. Your baby just needed a little tender loving care, and Sydney gave it to her."

"I hope he knows what he's doing." Zach's words carried a warning.

"Syd is a girl. A stunning brunette. Smart. Not at all your type."

He chuckled. "I've really missed you picking on me. I wish you'd called sooner."

"I've been in touch with Mom and Dad."

"I heard. They also said you wouldn't tell them where you are or where you've been," he pointed out.

"I needed some time."

"Say the word, Kate. I'll beat the bastard up for you." Zach clearly believed her time-out was about the aborted wedding.

She laughed at the big-brother posturing, the warm, familiar feeling it gave her. "It's so good to hear your voice."

"I mean it. If it will make you feel better, I'll mess up his pretty face."

"Ted would probably file assault and battery charges against you."

"I'd risk it."

"So not worth it to me. He's done enough damage." She'd been stupid and wouldn't be again.

Zach let loose with some colorful language before saying, "So you're not over him."

"Actually, I am. And to put a finer point on it, I don't think there was anything to get over."

"That's a little subtle for me. You're going to have to spell it out for those of us who are touchy-feely challenged."

"I never loved him."

"How can you be so sure?"

Because everything she felt for Cabot was so much clearer, so much stronger. If she had truly loved Ted, that wouldn't be possible. "Catching Ted kissing another woman at our wedding was a blessing. Fortunately it happened before we exchanged vows. Marrying him would have been a mistake. A disaster."

"You're not just being spunky, are you?" he asked skeptically.

"Spunky? Did you seriously just call me that?"

"No."

"It sure sounded that way," she teased. "But the answer is no. I'm not putting on an act. I truly believe he did me a huge favor."

"That's a new one." Zach's tone was wry. "Cheating as a good deed."

"I'm telling the truth. Cross my heart."

"I'm glad that your heart is unscathed," he said fervently.

That wasn't completely true. Her ex hadn't touched it, but the same couldn't be said of Cabot. The only question was how much damage he'd done.

"I'm fine. Really," she emphasized.

There was the slightest meaningful pause on the other end of the line. "That sounded as if you're trying too hard to convince me."

"Trust me, Zach. Ted is so yesterday." Cabot was

today. Probably tomorrow. And as many days after that as there were until summer was over.

"So, are you ready to come home?" he asked.

"No."

"Wow. Whatever beach you're sitting on must be truly awesome."

Thinking about the nearby cabins with kids and camp counselors, Kate laughed. "You couldn't be more wrong about that."

"Okay. But wherever you are, it's obvious that you needed a break."

"Yes." She remembered that day at the church, catching her fiancé kissing one of her bridesmaids and feeling the need to run from the betrayal she'd seen with her own eyes. Maybe if she hadn't been working so hard for so long she wouldn't have run. But she simply didn't have the reserves to rationally deal with what he'd done to her. "I don't think I even realized how much I needed to get off the wheel until I got to Blackwater Lake—"

After a very long silence on the line, Zach asked, "Where are you?"

She hadn't told anyone where she was; she'd just wanted to be alone to lick her wounds without an audience. Or press. She'd only told them she was okay and would be back at the end of the summer. That was so close now that keeping her whereabouts secret didn't seem to matter anymore. In two weeks she'd be headed home because camp would be over and her verbal contract with Cabot satisfied. Emotionally not so much, but the man knew what he wanted and it didn't include her.

"I'm in Montana," she told her brother.

"Good Lord." And then he asked, "What in the world are you doing there?"

Trying not to be a romantic fool over a handsome rancher, she thought. "I'm keeping busy."

"Doing what?"

"Oh, this and that."

"Well, there's something you need to know. It's about work. Someone has been trying to get in touch with you—"

She heard a knock on her cabin door. Although it was a little late, it was probably one of the kids. Sometimes one of them wandered over with a question. "Hold on, Zach."

She opened the door, but there was no child there. "Cabot."

"Hi," he said. Then he saw the phone and said, "Sorry. Didn't mean to interrupt."

"You didn't."

In her ear she heard a sharp tone in her brother's voice. "Who's there, Kate? Is that a man?"

"Come in," she invited Cabot. Into the phone she said, "I have to go."

"Don't hang up. I want to know what's really going on with my little sister."

"I'm fine. Stand down. I'll be back in a couple of weeks. We'll talk then."

"Kate—"

She hit the end button and met Cabot's gaze. "So, what's up?"

He nodded at her phone, which vibrated in her hand. "Someone from home?"

"Just my brother." She glanced at the caller ID and confirmed her guess. After hitting Ignore, she shut the thing off. "I'll talk to him later."

Zach no doubt had a lot of questions and she owed her family answers, but now wasn't a good time. She would see them all soon enough. Right at this moment she was just so darn happy to see Cabot. It felt like forever since she'd seen him, his handsome face, the small smile that teased the corners of his mouth.

"Are you going to let the bugs in?" she asked, pointedly looking at the open doorway where he was still standing.

"I won't be here that long." His intense expression was completely at odds with his words.

"Okay." Disappointment pressed against her heart. "Then why *are* you here?"

"I saw your light still on."

She glanced over her shoulder at the book on the bed. "Yeah. I was reading."

He shoved his fingertips into the pockets of his jeans. "Just wanted to let you know that I had a talk with Ty. About you leaving."

"And?"

"To be honest, he got a little defensive. Said he's not a little kid and everyone should stop treating him like one. He knows the campers and counselors are all leaving when summer's over." She saw a troubled look in his eyes when he added, "But he's going to ask if he can email you. To stay in touch."

"Of course he can. I'd love to hear from him." *And you,* she thought. With the end of her stay so near, she tried to memorize every line on his face. The shape of his nose. The strong, handsome curve of his jaw.

"Okay. Like I said, I just wanted to let you know so you wouldn't worry." But he still didn't close the door.

"Was there something else?"

This was killing her. So near, yet so far. She probably shouldn't have asked him if he was going to miss her, but she had. And all he would tell her was that it went without saying. Well, she wanted to hear him say it. Better yet, she wished he would ask her to stay.

"No. Nothing else," he said.

A jab of rejection pierced her heart, proving what she'd thought earlier—that it likely wasn't getting out of Blackwater Lake completely unscathed.

"Okay, then. You should probably get back to Ty. I know you don't like leaving him alone up at the house too long."

"He's not at the house." His voice was on the ragged side. "He's sleeping over at C.J.'s."

"Oh. Well…" He had nowhere he had to be. But he didn't want to be here. She moved to the door and started to close it. This was making her crazy, and she wished he would just go. "Anyway, it's getting late."

"Yeah. A rancher's day starts early."

"Thanks for letting me know about your talk with Ty."

He nodded but still didn't back out of the doorway. Conflict sparked in his eyes, an intense expression that revealed a battle raging inside him.

"Cabot?"

"Oh, hell—"

He stepped inside and closed the door behind him. Then he pulled her into his arms before turning to back her against the wall. At the same time he took her mouth and pressed his lower body to hers, letting her know what he wanted. His arms cushioned her back and her heart soared with the knowledge that he was protecting her. He'd lost control enough to kiss the living daylights out of her but was still taking care of her. Heat radiated through her, setting fire to her nerve endings as she kissed him back.

His mouth nibbled over her jaw and down her neck,

where he touched his tongue to that spot just beneath her ear. Then he blew on the moist, sensitive place and shot tingles straight to her female core.

"I want you, Kate." The words vibrated against her skin. "I tried not to—"

"I'm glad you're here now." She shouldn't be so happy he'd failed, but she couldn't help it. "I want you, too."

His gaze searched hers for several intense moments. Both of them were breathing fast, and the harsh sound filled the tiny cabin with escalating need. Then they both moved at the same time, pulling off shirts, undoing buttons, removing pants. He'd pulled a square packet from his jeans and she recognized it as protection.

"Didn't trust your willpower?" she asked breathlessly.

"Not with you." Then he handed it to her before swinging her into his arms.

"Always be prepared?" she teased.

"Yeah, I'm a real Boy Scout. I really did want you to know I'd had a talk with Ty." Intensity simmered in his eyes. "I just wasn't sure I could say that and keep walking. If I didn't… I don't take chances."

"And you were taking me for granted?" She lifted one eyebrow teasingly, questioning.

"Not really. Never let a condom go to waste. I figured we could always wait for the sun to come up and use it to start a campfire."

"So you weren't sure about me."

"No. Yes." Need swirled in his eyes. "Am I wrong?"

"Absolutely not."

He took a couple of steps over to her bunk and gently placed her there. It was wider than a single bed, but not by a lot, so when he joined her they were skin to skin. His big hand slid over the curve of her waist and down her thigh, squeezing gently. Then he moved to her abdomen and down lower while she held her breath in anticipation.

When he touched her, she thought she would go up in flames. Reaching out a hand to the scarred pine nightstand, she found the condom and handed it over.

"Now, Cabot—" She was so breathless, the words were nearly trapped in her throat.

"I know, honey."

After putting it in place, he rolled over her and settled his weight on his forearms before slowly entering her. She wrapped her legs around his waist as he thrust into her, then matched his rhythm. He drove her higher and higher and too soon she cried out as release roared through her.

Another push, then two and he groaned, pulling her even tighter against him. They held each other for what seemed like forever as their breathing slowed and shock waves subsided.

"Oh, my—" She smiled up at him, enveloped in a warm glow.

"That goes double for me." He kissed her softly, tenderly, then levered himself off. "Hold that thought."

Completely spent, she dropped her forearm over her eyes as he walked into the tiny bathroom. Several moments later he turned off the light and returned to her bed. He lifted her enough to turn down the sheet and blanket, then slid in beside her and pulled the covers over them, curling himself around her.

The last thought she had before falling asleep in Cabot's arms was that she'd finally found the place she belonged.

* * *

The next morning Kate woke up alone in her bunk. She remembered Cabot gently easing out of the bed, trying not to wake her. She also remembered that he didn't kiss her goodbye, not even a soft touch of lips anywhere. So much for belonging.

As she showered, brushed her teeth and prepared for the day, she tried to shake the feeling of dejection, of giving up. She'd been so darn happy when he couldn't walk out the door last night without kissing her and happier than she could ever recall being when he'd made love to her. But she couldn't bury her head in the sand any longer. That wasn't love.

What they'd done in her bed was nothing more than a physical act between a man and woman. It was just sex—really fantastic sex, but without any complicated emotions—and she knew that because even casual feelings would have compelled him to kiss her goodbye. He might as well have left money on the nightstand beside the empty condom packet.

That part wasn't fair, but she wasn't in the mood to be fair this morning. She was crabby. And how could she have been so starry-eyed and spineless last night? The man had come prepared to sleep with her, for goodness' sake.

But that wasn't fair, either. She'd seen the conflict in his eyes and had felt the tension in his body. She felt a teeny, tiny bit of satisfaction that he'd given in, that she was a temptation he couldn't resist. At least last night. This morning he'd resisted her just fine.

She recalled their conversation in his bed the other time and wondered if *he* hated himself this morning.

She gave her appearance one last look in the mirror and thought at least it had been good to talk to her brother last night. By now the whole family would know she was in Blackwater Lake, Montana. That was okay because she wasn't hiding anymore.

She joined the other counselors for a busy morning of relay races, scavenger hunt and ceramics. When she walked into the kitchen for a cup of coffee just before lunch, she was hot, sweaty and covered with dried clay.

Caroline was stirring a big pot of soup and glanced up. "You look like the mud wrestler who lost. Or did someone just pull you out of quicksand?"

"Ceramics are not my best event." She sighed and looked down at the dried splotches all over her front. "Those pottery wheels can get away from you if you're not careful."

Caroline grinned. "Happens with every group. Always someone who doesn't pay attention and that stuff goes everywhere."

"And I'm a horrible warning." Kate grabbed a mug from the cupboard and poured coffee into it. "You'd think after all these weeks I'd know when to duck."

And she didn't just mean the crafts activities.

"It happens fast," the other woman said. "You can't always see it coming."

"You'd think I'd know that, too." Absently she blew on the hot dark liquid in her cup. "I guess I'm just a slow learner. Apparently I keep making the same mistakes over and over."

Caroline put down the wooden spoon on the stainless-steel counter. She leaned back and studied Kate. "You're not just talking about ceramics now, are you?"

"What else would I be talking about?"

Kate realized this would be the perfect opening to discuss what was bothering her, but she didn't think it was professional to discuss their mutual boss, who also happened to be Caroline's good friend. Kate also knew she'd crossed the line into unprofessional territory by sleeping with him in the first place. Still, there were just a couple of weeks left. Why beat to death a situation that would soon be over?

"What I would be talking about is Cabot," the other woman said pointedly.

"I'm not sure why you would think that," Kate bluffed. "But he's not... We're not—"

"Oh, please. I'm a high school teacher and have been for a lot of years. I can tell when someone is dancing around the truth." Caroline fixed her with a teacher look that would have made the average person sing like a canary.

But Kate wasn't a teenager and didn't want to put this woman in the awkward position of taking sides. "It isn't fair or right to discuss this with you. You've known him for a long time, and it's not appropriate for you to be caught in the middle."

"Why don't you let me worry about all that?" Caroline said gently. "He's my friend, yes, but so are you. I've grown fond of you. It's obvious to me something happened that's bothering you. And if the choices are ceramics or Cabot, my money is on him. What did he do?"

If Kate said he hadn't kissed her goodbye when he'd left her cabin that morning, it would open up a whole messy can of worms. *Keep it simple.* "Well, I guess you could say I'm attracted to him."

"Tell me something I don't know." Caroline's tone was teasing. "In fact, everyone knows. One look and it's pretty clear that the two of you have the hots for each other."

Really? Everyone? Diane had noticed differences in

Cabot and clearly suspected it had something to do with Kate. Yes, she quivered like crazy when she was around him. If that qualified as "the hots," she was guilty as charged. But she wanted more, something deep and lasting. This conversation was pointless.

Kate took a sip of coffee. "Oh, well, I don't know about that—"

"I'm really going to stick my nose in where it doesn't belong," Caroline interrupted. "But I think you've slept with him."

Kate wanted so badly to say he'd started it, but she wasn't twelve. And she'd enthusiastically participated.

Cheeks hot with something that was a mixture of guilt and shame, she met the other woman's gaze. "I have."

"I didn't really know for sure. Just took a shot." Caroline smiled, a pleased expression on her attractive features. "I'm so glad."

Now she was confused. "You are?"

"Absolutely. What?" the other woman questioned. "You thought I'd be upset?"

"Maybe." Kate shrugged. "At the very least I thought you'd be protective of him."

"Oh, I am. When the situation calls for it. But this isn't one of those times." Caroline's expression was soft and maternal. "You're good for him, Kate."

"I am?" She blinked, then gripped her coffee mug so tightly her knuckles turned white. "Could have fooled me."

"He's very closed off since his wife left. She really did a number on him."

"She still is doing a number on him," Kate corrected.

"You know she passed away?"

"I do." No way would Kate share about being with

him when he got the call because of having spent the night in his bed. "And he wanted me to stand by when he broke the news to Ty."

"You're good for that boy, too," Caroline observed. "So explain to me how that woman is still messing with him."

"He's in love with her and always will be."

"Did he tell you that?" Caroline's blue eyes narrowed skeptically.

"Almost. He told me his father never stopped loving his mother even though she left. He was a one-woman man and Cabot takes after him."

"In a lot of ways he does," Caroline agreed. "They both have a connection to the land and family. But not in relationships. That woman walked out and left him with a newborn. It took him a while to get through all the steps of grief over it, but I'd bet everything I've got that he stopped loving her a long time ago."

"I'm not so sure."

"He's different with you," Caroline persisted. "He's lighter somehow—his spirit, I mean. He hired me to run the camp when Ty was a baby and he had his hands full with everything. But this is the first summer I've seen him so involved. And Diane told me how he acted on the campout. The only difference around here is you."

"I'm having a hard time believing that," Kate confessed. "He's really resistant."

"He's built up some pretty high, thick walls, but if you give it time, I think they can be penetrated."

"If it's not in the next couple weeks, I won't be around to see that."

"Why not? You could stick here if you wanted to. After all, if your life was firing on all cylinders, you wouldn't be here in the first place."

Kate couldn't dispute that. And she wasn't looking forward to leaving, which was pretty telling. She loved Blackwater Lake, and that had nothing to do with Cabot and how she felt about him.

"You have a point about that. But two wrongs don't make a right."

"And giving up without a fight is the coward's way out. What if he's your soul mate?"

"What if *she* was *his?*" Kate shot back.

"Sometimes you have to take a leap of faith to get what you want."

"A little encouragement from him would make it a lot less scary."

"No pain, no gain."

Kate knew the other woman was sincere and began to wonder if she might be right. Caroline certainly had known him a long time. What if Kate was giving up too soon?

"I'll give it some thought," she agreed. "And thanks for talking with me. I really do feel a lot better."

"Good." Caroline smiled. "I love playing Cupid. It's so rewarding when—"

A strange sound interrupted her, something completely out of place. Usually the quiet here by the lake and mountains was absolute, but Kate swore the noise was the *whap whap* of helicopter rotors and it was moving closer and getting a lot louder. She and Caroline looked at each other and without a word walked to the door, then went outside onto the porch.

Sure enough, they weren't the only ones who'd heard. All the kids and counselors were gathered outside, watching as a helicopter set down in the open area by Cabot's house. On the side of the chopper were the letters *ESPN*.

Kate made an educated guess that this had something to do with her and took off at a run up the slight rise. She stopped beside Cabot, and both of them watched as a man in an expensive suit and tie stepped out of the chopper. He approached with hand outstretched to Cabot and the two shook.

"I'm John Crowley, vice president in charge of televised sports for ESPN." He looked at her. "You're not an easy woman to locate, Miss Scott. But I've got a proposition for you, and I think you're going to like it."

Chapter 14

"Dad, is Kate going to fly away on that helicopter?"

Cabot saw the anxiety in his son's eyes. The boy had come running with everyone else from the camp when the guy in charge of sports for ESPN had arrived. He'd asked to speak with Kate privately, and Cabot had offered his house. They were still talking, as far as he knew. He was in the barn with his son, fielding questions that he had no answers for.

"I don't know, Ty," he said. "I could sure use your help mucking out this stall."

The boy only nodded, but the wheels were turning. Cabot had no illusions that the interrogation was over. This was just the eye of the hurricane, and he was bracing for the storm to come.

He and Ty assembled shovels, a wheelbarrow and a pitchfork to remove the dirty hay and replace it. The work was messy and sweaty, but sometimes a guy needed something like this. Now was one of those times.

Ty shoveled up some muck. "That man must be pretty rich if he could come here in a helicopter."

That thought had also occurred to Cabot. "Yeah."

"Why do you think he wants to talk to her?"

"He said he's in charge of sports broadcasting, so it probably has something to do with that."

Cabot had quickly realized that Kate was an even bigger deal than he knew. One picture was worth a thousand words, and the helicopter was quite a visual pointing to the fact that she was way out of his league.

He dumped a shovelful of dirty hay into the wheelbarrow. "Remember I told you she won Olympic medals in skeet shooting?"

"Yeah. That's her best event."

"Well, when someone is an expert and a competition is on TV, they like to get that person to explain things to the people watching."

"Oh." The boy leaned on his shovel, obviously thinking that over. "If she does that, will she have to go? I mean before summer's over?"

"It's probably best not to speculate about that. We don't even know for sure that's what it's about." But he was pretty sure they wouldn't send a suit in a helicopter to discuss the summer-camp program.

This was a big deal.

"I don't want her to go, Dad."

"I know, son."

It was official. The talk he'd had with Ty had not prepared the kid for her leaving. Cabot knew better than his son that there was no way to prepare yourself for the void of losing someone you cared about. Tyler cared about Kate and he wasn't the only one in this family who did.

He'd known that when he stuck that condom in his pocket last night in case he couldn't make himself walk away after telling her about his talk with Ty. But as soon as he'd pocketed the thing, there was no way he could keep himself from having her. He realized that now. On some level he'd already made up his mind to take her to bed.

Some indefinable thing about Kate Scott drew him like a moth to a flame. And it wasn't just sex, although that was fantastic. He just really liked her, everything about her. Especially the way she'd taken Tyler under her wing.

"Dad, I have an idea."

"Oh?" Cabot knew he wasn't going to like this. "What is it, son?"

"You should talk to her. Tell her you want her to stay."

"I didn't say that." He saw the boy working up to a protest and jumped in before the words came out. "You said you don't want her to go and I said I understand how you feel. That's all."

"It's the same thing."

"No, it's not." Cabot couldn't let himself want her to stay. He couldn't cross that line; he couldn't take the chance. If it went badly, and he had every reason to believe it would, he might never make it back. "But that doesn't mean you can't tell her how you feel."

He heard muffled footsteps on the hard-packed dirt path that ran down the center of the barn. Seconds later Kate appeared.

"Here you are," she said to Cabot, then smiled at Ty. "I've been looking everywhere for you."

"Hi, Kate. What did that guy want?" The boy was clearly happy to see her.

Cabot wanted to think he wasn't, but it would be a lie. He couldn't look at her hard enough or long enough.

"The helicopter was pretty cool, no?" An undeniable undercurrent of excitement hummed through her. "I talked to my brother, Zach, last night. Apparently he told them where to find me. It was about a job offer."

"They didn't waste any time." They must've wanted her bad. Cabot knew exactly how that felt. "What's the proposal?"

"A national championship is coming up in a couple of weeks, and they want me to provide color, context and commentary on my sport."

"I see."

"He said they saw the magazine cover and liked my look. They think that people will be interested in my story, and that will boost the ratings for skeet the way Danica Patrick has done for NASCAR. The objective is to get airtime experience before the summer Olympics, which aren't that far away."

"You sound excited." That was the exact opposite of how he felt.

"I'm flattered, for sure. And it's always nice to be asked." She glanced down at the front of her legs, the dried dirt on her shirt and shorts. "And they still wanted me, even though I look as if I've been dipped in quicksand."

He thought she'd never looked more beautiful than she did at this moment. But he couldn't afford to give in to that feeling. "So you accepted."

"That's what I'd like to talk to you about." She grew serious and looked at Tyler, who was listening to every word and soaking it up like a sponge. "Kiddo, could I talk to your dad alone for a few minutes?"

"You're going to leave, aren't you?" His voice had threads of anger and hurt mixing together.

"There's a whole lot to consider, sweetie."

"Ty, we talked about this. You knew Kate was only staying until the end of summer."

"But she likes it here," he cried. "I know she does."

"You're right about that, Ty. I do love Blackwater Lake and the ranch. But—"

"She has a career," Cabot interjected. "And this is a really good opportunity for her. Do you understand?"

"Yes." But the expression in his eyes said different.

"Just let me talk to your dad for a little bit," she pleaded. "Then I'll come find you and let you know what's happening."

"You won't leave without saying goodbye?"

"Of course not. I promise," she said. "If I go."

"Okay." The tone said he would do as requested but wasn't happy about it. He dragged the shovel behind him as he walked out of the stall and toward the barn door, leaving them alone.

Cabot set his own shovel against the stall fence, then turned back, carefully and deliberately standing a few feet away from her. "So, what did you tell them?"

"I turned it down."

That shocked him. "Why? Isn't it a really good opportunity?"

"It's what I've been working for."

"And you told them no?"

"I did."

He shook his head. "But you're ready to go back. All set to rat out the cheating scumbag about what he did. Face the world."

"But I don't want that world anymore." Her eyes pleaded with him to understand. "Staying here on the ranch, here in Blackwater Lake, is what will make me happy."

Call him cynical, but his wife had said she wanted to stay, too, and that hadn't worked out so well. "What would you have said to this offer if you'd never come here?"

"But I did."

"Humor me. Think about this. What if you hadn't driven into Blackwater Lake in your wedding gown and stayed for the summer camp? What would you have said to a sportscasting gig that you've worked really hard for?"

She thought about it for a moment as emotions swirled in her eyes. "I would have said yes. But I did come here and stay for the summer—"

He held up a hand to stop her. "That's what I thought."

"Cabot, listen to me. Being here with you and Ty has changed my perspective and priorities. What we have is special and I'm not willing to give that up."

"It's a summer fling."

"You don't mean that. Not after last night."

He met her gaze and forced himself not to look away so that she would see this was for the best. He also fought the overwhelming urge to pull her into his arms and beg her not to go. But if he did that and she stayed, missing out on all the opportunities waiting for her, eventually she'd resent him. He would lose her either way, so why prolong the inevitable?

"Yeah, I do mean it. We both know this isn't going anywhere. You have a once-in-a-lifetime opportunity and should take it. You should go."

"You're only saying that because circumstances made ranch life your career choice. Maybe you feel deprived of having the option or this is about the fact that your wife wasn't satisfied with her decision. But for some people, the life you live every single day is a dream."

"Dreams are nothing but a romantic notion before reality hits you where it hurts."

Kate stared at him for several moments, surprise and hurt filling her eyes. Then a single fat tear rolled down her cheek, and he nearly lost his resolve.

"Don't, Kate," he pleaded. "You'll see. This is the best thing for both of us. A clean break."

"There's nothing clean about this." Anger chased the wounded expression from her face. "You think you're being noble, preserving that nice-guy image by helping people who are down on their luck. And when you didn't know about me, everything was fine. I fit into the mold of acceptable, someone who got through the barrier."

"Look, this is—"

She held up her hand. "You had your say—now it's my turn. All was well until you found out I could actually take care of myself, but you started putting up different walls. Taking me to bed was okay as long as it was just temporary. But you're so worried about taking another chance that I think you're glad about this offer. It takes the heat off."

Her words hit very close to the mark, and he didn't like that at all. "Is psychobabble part of your Olympic regimen? If so, you need more training. You're way off target."

"Is that so?" She glared at him. "Well, even Olympic gold medalists miss what they aim at from time to time."

Without another word, she turned and walked out of the barn, head held high.

Cabot stared at the space where she'd been standing just a moment ago. He had that feeling of making a spontaneous purchase, then having buyer's remorse. Before he could puzzle that out, he heard a noise.

"Is someone there?"

"It's me, Dad." Tyler walked into the stall.

"I thought you went back to hang out with the other kids."

The boy shook his head. "You're probably gonna be mad and I'm sorry, but I had to."

"What did you do?"

"I listened to you and Kate talking."

Cabot read disappointment and censure in the eight-year-old's eyes. He saw a maturity far beyond his years, something Cabot had had in his own gaze as a kid.

"You know it's wrong to eavesdrop," he scolded.

"I had to," Ty said again. "No one tells a kid what's going on and I really needed to know."

"So you're aware that Kate is leaving."

"You told her to go," Ty accused. "She wasn't going to take that job. She told the helicopter guy no. She wanted to stay here because she cares about us."

"It's complicated." He winced as the words came out of his mouth. He'd proved what his son had just said about adults talking down to him.

"Yeah. That's what grown-ups always tell kids. And maybe I don't understand everything, but I get this. You really blew it, Dad. Girls sure aren't *your* best event." Then he turned and walked out, too.

Cabot lifted his Stetson and dragged his fingers through his hair before replacing his hat. He looked at the dirty hay around him and thought it was ironic that the whole crappy scene had happened here.

Ty was right. Love wasn't his best event, but heading off trouble was, and that was just what he'd done. Although the sinking feeling in his gut was starting to feel like a different kind of trouble.

The day after Kate left the ranch, Cabot was getting the cold shoulder from his son and dirty looks from everyone else. Or maybe he was imagining that because he felt lower than a snake's belly. Ty did say that Kate had kept her promise and said goodbye to him. He also shared that she'd told the boy she was taking the job and if he wanted to know why she couldn't come back here when it was over he should ask his dad.

But Ty hadn't asked him anything, apparently assuming that Cabot was completely hopeless with girls. That was what he'd been trying to tell everyone, so why was it such a big surprise when it all imploded?

For the first time in his life, the wide-open spaces were closing in on him, so Cabot had decided to go into Blackwater Lake for lunch. Ty declined the invitation to come along, opting to hang out with the camp kids, so Cabot walked into the Grizzly Bear Diner alone. It was half past noon and the booths were mostly full. People here and there occupied the swivel stools at the counter.

He took his usual seat, the one where he'd been sitting when Kate had shown up in her wrinkled wedding dress. Michelle Crawford was there, just as she'd been that day to interview the beautiful stranger who'd ended up making such a ding in his life.

The diner owner gave him a big smile. "Cabot, it's good to see you."

"You, too, Michelle." Even more, it was nice to see a friendly face. "How's the family?"

"Good. Emma and Justin are planning their wedding."

"I hope to get an invitation."

"The whole town will get one," she promised. "We have so much to celebrate."

A year ago Michelle, her husband and their three sons had been reunited with the daughter/sister who'd been kidnapped and taken from them as a baby. She'd come looking for her family and found the love of her life in Dr. Justin Flint, who worked at the medical clinic in town. It was nice to see good things happen to good people. Cabot considered himself an upstanding guy, but he held out no expectation of rainbows and roses. It just wasn't in the cards for him.

"Coffee?" Michelle asked.

He nodded. "And a burger."

"Coming right up." She wrote out the order and handed it to the cook working the grill behind her, then grabbed the coffeepot and a mug. "So what's up with Kate?"

"Why do you ask?"

"Seriously?" Pouring his coffee, she glanced up quickly and met his gaze. Her own was wry. "You did see the helicopter, right?"

"Yeah. I was there." He'd have been better off rounding up strays in an isolated canyon far away from what had happened yesterday. Especially the part where he'd talked to Kate in the barn. "How did you know about that?"

"Caroline called me." She rested the pot on the counter. "We knew Kate was a big deal when her picture was on that magazine cover. But who sends a helicopter? That really makes a statement."

"Yup." He lifted his mug and blew on the hot coffee.

"I'm dying to hear about it. So, where is she?" Michelle persisted.

Cabot figured there was no point in beating around the bush. If he did, the woman would just call Caroline and jump-start Blackwater Lake's very efficient information network. "She's gone."

"What?" The woman looked genuinely surprised.

"She left."

"For a job." Michelle studied him intently. "She'll be back, right?"

Cabot shook his head. "For good."

"Why would she do that? She loves this town."

"How do you know?" he asked.

"You could just tell. And she said so more than once." She frowned. "Everyone liked her. She's not a stuck-up city girl who couldn't stand being in a town where the closest mall is an hour away."

Like his wife, he thought. "I didn't realize you knew her that well."

"Actually, I don't because you kept her pretty busy at camp. But I heard. Sydney McKnight got to know her, though."

A woman had just walked in the door and sat down on the swivel stool beside him. "Did I hear my name? Are you talking about me, Michelle?"

"I never miss a chance to talk about anyone, and everyone comes in this diner sooner or later. It's gossip central. You should know that, Sydney."

"Right." Sydney looked at him. "Hi, Cabot. I haven't seen you since the day Kate's truck broke down. How are you?"

He'd been better but was glad she'd interrupted the conversation. Kate was the last person he wanted to talk about today. "I'm great. How's business at the garage?"

"Good. We're really busy." The pretty brunette glanced from him to Michelle. "So, I'm dying to hear about the helicopter at your ranch yesterday."

And here we go again, he thought. He looked at the two women, then sipped his coffee without answering.

Michelle had no problem filling the silence. "He was just telling me that Kate is gone and she's not coming back."

"She is?" Syd sounded surprised. "I don't believe that."

"Believe it." Cabot remembered the anger and hurt on Kate's face, the tear that had rolled down her cheek. He would never forget how she'd looked and his part in it. What he'd done was for the best, he repeated to himself. She would realize that soon enough.

"I don't understand," Syd said. "I saw her not that long ago, and it sounded like she would be here for the long term."

"You probably misunderstood." If there was a God in heaven, his hamburger would come any second now. Although when women were determined to get information, a man wanting to eat probably wasn't going to stop them from asking questions.

"I'm sure I got what she was saying. She was very clear that Blackwater Lake felt like home to her." The young woman looked puzzled. "That leaves only one possibility."

"That's what I'm thinking," Michelle chimed in.

"Do I want to know?" he asked, already knowing the answer.

"Probably not," Syd said. "What happened with you two?"

"I'd like to know, too." The diner owner stared at him.

The real answer was that it was his fault Kate wasn't here. He couldn't be the right man, couldn't tell her what she wanted to hear. But that was better kept to himself.

"The simple truth is that ESPN sent somebody important to offer her a job. She took it." He cradled the coffee mug between his palms and looked at each woman in turn. "End of story."

"I don't think so." Syd's dark eyes narrowed suspiciously. "What did you do to her?"

"Nothing."

Well, he'd slept with her, but he didn't think that counted. These two were digging for relationship stuff and there wasn't one between him and Kate. He'd been careful to make sure she knew that up front. Technically he hadn't done anything but stick to the established rules.

"Not buying it." Michelle shook her head as if he was dumb as a post. "She fit in here. I, for one, would never have predicted that she would, what with her being a runaway bride and all."

"I wish I'd seen her that day," Syd commented wistfully.

That was a sight Cabot would never forget. Along with her and Ty laughing together. The sight of Kate standing by the lake with moonlight shining in her hair. Memories of waking up beside her in his bed. The disappointment in her eyes when he'd trashed her romantic notions.

"I guess she changed her mind," he said.

"Michelle is right. She fit seamlessly into Blackwater Lake, and not everyone does. People really liked her. She never played the cover-girl card, never acted like a diva. Always down-to-earth. I'd have bet money on her sticking around. Unless..." Sydney gave him a pointed look.

Cabot gave it right back. "What?"

"You're the variable." She toyed with the straw in

the diet soda Michelle had set in front of her. "Something happened between you and Kate. What did you do to her?"

Nothing that he wanted to talk about, but he wasn't going to get to wiggle off this hook that easily. Walking out was an option, but he was no coward. He might as well give them the facts so that when the story spread, and it would, at least the truth would be out there.

"The fact is, she got a job offer. ESPN wants her to do commentary on a nationally televised competition. It's sort of an audition for the summer Olympics in a couple of years. I gave her my blessing."

He'd told her to go. If he'd understood the emptiness of her leaving, he wasn't so sure he would have sent her away.

"I get it now," Michelle said, shaking her head again.

"Me, too." Sydney sighed, and the way she looked at him now was similar to how the summer-camp staff did.

The only way to describe it was *pity*. And the only satisfaction he got was that they stopped grilling him like raw meat. That was small comfort when he felt as if he was losing everything. When had this community, the one he'd always loved and counted on, started working against him?

The answer was simple. It had happened the day a woman with light brown, sun-streaked hair walked into the Grizzly Bear Diner wearing a strapless wedding dress and four-inch satin heels.

As badly as he wanted to put her down as being a runner, that wasn't the case. After all, he'd given her his blessing to go.

Chapter 15

Cabot left his house and headed down the rise to the camp compound. He was glad that only a few days were left until the last group of kids would be gone. Then he'd help Caroline and the counselors close everything down until next year. Equipment, linens and mattresses had to be inventoried and stored for the winter. Also, he always readied the stray cabin in case someone needed it.

And that made him think of Kate. Of course, it didn't take all that much for his thoughts to go there.

Just thinking her name sent a stab of pain and loneliness shooting through him. She'd been gone more than a week, and the feelings of missing her just kept getting worse. Those flowery sayings about time healing all wounds was pure crap, in his opinion. Time wasn't helping at all.

People in town thought he had a screw loose for letting her go. They were entitled to their view, but not one had a wife who'd walked out because she hated her life on his ranch. Ty was speaking to him again, but clearly he missed Kate and talked about her a lot, which was its own kind of hell.

Until that day when the helicopter had touched down and the kid had eavesdropped in the barn, Ty hadn't even been aware of what was going on between Cabot and Kate. The irony was that he and his son were drawn to the same woman, but that was no comfort.

He walked into the dining room, empty now until dinner in a couple of hours. There were no warm bodies or noise in here, but it was still full of memories. Eating dinner with Kate on the patio. Watching the kids soak up every word about surviving in the wilderness. Cooking bugs. That made him smile, and it was about the only thing that could have.

"Something amusing?"

Cabot looked over at Caroline. He'd been so wrapped up in thinking about Kate that he hadn't heard the woman approach. "No. Nothing's funny."

"We're a little short-tempered this morning, aren't we?" Her eyebrows lifted questioningly. "Did someone get up on the wrong side of the bed?"

If he'd known how empty his bed would feel without Kate in it, he would never have taken her there. Those memories were some of the most tormenting. And it wouldn't do any good to bunk in the stray cabin to escape them because he'd held her in his arms there, too.

"I'm fine." But even he heard the edge in his voice.

"Yeah. I can tell."

"Everyone's got an opinion, but no one is walking in my boots. Don't start with me, Caroline."

"Start what?" she asked innocently.

"Kate," he all but growled. "I don't want to talk about her."

"Okay. So what are you doing here?"

"Just wondered if you have enough help for shutting the operation down after these kids leave."

"We could probably use one extra pair of hands," she acknowledged. "Seeing as we're suddenly a body short."

Accusation was in her tone, but he managed to ignore that. "Okay. I'll bring one of the hired hands with me to help when the time comes." He glanced out the sliding glass door leading to the patio. The kids were wearing bathing suits and drifting back from the lake with towels draped around their necks. "How about now? Are things okay, with one body short, I mean?"

"As good as can be expected."

He knew how that felt because he missed that spectacular body, along with her sassy sense of humor and quick wit. But he wondered what Caroline meant. "What's going on?"

"I'm bummed that the kids who came here for a ranch experience will get their money's worth, but it won't be as rich an experience as it might have been. If Kate was still here to teach survival skills, I mean."

"They'll get enough. It always was before she ever showed up." In her damn wedding dress looking like a fashion-show refugee.

"What about Ty?" Caroline leaned a hip against one of the long picniclike tables.

"I don't know what you're getting at." He'd come here to talk about camp shutdown, but this was wandering off the trail into personal territory. He was lost and no amount of survival skills would help him find his way out. "Frankly, I don't think I want to know where you're going with this."

"Ask me if I care." She was obstinate, no question about it, but the pigheaded look on her face was new. "Your son is hurting, Cabot, and you know it."

"He'll get over it."

"Yeah. Life has a way of moving on, but it will change him. As you well know."

"He barely knew Kate." In fact, his son had known her longer than his own mother. "And I'm not sure what you want me to do about it. She left for a job."

Caroline ignored that. "Kate wasn't here a long time—I'll grant you that. But Ty got a glimpse of what it would be like to have a mom. She was good to him and good for him."

Cabot shifted his feet, feeling not only his own hurt and betrayal, but also his son's. "I can't force someone to stay. People move in and out of his life and I have no power to control who he does or doesn't become attached to."

"In most cases that's true. But it's different with Kate."

"No, it's not." He already knew she was unique, but he would argue the point all day long. "She was always only temporary and Ty knew that. I talked to him about it." Because Kate had insisted so that his son wouldn't get hurt. Fat lot of good the conversation had done.

"She didn't act temporary." Caroline shook her head sadly. "And she didn't feel that way. It's just not the same without her here."

Cabot knew exactly what she meant, but no way would he say anything to agree with her. It was better to let her believe he'd gotten up on the wrong side of the bed than confirm how miserable he was. And she would know. He couldn't put anything over on this woman.

"She's not irreplaceable," he said defensively.

"You're so wrong about that." The stubborn look shifted into her eyes again, and around the edges he saw pity. "And if you don't go after her, you're a damn fool."

"No. It would be foolish to chase after her just to get smacked down a second time."

"That's your father talking, Cabot," she said gently.

"What are you saying?" As soon as the words were out of his mouth he knew it was a mistake. Walking out rather than listening to this would have been a better option. The only reason he didn't was out of respect for this woman.

"When your mom left, you were just a vulnerable kid and your dad was shocked and hurt. Everything he was feeling got passed down to you. All the betrayal and bitterness. The wariness and lack of trust, even though he never stopped loving her."

"It wasn't his fault."

"I know," she said softly. "But the damage was done and he couldn't help it. It's just bad damn luck that your mom didn't love him enough to stay and he couldn't love anyone else and move on. He was a one-woman man."

"Yeah."

"And to make matters worse, you finally took a chance and, as luck would have it, picked someone cut from the same cloth as your mother."

"Dixon curse," he said angrily.

"Maybe. Or it could just be you were young and stupid. Ready to settle down and decided to settle for her and called it love."

Her words had a ring of truth. "And your point? I know you've got one."

"I'm willing to bet that you weren't really in love with Jennifer." She met his gaze, and her eyes clearly said *pay attention.* "Sometimes you don't get it until you fall hard and fast for real."

"There might be something to that," he conceded.

"The problem is, Kate thinks you were in love with your ex and still are. Pining for her like your dad did for your mom."

"How do you know?"

"She told me." Caroline shrugged. "We were in the kitchen together a lot. Women talk and she came right out and said it."

Cabot knew Kate thought that and he hadn't tried very hard to set her straight. On some level he'd assumed if she was under that impression, they could avoid a mess like he was in now. He no longer qualified for the young-and-stupid defense. He was older but definitely still not wiser where women were concerned.

"It doesn't matter, Caroline. She still left."

"Because you told her to go."

"It was the right thing to do." Although he wasn't so sure he believed that anymore.

"Maybe. To a point. The truth is she has a career and obligations, but that doesn't mean compromises can't be made. Things worked out. It makes a person glad that you don't work for this country's diplomatic corps." She gave him a wry look. "Kate did what you told her to because of what she believes, that there's no hope of having a life with you."

"She walked out. Nothing can be done now."

"Oh, please, Cabot Dixon. If you really believe that, you're as dense as they come."

"I hope you don't say that to your high school students."

"It gets some sugarcoating and a gentler touch," she admitted. "But the same message."

"Which is?"

"If you don't go after her, you're not nearly as smart as I know you are." She straightened away from the table and put a hand on his arm. "The two of you love each other."

"How can you be so sure?" Cabot knew what she said was the truth but wondered what had given him away.

"Just the way you look at each other. It's right there on your faces. And what a shame it would be to miss out on all that could be yours just because you're too stubborn, stupid and scared to go after her and admit you made a mistake when you sent her away."

Suddenly it hit him. Caroline was right. About everything. "I don't even know where to find her."

"I do. When she said goodbye, she gave me her contact information, including her mother's phone number. She said from now on they would always know where she is. I've talked to the woman. She's very nice, by the way." Caroline grinned. "What can I say? I'm a people person. It's a gift. You can thank me later."

"Caroline, I could kiss you."

"I'll take it." She lifted her cheek, then gave him a teacher look. "I just hope you haven't messed this up so badly it can't be fixed."

He planted one on her at the same time he prayed that Kate would hear him out.

A couple of weeks after leaving Blackwater Lake, Kate was in Nevada for the Western Regional Championships at the Clark County Shooting Complex. This would be her first on-camera experience and she was nervous. The sports network had given her a crash course in the basics of broadcasting, and a commentator would be running the show. He would ask questions and prompt her to provide context and color to the program. She liked him; he'd told her to just talk about the sport she knew and loved.

She could do that; it was the adding-color part that concerned her. Since she'd left Cabot's ranch, it felt as if all the color had seeped out of her life. She ate, drank, talked, laughed, worked. She went through the motions of living, but it was all in black and white. *Miserable* didn't begin to describe how she felt, but she still had a job to do.

Right now she was sitting in the mobile hair-and-makeup trailer, which was a big tricked-out motor home with beauty stations set up. Except for Andrea, who was getting her camera ready, she was alone. Through the window in front of her she could see the cloudless blue sky and mountains that looked as if they'd been carved from rock. Pretty in their own way, but not a single evergreen tree in sight. It wasn't Montana.

She missed Blackwater Lake desperately, and the thought brought tears to her eyes. Crying couldn't happen. It would ruin her makeup, and Andrea would have to fix the damage. Some professional she was.

The young blue-eyed blonde was applying her mascara. She frowned. "Do you have allergies? Nevada is different from California, and something could be making your eyes water."

Something was, but it had nothing to do with flora, fauna or the fact that it was dry as a bone in the desert. She simply missed Cabot, and her heart hurt every time she thought about not being able to see him.

"I'm so sorry, Andrea."

The other woman waved a hand. "No big deal. It's nothing that can't be touched up."

"I don't mean to be so much trouble."

"Are you kidding?" The young woman took a small makeup sponge and blotted under Kate's eyes. "I've worked with trouble, and you don't even rate in the top ten."

"Still, I don't want to give you more work to do."

"It isn't allergies, is it?"

Not unless she was allergic to loving and losing.

Andrea took another sponge and ran it through a small container of light tan–colored concealer. "I heard rumors. About you and some rancher in Montana."

"How could anyone know about that?" Kate had told her family what had happened, and Zach had wanted to beat up the rancher in question. The thought made her tear up again.

The other woman noticed. "I'm sorry. I have no idea how this stuff gets started."

"Rumors and gossip remind me of Blackwater Lake."

"Where's that?"

"Montana."

"Where the rancher is?"

Kate nodded. "It's a small town and news travels fast. The people who live there take great pride in that."

"How did you find this place?" Andrea shrugged. "We might as well talk about this. Get it out of your system and maybe you'll stop crying."

She didn't think that would happen, but it was worth a try. "You know that I ran out on my wedding?"

"Yeah. When you dropped off the radar it was a big story. For what it's worth, you did the right thing, walking out on the cheating jerk."

"Sure dodged a bullet there."

When she'd returned from Montana, one of the first things she did was a series of interviews to set the record straight. Some of the fallout was that her ex lost a fair number of high-profile sports figures he represented, including Kate. It hadn't taken her long to find excellent representation, a guy who made sure she took advantage of this opportunity for some terrific publicity that highlighted her new gig as a sports commentator. Now it occurred to her that the press might have been digging into her Blackwater Lake experience, which was how the romantic rumors had started.

She continued her story. "After I caught him kissing another woman, I grabbed the first set of car keys I saw and they happened to belong to my brother's old truck. I got in, still wearing my wedding gown, and drove until I was too tired to drive anymore. That happened to be Blackwater Lake."

In spite of how badly things had turned out with Cabot, she would never regret finding the town, the beauty and majesty of the lake and mountains. Knowing the people. She was keeping in touch with Caroline and Sydney.

"Is the rumor about the rancher true?" Andrea asked.

Kate nodded. "Cabot Dixon. He's smart, funny, a little brooding, which is sexy. Wonderful father to an eight-year-old boy. Tyler."

She missed him, too.

"What happened?" The other woman was teasing and tweaking her hair.

"I worked at his summer camp. He felt sorry for the runaway bride and took me in."

"No. I mean personally—between the two of you."

Kate had fallen in love with him—that was what had happened. And he'd broken her heart. "I was supposed to stay until the end of summer, but the network sent a helicopter to find me."

"I heard about that." Andrea frowned. "Cabot didn't try to stop you from leaving?"

"He urged me to take the job." *Because he didn't want me.* It was as simple as that. Her eyes filled with tears again. "I don't think the talking-about-this therapy is working very well. Probably we should change the subject."

"Too soon?" When she nodded, Andrea said, "Okay. Then let's talk about your brother."

"What's there to say? Like all brothers, he's annoying and endearing in equal parts."

"Don't forget cute." Andrea had a dreamy look in her eyes. Apparently Zach's visit to the sports newsroom had made an impression. "Is he single?"

"Yes, but you don't want—" A knock on the door interrupted.

"Probably they want you in the booth. Come in," she called out.

The door opened and a man wearing a formal black tuxedo walked in. Kate saw him in the mirror and her heart started hammering in her chest. "Cabot—"

Andrea gasped and gawked. "The rancher?"

He held out his hand. "Cabot Dixon. Nice to meet you."

"Andrea Tillson. Where's the cowboy hat?" She looked him up and down. "You look like you just filmed a champagne commercial or ran out on a wedding."

"There's a good reason for that."

He looked awkward and uncomfortable but so incredibly handsome that Kate could hardly stand it. "Where's Tyler?"

"With C.J.'s family."

"How did you find me?"

"Caroline shared your contact information with me. I talked with your brother and he told me where to go."

That was when she noticed the bruise near his eye. "He made you work for the information, didn't he?"

Cabot brushed a knuckle over his cheek. "He's everything a big brother should be."

Kate didn't know whether to laugh or cry. "Why did you come?"

He looked at Andrea. "Would it be all right if I talked to her alone?"

"Sure. Of course." She looked at her watch. "You've got about a half hour before your call."

The girl walked out, and Kate was alone with him. She took off the plastic cape protecting her silk shirt and denim jacket from the heavy makeup and stood to face him. If there was a God in heaven she would be able to keep him from seeing that she'd been crying over him just minutes ago.

"It seems as if you've gone to a lot of trouble to find me and I really can't figure out why." She tried to be cool as she stared at the face she'd missed so much. The one she'd never expected to see again. He had a point to make; the tuxedo was a big clue. "We said everything necessary that last day on the ranch."

"No, we didn't." He ran his index finger around the starched collar of the formal white shirt. "I have more I want to tell you."

She looked at her wristwatch. "Okay. You've got twenty-eight minutes."

"Then I'll get right to the point. I'm not in love with my ex-wife. That was over long before she died. If I grieved at all, it was for Ty and the fact that he might miss her being part of his life."

He looked sincere and she believed him. "Okay. If that's all—"

"It's not." He took a step closer and looked down. "I found out that I am a one-woman man just like my dad was. But my wife wasn't that woman."

"Who is?" Her head was spinning at the pace of the revelations.

His brown eyes darkened with intensity. "You are."

"I am? You sure have a funny way of showing it."

He moved his shoulders uncomfortably. "I feel stupid in this tux but not as stupid as when I told you to go." He reached out and took her hand, linked his fingers with hers. "I was telling the truth about not wanting to stand in your way. I never want you to have regrets or give up anything for me."

"Oh, Cabot—"

"The thing is, I completely blew that. Shut the door because of my hang-ups. I've since been educated about the fact that couples make things work by reaching compromises. I want you to follow your dreams—as long as you always come home to me."

"Are you sure?" Her heart nearly stopped. After all the unhappiness, it was hard to take in what he was saying. "I understand why this is hard for you—"

He touched a finger to her lips. "Very sure, and I'll tell you why."

"I'm listening."

"I take after my dad and it's not in my DNA to stop loving you. And I *do* love you, Kate. I think I have from the first moment I saw you in that wedding dress at the Grizzly Bear Diner. So, I really hope you can forgive me for being so stubborn and stupid."

If anyone needed forgiveness it was her, for enjoying his groveling just a little too much. She was only human. She was also unbelievably happy. "There's nothing to forgive, Cabot."

For the first time since he'd walked in here today, the tension drained from his face and he smiled. "I'm glad."

"But I'm curious. What happened after I left?"

"Besides the fact that I missed you like crazy?" He looked out the window, a thoughtful expression on his face. "The community I've always loved and counted on to be there for me did exactly that. The people at the diner were sure I'd lost my mind. Caroline said, and I quote, that if I didn't go after you, I was a damn fool. And dense as they come. Tyler told me girls aren't my best event."

She laughed. "Did he really?"

"Oh, yeah. Kind of pathetic when your eight-year-old son knows more about women than you do." He grinned. "The thing is that all of them were just saying what I already knew deep down inside. I fell for you hard, fast and forever."

"Does Tyler know where you are?"

Cabot nodded. "I told him I was going to find you and tell you I love you. He gave me a hug and a high five. He misses you, Kate."

She still remembered the sad look on his little face when she'd said goodbye. For all her worry about him getting attached to her, she was really glad he cared because he'd stolen her heart. It was nice to know he was in her corner, along with the rest of Blackwater Lake. "I feel like the luckiest person in the whole world."

He shook his head. "I'm the lucky one. Of all the diners in all the world, you walked into the Grizzly Bear and answered my Help Wanted ad. At the time, I didn't know how much I needed you. Now I do."

She trailed a finger down the fancy buttons on his

crisp dress shirt. "So, why *do* you look like you just ran out on a wedding?"

"I hope I'm running *to* one." He tugged her close and put his arm around her waist, holding her against him. "Will you marry me, Kate?"

"Yes." Her heart filled to overflowing. "I love you, too, Cabot. And this is one wedding I won't run away from."

"Good."

"How does Ty feel about us getting married?"

"I didn't tell him about proposing to you in case the answer was no. But I have a sneaking suspicion that he'll be pretty happy." He kissed her mouth softly, then said, "He set us up, remember?"

"Yes, he did." She sighed. "Nothing would make me happier than spending the rest of my life with you and Ty and putting down roots on the ranch."

"I'm glad."

"And it's all because you took pity on me and gave me a job."

"Best decision I ever made." This time when he kissed her it was long and thorough.

Andrea would have to fix her makeup, but Kate didn't have the will to worry about that. All she cared about was spending the rest of her life with Cabot.

Epilogue

On the chilly October evening Kate got married, she wasn't nervous at all. It was a sunset event and couldn't have been more different from her last wedding. Except for one thing. She did run again—straight into Cabot's arms.

Their wedding was a small affair at Cabot's house on the ranch with her family and their closest friends in attendance. Ty was the best man and ring bearer. Cabot teased that it was a twofer. Kate's sister, Amy Scott, was maid of honor. It was casual, personal and perfect.

They said their vows in front of the big stone fireplace in the great room. After the minister from the local church pronounced them husband and wife, Cabot cupped her face in his hands and smiled with satisfaction, then proceeded to kiss her soundly.

He reluctantly pulled back and looked down when Ty tugged on his suit coat. "What is it, son?"

"When do I get to make my best-man speech?"

Cabot looked at her. "What do you think? Is there a specific schedule?"

She shook her head. "Do you want to do that now, Ty?"

"Yes."

"Okay. We just need to get champagne poured and make sure everyone has a glass." She looked at her brother. "Zach, can you handle that?"

He nodded. "Mom, Dad, Amy, can you give me a hand?"

The Scott family mobilized in the adjacent kitchen to pop corks and pour the bubbly. Tyler and his friend C.J had apple cider. Kate didn't want anyone left out of the toast.

Finally she and Cabot stood with the cheerfully crackling fire behind them and flutes of champagne in their hands. Ty was beside his father, and everyone was quietly gathered around to hear his words. Kate knew Cabot had talked to his son about this moment, but they had no idea what the little boy was going to say.

"My dad told me to thank everyone for coming. So, thanks." He looked around at Caroline and Nolan. The Crawfords, who owned the diner. Sydney McKnight and her father, Tom. The wedding guests faded to a blur as she concentrated on this sweet, precocious child who was now her son.

"Dad said I should say what I feel." He hesitated a moment, as if trying to figure it out. "I'm really glad Kate didn't marry that other guy. I'm glad she ran away and came to Blackwater Lake. My dad told me she makes him really happy and he loves her." He glanced up at them and grinned. "And I'm real glad that she's my mom now. I love her, too."

Kate's eyes filled with happy tears when she bent to

hug him. "That was the best best-man speech ever. It was beautiful, Ty."

"Then why are you cryin'?"

She sniffled. "Because what you said was wonderful, and I'm so happy."

Spontaneous applause and laughter erupted from everyone present, but Ty still looked confused.

Cabot put a hand on the boy's shoulder. "Kate loved it."

"Really?" The boy looked skeptical.

"Really." Her husband met her gaze and said with conviction, "You just have to trust."

"Okay." Ty shrugged and then gave her a pleading look. "Can I go play with C.J. now?"

"Of course. Go have fun."

He didn't waste any time and disappeared while the adults moved close, forming an unofficial receiving line to offer congratulations and wishes for a long, happy life. Sydney McKnight was the last one and gave her a big hug.

The pretty brunette smiled. "See, I told you the very first time we met that Cabot was sweet on you."

"When my brother's truck broke down."

Syd glanced at the brother in question, who was now talking with Cabot. "He's not hard on the eyes."

"Please, I beg you, don't have a crush on my brother."

"It was just an observation. I've sworn off men." Syd held up a hand in protest. "But why the warning? You're deliriously happy with your handsome rancher and I'm glad for you. But when people are sappy in love, they try to fix up their friends. Is there something wrong with me?"

"Absolutely not. Any man would be lucky to have you." Kate was adamant.

"At least one guy didn't think so."

"Then he was stupid. But if Zach broke your heart, it might affect our friendship."

"That wouldn't happen," Syd guaranteed. "As your husband so eloquently said to his son, you have to trust."

"Husband." Kate sighed dreamily. "I love the sound of that."

She met Cabot's gaze and saw the tender expression he wore only for her. He was no longer that cynical, guarded man who wouldn't believe in forever. Who'd ever have thought anyone would use *Cabot* and *trust* in the same sentence?

Just a little while ago, Kate had vowed that he would never have cause to regret trusting her, and he'd made the same promise. She'd expect nothing less from her hero, the rancher who took her in.

* * * * *

When Laurel Hudson is found—alive but with amnesia—no one is more relieved than Adam Fortune. He will do whatever it takes to reunite mother and son, even if it means a road trip in extremely close quarters. Will the long journey home remind Laurel how much they truly share?

Read on for a sneak preview of the final book in
The Fortunes of Texas: Rambling Rose continuity,
The Texan's Baby Bombshell *by Allison Leigh.*

He'd been falling for her from the very beginning. But that kiss had sealed the deal for him.

Now that glossy oak-barrel hair slid over her shoulder as Laurel's head turned and she looked his way.

His step faltered.

Her eyes were the same stunning shade of blue they'd always been. Her perfectly heart-shaped face was pale and delicate looking even without the pink scar on her forehead between her eyebrows.

Her eyebrows pulled together as their eyes met.

Remember me.

Remember us.

The words—unwanted and unexpected—pulsed through him, drowning out the splitting headache and the aching back and the impatience, the relief and the pain.

Then she blinked those incredible eyes of hers and he realized there was a flush on her cheeks and she was chewing at the corner of her lips. In contrast to her delicate features, her lips were just as full and pouty as they'd always been.

Kissing them had been an adventure in and of itself.

He pushed the pointless memory out of his head and then had to shove his hands in the pockets of his jeans because they were actually shaking.

"Hi." Puny first word to say to the woman who'd made a wreck out of him.

Still seated, she looked up at him. "Hi." She sounded breathless. "It's…it's Adam, right?"

The pain sitting in the pit of his stomach then had nothing to do with anything except her. He yanked his right hand from his pocket and held it out. "Adam Fortune."

She looked uncertain, then slowly settled her hand into his.

Unlike Dr. Granger's firm, brief clasp, Laurel's touch felt chilled and tentative. And it lingered. "I'm Lisa."

God help him. He was not strong enough for this.

Don't miss
The Texan's Baby Bombshell *by Allison Leigh,*
available June 2020 wherever
Harlequin Special Edition books and ebooks are sold.

Harlequin.com

Brooklyn K-9 Unit officer Belle Montera glanced back on the shortcut through Cadman Plaza Park, her K-9 partner, Justice, a sleek German shepherd, moving ahead of her as she held tightly to his leash. She had a weird sense she was being followed, but it had to be nothing.

Justice lifted his black nose and sniffed the humid air, then gave a soft woof. He might have seen a squirrel frolicking in the tall oaks, or he could have sensed Belle's agitation. Still on duty, she kept a keen eye on her surroundings.

"No time to go after innocent squirrels," she told Justice. "We're working, remember?"

Her faithful companion gave her a dark-eyed stare, his black K-9 unit protective vest cinched around his firm belly.

They were both on high alert.

"It's okay, boy," she said, giving Justice's shiny black-and-tan coat a soft rub. "Just my overactive imagination getting the best of me."

She had a meeting with a man who could have information regarding the McGregor murders. The DNA match from that case had indicated that US marshal Emmett Gage could be related to the killer.

The team had done a thorough background check on the marshal to eliminate him as a suspect, then Belle had been assigned to meet with him.

Justice lifted his head and sniffed again, his nose in the air. The big dog glanced back. Belle checked over her shoulder.

No one there.

She slowed and listened to hear if any footsteps hit the strip of pavement curving through the path toward the federal courthouse near the park.

Belle heard through the trees what sounded like a motorcycle revving, then nothing but the birds chirping. Minutes passed and then she heard a noise on the path, the crackle of a twig breaking, the slight shift of shoes hitting asphalt, a whiff of stale body odor wafting through the air. The hair on the back of her neck stood up and Belle knew then.

Someone is following me.

Don't miss
Deadly Connection *by Lenora Worth,*
available June 2020 wherever
Love Inspired Suspense books and ebooks are sold.

LoveInspired.com

LISEXP0520